# Sun-Painted Man

6/26/11

For
Eric Nisley
with Justice
and Best Wishes

Mie Schuster

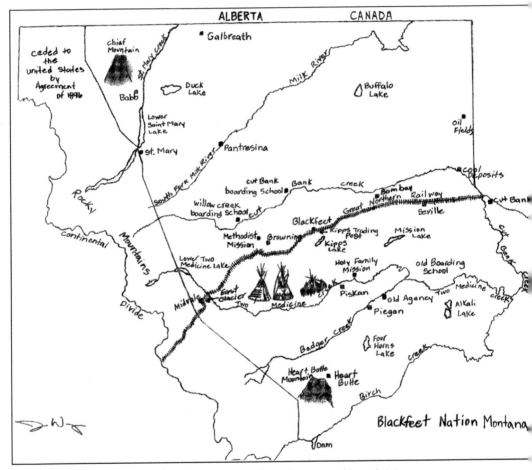

Map of Blackfeet Reservation. Courtesy of Joseph Wagner.

# Sun-Painted Man

>>>→ • ←<<

Philip F. Schuster, II

Foreword By Curly Bear Wagner

CLEAR LIGHT PUBLISHERS
SANTA FE, NEW MEXICO

© 2010 by Philip F. Schuster, II
Clear Light Publishers
823 Don Diego, Santa Fe, New Mexico 87505
www.clearlightbooks.com

This novel of historical fiction was inspired by the life of Red-Boy, Peter Stabs-By-Mistake, a Blackfeet Indian (1892-1974). Any similarity of the fictitious characters in this novel to real persons, living or dead, is coincidental and not intended by the author. Some events, involving historic or real persons, have been fictionalized in tribute not only to the gallant service performed by Blackfeet natives during World War I, but also in tribute to the suffering and survival of the Blackfeet People.

First Edition
10 9 8 7 6 5 4 3 2 1

**Library of Congress Cataloging-in-Publication Data**

Schuster, Philip F.
Sun-Painted Man / Philip F. Schuster, II.
    p.  cm.
Includes Index.
ISBN-13: 9781-57416-097-0
ISBN-10: 1-57416-097-4
1. Piegan Indians--Fiction. I. Title.

PS3619.C4833S86 2009
813'.6--dc22        2009032776

Cover Photograph courtesy of
Paul Foster Photography
Cover design: Gregory Lucero
Interior design & typography: Gregory Lucero

# SPECIAL MEMORIAL DEDICATION

## For Curly Bear Wagner and Thomas Blackweasel

Curly Bear Wagner, founder and president of Going-To-The-Sun Institute, first introduced himself to me in Washington D.C. in January, 2003. He knew I was working on *Sun-Painted Man*, and I took an immediate interest in his Institute. Internationally respected as a cultural spokesperson, Curly Bear was also a virtuoso storyteller in the Blackfeet oral tradition, always lacing his storytelling with a wonderful sense of humor.

Thomas A. Blackweasel (Gray Horse Rider) was introduced to me by Curly Bear. A widely respected Blackfeet historian and linguist, this Elder's guidance with the Blackfeet language and cultural issues proved invaluable. Thomas Blackweasel also designed the traditional Blackfeet frame for the painting that inspired this book and which is depicted at the beginning of Chapter 25.

I soon learned that Curly Bear was related to me through adoption. Curly Bear's great-grandfather was the revered Blood leader, Red Crow. Red Crow's sister, Small Woman, was the mother of Chief Curly Bear, Curly Bear Wagner's namesake. In 1923, at Glacier National Park, Chief Curly Bear adopted my Anglo great-uncle Christian F. Schuster, a New England businessman, giving him the Blackfeet name, Morning Eagle.

*Sun-Painted Man* tells the story of Morning Eagle and Red-Boy, Peter Stabs-By-Mistake, a young Blackfeet man. The story tells of the injustice done to Red-Boy that led to his imprisonment at Leavenworth Penitentiary in the 1920's and his survival. My great uncle, Morning Eagle, worked tirelessly to secure Red-Boy's freedom.

Without the friendship and generosity of Thomas Blackweasel and Curly Bear Wagner, Red-Boy's story could never have been told. Along the way, my connection to Curly Bear, through my great-uncle's Blackfeet adoption, led each of us to call one another "brother."

Now, the Creator has taken Thomas Blackweasel and Curly Bear to be with their ancestors. Here were two good men who honored their Blackfeet people and ancestors and became the embodiment of the values they taught: hope, faith and love. It is with the deepest gratitude for both of these good men's lives that I dedicate *Sun-Painted Man* to them.

Phil Schuster

# TABLE OF CONTENTS

Curly Bear Wagner. (October 31, 1944-July 16, 2009)  Photo by Marcia Keegan

# Foreword

## By Curly Bear Wagner

When you start reading this extraordinary story, you're not going to stop and set it down. It tells a realistic story of my people. Looking back at the roughly 5,000 years or so that my people and First Nations people have been here, those who know only written history don't really know who the Native peoples were and are.

We are who we are because of the land, the land given to us by the Creator for our survival. We were taught to observe what was around us, to follow the laws of the land—what was right and what was wrong, what to hunt and when not to hunt, what to hurt and what to protect, when to go on horse raids and when not to. The land gave us our stories, which were told to generation after generation so that we knew we were connected to the land, the Creator and could survive.

When the whiteman came, they knew nothing of our system of government, our educational system or how we cared for our sick. They saw only what we seemed not to have; our differences were called inadequacies. At first, we ignored their judgment of our ways.

The missionaries were the first to come with their school system. They taught our children that the traditional ways of our people were no good. Even our language was forbidden to our children. They made us pray to a "new" god in a new way. We were to pledge allegiance to a flag that had no meaning to us. In this way, our children were torn from their roots.

Then came trappers, settlers, farmers, hunters, governments, the railroad. We were crowded into a smaller area; then, even the Buffalo were gone. In this way, holes were torn in the beliefs and values that lived in our land and way of life. Our people were left to struggle with new rules and new meanings.

We learned to want the fancy homes and fancy clothes of the people working for the government. This was also denied to us. The flag became a symbol of our hardship as we were cut off from our traditions and left without a meaningful role in shaping a new life for ourselves and for our children. The deeper our striving the greater our confusion.

All that was, was no more; what was new did not work. Our children were taken away to school where they were abused both physically and mentally. Our hair was cut, our dances, songs, pipes and rituals were denied us.

We were put to farming and living sedentary lives, but white ranchers were allowed to run their cattle on our land.

>>>→ • ←<<<

*Sun-Painted Man* tells the story of Red-Boy, Peter Stabs-By-Mistake, who, like many Native young men during World War I, stepped off the Reservation into a world he knew nothing about, then returned and saw the injustice. He sought to right the injustice and was caught in the lies and manipulation of corrupt others.

Although the story is historical fiction, many of the characters in the story include our most revered ancestors, including my great-grandfather, Red Crow. *Sun-Painted Man* tells of the traditional values of our people and shows the strength of the conflict of trying to survive in times of unending poverty and cultural clash.

My people saw Christian Schuster on the Blackfeet Indian Reservation — how he conducted himself, how he treated the people. He always spoke the truth about the things he was doing. The people, including my great-uncle, Curly Bear, took an extreme liking to this man and they gave him one of the most honorable and powerful names that could be given to any person — Morning Eagle.

Morning is a very important time of day in our lives. Morning is when we leave our offerings to the Sun. The Sun is considered one of the most powerful, most sacred things that the Creator has given to us. Its light, heat and energy force, to make all things grow, first occur in the morning.

Pita — the eagle — is the sacred bird of our people. We use the feathers of the eagle in ceremonies and in conducting some of our most important prayers and dances because Pita flies the highest and carries our prayers to the Creator.

So my people laid honor on Christian Schuster. They were hoping he might help Peter Stabs-By-Mistake, and that the injustice done to Peter might be told to the world.

And it happened that Morning Eagle's deeds were passed on to Phil Schuster, his great-nephew, that he might finish the story.

Phil has done a terrific job of working with the Blackfeet people through interviews, through meetings, through seeing, through observing our people. His research has been done to get the essential historical facts correct—to make sure the story is done in a traditional manner.

This man is very well-accepted on the Blackfeet Reservation, such as his great-uncle, Morning Eagle, was. The people think the world of this man. He has furnished to us the story of one of our own people, which although it happened 80 years ago, has meaning for my people even today.

*Curly Bear Wagner*
Blackfeet Cultural Consultant and President,
Going-To-The-Sun Institute
Browning, Montana

# List of Characters

## Principal Historical Characters

| | |
|---|---|
| *Red-Boy* | Ii ko tsi saah ko ma pi aka Peter Stabs-By-Mistake (Pah tsi si ma ki)<br>Son of Thomas Stabs-By-Mistake |
| *Thomas Stabs-By-Mistake* | Piegan Chief and father of Red-Boy |
| *Steals-in-the-Daytime-Woman* | Ksi stsi koi ka mo' saa kii<br>Daughter of revered and honored Big Brave-Frank Mountain Chief, wife of Thomas Stabs-By-Mistake and Red-Boy's mother |
| *Curly Bear* | Kia yao soi sksis si<br>Piegan Chief and adoptive father of Christian F. Schuster |
| *Christian F. Schuster* | New England businessman and resident of Holyoke, Massachusetts; on September 4, 1923, Christian Schuster was adopted by Curly Bear and given the Blackfeet name Aapinakoi Píítaa (pi ta) (pronounced Aa-pineck-way-Pita) (literally, Morning Eagle) |
| *Mountain Chief* | Ni nais tá ko<br>Revered and honored Blackfeet Chief and leader of his people |
| *Big Brave-Frank Mountain Chief* | Son of Mountain Chief, father of Red-Boy's mother and leader of his people. |
| *Bear Head* | Ki áá yo to kaan<br>Pikuni friend of Christian Schuster (Morning Eagle) |
| *A-tso-tsi-ni* | Bear Head's sits-beside-him-woman (wife) |
| *Black Horse Rider* | Si ki mioh ki to pii<br>Son of Mountain Chief and brother of Steals-In-The-Daytime-Woman (Red-Boy's mother) |
| *Fish* | Mamíí—revered and powerful Piegan Elder |

| | |
|---|---|
| *Turtle* | Sspo pii—honored Blood Elder pardoned for the crime of murder by President Woodrow Wilson in 1914. A younger, better-known man named Turtle (whom C.F. Schuster referred to as "Spopia") was a full-blood Piegan and unrelated to Sspo pii |
| *Calvin Coolidge* | 30th President of the United States, whose friendship with Christian F. Schuster stemmed from the days when Mr. Coolidge was mayor of Northampton, Massachusetts |
| *Ruth Muskrat Bronson* | Cherokee woman; graduate of Mount Holyoke College and Indian activist |
| *Red Crow* | Powerful and revered Blackfeet Chief and leader of his people |
| *Frank (Fred C.) Campbell* | Superintendent of the Blackfeet Indian Reservation from 1921-1928 |
| *Senator William M. Butler* | Senator from Massachusetts and Republican National Chairman, running for reelection in 1926 |
| *Art Chapin* | Fraternity brother of Christian F. Schuster and friend of Senator William M. Butler |
| *Senators Thomas Walsh and Burton Wheeler* | Montana Senators and acquaintances of Christian Schuster |
| *Ted and Nellie Running Crane* | Parents of Annie Running Crane (fictional character) |
| *Frank Stearns* | Coolidge's closest political advisor from Massachusetts days as governor |
| *Emma Running Crane* (given the fictional married name of Emma Bull Child in the story) | Annie's younger sister and daughter of Ted and Nellie Running Crane |
| *Louise Red Fox* | Friend of Annie Running Crane |
| *Maggie Wolf Plume* | Friend of Annie Running Crane |
| *Mary Horn* | Friend of Annie Running Crane and daughter of Thomas Horn (Yells In The Water) |
| *Gertrude Bonnin* | A Sioux writer (Sioux name: Zitkala-sa) |

| | |
|---|---|
| *Bow Maker* | A Tobique Indian from New Brunswick who befriended Christian Schuster at an early age |
| *A.A. (Albert) Grorud* | Attorney from Helena, Montana who assisted Christian F. Schuster with his investigation of Red-Boy's trial and conviction for rape |
| *Wolf Plume* | Honored Piegan Elder and friend of Christian F. Schuster |
| *James Vielle* | Childhood friend of Peter Stabs-By-Mistake |
| *W.I. Biddle* | Served as Leavenworth's fifth warden during Red-Boy's incarceration |

## *Principal Fictional Characters*

| | |
|---|---|
| *Marilyn Deer Child Sanders* | Daughter of Oliver Red Bird Tail (Oliver Sanders in the story); she works for Pardon Attorney James A. Fry in Washington D.C. |
| *James A. Fry* | Pardon Attorney who processes Red-Boy's application for pardon |
| *Victor Sanders* | Half-brother of Marilyn Deer Child Sanders |
| *Annie Running Crane* | Young Indian girl who is the alleged victim of the crime of rape; the accused is Red-Boy, Peter Stabs-By-Mistake (This fictional character is based upon an actual relative of the Running Crane family; her true identity has been changed to protect family privacy) |
| *Richard Sanders* | Government translator and informant; brother of Oliver (Red Bird Tail) Sanders |
| *Coombs, Gunny, Big Ed, and Shake Spear* | Leavenworth penitentiary inmates who are friends and acquaintances of Red-Boy |
| *Krankk* | Leavenworth cell boss and enemy of Red-Boy |
| *Monroe* | One of Krankk's minions |
| *Oliver Red Bird Tail Sanders* | Mi' ko tsi sóó a' tsis (Red Bird Tail) Blackfeet translator and father of Marilyn Deer Child Sanders and half-sister of Victor Sanders (both fictional characters) (This fictional character as well as Richard Sanders are based upon real people whose true identities have been changed to protect family privacy) |

| | |
|---|---|
| *Rosa Diabo* | Mohawk young woman; graduate of Mount Holyoke College and friend of Marilyn Deer Child Sanders |
| *Maxine Sanders* | First wife of Oliver Sanders and mother of Victor Sanders |
| *Miggs* | Assistant US Attorney in Helena, Montana, charged with investigating Red-Boy's pardon request |
| *Yessup* | Investigator and law school graduate who works for Miggs |
| *George Bernard Whiting* | Federal Judge presiding over Red-Boy's trial [archival records disclose that Federal Judge George M. Bourquin presided at the trial] |
| *Ed Elliott* | Red-Boy's defense attorney |
| *Miles O'Donnell* | Assistant U.S. Attorney prosecuting Red-Boy |
| *Sullivan* | African-American porter befriended by Christian F. Schuster during his travels on the "iron horse" to Montana |

...g Brave-Mountain Chief holding his last Tobacco Board and handing Morning Eagle a sacred Buffalo-Stone. ...o the left of Morning Eagle sits Thomas Stabs-By-Mistake. Behind Morning Eagle sits Red-Boy. Bear Head ...i áá yo to kaan) is seated to Mountain Chief's immediate left. (Mountain Chief gave Morning Eagle his last ...obacco Board and the sacred Buffalo-Stone at the time of the lodge-painting ceremony.)

(left) Red-Boy Peter Stabs-By-Mistake; (right) Thomas Stabs-By-Mistake (father and son), dressed for a dance, ca. 1920 (From a photo postcard.)

# Red-Boy

is legs were cold and sore from the hard ride from Heart Butte. His war-wounded right hand throbbed from clutching the reins in the cold. A long swallow of whiskey would make him forget the pain. That feeling lingered for an instant, then vanished. He thought back over the past year and how he had stayed sober.

He tethered his sorrel pony next to a bony gelding beneath a crude wooden pole shelter. Frozen tufts of needle grass lay trampled under pawed-away snow. Icicles hung like coyote fangs from the cross poles of the structure, stark reminders of Snow-Maker's craft. A skinny black dog approached from beneath some rabbitbrush. The man fed his mount a handful of partially frozen hay and bits of cottonwood bark from a wooden trough on the ground as he bent to pat the dog. The horse's crisp breath met his own and wisps of steam were snatched away, devoured by Cold-Maker's greed. Nearby, an aspen shivered under a tattered shawl of snow, shaking its spindly fingers, scolding Cold-Maker for the misery he had brought to the tiny Piegan-Pikuni settlement of scattered cabins, wall tents and lodges along frozen Cut Bank Creek.

Cold-Maker had descended from Canada into Cut Bank, Montana with a bitter 30-degree-below-zero breath in this January of 1921. The man looked out at the great shadows of snow-filled clouds that rolled over the silver-topped Crown-of-the-Rockies, bringing a white stillness over the barren vastness of the plains.

There, nestled in a shallow draw stood the Niitóyis — the winter lodge — of Chief Thomas Stabs-By-Mistake, who had seen fifty-two winters. The lodge of seasoned mountain pine poles crossed and strapped together at the top, all covered with canvas and gray Army blankets cinched together with rawhide, rested on the hard-packed earthen floor, as if in prayerful obedience to the Great-Unseen-Above-One.

Unbuttoning the top of his olive-drab army jacket, he shook the snow off his flat-brimmed, Carlsbad hat. His long black hair, threaded into two braids, hung down to his chest. Over the left breast pocket of his coat were stenciled the faded gray letters—"U.S. Army—Stabs By Mistake, P."

The old black dog gave a half-hearted bark. Inside, Thomas knew that his son, Red-Boy, Peter Stabs-By-Mistake, had come as requested. In the warmth of his Otter Medicine Tipi, sitting cross-legged on his frayed Buffalo robe, he waited for his son to cross the red earth band, the row of yellow dusty star circles, the faded triangular mountain peaks and the nearly obliterated otters and wolves outlined on the few Buffalo-hides stitched into his lodge cover. All these symbols of the old ways and old power were no longer part of his son's modern life.

Now in his twenty-eighth year, the Indian veteran was a young man caught between the old world of his youth here on the reservation and the outside world that had wounded his body in a distant war.

Red-Boy wondered why his mother and father still lived in a lodge, in sub-zero freezing cold. Still, he was proud of their ways. He knew that the Indian Agency's plan for his people to live in small wooden houses, raising livestock or farming, did not run through Thomas's stubborn, nomadic, full-blooded Blackfeet veins. Besides, one of Montana's harshest winters a year ago had left thousands of cattle, horses and crops frozen to death on withered land. His parents' meager vegetable garden was tended by Red-Boy's mother, Steals-In-The-Daytime-Woman. Thomas's only interest in planting was overseeing the growth of his tobacco seeds.

Stooping low, the young man entered his father's lodge, again patting the old black mutt before closing the lodge-flap. Steals-In-The-Daytime greeted her son and brought him close to the lodge fire. She expressed concern on seeing him rub his hand. Red-Boy gave his mother a hug and whispered, "Hurts only a little, Mother." He stretched in the warmth, filled with the thick resinous scent of pine mixed with the sweet fragrance of cottonwood.

Red-Boy watched his mother limp away from the fire—her lame knee the result of a poorly healed break from a fall off a horse. She carefully moved the ear-poles on the lodge now that the wind had shifted. The lodge quickly cleared of smoke. His mother's bull berries mixed with bitterroot were bubbling in a stone bowl set in the fire. Small wild turnips were simmering in a black kettle suspended from a wooden tripod. Steals-In-The-Daytime set out pemmican, pounded strips of dried deer meat mixed with chokecherries and fat. He watched her, her dress of faded blue trade cloth reaching to her ankles, tattered at the hem. A quarter-inch thick belt of harness leather, tied with buckskin, accentuated her broad hips.

"Ó ki," greeted Thomas with a short, level tone in his Pikuni tongue. "Son, I am glad you have come. My heart is good towards you, but sadly I have covered my head with my robe." His father's brow wore sharp creases of worry.

"What's bothering you, Father?"

Warmed from the lodge fire, Red-Boy removed his overcoat, revealing a dull khaki Army shirt still emblazoned with the red and black rifle insignia of the Machine-Gun Battalion of the 77th Division of the 307th Infantry. Many of the veterans of Pershing's American Expeditionary Force instantly recognized what it meant. Red-Boy's unit had crawled and killed their way through the German lines, finally reaching the "Lost Battalion" in the pitch-black Argonne Forest. Thomas nodded at his son with obvious pride, momentarily masking his worry.

"Since you have returned among us, you know we have seen much sickness and suffering up here. This last moon, we have seen two babies die. We have seen the clouds press down upon us. The brightness of the Sun is not with us."

"I know, Father," replied Red-Boy. "I tried finding a doctor for some sick little ones in Heart Butte, and all I was told at the Agency was the doc had gone to Helena for a day." The young veteran paused and jabbed at the fire. "Little girl died," he continued with clenched jaw. "Then life left two more little boys with the flu four nights later. 'No doc,' we were told!"

His father nodded, then slowly held up his hand, hoping to calm his son's growing anger.

"I have visited many lodges and seen little food there," continued Thomas. "Many without flour, beans, or coffee. The helpless are given no meat." He paused, staring into the lodge fire, then directly at Red-Boy. "Son, you are young and a great warrior. Many of our people look to you."

"Unh," uttered the young man. "If only I could understand why the whiteman government doesn't handle supply problems on the reservation like the military quartermasters did."

Both father and son knew that on the reservation the enemy was a hidden bureaucracy; the problems of the people were deemed less urgent.

Red-Boy had been one of the first of the Blackfeet to enlist to fight in the whiteman's Great War. It wasn't until he returned home that Red-Boy realized the Indian Health Services had been cut to the bone to support that war. He saw the hopeless faces of the old, the blind, the betrayed.

He'd seen those same bitter, hopeless faces in Europe—faces that lit with hope when his unit handed out candy bars or cigarettes in small French towns. Here, the faces were unchanging.

More than once, the usually quiet young veteran had lost patience with the Indian Agency. Harsh words had been spit at Superintendent Frank Campbell when direct answers were not forthcoming. Thomas Stabs-By-Mistake and other Elders had interceded, keeping Red-Boy at bay, hoping the young man's anger would cool.

Once, when Campbell again offered double talk instead of rations and medicine, Red-Boy's frustrations had flared into a hasty threat to torch the sub-agency. An answer soon arrived in the persons of two BIA policeman who warned that any damage to the sub-agency could result in Red-Boy's cabin being accidently burned to the ground.

>>>→ • ←<<<

Red-Boy looked across the lodge fire as his father unwrapped his large pipe. A faraway look replaced worry in the old man's eyes. Thomas-Stabs-By-Mistake fitted the worn, sandstone bowl to the seasoned, wood stem of his pipe. He lit the tobacco with a burning twig and blew four short puffs to the Sun and four more to the Earth.

Father then offered the pipe, bowl first, to his son, who took a long draw and repeated his father's actions. This exchange was repeated four times before Thomas replaced the pipe on his tobacco board.

Mother now set forth the meal of pemmican, berry soup and turnips.

"Is your hand feeling better?" she asked.

Red-Boy nodded and smiled. "Better, Mother."

"We must thank the Creator for everything we have," she whispered.

With bowed head and eyes looking into the banked coals of his lodge fire-ring, Thomas spoke softly in the Pikuni dialect, almost in a whisper:

"Oh Great-Unseen-Above-Mystery—O Father, Sun—pity us. The Pikuni thank you for the food which you have given them. We thank the Sun, Giver-Of-Light, for letting us have life. We put the bit of Dried Meat in Mother Earth, Womb of all life. We ask you, Great-And-Merciful-Unseen-One, to heal our old people and children from their sickness. We ask that the Blind People may see the Sun again."

The trio—father, mother and son—slowly ate in silence.

Red-Boy noted with satisfaction that even when eating boiled turnips, Chief Stabs-By-Mistake exuded a quiet dignity. A man with a proud bearing, Thomas's long, coal-black hair was swept back from his high forehead. His strong nose and broad mouth were framed by slender braids resting on his red flannel shirt. His faded, black trousers almost covered his favorite porcupine-quilled moccasins.

Thomas smiled at his sits-beside-him-woman, watching her carefully spoon the soup to her lips, her elbows showing through the holes in her wool sweater.

Red-Boy was proud too of his mother and her blood ancestry. Having now seen forty-nine winters, Steals-In-The-Daytime-Woman revered her father, Big Brave-Mountain Chief, whose father, in turn, was the great Mountain Chief. Steals-In-The-Daytime's mother, who was called Bird Sailing This Way, had been chosen as the sacred and virtuous Medicine Woman for a Sun Dance at Two Medicine Lodge. Like her mother, Steals-In-The-Daytime was trusted by other Piegan women who knew they could confide in her. For this honor, Thomas teasingly called his wife Many Ears.

Red-Boy's mother and father had lived a hard life. Yet his parents knew how to laugh with an earthiness that often overcame suffering. Red-Boy, once imbued with this gift, had returned from the war with his laughing spirit extinguished. Only recently had this spirit been rekindled by Annie.

After Thomas finished eating, he looked at his sits-beside-him-woman, then fixed his eyes once more on his son. "My faith in Great-Unseen-Above-One is powerful. To have much anger is bad. A man who talks much about his sorrow is a coward and the heart of a coward is weak." Red-Boy waited; his father had not summoned him to speak of anger or sorrow or weakness.

The wind outside buffeted and pounded the blanketed walls of the lodge. Red-Boy's mother held fast to the lodge-pole rope fixed to the center, helping to hold the structure in place. Long ago, he had watched his mother scrape and cure the scarce lodge hides. Now, fleshy brown arms and stout frame reminded Red-Boy that his mother had moved many lodges and was thankfully one of the still healthy people. "Father, you know I have built a fine log cabin in Heart Butte with my friend James. It has heat and a wood floor and the roof is laid with shingles. With it, we are helping to shelter and care for as many of our older, sick people as we can," said the young full-blood with a confident voice.

Then he stopped and smiled proudly at his father. "And of course you know Annie Running Crane, who helps care for our people, is going to become my sits-beside-him-woman, Father."

"Unh!" came a curt, explosive protest from his father. "The young men of today do not know where it grows," said Thomas, looking pointedly at Peter's mother.

The young man was, at once, perplexed and taken aback by his father's protest.

The wind continued to shake the skins and blanket coverings on the lodge. A violent gust of Cold-Maker's breath shook and whipped overhead. Smoke from the lodge fire swirled, drowning out the lingering smells of the meal. Red-Boy could hear lowing cattle and the intermittent nicker and whinny of horses.

The wind pounded and blew the lodge door-flap open. Through the open flap, a whining, nasal bark came from the black dog. Steals-In-The-Daytime gave a startled look at her husband.

"Thomas, the ghost-bark!" She quickly reached over and cinched the door-flap tight with a rawhide tie.

Red-Boy smiled at his mother, knowing that she was frightened by the dog's ghost-bark—a warning that the harmful spirit-ghosts cast about by Cold-Maker's power were near and could enter the lodge. But Thomas sat before the hiss of the lodge fire, expressionless.

"Why do you disapprove? Father, you know Annie's grandfather, Running Crane, was an honored Piegan Chief. Her father, Ted Running Crane, is a chief, too."

"Son, Annie comes from an honorable family." Thomas paused, catching his son's eyes with his. "But taking Annie as your woman— it is dangerous."

"What?"

The wind rose again, thumping and battering against the lodge, drawing Red-Boy's mind back several years.

>>>→ • ←<<<

Home from the Great War, he and Annie had wandered about alone on horseback, out into the fluttering wheatgrass meadows and fescue grasslands of the upland prairies surrounding Heart Butte. They had tethered their mounts beneath cottonwoods ensconced as rotund sentinels beside isolated Badger Creek. They had rested and counted the turning leaves, walked to where they could see the tinge of goldenrods and wolf willows smoothly change their patterns with the breezes. Lying in the long waving prairie grass amidst the sparkling rainbow drops of wildflowers, they had watched the gatherings of crook-backed, blue grama flower clusters sway and nod in the gentle breezes, imagining conversations the tall-stemmed grasses were having with each other and with the birds.

Red-Boy's favorite escapes with Annie were late spring in the swales and foothills surrounding Heart Butte, which blended into cloudless open sky — rolling hills blooming with millions of delicate, silky, blue lupine and dotted with yellow, cinquefoil shrubs. Annie loved the colors.

At the Sun Dances, Annie wore her mother's sinew-sewn, doeskin dress. Tiny brass bells hung from the beaded thongs. He loved to finger her favorite necklace of thimbles and cowrie shells warm against her neck.

One afternoon at the Sun Dance, he was with Annie on horseback when they spotted a golden eagle slowly circling, resting on a high current of air, patiently waiting — hunting — for the ground squirrels and badgers to scurry from beneath their underground shelters. Annie remarked how the nodding fingers of grama grass must have forewarned all the little four-legged ones — the grassland prey animals. Unsuccessful, the eagle finally soared away towards the Shiny Mountains. Red-Boy and Annie watched the eagle disappear into the strong, granite face of Chief Mountain.

On a grassy knoll, they listened to the singing of larks, thrushes and Savannah sparrows till the Sun Chief was no more.

They spent nights alone, lying together in the log cabin he and James Vielle had built. The sturdy log structure was a kind of coming-home-from-the-war celebration, a safe place that he told James would survive at least two hundred winters.

Red-Boy had tagged his childhood friend James as "Drags Behind". He forever teased James with this nickname every time he outraced him on horseback. The veteran smiled to himself as he recalled how the moniker had stuck, especially when he discovered upon returning from the Great War that James had enlisted after him, but had missed his chance to go overseas. Yet, Drags Behind could pound a nail and work a saw long after Red-Boy's war-wounded right hand told him the day's cabin-building was finished. Upon completing the cabin, Red-Boy joked with his friend that he would one day crawl inside between the legs of his sits-beside-him-woman, plant his seed and watch his children grow to old age here.

The war for Red-Boy had embodied the defining moments of his life, a kind of test above all tests. He had become the ultimate Piegan warrior among the full-blooded Blackfeet young men of his Nation. Often, without wanting to, he would look back on the suffering and sorrow of France. Afterwards, he found comfort in the soft bosom of Annie, his only true sits-beside-him-woman.

He noticed when Annie was healthy, her pouty full lips were accentuated, her long, coal-black hair, cascading on either side of her beautiful full dark eyes, was silky smooth to the touch. When they stole off together, her innocence overcame him. Resisting his touch at first, she soon relaxed, feeling safe within his protective presence and the warmth of the log cabin.

When she let him undress her, he caressed her small bare breasts and kissed her tiny ears and soft, scented neck. Finally, the earthy smell of her body and the pounding within him overcame them both, drowning them in the passions of love. Then, exhausted and content they slept...

>>>→ • ←<<<

"Has the pemmican your mother prepared made you fall asleep?!" His father's sharp question jarred Red-Boy from his thoughts. The wind was still howling outside. Thomas stoked the glowing logs with a fire-hardened stick. Gradually, Cold-Maker's breath relented.

Thomas fixed a penetrating eye on his son. Behind his look lay knowledge of unseen danger, forces one could not physically grasp.

"Father, there's no danger in my taking Annie as my sits-beside-him-woman. You forget I enlisted and went to France and fought. There, I knew danger."

The Great War had been no Piegan game-war or horse-raiding party upon the Crees, the Crows or the Kootenays in the times that were furthest back when one could "count coups" against the enemy. This modern war was not about coming back home and reciting great deeds of bravery.

As happened when Red-Boy returned from the war, Thomas knew he must again remind his son that not all danger is visible to the eye. When Red-Boy returned to the reservation, he had tried to drown the recurring visions of war with whiteman's alcohol. Still, the outstretched arms of war appeared, the bloated mouths agape, the steely eyes unseeing—frozen in death's last suffocating, poison gas breath before entering the Sand Hills— the eternity of death. Although they had not been able to replace the visions, his father and the Elders had helped him overcome the danger of demon liquor. Now his visions were of his people's suffering, which fed a simmering anger, a deepening resolve.

"Father, why do you protest my being with Annie?"

"Nellie Running Crane has come to your mother and has spoken from her heart. She has told your mother that you do not court her daughter in the old way. You are seen holding hands with Annie. Son, you know no lover of a young woman can touch her hands without the parents' consent." Thomas's eyes narrowed, his mouth set with a stern frown. His son cast off a whimsical grin.

Red-Boy shook his head, his grin widening. My God, he thought. The men of my company would laugh at this. "Father, few court in the old way. So what is the problem?" he persisted.

Red-Boy's grin faded when his mother solemnly shook her head. His mother had taken Nellie's talk and had shared it with his father.

"Victor Sanders paid much attention to Annie while you were gone to war," his mother softly interjected. "Victor helped when Annie was down with sickness. He would meet and talk often with Nellie. He is closer to Annie's father than you are, and Nellie Running Crane favors him for her daughter."

"What?" broke in Red-Boy. "That's a switch. Courting a girl and talkin' to her mother? Nellie speaks of the old ways but forgets that a young woman's husband never speaks to his mother-in-law. Besides, Annie doesn't even like Victor."

"I know, son," she said. "I told Nellie I was suspicious of Victor's heart. Seems Victor has been bold enough to break traditions. Still, it's not wise to leave good tradition behind.... it always kept peace in our family," his mother added, presenting her husband with a warm smile.

"Unh! The coward Sanders," gritted Red-Boy, "was never brave enough to go off to the war." He stared at his father. "His mouth is brave. His heart is a coward."

Victor had never really left the reservation. He had never counted the lethal-leaded coups that Red-Boy had counted in the Argonne forest in 1918. Victor didn't even possess the courage of his half-sister, Marilyn Deer Child.

It had all come crashing down before he left for the war. Marilyn Deer Child, his first love—the one who was to become his sits-beside-him-woman—was left behind, filled with grief. Despite his desperate rides to find a doctor, their infant boy died.

He wrote to her only once from France. She never wrote back. The war and their unshared sorrow separated them. Like a magnet, he was drawn back to see how she was, only to find her gone. Demon liquor became his soothing pastime.

When the haze finally lifted, Annie Running Crane was there. Annie had known the older girl—Red-Boy's first love. Red-Boy and the older girl had grown up close together, both of them regarding Annie as their younger almost-sister. Chronic fevers and coughing had kept the young girl at home. Later, Red-Boy and his girlfriend would visit Annie's parents, bringing blankets and fresh meat when they could.

Victor Sanders had stayed home during the Great War courting the young girl that Red-Boy now loved. Victor Sanders was a long-tailed rat. A thief.

Red-Boy's father leaned forward.

"I want you to take my talk and listen to me now." Thomas looked intently at his son. Red-Boy exhaled and was patient.

Red-Boy nodded slowly and remembered taking his father's talk in the sacred sweat lodge at the Heart Butte Sun Dance in July of 1919, that first summer following the war. His head had been throbbing from booze. "Listen to me now, son. Listen to your heart, not to your head," his father had told him over and over. "Give the whiteman's liquor to Naa-tó'si (the Sun)."

Red-Boy knew, too, that his father had given him his name, that he possessed the name of the son of an honored Piegan Chief. The giving of a name was a proud but private matter to be told only if someone you trusted asked.

»»—→ • ←—«« 

Peter Stabs-By-Mistake was given the name Red-Boy after his father, many winters before, went with his friend, Looking-For-Smoke, to the lodge of Three-Moons to put up a sweathouse. After the three men had entered it and purified their minds and bodies with the ceremonial prayer and sweat-bath, Thomas Stabs-By-Mistake called the old people. Then he filled his medicine pipe, passed it to Three-Moons and said, "I have a brown horse and other presents that I give to you. I want you to give my son a name."

Three-Moons took the pipe and prayed that the boy would live to be old like himself, that he would have good health and a good life. Then he said, "Bring your boy to my lodge." Red-Boy's mother brought her son to

Three-Moons' lodge. Three-Moons sat at the back of his lodge with paints, sweet grass and Buffalo Stones in front of him. He burned sweet grass and purified his hands. He painted the boy's body with sacred Earth paint. He prayed:

> *"My son, I pray that you live to be a very old man.*
> *To you I now give my life."*

Then Three-Moons said, "I now say two names—Red-Medicine-Star and Red-Boy. Pick the one you like."

The father nodded to his son and said, "I like Red-Boy. Give my son that name."

"I am going to tell you about the name Red-Boy," replied Three-Moons. "When I was at Two Medicine Water, I dreamed of Under-Water-Person. In my dream, I took buckskin, beads and presents and made a Bundle and threw the Bundle into a deep hole in the lake. Under-Water-Person came and said 'my name is Red-Boy.'"

Three-Moons paused a moment as if remembering, then, finally, spoke to the boy's father. "You have paid me well. You have paid for that name and Under-Water-Person hears you. Now I give the name of Red-Boy to your son."

Then, Three-Moons gave a small Buffalo Stone to Red-Boy's mother and told her, "Put it in a buckskin bag. Bead the bag with dark blue beads for the deep water and with red beads for the Sun's power. Let the boy wear it as a necklace."

"Your son's name will bring the power of fire from the Sun, which must be cooled with the depths of water and guided by the long vision of the night stars."

>>>→ • ←<<<

With a soft smile, Red-Boy remembered. Then he leaned forward and listened carefully to his father's words, spoken in his Pikuni tongue, the now worn, beaded necklace his mother had made for him swinging forward. The lodge fire filled him with warmth.

Indian with woodpile on Flathead Lake, ca . 1902.  Image No. 82-226, courtesy of Archives & Special Collectio
The University of Montana – Missoula.

# II

# A Warning From
# Stabs-By-Mistake

"Óki. Red-Boy, my story comes from Mountain Chief through his relatives. A long time ago, down on the flats, Mountain Chief, of the proud Blackfeet, set out to find a band of wandering Crees, who he knew were hunting and fishing close to the Blackfeet land."

Thomas paused and grinned at the traditional contrast. He leaned against his A-shaped backrest of peeled willow rods bound with sinew cord. Looking intently to make sure his son's eyes were with him, Thomas began the story, now and then giving shape to his words with his hands.

"Mountain Chief remembered when the Chinook winds came out of the south and, with the spring moon, melted the snow. Black Bear, his brother and second in command, became restless then and went on a journey. He traveled far into the north, to the lake of Pakowki, the home of the Cree. There he saw the son of Otter Robe; he was called Straight Shooter, who was strong, quick and fearless."

"Black Bear had seen a young girl among the Crees. She was beautiful like a flower that grows among the grass. He had wanted her for his own."

Hearing this, Red-Boy now knew the story would be linked to Annie Running Crane. The same old story of rivalry between two warriors over the girl they both loved, he figured. Red-Boy wondered if his father's story was meant to tease him. Glancing down at the red coals slowly pulsating, his father's voice sank into the background as he thought of Annie.

With an abrupt grunt, Thomas leaned forward, eyebrows raised, his gesture stopped in mid-air. The Piegan Chief's grunt and scowl prodded Red-Boy to straighten and nod respectfully; his father resumed his story.

"Black Bear said to his brother, Mountain Chief, 'I tried to court the young girl, but she cared only for Straight Shooter and would not be seen with me.

I meant to steal her and bring her back to my own people, but Straight Shooter hid and watched on that night as I entered silently into her lodge. I was attacked by him and barely escaped with my life...I knew that I must kill Straight Shooter for he had hurt and shamed me.'

"'Men fight much for glory, but fight hardest for what is almost in their hands and what they most desire,' said Mountain Chief. 'You shall have the Indian girl if you can take her.' And they sat in front of the warmth of the fires.

"Old Otter Robe was a strong Cree Chief who spoke with a straight tongue and firm words to Straight Shooter. 'My son, I have seen you many times with this young girl, looking fondly upon her. I have seen you run with her in childish play, this lowly stray child of our tribe. You know her mother was a captive who gave birth to this child and then passed over to the land of her fathers. My son, have you lost your heart to this young girl...Áwákaasii Pokaa (Deer Child)?'"

Instantly, Red-Boy's stomach tensed to a knot which rose to his throat. Not Annie after all. Hearing the Blackfeet name—Áwákaasii Pokaa—his temples pounded, tides of ancient memory flooded back. Marilyn Deer Child. His breath caught in him; before him swam their dead son, then the face of the young woman gone when he had returned from France.

His long exhale brought his mind back to summer afternoons when he snuck away with his first love and rode horseback into the tall grasslands—the soft fleshy curve of her undulating backside, gently rolling and bouncing with the trod of her mount—reminding him of his first lovemaking.

Then, his father's metallic-eyed gaze was a piercing arrow which reflected the smoldering gray embers of the lodge fire. Perhaps his father's spirit-power really did give him the cunning of the wolf, the potency of the otter.

Red-Boy shook off that notion and wondered what his father's tale was about, for the legend bore no resemblance to his Annie now or to the Deer Child, Áwákaasii Pokaa, he had known before.

Red-Boy listened more intently now, for Thomas's words and gestures cast different personal reflections on the walls of the lodge, as firelight flickered.

»»—→ • ←—««

"After Chief Otter Robe spoke to his son, Straight Shooter, the son answered, 'Father, the gentleness of beautiful Deer Child makes my heart cry out that I love her. She is a part of the light that our Creator gave to me.'

"The old Chief spoke with command, 'Son, you are young. You must have a victory over yourself. Deer Child is not the daughter of a chieftain. You know I have chosen for you another good and obedient daughter of a great hunter and mighty warrior, one who would please our Great Spirit.' The old man stopped talking and looked hard at his son. Then he spoke with a firm, straight tongue. 'Deer Child must be forgotten. I have spoken. Son, you must obey.' "

Catching Red-Boy's glance, Thomas paused. "To follow the words of your father still remains tradition," he said. Thomas slowly nodded and smiled at Red-Boy, then continued.

"Suddenly, while Deer Child was dancing at the side of a tall butte, some moving objects on the flat country attracted her attention. Deer Child took a step forward and her eyes blazed at the sight: 'Blackfeet!!' she cried. She turned and ran down the steep side of the butte to warn Straight Shooter.

" 'So,' muttered Straight Shooter, 'the warriors of Mountain Chief walk on the trail of the Cree. They bring us no good.'

"The Crees down in camp quickly took up their weapons. Soon, they came within sight of the moving horsemen. Chief Otter Robe, first of the Crees, saw the Blackfeet and stopped, watching the group with fierce, gleaming eyes.

"The approaching party of Blackfeet stopped when they saw the Crees. One horseman left the rest and rode out within speaking distance with his strung bow held high over his head, a sign that he wished to talk, but only with a serious purpose.

"Old Chief Otter Robe nodded at his son, who quickly walked out to speak to the lone horseman. They stopped, carefully measuring each other with the eye.

"Then, Straight Shooter spoke with angry words. 'What do you sneaking Blackfeet want, following on the trail of the Cree?'

"The face of the Blackfeet warrior darkened and he spoke back. 'You Cree carry much meat and game from the hunting ground of the Blackfeet. You are taking our winter food back to the lake of Pakowki out of the land of Mountain Chief.' Then he lifted his head and stood tall and announced, 'I am the Black Bear. I have taken many scalps. I am the brother of Mountain Chief. I have come with words to be given to Otter Robe, Chief of the Cree, from my brother, the mighty Mountain Chief. He tells Otter Robe that he may go on to his lodges in peace, but that he must leave part of his meat and all of his wives and daughters to the Blackfeet. There is one girl among you who is of our people . . . a fair flower, the prettiest among our young girls. This one, the Black Bear will have for his own. Go sneaking Cree with these words to Otter Robe.'

>>>→ • ←<<<

Like the arrogant "Black Bear" in his father's story, Red-Boy remembered the half-blood Victor Sanders boasting to him after the war that "I will have Annie Running Crane for my woman." Red-Boy figured that Victor's becoming a government interpreter had impressed Annie's parents.

After the war, James Vielle told Red-Boy about Victor, the sly government interpreter, the "puppy" who would ply the women with whiteman's water — liquor — and, at the same time, curry favor with the whites at the Blackfeet agency at Willow Creek and Browning. They shared a common disdain for Victor Sanders.

>>>→ • ←<<<

Thomas's voice, now slightly higher pitched and resonating, burst through his son's brooding.

"After Black Bear spoke, Straight Shooter spoke back with angry words. 'I will tell my father, the Chief of the Cree, that if he should ever say yes to the demands of the Blackfeet, I will kill him with my own hands and die before you ever breathe with snake's breath upon any woman of our tribe. Tell this to your Mountain Chief.' With these words, their talk was ended.

"Reaching his people, Straight Shooter walked over to his father, old Otter Robe, his fierce eyes burning as he spoke to his father. 'Will you, father, give half of your meat and all of our women to the Blackfeet, that the Cree may travel on to our lodges in peace or shall we keep the traditions of our fathers, save that which is ours?' "

>>>→ • ←<<<

Now, Red-Boy half stood, holding up his hand.

"Father, wait."

Thomas stopped, his eyes igniting with dark indignation.

"Father, you know your story is backwards. Why are not the Crees, instead of our Nation, the ones who are violating the honor of Blackfeet women? And my ancestor Mountain Chief — our family's honor — doesn't that matter?"

Thomas's scowl softened. Nodding and giving his son a sly, knowing smile, he replied, "Red-Boy, you know that our people and the Cree are at peace. The bones of our warriors are buried. I know in your heart you have picketed ten ponies at the lodge of Annie's father. You want the girl. But you are too quick with your affections." Thomas paused, stoking the lodge fire. "The half-blood Sanders also wants the girl. The way he courts her pleases her parents." Chief Stabs-By-Mistake stared into the lodge fire for a long minute. "But Victor has eyes that tell what the tongue would hide." Thomas locked his gaze squarely on his son's eyes. "Look twice at a two-faced man, Red-Boy. It matters not if you are Cree or Piegan. This two-faced man who woos your woman will not use the laws of our fathers. He honors not our tribal traditions nor cares about our family honor. The whiteman's law now rules, Red-Boy. Believe what I tell you. Sanders has taken the whiteman's ways. He is never to be trusted."

Red-Boy crouched, then sat back down in silence, transfixed by his father's penetrating glare. The young man lost himself in the patterns of the lodge fire. He finally glanced over at his mother. Red-Boy smiled at his parents.

"You know we have always shown you our hearts, Red-Boy," his mother softly offered.

"Save that which is ours?" Red-Boy repeated Straight Shooter's last question from his father's story. Beckoning, now, with an outstretched hand, Red-Boy implored his father to continue the strange tale, where it mattered not if you were Blackfeet or Cree.

His father's voice rose, mimicking Deer Child's cry, " 'Let us fight with our men!' ...And then to the man she loved, 'I will fight at your side, Straight Shooter!' "

Red-Boy recalled how Annie stood next to him, her chin high and a dark, defiant look, as he angrily confronted the Bureau agents at Browning and ridiculed them for not sending doctors to tend to the elderly tubercular victims down at Heart Butte.

Suddenly, his father gestured ever more fervently, his gray eyes blazing into the lodge fire.

"The Blackfeet charged on foot up the sloping south side of the butte where Deer Child had first spotted them. The battle raged until the Sun began to lower in the west. Blackfeet and Cree fell alike. They crawled to each other when wounded and locked in a death grip, fighting until the very last.

"Old Chief Otter Robe fell early in the fight, but his warrior son carried the battle — sweating, bleeding, striking, fighting, running to the side of some warrior in distress — always standing where the battle was thickest. His constant companion was Deer Child, always carrying his arrows. When these failed, she grabbed a spear or war club where they had fallen and held them for her warrior, Straight Shooter. Deer Child fought hard, striking or thrusting with willow spears where she could. Many fell dying.

"As the Sun neared the edge of the earth, Straight Shooter came face-to-face with Black Bear. The Blackfeet warrior cried, 'Ah, skulking Cree, a woman bears your weapons! A woman fights your fight! Now, coward, if you will fight, I will fight you for that woman!' With wickedness on his face, he pointed his arm at Deer Child.

"Hearing these words, Deer Child sprang forward and struck him with the club that she held. Black Bear staggered backward and looked as though he would sink for a moment. Then, he stood up and, with a howl of rage, sent an arrow into her body."

>>>→ • ←<<<

Red-Boy's gut was pierced at the thought of his long ago Deer Child and their son, both gone. Annie, his new flower, was his sole reprieve, blossoming from the frost overlaying sorrow, war and death.

For Red-Boy, Victor Sanders had become like "Black Bear" in his father's story. He drank too much whiteman's water and got too near Annie. Once, the slender young woman had, with a furious shove, sent the flabby half-blood back-peddling over a bucket of slops. Humiliated, the drunken young man had staggered after her with menacing fists, striking her several times. Red-Boy had seen this and had quickly flattened Victor using the hand-to-hand combat he had learned. Sanders glowered at Red-Boy with a black, dagger-look of hatred and rage. It took a complete moon for Annie's bruised face to heal. She told her mother she had taken a bad fall from a horse. Nellie blamed Red-Boy for her daughter's fall.

>>>→ • ←<<<

"Unh!" Thomas's excited burst startled Red-Boy. He watched his father's skillful hands as he re-enacted the story of the death struggle between "Black Bear" and "Straight Shooter."

"With the cry of a wild beast, Straight Shooter jumped at Black Bear. Other warriors on both sides drew back at the sound of the cry, to watch the hand-to-hand fight that would end the battle. Black Bear was now leader of the Black-feet, for Mountain Chief lay wounded with life leaving him. Straight Shooter was the leader of the Cree.

"They battled fiercely for a death hold that would crush or tear the life from the other. The teeth of Black Bear were white and gritting as his face twisted into a wicked snarl. The face of Straight Shooter was grim and set. Black Bear fought from hate and fury that lived inside him. Straight Shooter fought to avenge his beloved Deer Child.

"Straight Shooter got one hand on Black Bear's chin and the other hand grabbed his thick black hair. Straight Shooter was slowly bending Black Bear's head backward. Black Bear fought to loosen the hold. Straight Shooter gathered all the strength left in his body and gave a mighty pull. Like a crack of thunder, Black Bear's neck snapped. Black Bear and life parted.

"The young warrior lay with his hands still on his dead foe. His wounded body shook and he drew in great mouthfuls of air. Then he rolled over and looked up into the eyes of his faithful friend, the old warrior Stone Face, who stood over him. A strange light came from the eyes of the old warrior. They had fought and won. The Blackfeet gathered their dead and wounded and returned to the big mountain in the West.

"Straight Shooter finally rose to his feet and staggered to where Deer Child had fallen. The young Indian girl had pulled the arrow from the ugly wound, but life was slowly leaving her.

"Straight Shooter bent down and lifted Deer Child carefully in his arms. With slow, weak steps, he carried her to the shadow of Black Butte, followed by Stone Face and his woman. He laid her down gently and fell beside her, burying his face on her breast.

"When the Sun went down, Straight Shooter still lay with his face buried on Deer Child's breast. Then, he felt her soft hand stroking his head. She whispered softly, 'Be brave my warrior, for I love you. Do not grieve. I can feel the presence of the Great Spirit. Surely the Great Spirit, he will not let us part. He knows that I do not want to leave you. I want to be with you forever, to have you always for my warrior.'

"Straight Shooter raised his arm and stroked the face of the girl. With a soft voice, he told her of his love for her. He told her how he had always wanted to have her for his own, how he was glad that he had fought for her. 'Now my Deer Child let us wait the will of the Great Spirit. He will take our sorrow away and make us happy. His power is great, his ways are mysterious. He is near to us.'

"Then Straight Shooter turned. 'Ah, Stone Face. You are a good and true friend. Watch for us till the light begins where the Sun comes forth. We now wait the will of the Great Spirit.'

"'I will stand and watch until my breath leaves my body,' said Stone Face, and he fastened his eyes on the eastern sky.

"Stone Face's sits-beside-him-woman pulled her Buffalo robe closely around her and waited patiently and silently with her husband. Night came, the air grew colder and frost began lightly touching the ground.

"At the coming of morning light, a warm breeze sprang up. For a moment, things were not natural. The Crees down at their camp felt a strange, soft wind in the air. A soft musical laugh floated out of the sky, and all was still. Stone Face started, stiffened, then shook and settled back, still. His woman then shook very slowly and also became still. At that moment Stone Face became true to his name—a tall stone, always looking into the east.

"The low laugh came again, then the soft humming of a bow string that died away as two great golden eagles spread their wings and climbed above the butte."

Thomas's outstretched arms accented the image. His voice grew higher-pitched, quavering, almost musical.

"The night watchers at the camp saw the eagles float in wide circles through the early-morning sky. The fierce male screamed a cry of joy, carrying for a moment over the camp. His great wings started to move with powerful strokes as he led his mate through the wind pathways of the sky toward the mountains in the south.

"When the morning light had fully come, the people approached the place where the silent Stone Face had stood and found only a stone pillar. A short distance from this pillar was another that resembled a woman. Straight Shooter and Deer Child were gone.

"The people then said firmly among themselves, 'The Great Spirit has been among the Cree and has rewarded the warrior.' As the Sun rose higher, the Crees gathered up the camp and slowly traveled on their way back toward the lodges in the north."

>>>—→ • ←—<<<

Red-Boy watched his father, the Piegan Chief, gently rock back and forth on his comfortable willow-reed seat. The wind had died with the story heroes. The fire had dwindled to embers.

"Red-Boy, remember to take my talk. The hand that scalps the reputation of the dead wears fine fur that may cover tough meat."

Still, Red-Boy scoffed at the idea that the deceitful half-blood Victor— like "Black Bear"—could ever steal Annie from him on this Earth. She had become too much a part of his mind and his heart, of his plans for them both.

For Red-Boy, the finality of tens of thousands of soldiers tossed in the wake of poisonous, metallic warfare had left its blood-searing stain. This, and the suffering he'd witnessed at home, had utterly erased any silly notion that noble spirits soar together as eagles when life leaves the body. Before his platoon sergeant had taken a bullet through the forehead in France, he had drilled into his men that there was only "the quick and the dead." The quick and the dead—

this was the rule of survival that existed everywhere. Red-Boy would not bear witness to his people becoming "the dead." Embedded deep within him was "the quick." He would jar action from the whiteman Indian Agency. Annie would share his life because, like him, she was a survivor and unafraid.

"A nice story, Father," replied Red-Boy, "but my plan is not to disappear with Annie and have our people remember us only by looking at stone pillars or flying eagles." Red-Boy chuckled while he watched his father's expressionless face.

"The son never listens to the father," said Thomas as he slowly nodded. "But my heart is always good towards you, my son." The lines etched in his father's face seemed smoother, more relaxed now.

The father knew all too well his son's restless, angry impatience. The father's spirit too was tempered with a quieter, but no less intense, distrust born of years of bearing witness to the failure of whiteman promises as well as the crop, cattle and sheep-raising programs for the reservation. A spirit fueled, moreover, with a mistrust of those mistakenly entrusted with the management of Indian tribal funds and lands.

Reaching over, Thomas retrieved his pipe from the tobacco board and relit it. Father and son smoked again. Mother busied herself with beadwork she had started on a shawl. As the two men smoked, Thomas prayed for good health and an abundance of things that grow in the Earth, the ground-of-many-gifts. Finally, the sandstone pipe-bowl was empty.

Red-Boy knew it was time to go and rose slowly from the gray Army surplus blanket spread before the fire.

"Have a safe journey son." The young man nodded at his father. "Remember, Red-Boy, watch behind you, especially with the young woman and Sanders."

Turning, Red-Boy gave his mother and father one last grin and a nod. Putting on his army overcoat, he bent low and raised the flap to the lodge. He peered out at the silent, murky sky and the puffy snow blanket. It was dusk. He buttoned the heavy jacket and lowered the front brim of his dark Carlsbad. He would think about the half-blood and Annie's mother, Nellie Running Crane, during the cold ride back. Or perhaps he'd spend the evening at Cut Bank in the humble, clapboard home of James Vielle's parents.

Slowly, silently, Red-Boy closed the lodge-flap behind him and flinched as Cold-Maker's icicle claw reached out, gripping and raking his face.

He wondered why his father had chosen the Blackfeet name Deer Child.

# APPLICATION FOR EXECUTIVE CLEMENCY

This form may be used in applying for *pardon, commutation of sentence, or remission of fine*, etc., but *not* for pardon to restore civil rights. A different form is provided for applications of that character. Petitions may also be presented, signed by a number of persons in behalf of the applicant, but this is by no means **essential**. *There must, however, be one petition signed by the prisoner or bearing his approval*. Note carefully Rules 2, 8, 12, 13, 14, and 16, and *directions about letters*, duplicate copies of petition, etc., printed on verso side of this page.

U.S. Penitentiary

Leavenworth, Kansas,

July 29th, 1926 ......................, 192

*The President of the United States:*

Your petitioner, ........Peter Stabs By Mistake........, a Federal prisoner, No. ..16986..

confined in the ......Penitentiary...... at ......Leavenworth, Kansas..

hereby respectfully prays your Excellency to grant him a ......Commutation of sentence..
(Pardon, commutation of sentence, or remission of fine)

for reasons herein set forth.

Petitioner states that he is a resident of .....Post office, Hard Butte.. State of ..Montana..

his correct address at the time of conviction being..Hard Butte, Montana...........;

that he is a citizen of ....United States...., a ....Indian.... man, and was ..29
(State whether white, colored, or Indian)

years of age at the time the crime was committed; that he had .....never..... before been convicted

of crime or indicted therefor, and his prior record respecting crime is as follows: ...................
(State criminal record, if any, prior to

present conviction)

-----------------------------------------

-----------------------------------------

-----------------------------------------

Petitioner states that he was convicted upon a plea of ..guilty.. guilty, in the U. S. District

Court for the ................ district of ....Montana...., at ..Great Falls, Mont..

of the crime of ......Rape..
(State specifically, accurately, and fully)

Petitioner states that he had had intercourse with the girl in

the case several times, and at all times with her consent, and

that furthermore, the girl was not at any time the complainant

Several Applications for Pardon were made on behalf of Red-Boy. Pictured above is Red-Boy's Application for Executive Clemency, dated July 29, 1926.

# III

# The Petition

t read: *Penitentiary at Leavenworth, Kansas. March ___, 1926. Plea of guilty... of the crime of Rape — imprisonment for twenty years.* The inmate had entered his plea back in 1921.

A bead of sweat trickled from his forehead, sliding down the side of his Roman nose beneath his glasses, blurring his vision. Wiping his eyes with his monogrammed handkerchief, he continued to read the unsophisticated wording: *The President of the United States: Your petitioner...a citizen of United States, a Indian man and was 28 years of age at the time the crime was committed...never before been convicted of crime or indicted therefore... hereby respectfully prays your Excellency to grant him a Commutation of sentence.*

"Just another Indian begging for an early out," he muttered. Then he saw the phrase "*a false accusation.*" "Jesus," he muttered, again, with a dismissive scowl, disgusted with this all-too-familiar con line.

Leaning back, the slightly balding pardon attorney wiped his forehead and tossed the Application for Executive Clemency on the stack of papers resting atop his mahogany desk. The dampness of James A. Fry's white shirt was a constant reminder that stifling-hot summer afternoons in Washington, D.C. were unrelentingly muggy. He fixed his eyes on the ceiling fan, its long blades pushing sluggish air around his cavernous office.

"Mind if I finish filing?" Marilyn Sanders' velvety-soft voice entered the room. The pardon attorney beheld the soft curve of her hips as his twenty-seven-year-old secretary cast a warm smile from his office doorway. "No, Marilyn not a'tall. C'mon in," he replied in his Boston brogue.

"Marilyn, when you finish, ah, filing those things, please humor me and wind my clock, okay?"

Unfamiliar with the double entendre, the young woman's smile broadened. She knew he'd be disappointed if she neglected every Friday to rewind her boss's gold-inlaid Westminster chime clock.

Taken with his clever request, he arched his upper lip slightly as his eyes followed her to the olive-green filing cabinet in the far corner of his office.

He loved watching her file his things. The girls in the office were envious that her skin required no makeup. He was enchanted with her short, black, bobbed hair and that warm smile, her full lips. The curve of her lovely derriere as she bent low. Marilyn didn't follow the flat-chested style of dress so popular with the young women. Her dresses flowed smoothly over the outline of her full breasts, soft beneath the silk as she turned to fetch each manila file-folder stacked on the table, inserting the thing gently into the proper crevice with slender, delicate fingers.

Indeed, when seeing her approach to rewind the chime clock atop his desk, he felt a stirring that he tried to push away. It was more the guilt of knowing that Marilyn had replaced Lucy Thayer as caretaker of his treasured timepiece — a wedding gift when he and Lucy had married.

Lucy had rented out their Long Island home when he was shipped off to the war, and moved back to her parent's home on Beacon Hill. Then the Spanish flu hit Boston.

He received news of her death while hospitalized for mustard gas poisoning. His own death would have been a relief from the realization that he had lost his beloved young wife.

But James A. Fry, pardon attorney, was raised with a patrician Boston upbringing — honor duty, overcome adversity, serve the higher purposes of life.

His father, a prominent Boston attorney, greased his only child's admission into his alma mater, Harvard. After the war, James relented to his father's wishes and earned his legal stripes at Harvard Law School, landing a job with the Department of Justice.

He thought his father uncommonly prescient about Mr. Coolidge, knowing that his home-state friend, now president, would well serve his son's ambitions. Public service for the Harding-Coolidge administration meant a top-ranking position in the small, but exclusive, pardon attorney's office. Not to mention, the pick from a bevy of lovely women in Washington, D.C.

At first, James Fry compared the women he dated to Lucy, shaking off anyone with ideas he considered remotely offensive to those of his Wellesley-educated, but conservative, wife. Such imperious exclusiveness came instinctively to Fry, the Boston Brahmin son of an unaffectionate mother and a self-absorbed father.

Yet the Great War had imbedded within him a tighter knot, an unshakeable cynicism that often startled, and sometimes put off, his colleagues at Justice and the women he had dated. More and more, Fry's female liaisons had become infrequent sexual couplings, transitory tactile fixes. He eventually stopped dating altogether, finding even the one-night stands a poor salve for his loss and the guilt he felt at having survived when Lucy had not.

>>>→ • ←<<<

Glancing out his white-valanced office window, Fry stared at the cherry tree limbs on Vermont Avenue, bare of their pink blossoms. Somehow, the slackened limbs reminded him of how he felt after the war. He took in, again, the young woman now returned to her filing.

In a less obvious way, Marilyn stood apart from all the other women. She had an elusive quality which rather beguiled him. Still, she was not his social equal.

The thirty-two-year-old pardon attorney's eyes snuck across the room as she leaned over the oak table to retrieve some files. As if sensing the touch of his gaze, she glanced over at him. He flinched, pretending to study the Indian's pardon application lying atop the pile on his desk.

She might be interested, he told himself.

>>>→ • ←<<<

He again picked up the Indian's application. *Your Petitioner, Peter Stabs-By-Mistake, a Federal prisoner.* Fry laughed. The inmate's name was his own alibi. "How convenient," he mumbled.

"Something the matter, Mr. Fry?" asked Marilyn.

"No," he said, his face reddening. "I'm just reading a young Indian's Application for Clemency. Seems he was convicted of rape. Name's Peter Stabs-By-Mistake."

"Oh." She dropped a file and looked away. Fry did not notice her shaking hands as she quickly picked up the papers to continue filing. She wondered, not for the first time, about the events surrounding Peter's conviction.

The victim, Annie Running Crane, was the violated Indian girl and the immoral deed had taken place on a Government Reservation at *Hard Butte, State of Montana.*

He stopped, reread the last paragraph—an earlier Application for Pardon that Stabs-By-Mistake had sent in December, 1925—Fry never saw it. His brow furrowed as he realized that the Indian's current petition had taken over three months to reach his desk. He wondered if anything really important had been similarly misplaced, picturing the myriad petitions for clemency, pardon and parole stuffed into long rows of filing cabinets down the hall. He flipped through several more pages, trying to ignore the stifling humidity and his fear of official carelessness with other files.

Seems Stabs-By-Mistake claimed he was unable to read or understand the "*english language.*" Shaking his head, Fry leaned back, soothed by the gentle cadence of the chime clock. Nodding self-assuredly, the pardon attorney surmised this application was some kind of a crackpot joke—the kind that occasionally annoyed him when a subordinate failed to be alert. Still, the Indian's name made him shake his head and smile.

Twenty years for an Indian pleading guilty to a first-time rape. Seems a little harsh, he mused, remembering that a conviction for interstate transportation for immoral purposes would net only five years, maximum.

*Yet, in the case of Your Petitioner, who in the eyes of our more civilized members of the human family, is a mere child, who in his intercourse with Annie Running Crane, was only following the dictates of a natural law, with her consent, Petitioner was given the cruel and unusual punishment of twenty years.* But the girl, Annie Running Crane, must have been under the age of consent. Otherwise, why would this Indian have been convicted? Fry mused.

Glancing further through the application, he spotted one of the affidavits attached to the application. Fry suddenly pursed his lips.

"*Mr. Victor Sanders, a government interpreter, had, with Annie Running Crane's mother, accused Peter Stabs-By-Mistake of rape.*" Victor Sanders… Fry's brow tightened as he glanced over at Marilyn Sanders, noticing her velvet-mahogany skin. The young woman from out West had only been with his office a short time. Nah, he thought to himself, dismissing the thought in an instant.

Still, the name, Victor Sanders, rolled around in Fry's brain again and again. A government interpreter, an "*employee of the Indian Bureau.*" The application, for all its clumsiness, had been artfully drafted, pitting the "*Honorable*

*Department of Justice"* against the Department of the Interior, Indian Bureau. Somebody had assisted Peter Stabs-By-Mistake to prepare this Application for Executive Clemency. If left unattended, those who sponsored the application could place an embarrassing smudge on the administration. Fry continued flipping through the application.

*For any further information about the Petitioner, he refers your Honorable body to Mr. C.F. Schuster, of Holyoke, Mass., who has interested himself in Petitioner's behalf, and with whom the Honorable Department of Justice has already had some correspondence in this matter. Signed—Peter Stabs-By-Mistake.* Attached to the application was a letter from the Holyoke businessman.

"There's the catch...really swell," he muttered contemptuously. That man from Holyoke. If that man was involved in the missing application of 1925, then the three-month delay in my seeing this...But with that name, the petition became politically delicate. He would have to do more than stamp and file this one.

The New Englander was on the warpath again and he was a friend of Coolidge's. The fellow citizen from the Commonwealth of Massachusetts was not just content to run his cracker box factory in Holyoke. This prominent businessman, this dilettante Holyoker who thought himself a do-gooder for the Indians, was now pulling strings for the likes of Peter Stabs-By-Mistake, a twenty-eight-year-old ne'er do-well inmate at Leavenworth. Fry was perplexed, annoyed, and a little anxious.

Glancing up, he was startled to see Marilyn standing directly in front of his desk. "Excuse me Mr. Fry. Do you mind if I take my break now?"

"Sure," Fry quickly replied.

"Well, if you need me, I'll be back in ten minutes." She was looking directly at him with those dark eyes. Catching his look, she quickly glanced down, as she always did. He was sure it was her innate coyness—an enticement nevertheless.

Sighing, he went back to the application. He read once more that, after all, Stabs-By-Mistake *"was only following the dictates of a natural law"* with Annie Running Crane's consent. He wondered again about her age as justification for the sentence. Still, he could not let the administration become even remotely preoccupied with the manipulations of Peter's sponsor, trying to pit the Indian Bureau against Justice.

Sitting back, he stretched his arms wide and squinted, recalling a story his father had told him. It seems that one of his father's biggest clients, a competitor of the Holyoke businessman, had tangled with the man. Uncharacteristically, Mr. Fry, Sr. had lost the case; his client went bankrupt.

Studying the wall photograph of sphinx-like Calvin Coolidge, James A. Fry grinned. The wonder was that both his Protestant Brahmin father and the Irish Catholics called themselves "Coolidge Democrats." The campaign slogan came back, as if re-electing him were somehow the recipe for ridding Washington, D.C. of all its troubles and the stifling humidity—"Keep Cool with Coolidge."

Fry owed his recent promotion as chief pardon attorney to the new president.

Fry emulated the president's cynicism toward favor seekers. It justified Fry's contempt and easy dismissal of most pardon seekers—ubiquitous opportunists, fawning whiners. But what to do about the Holyoker . . .

Staring back at the black and white photograph of the aloof-looking president—his mouth set in an almost expressionless line—Fry knew that beneath the veneer, the president—like himself—did not suffer fools gladly.

Yet, uppermost of Fry's concerns this early summer of 1926 were the mid-term elections. The new attorney general and the president must not be exposed to any political embarrassment unleashed by the maneuverings of Stabs-By-Mistake's Holyoker. The Harding scandals still echoed off the walls at Justice. Fry would find a suitable answer, a clever pigeon-hole which would completely neutralize this lesser New Englander, and quickly. This is why he had been chosen to serve at Justice. To do one's duty. To protect access to the highest centers of power and prestige. Find the most prudent—the most clever—solution. Do the proper thing. Above all, avoid embarrassment for Mr. Coolidge.

Arising from his leather-upholstered chair, Fry arched his back. At nearly five-feet-six, he proudly tucked both thumbs under his suspenders and strode purposefully from behind his desk, prodded by urgency to show this Holyoker his place. Opening the door to his office, he crossed the ornately-decorated dark blue hall carpet, a plush pageantry emblazoned with fierce-eyed golden eagles and oak-leaved branches. He leaned across the doorway to Marilyn's office; his young secretary had returned. He strode quietly up behind her as she clicked away at her typewriter. Her lilac perfume drew him. He stifled an urge to touch her, just the shoulders of her silk dress.

"Marilyn, I need you to take a letter. Can you come in?"

"Sure," she replied, reaching for a stenographer's pad as she stood.

Turning, Fry almost smirked. His Harvard-educated mind had thought of the perfect sleight-of-hand: Employ the bureaucratic natural law. Peter Stabs-By-Mistake's Application for Executive Clemency would be properly pigeon-holed. And magically mired down in bureaucratic shuffling.

He seated himself behind his desk. Marilyn rested her pad on her lap, pencil poised, ready to obey the dictates of his natural law. As she delicately crossed her legs, James Fry tried to ignore her exposed knee and looked instead at her sparkling, dark eyes beneath even darker eyelashes.

"This will be a letter to Mr. C.F. Schuster of Holyoke, Massachusetts."

*"Dear Sir:*

*Regarding your letter of March 2, 1926, addressed to the Attorney General, together with the Application for Executive Clemency of Peter Stabs-By-Mistake, I have to state that your communication has today been referred to Assistant United States Attorney Miggs, at Helena, Montana, with the request that he give the suggestions contained in your communication careful consideration and report promptly his views in the premises. When his report has been received, it can then be determined what further steps should be taken with respect to the investigation suggested by you and through what source it should be conducted.*

*Respectfully,"*

"There, that should take care of it." He wasn't about to honor the Holyoker's request to have Justice open an investigation of Indian Bureau officials. Miggs, the fiery little Assistant U.S. Attorney in Helena, would close that door.

Noticing her distant look as she slowly rose from her chair, he wondered if Marilyn might somehow be harboring a secret. Was she interested in him? He should ask her to dinner. It might be interesting.

Would she be willing to accompany him to a speakeasy? Wouldn't be proper, he decided.

Pursing his lips, he reached over to the sheaf of papers on his desk, dutifully pulling another application off the top. "Your Petitioner hereby respectfully prays your Excellency...."

Morning Eagle's painted lodge is complete. In foreground Wolf Plume's daughters. (From a photo postcard

**IV**

# Deer Child
# (Áwákaasii-Pokaa)

The sticky humidity of Washington D.C. in late June of 1926 was only slightly relieved by the occasional breeze off the silver Potomac, or a ceiling fan if you happened to be lucky enough to occupy a high-rent flat. This late afternoon, a breeze was blowing in from the river, fluttering the broad green leaves on the maple trees fronting the Early-American townhouses in Georgetown. There, Marilyn Sanders sat by the open window of her small studio apartment overlooking the shores of the Potomac.

Marilyn tasted more of the bannock bread she had made earlier that Sunday morning. It had been good therapy—kneading and rolling the dough and bacon together and baking it to a special texture and thickness that only her mother and grandmother were able to bestow.

Mary Crow Woman had taught her daughter all of the home-making skills Marilyn needed on the plains. And they served her well in Georgetown; Marilyn's Friday "bannock bread surprises" made her popular with the staffers at Justice.

Finished with bannock and fruit salad, Marilyn glanced down at her stomach, remembering that the French named the Gros Ventre after their large bellies. Bellies full of women's wisdom. Her abdomen, though, showed only a slight bulge. The only female relation whose stomach bulge protruded more than Crow Woman's was her grandmother's. Grandma Mary Sheep Woman was full-to-the-brim with knowledge of the traditional ways. For a young girl of seven, the daunting tasks of food preparation, housekeeping and baby care had became far less complex under the skillful stewardship of her physically imposing but patient grandmother. Especially since her grandmother knew how to make true beauty.

One spring afternoon while collecting firewood, seven-year-old Marilyn had watched intently as Mary Sheep Woman made her young granddaughter a doll. She cut a birch limb about a foot long and four inches in diameter. Grandma then cut a groove with a butcher knife around the limb about four inches from the end, forming the doll's shoulder-line. Above this line, she carefully whittled a knob-like head, boring holes for the doll's eyes, nose and mouth. Absent any ears, hair or legs, the doll was dressed when Sheep Woman wrapped buckskin around the birch cylinder.

After much prodding from the impatient youngster, Sheep Woman made arms and legs of birch strappings. The doll's head became bigger when the knob was covered with red trade cloth stuffed with grass and trade beads were stitched on for facial features.

Then Mary Sheep Woman sat her attractive young granddaughter down for one of her first lessons in womanhood.

"You know why your doll had no face? Only holes to begin with? You must listen carefully to me now about the young girl from times-far-back. She was given the gift of beauty. And she spent all of her time looking at herself in a pond."

"Who was this girl?" asked Marilyn.

"My grandmother taught me about her. She was like you, child—in beauty and spirit. But when her mother needed her to help prepare the meals, she couldn't be found. When it was time to prepare the Buffalo hides for clothing, she was not found. When her mother wanted her to watch the younger children, she was never around."

"Did she run away, Grandma?" asked the wide-eyed child.

"Oh, no," Sheep Woman chuckled. "When it was time to serve the meals, she was the first one to eat. She got the best hides for clothing. At the Sun Dance, she was always the first in line to dance and sing. All the people were very unhappy with the young girl. And Ná pi, he saw this and Ná pi was not pleased."

Sheep Woman's young granddaughter lowered her head, glancing up at her grandmother while biting her lip. "Ná pi, he's the trickster, isn't he?"

"Yes, child. Ná pi taught us many things."

"What does he look like?" the little girl asked.

"Well, he's very, very old. He looks like some of your mother's Gros Ventre relations—her fat uncles." The old woman smiled and winked at her little granddaughter. "Has a big pot belly with thin little stick legs!"

Deer Child smiled, then giggled. "I like old Ná pi. He's funny."

"Aaee, child. Ná pi, he could be kind and funny . . ."

Mary Sheep Woman stopped, drawing her granddaughter's eyes to hers. "But...Ná pi, the trickster, he could also be mean and hurtful, child."

"Oh," the little girl exclaimed, lowering her eyes. "What did Ná pi do to the girl at the Sun Dance, Gra'ma?"

"Well, Ná pi, he came to the young woman one day and said to her, 'I gave you the gift of beauty and you have used it the wrong way. I will have to punish you.' Ná pi reached out and took the young woman's pretty face and hid it. That is why I first made your doll with only holes for a face. A woman with only a plain face is as good and pure as a woman with a face of beauty. So you see, no one is better than any other person because of how they look. You must not use your gift of beauty to be lazy and selfish. We must all help one another to survive."

Sheep Woman's stick doll and her Old Ná pi stories taught the young girl much more about the wisdom of the Elders: about giving thanks to the Creator, even in the face of loss; about preparing meals and making clothes and taking care of the younger ones. And later, she taught her granddaughter about taking care of the older ones and, when time permitted, about sewing hides with sinew into parfleches, and decorating dresses and horse headstalls with beadwork.

Oliver Red Bird Tail and Mary Crow Woman had encouraged their daughter's artistic talent, which Grandma Sheep Woman had sparked and which Marilyn took with her to the boarding school and shared with one or two of her other almost-relations — friends who were closest to her. Peter had been one.

The old birch doll, dressed in buckskin, now sat propped in the window of Marilyn's Georgetown flat. Grandma Sheep Woman had died during her granddaughter's twelfth winter.

As Marilyn surveyed her small living room, she admired her bead work, which decorated two prints hung on either side of the couch.

In the middle of the wall, above the couch, hung a silk painting of a Piegan Chief dressed in full-feathered war bonnet. Marilyn had completed this latest painting after coming back East. Since leaving Montana, she had not seen her father. Oliver Red Bird Tail, now having seen sixty-seven winters, was the man whose image was depicted on the white silk painting hanging from her wall.

She studied the painting carefully, noticing the darker outlines of his face blending and melting into fainter hues and shades and how the wrinkles became character tones. His image evidenced a subtle change of mood or expression with the changing of the light or casting of shadows—serious and deep in the dark, bold and honest in light. The fingers of her imagination continually repainted the thing, giving her comfort.

Oliver's skill as a principled, honest translator had always held Marilyn's deepest pride and respect, as well as that of the Elders and full bloods. But she shunned her uncle, Richard Sanders—an ambitious agency translator and opportunistic informant for the whiteman Indian Bureau. Oliver and his younger brother Richard had always been at odds.

Marilyn had lost contact with her closest friends, mostly because of boarding school. A few had died. Most had had children and became occupied with family life and survival.

Oliver, her father, was her only real link. Her mother, Mary Crow Woman, had died from tuberculosis after Marilyn saw twenty winters. The other old-timers on the reservation—the friends of her father—had kept to themselves. These Elders had long ago been folded inside a distant curtain that separated her world on the east coast from the curtain's other side. Yet she felt herself still connected to the other side.

Her favorite elder, Big Brave-Mountain Chief, had given Marilyn her name after Crow Woman gave birth to her in a small hovel of a log shack at Browning twenty-seven winters ago. Upon seeing the newborn, Oliver held her up, away from her mother. Mountain Chief remarked at the slimness of her features—"like a hungry little newborn deer that leaves no scent— Áwákaasii Pokaa." Deer Child. Oliver and his friend Bear-Head thought it a fitting name.

Feeling the humid breath of the infinitesimal breeze licking her shoulders and neck through the open window, Marilyn Deer Child let her tired limbs sag. A party with her girlfriends from Justice had lasted way past midnight. Her visit with Ruth Muskrat—whom she hadn't seen in weeks— brought back her days in Montana. Drawing a cool bath seemed more attractive than sitting by the window with the pressing humidity.

Walking into her small white-tiled bathroom, she slowly bent down and turned on a cool stream of water. As it gushed into the high, white porcelain bathtub, the young woman thought of her father and her half-brother and what life must be like for them now, back on the reservation.

Oliver had sired her older half-brother Victor by a young white woman, Maxine—a boarding-school teacher at the Willow Creek agency. As far as Marilyn knew, Victor had always lived with his mother. Marilyn rarely saw him except at Sun Dances. Then, at Crow Woman's urging, Marilyn would ask Victor to come stay with them. He never came and his weak excuses always hurt. Yet when she was older, while they both attended boarding school, Marilyn and her sibling grew closer. She finally realized that Oliver had missed raising his son, not out of any neglect but because of Maxine's hostility. Forever afterward, Marilyn felt sadness for her father rather than any real animosity towards Victor. The animosity she saved for Maxine.

Turning the bath water off, she caught a glimpse of herself in the mirror. She had cut and bobbed her long, silky black hair right after coming East. The latest "flapper" style. It seemed the thing to do. But flattening her bosom, like the other young women at Justice did, seemed strange and unwomanly—something Pikuni women just didn't do.

She was proud of her promotion, from a senator's lowly file clerk and staffer to the pardon attorney's secretary at Justice. But she never really felt drawn to the Washington party scene. Cutting and bobbing her hair and wearing the shorter, flimsier "flapper" outfits was an artistic novelty, not an expression of her life-style—who she really was. The mere familiarity born of the passage of years made her fit in. Except when she was naked, as she was now.

She felt the coolness of the water slip over her submerged legs and hips, and hummed as she sponged her shoulders. She recalled the times spent with friends cooling off in the hot Montana summers, running and splashing in the small creeks back home, especially Cut Bank Creek. She missed how long her black-braided hair had been, like Ruth Muskrat Bronson's hair.

A student at Mount Holyoke College, Ruth Muskrat was her idol.

When it came time for the Committee of One Hundred to present its recommendations on the future course of the Bureau of Indian Affairs, the committee met with the president in 1923. Marilyn had attended the outdoor ceremony. Ruth Muskrat and the president had simply stared at each other. Dressed in a traditional Cherokee Indian princess dress of beaded white deerskin and muslin, Ruth Muskrat approached President Coolidge. Her beautiful dark eyes flashed, her long black braids hung down her chest to her waist. Marilyn remembered how the young Cherokee woman had delivered a short, passionate speech and called for renewed support for the Indian.

Marilyn first met her best friend in Washington at a reception arranged by Montana's Senator Walsh. Impressed that Ruth Muskrat had already become experienced in reservation social work through participation in YWCA programs, Marilyn soon spent her own Saturday mornings and early afternoons at the YWCA near Howard University.

Marilyn Deer Child had been right about Ruth Muskrat Bronson; her spirit was catching.

The young woman gracefully stepped out of the tub and carefully dried her hair, arching her back with pride at the knowledge that she, too, had come a long way, graduating from boarding school in Montana, and then finishing a year-and-a-half at the Corcoran School of Art in D.C.

Toweling herself off, she felt the puckered skin and glanced down at the scar—evidence of an emergency appendectomy and her stay in a D.C. hospital. She knew she had been lucky. On the reservation, she would have died for lack of medical care. Like the old people, she would have been placed down on robes and frayed blankets in their lodges—sick, blinded or tubercular, waiting to die. No doctors.

Glancing over, she beheld her profile in the mirror behind the bathroom door. She was not usually prone to linger here very long. Turning slowly to observe her full nakedness, she walked towards the mirror. She noticed the scar, the few stretch marks on the soft sloping curve of her abdomen, her breasts.

She suddenly began to weep. She gulped several times, trying to swallow the hurt. Marilyn Deer Child's heart still carried the infant she had borne more than eight winters ago back in Montana.

The little baby boy had come out too early, in the dead of winter, in her parent's cabin at Browning, before Crow Woman had passed over to the other world.

She squeezed herself slightly now, thinking how the small infant would not take to her breasts, no matter what she did, no matter how she tried, no matter how many times she cried. Crow Woman tried to reassure her.

Her son grew weaker, she grew more desperate. No milk or formula was available. With Crow Woman's reassurance, she tried expressing milk from herself. But the infant ate little and grew listless.

The infant's father was there, too. He and his friend rode for days to find a doctor. No doctor came. The terrible influenza epidemic had completely taxed whatever money the Indian Bureau had allotted to the subagency for medical attention on the reservation. This is what her baby's father was told. His rages at his helplessness came more often, the sicker their baby boy became.

Red-Boy was the father—his consuming involvement gave him ownership as the father. She confided this to her mother. Oliver thought it proper that they be married in the church. Red-Boy agreed. Yet Marilyn did not want to keep Red-Boy there for any wedding, preferring instead to see him honor his commitment as a warrior.

One of the few on the reservation to enlist, Red-Boy, like other Indian enlistees, had been rejected outright by the whiteman's army. Then, as casualty lists grew longer, a few of the persistent ones, like Red-Boy, were finally allowed to go. Marilyn's pride in Red-Boy was brief in the face of a dying child.

At first Red-Boy refused to leave for the war, thinking that staying with her and the baby was the best thing to do. She tried to reassure him. It was better for him to fight for his country and his people. She and Crow Woman would find a doctor. Beyond-Sun-Person would protect them all—they would give thanks to Naa-tó'si, the Holy One, at the Sun Dance when he returned.

But before he was to leave, Red-Boy's baby boy died. In his grief, he wandered alone on horseback for two days. Marilyn, lost in her grief, urged Red-Boy to go. She could not bear the double burden of their grief.

His leaving was the right thing for them both.

>>>—→ • ←—<<<

By summer, Crow Woman was buried in a similar unmarked grave beside the infant grandson she had tried so hard to save.

Marilyn felt guilty to have survived.

She resolved then that she would escape, like Red-Boy had done. The grief Marilyn and her father shared—the death of a son and a grandson, the death of a mother and wife—wove a tight bond between them. He understood her desire to go. Unselfish as he was, Oliver impressed upon Marilyn the idea that, although her leaving the reservation would sadden them both, he knew that such an opportunity would make her a stronger woman.

The opportunity came when one of Senator Thomas Walsh's staffers asked Oliver if he knew of someone from the reservation boarding school "smart enough" to serve on the Montana senator's staff. Walsh wanted to showcase how educated "these young Indians were from Montana's Indian schools." Immediately, Marilyn had offered to make coffee, buy donuts, run errands and do whatever else it took to keep the senator's staffers happy. Her father, Oliver, had been her conduit out.

The young woman first moved to Helena and worked at the senator's office with a staff of three other females.

Smart enough to keep her counsel about Indian boarding school abuses, Marilyn finally persuaded a senior Walsh staffer that he needed a research assistant—a trusted Montanan—if the senator really wanted to showcase Indian policy back East. Marilyn rode the iron horse back to the senator's D.C. office after a three-month grooming period in Helena, during which time Marilyn worked hard to improve her office skills.

>>>→ • ←<<<

When Deer Child was ten, Grandma Mary Sheep Woman gave her the small hunting knife which she had used for preparing hides and for cooking. She taught her granddaughter to define her own tipi ring of protection with the use of Grandma's knife. Deer Child would sit near her parent's small cabin and draw, with the point of the knife, a large circle in the dirt so that no one would enter her space. For hours she worked on the ground—scraping small pieces of deer hide with her knife. She made horses or Buffalos, whittling cottonwood branches for legs.

The knife had accompanied her to D.C.—now a letter opener and reminder that there could always be a magic circle around her.

Few really entered that circle. Ruth Muskrat Bronson was safely there, helping Deer Child gatekeep the circle. She brought to Marilyn new acquaintances and friends from Mount Holyoke College and beyond who shared Marilyn's interest in Native art.

Marilyn and Ruth talked politics, art, men. One discussion of woman's suffrage involved the argument of women as "intelligent human beings," and finally to H.L. Mencken's small book, *In Defense of Women*.

"The man's never lived with my people and seen the work our women do." Marilyn wasn't smiling. "The man's disgusting! Why did you even give me this whiteman's book?"

Ruth Muskrat rolled her head back and laughed. "Mencken's not very likable, is he? Had to read him for an English class." Ruth got up from the couch and strode to Marilyn's kitchen to get her second glass of iced tea. "But you missed the point, girl."

"What point?"

"Women are ungraceful, misshapen and women need to be put in their place," announced Ruth Muskrat. "Women are flawed, incompetent, devious, weak, more uncivilized."

"What?!"

"But I guess you didn't read his punch line."

"What punch line?"

Ruth pointed to a line in the beginning of the chapter entitled 'Woman Suffrage':

'...I am convinced that the average woman, whatever her deficiencies, is greatly superior to the average man.'

"A back-handed compliment to women—even Indian women—huh?" Ruth had on a wide grin. "Mencken's a little strange, I know." Both women laughed.

A knock on Marilyn's door brought in their friend Rosa Diabo, wearing her familiar, mischievous "Saturday nite smile." A graduate of Mount Holyoke College, Rosa was a young Mohawk cultural researcher for the Smithsonian. She hailed from the Brooklyn Caughnawaga community, and most of her male relations were New York steelworkers or lived in Canada, a place where one could easily obtain "giggle water" during Prohibition. Rosa reached inside her black-beaded tote bag and drew out a green bottle.

"Swell time for a little private créme de menthe, don't ya think? My treat, girls."

More laughter and talk of H. L. Mencken prompted Ruth Muskrat and Rosa to introduce Marilyn to Hemingway's *The Sun Also Rises*, which portrays a group of Americans and Red-Boy's "lost generation," disillusioned by the war. Talk of Hemingway led to a discussion of Theodore Dreiser's *An American Tragedy*, about a weak young man executed for murdering his pregnant girlfriend. Dreiser took to task the society that had produced and destroyed the young man. Deer Child, seeing her own Piegan-Pikuni society, was thrust back to the ghost-trail of evils which had destroyed their baby boy and wondered if those same evils had finally destroyed Red-Boy.

Even as the women wrestled intellectually and emotionally with these writers, Marilyn's friends were never privy to the deepest secrets and sorrows that lay at the core of her carefully created and guarded woman's circle.

>>>→ • ←<<<

e looked at herself fully in the mirror now, wondering what would ...........  to her as she aged. She looked to see the faintest trace of crow's feet. Finding none, she scrutinized her stomach, proud of her smooth soft-textured bronze skin. The scar and a few stretch marks left their footprints of fear and pain on her body. Still, her full hips framed legs which descended past strong calves to sturdy ankles. She admired her long, athletic legs that had outrun most of the boys back at boarding school.

When she first arrived back East, she tried wearing the fashionable patent leather heels, but had grown tired of the constant pain in her feet and back and had compromised by wearing more fashionable versions of flats she had worn on the reservation.

Turning from the mirror, she slipped into her lavender bathrobe and cinched the drawstring tightly, deciding that it was better to face in a new direction, away from her past.

At the living room couch, she flopped down and gave a deep sigh. Again she thought of Red-Boy and the way her boss had almost choked with ridicule when he read the name Peter Stabs-by-Mistake.

She didn't dislike Fry. Around her, he possessed a kind of shyness that made him seem vulnerable. She laughed out loud, thinking how the man would be offended by her own people's earthiness and sense of humor. The smell of his strong deodorant in the morning meant that he would certainly be put off by the smoky-willow odor of her male relations.

Still, he was professional and polished and spoke with that strange Boston accent she found so foreign, yet intriguing and appealing. His world seemed far away and alien to her. She could not imagine what his parents were like or what his life growing up in private schools had meant. She thought of her boarding school days and wondered if there might be any similarity.

But for all of the man's wealth and education, his face at times betrayed a deep, burrowing sadness that made him seem defenseless. She understood that feeling. One moment, he would be intensely focused on processing case files, dictating letters, giving orders. At other times, mostly in the afternoon, she would find him staring out the spacious windows from behind his large desk. Then his jaw sometimes slackened, a man lost, forlorn, beyond the reach of ordinary man.

She smiled as she thought of times when she caught him drowsing at his desk; he would snap upright and resume the proper pardon attorney position. His attitudes and precise mannerisms also amused her. She found him interesting and often charming but, well, he was older than she and so much better educated. She couldn't imagine what his friends were like or what they did for fun.

Her thoughts of Fry evaporated when her eyes came to the maplewood dresser opposite the couch. The bottom dresser drawer, slightly open, seemed to be beckoning to her. She hesitated. Along with her undergarments, therein lay pieces of and keys to her past, letters that evoked memories and emotions she kept near to her but safely hidden. Deep in the bottom of the dresser, they could not inspire curiosity in others or unexpectedly grab her attention.

Without deciding to do so, she opened the drawer and reached the small packet in the bottom to reexamine certain of its contents, to confirm what she already knew, to look for clues to what was happening. Old letters she had read and reread and carefully tucked back fell into her lap when the ribbon holding them was untied. There was a letter from Red-Boy at war, which she never answered. One from her half-brother written at Red-Boy's trial, also never answered. More numerous were the letters from her father. All filled with things she would never tell her friend Ruth, much less her boss, James A. Fry, pardon attorney.

She slowly opened the worn letter from her half-brother, Victor, and reread it once again:

*Great Falls, Montana*
*September 26, 1921*
*Sister Marilyn,*

*I received your letter of August 26th in reply to my letter. So good to hear from you. Father is well and taking work as Indian interpreter for white folks in court and on the reservation. We were all worried about you dying in the hospital back there at the whiteman's capital in D.C. Our hearts were truly glad to hear that the doctor pulled out the poison from your side. Hope you are feeling well.*

*I am happy to tell you the good news that Red Boy is finally being sent away. I always knew he was a trouble maker, no good coward. I am sitting in the court of the federal judge now looking at the coward. He stands before me like a frightened badger. Leavenworth will soon be his home. After all he did before he tried to rape Annie Running Crane and was caught with her. He never could keep his hands to himself. The Indian police acted quickly. He still had no respect for the women when he came back from the war. He will soon be with his other soldier cowards at Leavenworth. It was a good thing that the judge asked Uncle Richard to translate for him.*

*Now Annie, she will soon want to be my woman. I will marry her. There is much sickness and shortage of food on the reservation. The agency is always doing its best. Red Boy always thinks he knows so much and has been critical of the ways of the Indian agency. Red Boy was always bragging about being in the war and he caused much trouble, threatening the agents. He made false statements and made everyone angry. Soon he will be gone. The whiteman's justice has served us well.*

*You will be proud to know sister that I am now official government interpreter for Commissioner of Indian Affairs Mr. Frank Campbell here on the reservation. I have a very important job. Some day I even plan to run for tribal council. Uncle Richard is very proud of me. I hope you are proud of me and all is well with you sister. Please write soon.*

*Victor.*

>>>→ • ←<<<

Look at the sneaking coward, Victor Sanders thought. Now he's sweating.

The twenty-eight-year-old Indian's brow was deeply furrowed. Dressed in worn, but clean, jeans and shirt—two dark braids on either side of his head—Red-Boy provided a sharp contrast with his lawyer's black suspenders holding up a pair of rumpled brown suit pants. The wrinkled pants ended, it appeared to Victor, almost four inches above the tops of the counselor's immense pair of scuffed and well-worn dress shoes.

A harsh breeze whipped rain pellets through the firs and cedars surrounding the three-story brown brick and ivory-trimmed Federal Courthouse in Great Falls, Montana.

It was September 26, 1921, and United States District Court Judge George Bernard Whiting, in his black robe, was perched on his loft. He peered out at those arrayed in his immense, high-ceilinged courtroom. Federal Judge Whiting was a balding eagle of a man in his late fifties. His sharp, dark eyes were piercing, intimidating, giving Victor a feeling of smug confidence. To the judge's left were the witness stand and the empty jury box. The jury men had just been temporarily excused by the judge, ushered back to the jury room by the bailiff.

Seated diagonally to Judge Whiting's lower right was a middle-aged, disheveled female court reporter, facing the raised witness stand and taking hand stenography of the criminal proceedings.

At counsel table sat Assistant United States Attorney Miles O'Donnell. It was still uncommonly hot in Montana, but the government prosecutor wore a crisp white shirt, red-silk tie and black pinstriped suit with vest. His wavy black hair was pasted back in layers from his high, sweat-free forehead.

Seated at counsel table to the right was the young Indian's representative, a tall, bushy, white-haired gentleman in his late sixties. He mopped his brow and rose slowly from his chair. His client sat next to him, head forlornly resting on his left palm, elbow propped on the armrest of the wooden chair.

The elderly counselor peered awkwardly around the courtroom, his furrowed eyebrows twitching. He was nervously manipulating his client's file with both hands, elbows going every-which-way.

"Are you ready to proceed, Mr. Elliott?" asked Judge Whiting. "Shall I bring the jury back in?"

"I...need one more minute, Your Honor...to confer with my client," requested Elliott. The judge nodded. The smartly dressed Assistant U.S. Attorney now turned to speak with those behind him—the victim, her family, friends and observers.

Directly behind the pinstriped prosecutor in the front bench sat Nellie Running Crane. A short woman with graying hair, she was listening patiently with arms folded on her lap, eyes lowered. Occasionally, she spoke in whispers to the young women seated to her right—Louise Red Fox, Maggie Wolf Plume and Mary Horn. All three young women had long-braided hair and wore brightly colored red and blue trade cloth blouses and their finest long muslin skirts.

Victor watched Nellie and the young women intently. Squirming and fidgety, they alternately turned towards the pinstriped suit and swiveled backwards toward Victor's uncle, Richard Sanders, an older Indian seated behind them. Sanders had been selected as court translator for these criminal proceedings. During breaks in the trial, they spoke in whispered tones with Nellie. At times, they seemed puzzled when talking with Richard Sanders, or appeared frightened when testifying. Sitting silently in the back of the courtroom was Richard Sanders' brother, Oliver, who had been passed over as translator. Nonetheless, he stayed.

Seated on the other side of Nellie Running Crane, closest to defense counsel, was the victim—Annie Running Crane. Victor's eyes never left her for long. Throughout the trial, her head remained bowed, her hands folded on her lap. He saw her cast a furtive glance around the backside of the bushy-haired man to see the seated Red-Boy. Ed Elliott was bent low, almost doubled-in-two with his angular rearend pointed back toward Annie and the pinstriped suit as he spoke to his client.

One row behind Richard Sanders, with eyes glaring and squinting, sat Victor. The high-arched ceiling of the courtroom would have swallowed the intensity and bitterness of Victor's look were it not for the return of his glare by Red-Boy, as he attempted to glance around the bent-in-two pillar at Annie.

Victor Sanders, government interpreter for Indian Superintendent Frank Campbell, leaned back and smirked. He and his uncle Richard had made sure that Superintendent Campbell received his subpoena and rearranged his busy schedule so he could testify for the prosecution. They had seen to it that Campbell pulled all the right strings to get Richard appointed as official translator at Red-Boy's trial. When his father, Oliver, learned that he had been passed over, he went straight to Judge Whiting's chambers. The officious judge, irritated with Oliver's sudden, unexpected intrusion, scolded the elder, then reluctantly threw him a bone—announcing that Oliver could serve as alternate translator if Richard became sick or if the defendant entered a plea of guilty. Or during sentencing.

Victor knew he had finally scored a fatal coup against Red-Boy, the troublemaker, this so-called soldier-warrior with the heart of a coward. This skulking violator of his women.

It had all happened so fast at the boarding school when Marilyn became with child. Victor felt a biting instinct that Red-Boy would not show his heart and come to him or his uncle with the truth. What festered inside Victor, though, was the notion that Red-Boy's eyes told what his tongue would hide. He was equally rankled that his father, Oliver, had not demanded justice for his own daughter from the sneaking coward. When the baby died, Red-Boy left his grieving sister for France. His convenient escape only deepened Victor's conviction that here was a truly dishonorable man. Victor had never bothered to hear of Red-Boy's futile attempts to find a doctor or Oliver's help when Red-Boy had to bury his son. Hearing the whispering in front of him and watching Annie intently, he thought how much she reminded him of his sister. Victor intended to picket ten ponies at her father's lodge; he wanted Annie Running Crane.

"Counsel, do you wish to take a recess before proceeding?" The sharp query from an obviously annoyed Judge Whiting interrupted Victor Sanders' thoughts. The bent-in-two pillar sprang erect, head slightly trembling and shaking.

"Your Honor, we would like about a thirty-minute recess," requested the pinstriped prosecutor, coming to Elliott's rescue. The young Assistant U.S. Attorney looked over at the aged pillar, smiled and nodded confidently.

Framed by the state flag of Montana to his right and the nation's stars and stripes to his left, the sharp-eyed Judge Whiting banged his gavel, imperiously announcing, "The court will be in recess until 9:30." The judge, now more predatory raven than eagle in his black robe, slowly rose and swooped off, disappearing into his inner sanctum, where he would remain ensconced for the time being.

Victor thought he heard a sigh escape Red-Boy's mouth, belying his nervousness.

Victor grinned to himself. The frightened badger actually thinks he's safe, so long as the black raven judge stays in his nest.

The court reporter sat impassively, frumpish in her impatience, eyeing the white-tiled ceiling.

Time inside the cavernous courtroom ticked by as slowly as the large hand on the wall clock.

Victor Sanders watched. The pinstriped suit was growing impatient with the young women seated just behind him. Two of the young women stood, whispered to each other and nervously gestured first to Richard Sanders, then to Oliver Sanders. They were agitated, perhaps frightened by some force with which they could not reckon.

From behind Victor, came his father. Without talking to his son, he stepped forward and beckoned to his brother. Victor noted his father's eyes fixed hard on his uncle. Oliver spoke softly but intently to his brother as the two men walked to the back of the courtroom.

Turning slightly, Victor could see his uncle standing close to his brother. With eyes glaring, Richard dismissively shook his finger in his brother's face, turned, nodded at the prosecutor, and strode back to the front. Oliver caught Victor's eye and stared at his son with disappointment and disgust. Victor looked away. Nellie and her daughter sat almost immobile—eyes lowered— reminding Victor that Indian women were usually very timid in a whiteman's world. Except, of course, his sister who had done well off the reservation. Beneath it all, Victor envied his sister's self-assurance, yet felt unappreciated that she was not here to witness his coup on Red-Boy.

It rankled the half-blood that Red-Boy was even allowed to converse with his bent pillar. He had hoped that Red-Boy would never return from France. To Victor, becoming a modern warrior was Red-Boy's naive way of becoming important. Why bother with that when the whiteman's government could give real power. He would be able to pick and choose many opportunities to grow powerful. Then he would have real respect. And today would witness his big coup, a step to becoming a true tribal chief like Annie Running Crane's father and grandfather. A much better, more powerful, tribal chief than Red-Boy's foolish tradition-bound father. He would make his family, especially Uncle Richard and his sister, proud. He would become as revered as Mountain Chief.

Taking a small tablet and pencil from his parfleche and crossing his legs, he put pencil to pad and began a letter to his sister, Marilyn Deer Child. At last, he had struck the fatal coup—the battle blow of victory—to avenge her honor and save Annie Running Crane for himself. A short time later, the door to Judge Whiting's chambers opened.

"Ladies and gentlemen, all rise!"

Judge Whiting strode back to his bench, perched again as the devouring Raven from high atop the hill of whiteman justice. Victor hid a small smile of satisfaction when he saw the judge's steel gray eyes glower at Stabs-By-Mistake, ready to accept his plea of guilty to the charge of raping Annie Running Crane.

»»—→ • ←—««

Deer Child looked at the nearly five-year-old yellow-faded letter. Wiping tears from her cheek, she pressed her lips tightly together. Victor talked with the tongue of a stubborn child, she thought. She hated how he flaunted his victory over a man she once loved and whose child she bore.

Victor's letter was as impossible to answer as Red-Boy's letter from France had been. She wished there were something in the lessons of wisdom and grace her Grandma Sheep Woman had shared that would have given her the wisdom to answer first Red-Boy's, then Victor's letters.

As she gathered the letters and reached for the ribbon, all she could feel was shame for her half-brother. She wondered what else he had done, who else he had become these past seven winters, who else he had deceived. She feared he never had or never would talk with a straight tongue to anyone — whiteman, Indian or himself. It wasn't just because he was a half-blood. But that half his blood was his greedy and lying white mother, Maxine. Oliver, their father, was a good, honest man.

But for Victor, like Maxine, the tomahawk was always raised towards anybody who was better than he was. Especially Red-Boy, whose father was a tribal chief. Deer Child knew that Victor hated Red-Boy because he believed Red-Boy had violated her, then deserted her. Victor's hatred had blinded him from the truth of her relationship with Red-Boy. Ignorance and jealousy fed this unfounded hatred.

Wiping her tired eyes, the young woman knew it was late. Darkness covered the Potomac and filled her room. She must get some rest, for to-morrow the endless petitions, requests for pardon and other favors asked of His Excellency, the president, would come streaming through. The quiet Coolidge, The Great White Father, who listened to others and liked to wear Indian headdresses. She liked that. It reminded her of the Elders who sat together around their lodge-fires smoking the medicine pipes of kinnikinnick — they too said very little.

Pulling down her Murphy bed, she slid softly under the covers, still holding the faded letter as she settled back on the pillow.

Glancing up at the silk painting of her father in the white eagle-feather war bonnet, Marilyn Deer Child felt isolated from her people, holding on to a last, fading yellow piece of flimsy linkage of shame and hatred to her past, yet missing the comfort of her father, her childhood, her home.

She listened to the breeze off the river, silence surrounding the intermittent rustling in the maple trees. She had taken the trail to the East where the sun-farthest-rises, promising herself never to look back. Yet just this once, Deer Child had taken a furtive, painfully exhausting glimpse back across the Ghost-Trail to the Sand Hills.

Drawing of east wall and portal of Leavenworth Penitentiary. Courtesy of Joseph Wagner.

# V

# Leavenworth-1921

He could hear it every so often—the faint rustle of wind beyond the iron bars silhouetted against the thick glass window. Peter Stabs-By-Mistake wondered if his cell at Leavenworth would have a window. Awaiting transport for over a month, he had decided that the only blessing of his holding cell here in Great Falls was the window.

"Lights out!" barked an unseen male voice from the end of the long hallway.

Peter stood there in the darkness by the window, letting his eyes adjust. Outside, tree limbs were waving, beckoning to him, beginning to yield their leaves.

He wondered again about Leavenworth. Would the inmates behave like his buddies did during the war in France? How would the confinement change him?

The bars of his cell window stood out as his eyes continued adjusting to the darkness. His gut sank once again at the realization that he was completely disconnected from everything.

The weight of Peter's helplessness drew him to his bunk, his mind full of the trial and his own angry undercurrents, fighting to strike back at all those who lied to put him here.

He knew poor folks in Montana, especially Indians, went without a lawyer when accused of a crime. Accusation of the crime of rape was no exception.

A month after being arrested, he had an unexpected visitor. A gaunt, elderly man dressed in an ill-fitting, dark suit gingerly entered his cell.

At first, Peter could not understand how his relations could possibly afford a "city" lawyer. Ed Elliott finally told the young Indian that he had been representing all kinds of folks, including Indians, during his forty-plus years as a lawyer. Claimed he knew many of the Elders on the reservation. Curly Bear and Peter's father, Thomas, had approached him. The lawyer's small retainer had been paid by the sale of some precious livestock. "Why can't my trial be with my own people, in our own tribal court back at the agency?" Peter had asked. The fact that his trial was about to take place far to the southeast of the reservation in a federal court—and a whiteman's court at that—baffled the young Indian.

The not altogether unsympathetic counselor looked down at his legal pad a long time before answering.

"Your father ever speak to you about when Crow Dog killed his cousin, Spotted Tail? You know Spotted Tail was Chief of the Brule band of the Lakota Sioux."

"Yes, I know," replied Peter, barely nodding his head. "Was sentenced to death in a whiteman's court. My father told me Chief Crow Dog showed great honor and bravery. He was allowed to go home to prepare his death song and white buckskin suit to die in. He went back with his sits-beside-him-woman to be hanged."

"Yes. Then our Great Court, the United States Supreme Court, threw out the conviction. The Great Court said that Indian nations, not whiteman's courts, have full control over their own people."

The young Indian's brow slowly furrowed in puzzlement. "But why are we not in an Indian court, then?"

"Because," replied Elliott slowly, "the Congress in Washington, D.C. was outraged by that decision."

"Why?"

"Because an Indian was acquitted of a crime and," the counselor broke off, glancing down at his note pad with an almost embarrassed look, "our government would not tolerate the idea of Indians controlling their own affairs."

Peter looked hard at the lawyer, slowly nodding his head. He already understood. "That's when they enacted a law in 1885," continued the counselor. "This law got rid of the Great Court's decision. The Major Crimes Act makes it so that major crimes are to be tried in the whiteman's federal courts."

"Yeah," interjected Peter, dropping his head. "Don't matter if my people consider just holdin' hands with a woman...major or not, huh? 'Cuz that's all

Annie and I were doin' when they arrested me." The Indian's voice trailed off in a resigned monotone, belied only by his look of disdain.

>>→ • ←≪

Weeks later, when the trial finally began, Peter was still bewildered by the workings of the whiteman's court.

"Mr. Elliott, I've heard of the crime of rape in the military," Peter whispered to his white-haired counselor. "But why do I plead guilty to rape? I would never hurt Annie."

The federal judge had just granted a brief recess during the jury trial. The tall, hunched-over attorney, a worried look cast on his sunburnt, wrinkled face, slowly shook his head.

"Peter," he whispered, "all of these witnesses seated here have testified against you. That's why I stopped the trial. Nellie Running Crane thinks you raped her daughter." Ed Elliott paused as his young client glanced over at Annie Running Crane, seated next to her mother.

"I had to pull the plug," the counselor muttered, almost to himself. "All we've been getting are hostile looks from the jury…just waiting to convict you." Nellie was now looking sternly at the prosecutor and gesturing in a deliberate manner as she spoke to Richard Sanders, who was translating.

Turning his head slowly, Elliott continued, "If Judge Whiting hears you plead now, he will be less harsh on you. If you finish your jury trial, that white jury will certainly find you guilty, and Judge Whiting is very harsh with those found guilty by a jury. Says it wastes his courtroom time." Elliott paused and tilted his head, frowning. "I have never seen a white jury acquit an Indian of anything."

"But I didn't rape Annie!" Peter insisted. Elliott held his hand up, firmly gesturing to the young man to keep his voice down. Peter glowered at his counselor. "I am a veteran. I have fought for this country, the whiteman's country!" he hissed, his sarcasm finally unleashed. "Doesn't that stand for somethin'?" Peter's jaw clenched as he continued to stare at Elliott.

"The best you can hope for is a light sentence. If your conduct in prison is good, they will let you out before the end of your sentence."

It had all come down to this. The dark irony pounded in the young Indian's head. Defeat reverberated in his heart. Although Victor's father, Oliver, had come to the trial to offer his reliable services as translator, he had been dismissed and the role of chief trial interpreter had been relegated to Victor's powerful and crooked uncle, Richard. Under solemn oath, the words of Nellie Running Crane and Annie's friends had been translated for the jury.

An Indian police officer named Peter White Man and Victor Sanders, the half-blood coward, had "seen him commit the act." Annie's friends had already testified against him.

Red-Boy had bristled with dark contempt when Superintendent Campbell had taken the witness stand with an imperious air, testifying for the prosecution. Lie after lie had spewed forth from the whiteman's mouth.

Annie had started to testify. But ten minutes into her testimony, Peter's attorney had asked for a recess to "discuss a matter with my client."

"Let Annie continue her testimony, Mr. Elliott. I know she will tell the truth."

"No," the counselor had firmly interjected. "She has already said you did it. There is no point in hearing more."

"But she's only saying that because she's frightened! Frightened of those Sanders over there. I know it! She'll tell the truth, I know she will!"

Elliott put up his hand, gesturing the young man to stop. "We can't change what she has already said, Peter." Peter, his eyes now glistening, leaned back, laced his fingers in his lap and turned to face the judge's empty bench. A long time passed. Peter's stare fixated on the shiny golden eagle atop the American flag, its proud head facing the window, fierce eyes fixed outside, as if imploring Peter to escape now, before it was too late. The whispering and occasional din of excited utterances carried across the hollow room as Peter and his elderly trial counsel waited for the inevitable to play out.

"All rise! Court is now is session. The Honorable Judge Whiting presiding." The bailiff took his place behind the frumpish court reporter sitting straight, both ready to proceed.

Peter glared at Richard, then his eyes met Oliver's. Oliver's lips parted as if to speak but instead he just sighed and looked away.

The imperious Raven once again took his position. Peter stared unmoving at the harsh Black Robe judge.

"Mr. Elliott, are you ready to proceed in the matter of The United States versus Peter Stabs-By-Mistake?"

"Yes, we are, your Honor. My client wishes to dispense with the trial and to change his plea to a plea of guilty to the charge of rape."

From across the room, the young women sat mute, their widened eyes now transfixed on Peter.

"Okay, counsel. Mr. Richard Sanders, thank you for serving this court as translator," announced Judge Whiting, to which the Government Interpreter smiled and nodded reverently.

The judge's eyes settled on the defendant standing next to his aged counselor.

"Peter Stabs-By-Mistake, please stand." Pausing, the judge glanced to the back of the courtroom. "Oliver Sanders, you can come forward. You may assist me, now, if it is necessary to translate for the prisoner — uh, excuse me — the defendant."

Peter caught Victor's eye as he turned to watch Oliver come forth. The flat glare of hatred added to the heavy shroud of gloom that had settled over him at the mention of the word "prisoner." The last time he had felt his legs tremble and weaken was in France, running over broken trees and through stinking trenches, lying in muddy foxholes as shells pounded and exploded right on top of him.

"Peter Stabs-By-Mistake, your lawyer has indicated that you wish to change your plea and enter a plea of guilty to the charge of rape. Is that your wish?" The courtroom went silent. The judge and the others waited.

"Yes," came the hollow voice of the young warrior, now with his head lowered.

"Has your lawyer explained to you what the maximum penalty for rape is?" Peter did not remember that Elliott had said the maximum sentence for conviction of rape was twenty years. He remembered only that the judge might be lenient if he weren't convicted by a jury. The judge didn't like trials "to waste time and money."

"Alright, then, I am satisfied that you understand the charges before you and the consequence of pleading guilty to the charge of rape. Accordingly, it is the judgment of this court that you be sentenced to a term of imprisonment at Leavenworth Penitentiary in Leavenworth, Kansas for a period of twenty years, which sentence shall begin on December 4, 1921. That will be the judgment of this court."

Peter stared, immobile, expressionless, unable to move.

"Bang!" The gavel came down hard on the marble throne, a shell exploding right above his muddy foxhole, startling him.

Turning, he looked at Annie, who met his look with the full embrace of her wide, glistening eyes. If only he had known his last touch would be a held hand, he would have said and done so much more.

There, the last he saw of her before being led to the holding cell, were her eyes, imploring him—a pleading sadness, a look of sorrow that penetrated so deep within him he knew he would never forget.

Her mother quickly jerked her away from his gaze and out of the courtroom.

Slowly, the Indian turned to his lawyer and removed his beaded necklace. He instructed the tall, old man to please have it returned to his mother on the reservation for safekeeping. His voice trembled.

>>>→ • ←<<<

The young marshal's continual slow, droning Kansas City drawl either put the Indian to sleep or jump-started him into a conversation about the war and veterans at Leavenworth who, the marshal reassured, would "look out" for him.

An unspoken camaraderie soon bonded the two men. Both had been infantry men, machine gunners. Both had come back to make their homes a better place to live for their families, trying to forget the war.

Yet, feeling his right leg and hands securely shackled, Peter's veteran pride drifted away. It seemed ironic, he and the other prisoners being transported to the Leavenworth prison train at Omaha in a surplus Army convoy truck from the Great War. Beyond the stories of war, the young marshal's continual chatter seemed to ease his own boredom but left Peter taxed and tired.

The prisoner transport drove hard hours through the rain and chill of late fall, past lone ramshackle farm houses. The towns exhibited an oppressive kind of poverty from the post-war economic downturn. Still, to Peter, the whiteman settlements seemed several steps above what he knew on the reservation. All the towns were littered with dilapidated or boarded-up taverns, a lone Christian church or two and neat rows of small, run-down clapboard houses.

Listlessly looking out at the endlessly crawling, brown landscape of central Nebraska, with every mile left behind and every mile closer to Omaha, Peter felt a heaviness weigh him down, taking his mind back to that immense courtroom and single-windowed holding cell in Great Falls.

Finally escaping the confines of the prison truck, he boarded the iron horse at Omaha for the trip south to Leavenworth.

》》→ • ←《《

"Over there," pointed the US marshal, spotting the penitentiary first.

At first, the flat grassland stretched to nothingness. Then Peter caught the hint of cleared land and low fencing. Then higher fencing went whizzing by. He blinked hard at the barbed wire and concrete and felt his heart pound.

All eyes inside the prison rail cars were glued to the thirty-five-foot-high stone and brick bulwark — The Wall. Laced on top were rolls of sharp-toothed barbed wire, reminding Peter of the jagged barriers atop the bluffs marking the German lines across "no-man's land."

The train finally slowed and made a left-hand turn.

Immediately, the shackled prisoners were confronted by the large, rectangular east wall gate. On either side of the steel gate, two immense stone and brick pillars stood like colossal sentries. Armed guards stood on top, peering down beneath derby-shaped roofs.

Across the stone pillars straddled a brick archway bearing a sign with peeling black letters: "USP Leavenworth."

The enormity of the thick-walled concrete behemoth struck Peter. As if trying to escape this new reality, he glanced down at the postcard the US Marshal had given him — "a keepsake for your relations back home." He stared at the artist's rendition of the still-unfinished main entrance to Leavenworth from Metropolitan Avenue. Huge stone lions guarded the front steps beneath the gun tower with "eyes that did not see." A wry grin crept over the Indian. He glared, transfixed, at the silvered, dome-capped Rotunda in the postcard, deciding that the whole hideous structure, guarded by dead-to-life stone animals, resembled the Capitol Building he'd seen in photographs of Washington, D.C.

The immense, inanimate thing seemed a mocking echo of so many of the whiteman voices he'd heard in the service, boasting that "America's laws were meant for everyone." The leviathan structure only confirmed what Peter knew the instant the Black Robe's gavel had come down like a gunshot; whiteman's law served only white men.

For Peter, the stone lions standing on claws of marble staring with death-like hollowness, underlined the complete absence of the Great Spirit here.

Thomas Stabs-By-Mistake had been right. In his rambling, old-fashioned way, his father had tried to steer him from an invisible danger. He hadn't listened.

The train crept into the prison yard, lurched to a stop. Stepping down from the coach—hands shackled—he glared up at two more towering pillars guarding the yard. To him, they were the silent, dead sentinels that guarded the cast-out veterans of the Great War. He felt a cumulation of so much loss— of Deer Child, his first-born, his faith in truth to overcome injustice. He saw the pleading sadness in Annie Running Crane's eyes. He shook his head to rid himself of the dark pain of separation from freedom.

The guard motioned him towards the processing hall with the other "new arrivals."

Peter watched as the iron horse slowly nudged its way through the west wall gate onto the freedom of the grass prairie lands beyond the Wall.

Would Annie come to visit him? Nellie would keep her away. True to tradition, he had never spoken much to Nellie, the one he saw as his future mother-in-law.

Leavenworth's stone pillars were too far away for Annie and her people. Red-Boy was now only Peter, now far-on-the-road-alone. Like going off to war, again, he had been taken to the place of the ghosts of his past, perhaps to the Sand Hills where death awaited.

>>→ • ←<<

Peter's long braids were sheared off even before the delousing bath and issuance of prison garb. Peter shuffled along with the few other admittees to Leavenworth's cell blocks. He was escorted to Block B by a bull guard, wearing a dark blue guard's uniform, both following a trustee with fleshy tattooed arms.

Metal reverberations within the walls—clanks and creakings, buzzers and bells—reached his ears and made him turn his head, only to stare at distorted faces and mouths spewing a chorus of cat calls and shouts. Somewhere from deep inside came occasional demented babbling. Sometimes, a guttural ghost laugh followed several sharp, crazed screams.

The guard finally finished escorting Peter to his cell on the lower tier of the three-tiered Block B. He peered inside. No window. Two steel double bunks were attached to one wall. A small, seatless toilet rested at the rear of the six-by-ten foot cell. Left of the toilet, a wash basin with a single faucet was suspended from the cinder block wall.

On the lower occupied bunk sat a middle-aged thin man, with reddened skin covering his pockmarked face and blemished arms. A cigarette hung slackly from the side of his mouth, smoke lazily drifting from the end. A stack of frayed and worn books lay next to him. Various drawings and pictures, some of nudes, some of probably family or friends, hung on the wall behind him. The dimly lit cell smelled of sweat mixed with the foul odors emanating from the toilet and the faint sweaty-sweet odor of semen.

Coombs slowly inhaled on his cigarette as he glared at Peter. The guard nudged Peter forward. Coombs exhaled and smoke curled up and slowly drifted through the bars. Peter nodded and placed his few belongings—a change of prison garb, a blanket, a piece of hard soap, a prison rule book, a roll of toilet paper—on the upper cot to the right.

The close, dank confines of the cinder-block cell began squeezing in. The container forced Peter Stabs-By-Mistake to shut his eyes. He thought of his inmate number: 16986. Still, he was a Blackfeet, the son of Thomas Stabs-By-Mistake, a Piegan Chief. Annie had been privy to the secret horrors of war his veteran soul carried, which he had let trickle out only to her. Yet, he doubted he would ever share this place with her.

He opened his eyes. Coombs glared at Peter, aware of just who his cellmate was. An Indian.

He flinched and spun around as the unearthly caterpillar-grinding of an approaching Hun tank grew louder, followed mercifully this time by the sliding of the gray-green, steel cell gratings.

"Clang-clank!" The guard briskly checked the cell door, making sure it was locked, and informed the two to keep it down or "privileges will be taken away." His domineering tone met with derisive sneers and catcalls. Coombs took one of the books beside him and turned his back to Peter, pretending to read.

Settling up onto his cot, Peter stared at the gritty pebbles embedded in the concrete ceiling. With thoughts of Annie Running Crane lying beside him, he relaxed and a wash of warmth flooded his privates. There in the pebble patterns of the walls and ceiling, he saw the etched faces of the suffering he and Annie had witnessed when he returned from the Great War.

>>>→ • ←<<<

Most evenings had been spent visiting the lodges. Knowing that her very traditional mother was meddlesome and overprotective, Annie always told her mother that she was helping Victor and the Indian Bureau, working with her people. Annie never let Nellie know she was with Red-Boy.

Her mother and Red-Boy had never spoken to each other since the young man's return from France. Nellie thought Red-Boy had been corrupted by the army and the war. But if Annie was with Victor, she would be safe.

Red-Boy pressed his lips together as he thought of his first visit to the Glacier Park hotels and chalets after the war, to apply for a job. The whiteman vacation spots were built on lands stolen from his people. They employed no Indians. Superintendent Campbell had shrugged and told Red-Boy there was nothing he could do. There was also no work on the reservation because it was isolated. So, with no game left to hunt, the gathering fields over-grazed by whiteman's cows and the most fertile land taken for whiteman pleasure and profit, the people had no way to survive but to try farming or stock-raising, which the Indian Bureau encouraged. Tuberculosis, trachoma and futility were rampant.

That's when he and James Vielle built their cabin at Heart Butte, to take in and shelter as many of the sick Elders as they could.

One bitterly cold evening at Cut Bank, he and Annie visited the lodge of a sick little boy. His neck and face were a mass of running sores. Strips from an old, soiled apron were bound about the boy's head. He wore no shoes or stockings. A torn cotton shirt and khaki trousers were all the boy wore.

The boy's sister, barefoot in the cold, had trachoma. Her irritated eyelids had festered to reddened orifices, oozing with puss. One basin of water soothed the misery of each child's face. One soiled rag was a towel. Annie gave the girl her own worn shoes. No doctor had come here. The old medicine had little effect on contagious diseases or dangerous infections. Hunger was everywhere. Supper time at this lodge was a pail of berry soup.

All winter, the harsh breath of Cold-Maker blew hard.

Again, the Indian Agent told Red-Boy there was nothing he could do — maybe tomorrow or next week. The young Indian cursed and threatened to break into the sub-agency to get rations and clothing. There would be "recriminations," he was warned. Rations would be withheld.

Taking in his prison cell, the foul smells and plumbed toilet and sink seemed closer to accommodations at the great Glacier Park hotel than they did to the lodges he and Annie had visited that cold winter.

A week later, they had visited another shack where a young widow with two small children, one of whom she was nursing, lived with her old father. The father was pure-blood Blackfeet, highly respected by his people. Despite the biting cold, the children's legs were bare. Their mother wore a thin cotton dress. The only food they had was a little smoked meat, given to them by a friend. The mother was tubercular. Red-Boy and Annie brought them warm, woolen army blankets.

That same evening, they saw another child infected with trachoma. Again, all shared the same wash basin. No one had come here to teach them to do otherwise.

Finally, he and Annie rode their horses back to his cabin at Heart Butte, after visiting his father and telling him what they had seen.

The glowing redness of the little fireplace filled Red-Boy's log cabin with a warmth which seemed a luxury. Snuggled warmly together in gray Army blankets and a frayed Buffalo robe, Red-Boy, shirtless, leaned forward and stoked the fire with a cast-iron poker, his beaded necklace swinging.

"Thanks for yer shoes," she chided, poking him in the ribs. Red-Boy turned, grinning, playfully pulling on her shoeless little toe. "Mom will know, though. I better take your old moccasins. She wont recognize 'em."

"Yer mom don't trust me girl," Red-Boy chuckled. "It's 'cause I'm a veteran!" Annie poked at him playfully. "No, I mean it. You know most of our veterans, the Indian soldiers, are into all kinds of rackets. Nellie probably has heard."

"What are you talkin' 'bout?" Annie asked with unaccustomed surprise.

"Oh, we learned in France 'bout the swell time money and liquor can buy. The booze gives all us veterans a bad name, even me." He scowled. "But I been off the booze since the Sun Dance at Heart Butte." He paused, looking directly at Annie. "But Annie, that's all I did wrong. Your mom's wrong to think I'm into some of the bad rackets other vets have gotten into since they've come home. I've heard all kinds a' stories."

"Like what?"

"Oh, the guys who lease Indian land to the whites. Or sell off livestock to the whites to get money for liquor and women and things."

"But you're not like that! My mother's wrong about you."

"But some say all vets are alike." Red-Boy winked and poked at Annie with a wide grin. "Yer mom's just careful. Careful but wrong." He paused. "I mean she's okay."

"I know," she replied. "She and father live in their own world."

"So do mine," he retorted softly, smiling. He studied the fire intently. Then he scowled. "It's the little ones that get to me. Same's I've seen in France in the little towns at the front. Rags for clothes, runny dirty noses, sore eyes, no food." He stoked the fire. "Only worse here since no war's goin' on." He turned and looked at her ruefully. "And maybe what's goin' on here is war, too, girl."

Annie smiled and reached for him. Wanting to take his mind away from war and suffering, she slowly traced Red-Boy's chest scars with her fingers. "Tell me again what it was like for you," she quietly asked.

"Well, the piercing was secret, ya know." They both knew that after the war Superintendent Campbell—indeed the Indian Bureau—had outlawed the illegal "torture" of Sun Dance piercing.

"At Heart Butte, things were different, I heard."

"Aaee," replied Red-Boy. "After the war, Father said I should give thanks to Beyond-Sun-Person for guiding me through. I said, 'okay.' I guess I just wanted to see if I could stand the pain. You know, I'd seen a lot in the war. So, my father and Curly Bear and the other Elders all arranged it. The piercing was done way early in the mornin' at the Medicine Lodge pole."

"Did it hurt when they pierced you?" Annie's eyes were wide.

"No—yes, when they first put the skewers in my chest, it hurt," he replied with a casual gesture of his hands and a shrug.

"Did you pass out?"

"No, but it was painful when I danced the Sun Dance. The pulling and yanking of the skewers was not as painful as in the war." Annie winced. Red-Boy was looking directly at the young woman, his eyes fixed. She was locked to his gaze. "When the skewers ripped out, I don't remember too much." He paused at Annie's grimace. "But that's when I felt the pain bring me protection."

Annie took on a puzzled look. "Why do you feel protected?" she asked.

"Because the pain makes me realize I'm alive, I guess," he laughed. Suddenly, he scowled. "Afterwards, Father told me that Victor had seen the piercing. He told his Uncle Richard, and the BIA police came to us. But all the Elders stood up and the cowards backed down." He nodded his head slowly, triumphantly. "That coward superintendent gave me a talking, but I didn't listen."

Tilting her head, Annie smiled wistfully and touched his chest again, fingering his beads. They were quiet for a time. Then, she slowly drew back, shaking her head. Beneath a furrowed brow, her dark eyes were tense. "Red-Boy, you must speak to Superintendent Campbell about what we've seen. The sick children. I will go with you." Her look of determination was resolute. "We have to make him understand."

The young veteran grinned at her seriousness, tugging at the top of her robe. "C'mon, I'll only peek once," he kidded. She flinched and drew back, giggling, then tried to look serious again.

"So the kids got to ya, huh," he remarked, returning her serious look. "I'd like to know where the doc is s'posed to be makin' his rounds." He spit into the fire. "Probably out bootleggin.'"

"Victor tells us all the time that Mr. Campbell is doin' all he can. Says he's been visitin' everyone on the reservation. Tells us, 'Not 'nough money to go around.' " Her sarcasm was barely contained.

Red-Boy threw his head back and exploded out loud, "Unh! Victor is no better than the agency whiteman, he is only out for Victor. His eyes only see the whiteman's way. My father has spoken to me about him."

"What has he told you?" she asked.

"Told me to be careful," he replied, poking the fire again. "Not to be trusted." He paused and looked at her. "He's after you, you know."

"Ah, that's just talk," she scoffed. "You're not like him at all. You're honest like your father, Red-Boy. You are a better man than Victor. I know." She lowered her eyes. "I want to be with you."

He reached over and held her smooth shoulders with both his hands. He touched her cheeks. He took her hands in his as they snuggled closer together. The warmth of the fire and his nearness were comforting, reassuring.

After a long silence, Annie told him she must leave and return home, her mother would be worried.

But he held her and she did not resist. They touched and kissed. He slipped off what under-things she had left on. Her breathing became heavy and long. He explored her softness. They felt the warmth of each other's naked bodies, each other's hair, shared each other's heart beats as they came together. Then, passion spent, they lay quietly in the warm firelight.

>>>→ • ←<<<

Now, within the small confines of his cell, he thought of that night and of Annie Running Crane, who would be his sits-beside-him-woman. He had resolved that very night to honor her in the highest way he knew how, by following the traditional way to keep peace in the family. The way his mother and father had followed. For one thing, he would never speak to Nellie, his future mother-in-law.

When Annie left that evening, they both knew they were bound together. Later, they secretly decided they would be married, both in the church and in a traditional ceremony.

Perhaps trying to honor the old ways had been his mistake, thinking it was better to keep his distance from her mother. After all, Nellie had favored Victor over him. Victor had been there during the war when Annie was sick and her family needed help.

Red-Boy now realized that his decision meant that Nellie had never been able to see his heart.

>>>→ • ←<<<

A week later, Annie and Red-Boy had visited Superintendent Campbell, anxious to confront him with the burden of suffering they had witnessed, cautiously optimistic that this time they would be able to convince him of the people's desperate need, idealistic enough to believe he would care.

A whiteman of unmistakable Scotch ancestry, Campbell was a commanding presence, over six feet tall, over 220 pounds and carrying no fat on his body. His face and demeanor bespoke a resolute man, determined to chart out a successful tenure as superintendent with his Five-Year Plans for small farming and sheep raising.

But Red-Boy, his father and others, including Oliver Sanders, saw Campbell's tenure differently. Within the Agency, there was ever more mismanagement of tribal cattle and livestock herds, of oil and mineral leasing rights, failed irrigation projects, misuse of tribal monies, fraudulent granting of patent lands, inadequate accounting of leasing income, domination of the Tribal Council by Agency officials.

To Red-Boy, Campbell was a strutting whiteman bureaucrat in a dark-vested suit, white shirt, tie, and a gray fedora to cover his balding, sandy-white hair. Campbell stood on legs that were too tall for his unbending torso and for his own good.

At first dismissive of Red-Boy's ongoing remonstrances, Campbell turned disdainful of the young Indian's "outbursts" and criticisms.

This time, the superintendent wanted "to hear it directly from Annie Running Crane"—her version of what she had seen and the events which had transpired. Annie, who spoke very broken English, "needed a translator," or so Campbell insisted. Quickly ushering her into another room, out of Red-Boy's presence, he had Victor Sanders translate for him.

When Annie finished her story in the Pikuni tongue as Campbell had requested, Campbell's mood changed. He nodded his thanks to Victor, then returned to explain to Red-Boy that what Annie had told him indicated that his Bureau was really doing all it could and that indications were positive. After all, he knew these people she spoke of to be the ones who had "just recently" received some government assistance.

The blood pounded in Red-Boy's head. Later, he was able to confirm that Victor had changed the names and locations of the lodges visited, had deflected Campbell's heartless mismanagement through his translation of Annie's story.

His friend, James Vielle, had warned him about Victor the translator. "What can you expect of an offspring of a Blackfeet and a greedy white woman poisoned by the whiteman's water?"

Red-Boy was resolved to expose Victor as a traitor and a liar. James Vielle and Red-Boy figured Victor was making money bootlegging liquor onto the reservation. Perhaps Victor's game was part of the racket some Indian veterans were into, siphoning off Indian Bureau medical funds and Indian land to purchase liquor for their own purposes. They both suspected Victor was currying favor with selected families and lodges, who would then benefit when Victor achieved his big goal. It was common knowledge on the reservation that this coward's wish was to sit on the Blackfeet Tribal Council. And the Tribal Council was just another way for the whiteman's Indian Bureau to keep control over the reservation.

>>>→ • ←<<<

Glancing down at the blanket covering his Leavenworth prison cot, he knew he had lost the chance to expose Victor and the corruption that was wiping out his people. Single army blankets that sold for $2.65 each were sold to the Indians for over three times as much. There was hardly an Indian on the reservation who owned a steer. Most were forced to purchase meat from the whiteman's ranches outside the reservation. Small children were not given milk or eggs. He and Annie knew children six to eight years old who had never tasted milk, butter or eggs. All this a result of the "help" of men like Victor Sanders and the Indian Bureau. His people were being backed further into a corner, beholden to liars and cheats, doomed to a slow death.

Now, here, locked up, Peter could do nothing.

>>>→ • ←<<<

Coombs, leaning against the bars, squinting and holding the book nearly at arm's length, was still reading. Looking over at his cellmate's back, Peter thought of the white stranger who had come among his people, squinting at a worn map he held at arm's length. They had often teased the stranger from the place-of-the-rising-sun for his early awkward ways when he first came to see his people. Yet his father and the others grew close to the man who spoke of wanting to "preserve" Indian stories.

Once, Red-Boy sat with his father and grandfather, Big Brave-Mountain Chief, while they repeated a story for the Easterner before a gathering of children near his parent's lodge. Oliver Sanders had been there helping with the translation. There had been much laughter and teasing that day. Like many other times, they sat in the fading heat of the late day sun, for the man from the East only came in the summer when days were long and hot.

It was the same story told to him by his grandfather—of how death came to his people and how it changed them.

>>>→ • ←<<<

"In times far back, there was no death. There were no wars and no sickness. The people, they lived to be old like the mountains. Trouble and sorrow never came into their hearts.

"One day while many children were playing their games, a stranger came among them. This stranger was a little boy. They asked the boy to tell them where he came from. The boy said, 'I do not know where I came from. It was in the night when I came. I was very lonely, but now I shall be happy for I have found many children and many people.'

"So the old people, they talked much about the mystery boy. They asked him his name. They asked if he had a mother and father and other relations, but the boy could tell them nothing. Then the Chiefs, they held a council. They too talked much about this stranger who had come among them. Some said that he was 'bringer-of-bad-luck,' and others said that he was 'a child like their own who had become lost,' and that they would pity him and see that no harm came to him.

"So they gave the boy food and robes. The children taught him how to play their games, and the stranger, he made many friends.

"One day a mother said to her man, 'Our son, he sleeps long, he does not speak, he is like a stone. What is it that makes our son sleep while other children play.' The son, he never woke up, but became dust and wind took him away.

"'What is this great mystery? Why is it that our son has gone away and never comes back? We love our son. Why did our son disappear to the clouds.' Then, another child became nothing, then another, until four children went to sleep and never woke up.

"'Enough,' cried the people.

"A great council was held. All the people said, 'It is the stranger who has brought bad luck to us. He has a Powerful Medicine. He has brought sorrow to us. He is Great-Evil. He takes our children from our eyes. We cannot feel their flesh. Our arms cannot hold our children. Our children, they become like smoke from our campfires.'

"'We will destroy Great-Evil, the stranger,' they shouted.

"One day their Chief said, 'Four times, after each one of our children was taken, we have chased Great-Evil away. We gave his blood to the waters. We covered his flesh with earth. We broke his bones in little pieces and crushed his flesh with stones. We sent Great-Evil to the darkness of the Great-Waters. We saw with our eyes, our dogs eat his flesh and bones. Then, That-Which-Destroys-All burned him till he was nothing and Wind carried him away. Still, we see his face with our eyes, he is among us, his Medicine is beyond all Power. Our hearts cry in sorrow for our children who have become nothing. All my people, let us pity the stranger who has great power, let everybody be kind to him, give him food and robes.'

"They looked for the boy, but he had gone away, he was not among them…Ever afterwards, there was death among all people. Many died when they were young and many lived to be very old, but death always came.

"And there came also kindness and pity. Even now a stranger is always given food and robes."

»»→ • ←««

Red-Boy remembered the fire late that same evening in his father's lodge, his grandfather telling the Easterner of the time when he had seen twenty-one winters and his father, Mountain Chief, told of the coming of the white-scabs disease—smallpox—to fifty Piegan lodges.

"The Piegans died like flies. Tipis were left standing with whole families who had died. Bodies everywhere. Mostly young people died, the very old did not. Spring came. Smallpox faded."

His grandfather had spoken. There was no greater kindness than that shown to others during the great death from smallpox. Before knowing a stranger's heart, whether it beat for good or evil, the stranger was always treated with kindness.

It was said by the Elders that strangers from the East—perhaps soldiers, perhaps whiteman doctors—had given Blackfeet at Fort Benton the smallpox. Whiteman settlers then moved onto tribal lands, rich with fur-bearing animals and the yellow dust—gold.

Now, another stranger had come among his people—the Easterner. Big Brave-Mountain Chief spoke of the goodness he saw in this man's heart, and said that the goodness would be returned with kindness.

»»→ • ←««

Peter Stabs-By-Mistake stared at the ceiling of his cell. The smell of stale cigarette smoke filled his nostrils. He wondered if the rough walls closed in on the inmates, making them abrasive and hard. Or did the inmates themselves make the walls cold and rough?

Here he was, among strangers. All he could do was to remember what his father had told the whiteman Easterner in the death story following the words of his grandfather. That ever after, an Indian always offers kindness to a stranger.

Sitting up on his cot, Peter noticed Coombs standing, gripping the bars, listlessly peering out. He took a deep breath. "Hello, my name's Peter."

"Shut the fuck up, Injun'!" the man blurted, not even turning his head.

Ruins of Old Fort Benton, Montana.

# VI

# Bad-Medicine Stone Pillars

"That's Krankk," Coombs almost whispered, glancing furtively across the room. The Indian had been at Leavenworth long enough to have heard the name. And, he had been there long enough for Coombs to have learned that the Indian was a veteran, entitled to respect. "You know he's the cell boss, right?" Coombs' eyes narrowed as he carefully studied Peter Red-Boy's expression. "I think you've pissed him off."

"Pissed him off? How?" asked Red-Boy.

"Cause he don't like darkies," Coombs replied.

Having taken his meals alone at first, Red-Boy had been sitting with Coombs and his new messmates for barely a week and was less than impressed by this introduction to the cell boss.

"Yeah," replied Big Ed with a serious look. "You don't piss Krankk off. He controls things on Block B and he don't like Injuns."

So began the midday meal in the immense, gray-walled prison mess—bowls and spoons banging and clattering amidst the muttering and curses of inmates and the sharp retorts of guards—all beneath large rectangular windows ushering in the light. Peter saw with more clarity the hard, sullen outline of the prison tribal group. It was both enemy and enforcer, making all others "tow the line," as Coombs and Big Ed were pointedly reminding him.

At first hostile to Peter's very presence, Coombs warmed when he learned that this particular Indian had seen combat. For a veteran like Coombs, an ex-sergeant, Peter's service record was more important. Peter soon learned who else were veterans. The ex-sergeant's unit had helped stop the German advance at Château-Thierry.

Coombs' Purple Heart dangling from the cell wall was evidence of his survival at Belleau Wood.

Big Ed, a lean infantryman with a square jaw and clever mouth, had served under Pershing. Now and then, he would brag how his unit "single-handedly stopped the Hun advance in France." He was in for armed robbery, clumsily holding up an armored car after a three-day drinking spree.

Gunderson was short and fidgety. During the summer of 1918, he'd been wounded in the Second Battle of the Marne. Gunny was in for grand larceny. Coombs said that's why Gunny had been caught, trying to haul an enormous gunnysack from a bank.

Both Big Ed and Gunny were alcoholics. Even today their faces were pinched and wrinkled, their noses red.

Peter glanced at Gunny to hear his take on the situation with Krankk. Gunny shook his head. "No, doesn't like yer kind, man."

"Why is he 'boss'?" asked Peter. This drew quiet chuckles from the others.

"Damn, yer dumb," replied Coombs. "Murdered six guys in Chicago. Plugged some guy between the eyes just because he was laughin' at him in a bar. Then broke a nigger guy's neck with his bare hands." The Indian frowned, wondering if this was just talk.

Peter finished his bowl of watery soup. Taking a swallow of water, he glanced up at the man they called Krankk—a huge, globular form seated four tables away. The form had massive, tattooed shoulders and arms. His face was a bald, gleaming mask—a grizzly bear with no hair. The thought of a bald bear struck Red-Boy as amusing and he fixed a long look at the man. Slowly the boss's glance cut across the hall, then fixed on the Indian, as if reading his thoughts. He continued glowering, staring down the Indian.

The man's bloodshot, beady eyes remained transfixed and unflinching, his small mouth pressed together as tight as an arrow. The bald bear's nose appeared to be two prairie-dog holes stuck in the middle of his face.

"But how is he the boss?" he asked again, shielding a snicker with his hand.

"Because, man, he controls things!" snapped Gunny. "Coombs here used to be boss till that fat fucker showed up."

"Shut up," Coombs spat out, obviously annoyed at the disclosure and Krankk's intimidating stare.

Peter glanced across the room. Krankk's eye-dots glared back.

"His boys collect dues," continued Gunny. "Dole out cigarettes. Get favors from the guards. Real good favors."

"Like what?"

"You name it. Any fuckin' thing he wants," whispered Big Ed. "Smokes, drugs from the prison pharmacy. Sex."

Peter glanced back at the bald glob, whose eye holes were riveted to the slender Indian, his black eyebrows pinched together.

"Listen, man, the animal goes after squaw boys and pussies and runs a real racket in here," offered Gunny. "The guards, they just turn the other way."

"Who's his other boys?" asked Peter.

"See that big son-of-a-bitch next to him, closer to the windows?" directed Coombs. "That's Monroe, his enforcer and snitch."

Quickly glancing over, Peter caught the image—an angular, tow-headed, pale-faced man bent over, shoveling soup, paying no apparent attention to those around him.

"Monroe, huh," exclaimed Peter. "Where I come from, you don't get any whiter than that."

"Listen, God-damn it, Monroe asks you for anything, you better not cross him. He'll go right to the boss," asserted Gunny.

Glancing back at Gunny, Peter wondered if Krankk had scored a coup on this little wisp of a man.

Peter could picture inmates sitting together smoking kinnikinnick. But the notion of sex with anyone other than a woman reminded Peter of one time before going overseas. His bunk mate had told him about a "queer" who had been cashiered after grabbing at another soldier in the shower.

"Is this Krankk a queer?" he asked.

"Keep it down for chrissakes," cautioned Coombs. "Of course not. He's just a fuckin' animal. He'll make you his 'wife' if you don't tow the line. You unnerstan?"

Peter glared at Coombs, then he glanced again at Krankk and said nothing. After all, his veteran tribe would protect one another. In the war, men's lives had depended upon it. The veterans of cell Block B would do the same.

"Time's up!" barked the large burly guard at the far entrance of the mess hall. Peter and the others got up and left for their cell to await their stretch time in the yard after Krankk and his minions took their turn.

»»→ • ←««

By December, Cold-Maker had swept across the table-flat plains of Kansas, bringing below-freezing winds and snow, blanketing Kansas City and

Leavenworth and slamming against The Wall-Leavenworth prison-, perched atop a bluff beside the Missouri river. Yet Cold-Maker's harsh chill brought a not completely unwelcome respite from the usual stifling heat of Leavenworth's concrete interior. Long empty were the nests of robins, meadowlarks and sparrows that had rested on the barren stone and brick fortress encircled with barbed wire. Only the guards now perched like hawks in their pillar watch towers or paced like coyotes stalking cattle.

As time for Peter became increasingly meaningless, the daily routines in the prison mess and yard, the construction duty or work in the brick plant, became mere shadow patterns in the otherwise formless prison life. Inmates silently washed down oatmeal or mush and biscuits with weak coffee every morning in the cavernous, gray-walled mess, while still sleepy whitemen in uniforms watched.

Lunch was a bowl of soup, another biscuit. Afternoons meant exercise, a half-hour in another dank enclosure, a space half the size of the stockade compound at Old Agency on Badger Creek. A dozen or so prisoners were rotated in and out, with little to do there but lift some weights in the yard, if you were lucky enough to be among the first ones to arrive. The rest walked around in circles, congregating with one or two others, bartering for cigarettes, sharing the latest rumors.

Dinner was at 6:00 pm sharp—a small piece of beef, bread and water. Lights went out at the jeering commands of the guards at 9:00 p.m. sharp, usually followed by catcalls and obscenities, cursing by the residents who insisted on extra time to finish reading a letter, or to complete a sketch on paper or a drawing on the walls. More artistic inmates made drawings of nudes for other inmates, in exchange for favors.

Yet back in his cell, Peter could almost always banish the vision of concrete and stone walls and the routine of prison life, thinking instead of Annie. He hated pestering Coombs to ghost-write letters to her, but the shrapnel wound in his right hand had damaged the nerves, making writing an excruciating task. Coombs insisted he'd only do one or two a week, grumbling that the Indian needed to learn to write with his left hand.

Peter never knew if the letters got to her. Maybe Nellie or Sanders interfered. The doubts gnawed at him, but prompted him to try writing with his left hand, enabling him to send a few more awkwardly-worded letters each month. Maybe after all the letters he sent, some got through.

When he thought of her, he thought of them both lying together at the Sun Dance in the yellow prairie grass quivering in a warm, Chinook wind. Or together in the rain-dark swales and washes or on the rolling hills. In his mind, they again visited those they knew who lived on the outposts of the reservation.

At night, he reconstructed his cabin fireplace, where he could see reflections of her face, the fleshy, yielding curve of her thighs as he touched her and felt her breathing.

Self-conscious, he often turned late at night in his bunk to the cinder block wall to avert any stare from his cellmate or a passing guard.

When the throbbing ceased, he rolled back, once again facing the harsh reality of the concrete ceiling.

>>>→ • ←-<<<

"Can you write a letter for me, Coombs?" Peter asked one evening. Perched on the edge of his bunk, he leisurely thumbed through one of Coombs' books while his cellmate sat hunched on the toilet. Finishing his business, Coombs dropped down on his bunk and glanced up at Peter.

"Jesus, you sure are persistent with that girl. Everyone knows why they sent you here. Shit, ya' won't even be eligible for parole until '28. 'Sides, she'll be married by then." He glared at Peter. "What's in it for ya, man?"

Peter scowled at the man. "Lonely, I guess. Just a short letter, my hand's killin' me."

"Been playin' with yerself, again, huh?" They both laughed. Coombs understood how the shrapnel from a land mine had nearly severed Peter's thumb. "Okay." Coombs reached for his pad and small, stunted pencil. "Just a short one though."

Peter started slowly.

*"Annie, I hope my letters have gotten through to you. I haven't received a letter from you in so long. I haven't forgot you. You know I keep on loving you. Maybe Nellie or others have destroyed my letters to you. I don't know. Please come down and visit me if you can. I am lonely for you and want to see you so much. Things here are pretty simple. I have made friends with some veterans. Coombs is my good friend."*

Coombs glanced up, a wry smile crossing his face. Peter continued.

*"Big Ed and Gunny are my buddies. My friends told me to be careful to look out for myself, though. There is a big ugly white man who they call the boss. He doesn't like me. He doesn't like Indians, I hear."*

Coombs quickly glanced up, "You sure you want to tell her all this shit?" Peter glared at his cellmate.

"C'mon, man, she hasn't even written you once. Don't ya' get it? She don't give a shit about you anymore!" Shoving the pad and pencil at Peter, the cellmate's patience ended. "Here, you finish the goddamned thing. Try writin' with yer left hand for chrissakes. Didn't they teach you nothin' in those schools?"

"I can take care of myself." Peter gave Coombs a cool, steady eye. Holding the pad in his lap, the young Indian began forming the letters and words slowly, deliberately with his injured right hand. Coombs turned indifferently to the wall with a worn paperback.

*"Annie, don't worry for me. I can take care of myself in here. I miss you so much. Please tell me if your mother and father is okay. I wrote to my father but haven't heard back. Please let me know how my friend Jim is. I wait here for your letter. You know I have no other place to go. Without you here, the Sun shines with no heat. I ask the Sun to give you long life."*

Peter leaned back on his bunk, chin on his chest. The fingers of his writing hand cramped in pain and would not move.

>>>—→ • ←—<<<

Twice a week, on Monday mornings after breakfast and Thursday evenings after dinner, the men were instructed to shower in Block B in groups of ten. Ten silver showerheads lined the long, narrow confines of the white-tiled shower room. In the middle, holding up the ceiling, were two concrete pillars about ten feet apart. Behind them were rows of wooden stalls where the men could change or towel off.

One Thursday evening, Peter sensed a sullen moodiness from Coombs and the others. He figured someone had been docked demerits. Getting a mark had seemed such a trivial thing—talking back to a guard, having "an attitude," making an obscene gesture or remark. Yet, accumulating "good time" was important. Not getting demerits or being reported by the guards meant serving less time. The older veterans understood the avoidance pattern; the newer ones like Peter quickly caught on.

"You guys sure are quiet today. What's goin' on?" Peter asked as he soaped up, lathering his face and hair, his back facing the stalls, head bent under the shower head.

"Just watch your ass, man," joked Gunny with a nervous smile. The others laughed.

"Aaee. The boss-man Krankk been givin' you guys bad dreams?"

"Careful, the walls speak around here," replied Coombs.

"I know that," replied Peter as he rinsed off, his eyes shut tight against the steady onslaught of soapy water running down his face. A long minute passed.

To Peter, Krankk seemed to control things within the walls in a mysterious sort of way. He soon learned that those who were not with the boss seemed to be receiving more demerits than others. Those who "towed the line" with Krankk seemed to accumulate "good time" quicker.

Peter had learned to keep his counsel in the presence of Krankk's boys. The verbal taunts went unanswered.

"The walls say that Krankk, he wants you for his woman, Peter-boy."

Peter was not sure who had made this last jest, as his ears were full of soap and warm water. But the word "woman" resonated in his head. His heart pounded.

Quickly clearing his face and eyes, the Indian looked for Coombs and the others. The knife tattoo stood out on the fleshy chest of the taller man. The thick giant grunted, "You're my bitch, now, sheep fucker!" Shoving Peter backwards, he sneered, "C'mon squaw bitch, squeal like a pig!"

Terrified, Peter looked for the others but the man's enormous bulk blocked all view. Ducking low and to the right, he immediately recognized Monroe's shock of blond hair, his outstretched arms shoving Peter down to the hard tile floor.

"No!!" cried Peter, knowing instinctively that he was in a fight for his life. "Aaiiee!!" he cried as he swivelled on his back, kicking out violently with both legs. His right heel landed a hard blow to Monroe's left eye, his left heel glancing off the man's jaw. From behind, Peter felt the steel trap.

"This squaw's a keeper! Yer mine!" the looming, fleshy brute growled, as he grabbed at Peter's arms and shoulders from behind with an overpowering agility and strength. Gasping, he was swiftly jerked to his feet. The giant bear-hugged him so hard he could gasp no air.

"Don't fight me, snatch, or I'll cut ya' wide open!"

The six-foot-four, completely naked mass of muscle and flesh now alternately lifted and swung Peter across the room, smashing his skull against the concrete pillar as the giant shoved past the others, smashing Peter's face into a corner stall.

"No!!" he cried as he whirled around, only to meet a fleshy fist. Stars. He crumbled.

Krankk gripped the back of his head, smothering his mouth and nose onto the hard floor tile.

There, behind the two concrete pillars in the long-tiled shower, Peter's desperate, gurgling gasps and moans echoed into nothingness.

>>>→ • ←<<<

The singular most frightening moment in Peter Stabs-By-Mistake's life had been that night during the Meuse-Argonne offensive. A German soldier had rushed at him with bayonet gleaming and was cut in two by Peter's machine gun. Then, dropping into a foxhole, he had come face-to-face with another German infantryman's hollow stare.

For an instant, he saw the unclipped hand grenade clenched in the Hun's hand. Seated upright, the soldier wore no helmet. Nor did he have a waist or legs. His torso had been thrown there, upright, by an artillery blast. The eyes were wide, direct and unknowing. In death, the man clung unflinchingly to his steel grenade as if that act alone could have somehow saved him.

>>>→ • ←<<<

Peter awoke, trembling in his cell. His left eye would not open. Touching his head brought sharp pangs as if scalding shrapnel were imbedded there. He felt a throbbing, burning from below. Turning, he saw blood on his pillow and down near his hips. A faint, fetid odor touched his nostrils. The blood and throbbing led him to the toilet to rid himself of the foul experience.

His legs, his arms trembled; the sickening dizziness spun the walls. He sat on the toilet with face lowered, hands at his sides.

"Pretty swollen," remarked Coombs. "Yer lucky we came back…told you, the boss makes everyone pay their dues. Didn't I tell you that?"

Peter said nothing. His temples pounded and his head and legs shook. He took a deep breath and slowly, through his one good eye, caught sight of Coombs carefully watching him, shrug and force a weak smile.

"Fuck you," Peter muttered through blood-stained teeth.

Coombs turned back to his book.

Krankk's guttural sounds pounded with every heart beat in Peter's head. He clamped his eyes tight.

He saw the swollen brute's beady eyes, then the dead German's eyes, penetrating. Peter clenched his teeth and hands, veins stretched taut in his neck. He sat there straining to remove the unrelenting fiends.

Over and over, as he rocked slowly back and forth, he vowed he would count a coup against the Krankk.

Exhaustion mercifully swept through him, draining his tensed muscles. He returned to his bunk without looking at Coombs.

He thought of the supernatural power of which his father spoke. Going forth to the battlefield dressed in battle shirts, covered with ermine, scalps, beads and paints as protection—he had scoffed at the idea.

Peter closed his eyes.

»»—→ • ←—«««

In sleep, he was a boy again at home in his parent's tipi, his father resting against his willow backrest. The Piegan Chief, his father, was the only man in the world he trusted unconditionally.

"Father, please tell the story of how the earth was made."

Turning to his sits-beside-him woman, Thomas said, "Call the others to come in and I will tell the story that Red-Boy wishes me to tell."

The Chief, with braided hair and arms resting on his long thigh bones, looked solemn. Red-Boy stared transfixed at his father. His father's friends, Curly Bear—Kia yao soi sksis si—and Rides-At-The-Door, sat on either side of his father. Red-Boy's mother sat next to him.

"Away, way back, in time of beginning of all things, then everywhere was water. There was no land. Floating on the water was a great raft. On that raft was Ná pi and all the animals and birds, but no people."

"Father, who is Ná pi?" asked the wide-eyed boy.

"Ná pi is the Old-Man Creator known to many tribes, Red-Boy. We look upon him as a teacher of wisdom."

"But Ná pi, he is also a trickster," remarked Rides-At-The-Door with a twinkle in his eye.

"In the long-ago, Ná pi played evil pranks. Many stories tell of his tricks," interjected Curly Bear with a smile.

Red-Boy looked, again, at his father, who resumed the story.

"Ná pi, he had great power. He wanted the animals and birds to have homes so he decided to make some land. On the raft with Ná pi was a Muskrat. Ná pi told the Muskrat to dive from the raft. He was gone so long that all of the animals and birds thought that he had drowned. But when after a l-o-n-g time he did come to the surface, they found in his paws a little mud.

"Ná pi dried the mud and scattered it upon the water. Soon everywhere was land.... Finally, Ná pi decided that people should live on the earth. He molded a boy and a girl from clay and covered them with a Buffalo robe. He waited one sleep. When he lifted the robe, he saw that the boy and girl had grown. The second day he looked again. He saw that they were large enough. The third day, he saw hair on their heads. The fourth day, they were breathing. 'Now,' said Ná pi 'stand up, you are people.'

"So it was that all the people that were on the earth in times farthest back, they had hands like bear-paws so they could dig the roots and live.

"Ná pi said to all the people, 'The meat of the Buffalo is good. That will be your food when snow covers the earth. I made the flies so that they will drive the Buffalo out of the brush into the waters where the people can kill them.'

"Many winters passed. An old woman said to Ná pi, 'Will the people live always? Will there be no end to us? If all the people live there will not be food enough.'

" 'That is something that we must decide,' said Ná pi. 'Pick up something from the earth, and throw it into the water. If it floats, then the people will live forever. If it sinks, then all people must die.'

"The old woman did not pick up a Buffalo chip. She picked up a stone. She threw it into the water. The stone sank.

" 'You have chosen,' said Ná pi. 'All people must die.'

"Ná pi spoke with a straight tongue," said Thomas Stabs-By-Mistake. "That is all I have to say."

Suddenly, the lodge fire crackled and a large spark flew out, just missing Red-Boy.

>>>—→ • ←—<<<

His eyes slowly adjusted as he glanced around his darkened cell, the cinder block walls pressed close. Pain and reality seeped back. His eyes burned. His life, the manhood he once held so proudly, had left him — had been stolen from him. Just as surely as if diving from the raft, looking for mud at the bottom for Ná pi, he had, instead, been swallowed whole into the murky depths at the very bottom.

Propping himself up on one elbow, he wondered why Coombs and the others hadn't heard his cries. The guards were gone, too. How did he get back?

Peter knew that Naa to yi ta pi—the Creator—never intended for this to have happened. He knew some tribes had not shunned mutual male-to-male sex. Yet, the violence committed by Krankk had never been part of his people's way, had never corrupted the bloodlines of the warrior class.

Peter went deep within himself. The shame pierced his heart and sank into his belly. He knew he would never speak of what happened.

He thought of killing himself. Perhaps those on the outside—his people back home—would think that some whiteman inmate had killed him because he was Indian.

Still, he had vowed to count coup. The tomahawk must meet with this coward. Krankk possessed the hand that scalps the reputation of the dead—he possessed an evil mind.

He relaxed and felt the tenseness move out of his body in waves, first from his forehead, then down through his shoulders and arms, finally leaving him through the soles of his feet. Sleep carried him into a dark, misty dream world devoid, this time, of all consciousness of the brutality which had seared itself into his soul.

>>>→ • ←<<<

Looking about, he knew that he was home, again, seeing the smoldering lodge fires. He glanced up at the Seven-Brothers—the Big Dipper and North Star—looking down from their home in the night sky.

His mother, Steals-In-The-Daytime, was bent over, kneading dough, flattening it with her hands, carrying it to the lodge fire and cooking it in a flat, cast-iron pan. His mother made the best pan bread. That and sweet marrow from roasted beef–cow bones always killed his hunger.

Now Red-Boy saw his grandfather—Big Brave-Mountain Chief—and the Elders.

Many-Tail-Feathers, the old warrior who had seen more than ninety winters, tossed a bone into the lodge fire and weighed each word as he said, "Ki á nni a yi, ii níí stá oo." The old warrior was thinking of Buffalo days.

Many-Tail-Feathers had counted many coups in the war days. The ancient teller of stories was now speaking directly to Red-Boy.

"Younger brother, now I will tell you why we always pray that the Buffalo will come back to the prairies."

Red-Boy found himself seated on the ground close to the lodge fire, next to Big Brave, Mountain Chief. Many-Tail-Feathers and Red-Boy's grandfather were about to tell a story that the boy would never forget. Many-Tail-Fathers spoke first.

"We Piegans pray for the Buffalo to come back because we believe that in times-furthest-back, the Buffalo were given to the Indians for food, clothing, shelter, and for many other purposes. When we killed Buffalo, no part was wasted. The skins made our lodges, quivers, bow-cases, moccasins, shirts and leggings. Our women tanned the hides and made warm robes that protected our bodies from Cold-Maker. We made glue from the hoofs. With the glue we fastened the feathers to our arrows. The sinew we used for thread and bow-strings. We braided long strips of skin into ropes to picket and rope our ponies. Rawhide we used for our parfleches, moccasin soles and knife sheaths. We made spoons and ladles from the horns.

Red-Boy heard them all singing. "I-ay, I-hay, a-a-a-a-I-a. Yes, that which our brother, Many-Tail-Feathers, tells us is straight," Big Brave called out.

"Now I have something more to say" announced Big Brave. "Now I will tell you how the Piegans made the War Shield so no arrow could go through it."

"We made our Shields from the thick, untanned skin of the Buffalo bull's neck. The skin was soaked in water and dried. This was done many times to make it thick and hard. We decorated our Shields with the long, black, beard hair. That hair is strong Medicine. Dream-Spirit told us in times-long-ago how to make and paint our Shields. Dream-Spirit told us to observe all of the ceremonies of the War Shield."

For Red-Boy, the only war shield he had known had been the doughboy's metal helmet and gas mask. But his war shield had not been impervious. Hunkered down in that fox hole with the torso of a dead German, the fecal-scented stench of death had reached out with a gag. He took his helmet off and vomited into it, watching, exhausted, while his vomit dribbled out through the long, jagged bullet hole which had creased, then penetrated, his helmet.

>>>→ • ←<<<

"Thunk! Thunk! . . . Bang!" The sound of incoming enemy mortar fire jarred the veteran from his trench dream. He lay immobile, sweating and staring at the concrete ceiling of his bunker-turned-cell.

The clanging of the doors and loud curses from the guards ordering the inmates to muster up in their cells for morning inspection brought instant relief.

Then, the pounding pain returned, and waves of reality brought back the horrific memory of the day before.

Still, Peter Stabs-By-Mistake knew he was a Piegan warrior. He had survived. He was a veteran who carried a War Shield within himself right down to his skin and bones. He had been given something more than a steel helmet and gas mask. He had been given the impenetrable guidance of wisdom of his father and his grandfather, Mountain Chief, and the others, Curly Bear and Many-Tail-Feathers—the stories of the Elders he had so often scoffed at when he came home from France.

Now he faced a far harsher reality. Now, above all else, Peter knew he must one day confront Krankk in battle within the confines of this prison.

He would either count a coup with this coward or life would leave him. He hoped to go the way of the Wolf-Trail as a Blackfeet warrior should, never fearing death.

"Bear Chief's War Lodge." Photo by J.H. Sherburne, courtesy of Sherburne Collection and William E. Farr.

# VII

# War Medicine Dream

The grating, iron doors slammed with a reverberating clang behind Coombs as he entered and sat on his bunk. Peter was slumped on the edge of his bunk, staring vacantly at the opposite wall. "Man, me 'n the others been talkin' 'bout you not eatin.' You need food, Peter-boy." Coombs stood and leaned closer. "Me an' Gunny an' Big Ed an' the others will go with you to dinner. Ya gotta eat, man."

Peter nodded, untouched by his cellmate's remarks.

"I need an answer, Coombs," the Indian said cooly. "I've asked you before and you've not given me a good 'nough answer." He slid down from his bunk and stood, locking his dark eyes squarely onto Coombs. His cellmate stared back.

The facial contusions and abrasions had healed. But the injury still brought on waxing and waning pangs of shame and hatred, paralyzing attempts at rational thought. Keeping out of sight as much as possible meant showering once a week and seldom eating. He had lost thirty pounds.

The Indian slowly lowered himself to the floor. His eyes were sunken, his cheeks slightly hollowed, his broad shoulders slackened. The gaunt Indian appeared in need of a meal. Soon.

"You know that the weak ones around here get made by Krankk. I told you, the son-of-a-bitch doesn't like your kind." Coombs eyed his cellmate closely, trying to spot an emotional opening.

"That whiteman is not a man," replied Red-Boy slowly. "He is not natural."

Coombs leaned back. "Listen, he hates yer kind. Yer a movin' target man!" Coombs paused, looking around the room as if searching for something. "Only Krankk doesn't give a shit if you raped a white woman or a squaw."

"Who told him that?" Red-Boy glowered. "That I'm in for rape?"

"Hell if I know, Peter. You know these fuckin' walls talk." Coombs grabbed hold of a worn, coverless paperback. "The man's a crazy bastard anyway. He wants the weak ones to be totally submissive to him like the others."

"What others?"

"Like I told you, the weak sissies, the faggots. His 'women.' That's why he attacked you, for chrissakes. That's the way it is in here." Coombs was looking at Peter now with a wry grin. "You just have to learn to live with it." He uttered a short, mocking laugh.

"Unh! No!" Peter suddenly shot back. He stood up, clenching his fists, as if trying to decide whether to pace up and down or smash the wall of the cramped cell. "You told me this Krankk isn't a veteran!"

"Yeh."

"You told me the others in his group are veterans!"

"So."

"Why don't they control things? Take charge?"

"Jesus." The cellmate slowly shook his head.

"Why didn't Big Ed and Gunny and the others see what happened to me?"

"Jesus Christ, man! You really don't get it, do ya." Coombs laughed again and continued shaking his head. "Yer a fuckin' 'rape-o.' Yer lower 'n shit in here."

There was a long silence followed by the nasal sound of Coombs slowly breathing in, out. "Just 'cause you're a veteran, Peter, don't mean shit to Krankk. Or his veteran shitheads, either. 'Sides, you haven't proven to any of us in here that you can take care of yerself." Peter flashed Coombs an angry look of betrayal. " 'Sides, Krankk's in tight with the guards."

Peter raised his eyebrows.

"Jesus man, didn't ya know that?" the cellmate continued. "The guards... hell, they're never around. 'Specially when Krankk's feeling a hard-on. He's got too god-damned much on the guards. He brings in the tobacco, deals the drugs. This is his racket. We fellows, ya know, us veterans, we wouldn't get a take of the smokes if it weren't for Krankk. We don't screw with Krankk. A guard sees somethin', he don't say nothin'. If he does, Krankk's whole fuckin' god-damned organization will go to the Warden with shit on the guards."

Big Ed and Gunny's raps for bank robbery seemed puny. The same with Coombs' stint for bootlegging and second-degree murder. A federal liquor agent had nailed him. The agent had mistakenly shot to death another agent when they had tried to arrest the drunken ex-sergeant.

Even the mean-spirited half-blood Victor Sanders and his schemes were nothing next to the evil that was Krankk.

Coombs explained to Peter what he had learned about Krankk. The cell boss's given name, Nathan Bedford Stone, had been chosen by his dirt-poor, tenant-farmer parents in Mississippi after Nathan Bedford Forrest, the infamous Confederate cavalryman and founder of the Ku Klux Klan. An avowed Klan member, Krankk held regular Klan meetings with other inmates during recreation. The guards found reasons not to notice.

"Krankk's not just some goddamned country bumpkin from Mizzippi, either."

Coombs laid out for the young Indian the trail marked by Krankk outside the walls. After the Great War, he had left the South for Chicago, where he got into bootlegging. The July 1919 race riots in Chicago interfered with his operation and touched off an already simmering hatred for blacks. His prison minions bragged that during the Chicago race riots he had "killed half-a-dozen niggers." The last one, a black veteran in uniform, brought Krankk his elite status as a convicted murderer.

Krankk despised those prison veterans who weren't with him.

Peter said nothing. He rose and climbed up onto his bunk, laid down facing the wall, closed his eyes. In his head, he tried to count the broken rhythms of his life.

$$\ggg\!\!\rightarrow \bullet \leftarrow\!\!\lll$$

Cold-Maker bore witness to Peter's day-to-day existence at the birth of 1922; the cinder block walls, the smells, the curses, all were suspended within the reptilian rhythms of a frigid shadow life. At first, there had been the three-times-a-day feed in the big, gray mess hall, punctuated by the daily tour in the exercise yard, with lights out at 8:00 p.m. Now, Peter seldom left his cell except for an occasional meal, a little exercise. The clang of steel to steel, the curses and jeering catcalls, the echoing ghost screams of the demented, the kicks and prods from the guards, all blended like the shadows on the walls, drifting in and out like light and darkness.

Weeks and months finally turned into another year, with only a single letter from Annie. He wrote every day, compulsively sharing every thought, every feeling, every nerve. Clumsily he wrote, till the throbbing in his hand became numb and he could write no longer. His left-handed attempts brought only frustration.

Coombs grew more impatient with his surrogate role, writing what, to him, were maudlin letters, letters that drew no answer. The letters from his father and the one letter from Annie were worn and soft from many readings.

Reaching under his pillow, Red-Boy drew out the crushed shoe box and lifted the letter on top, written many months before for Annie by one of her close friends from boarding school.

*March, 1922*
*Red-Boy,*

*I want to tell you that your father and mother are in good health. The winter was hard. Three babies died. I have been sick with coughing.*

*My mother and father are planting the garden. Father has some cattle. Two were frozen during winter. But the grub box feeds us. We thank Above-Person.*

*I got your letter telling about gunny sak. The prison boss sounds like he means trouble. I hope you are fine and strong. I think about you. My heart grows heavy. I wait for your next letter.*

*Annie Running Crane*

Peter had written the letter telling about Gunnysack and the others more than a year earlier. Still, her letter gave him hope; she had thought about him. He held Annie's letter above his reclining head, following the lines, as if by doing so he could somehow touch her presence.

He gained comfort in the daily routine of touching her letter.

Still, the comfort was brief. The throbbing shame and hatred for Krankk defined each day, smashing the gentle shroud until the young Indian desperately sought the only path to escape, to nothingness.

So he slept. Hour after hour, day and night.

>>>→ • ←<<<

Cold-Maker's breath pummeled against the blanketed hides and canvas of his father's lodge. Steals-In-The-Daytime-Woman was stirring the large soot-blackened kettle next to the lodge fire. Seated next to Thomas was Chief Running Crane, Annie's father. He wore a white bandana around his thick neck. The tie seemed an extension of his white hair, neatly smoothed back from his high forehead. His dark-gray eyes and imposing nose framed a mouth, set and closed in a wide, fleshy jaw. No one spoke.

Red-Boy felt as if Annie were near, yet out of vision. He felt her pressing next to him, her breathing.

Red-Boy sensed that Chief Running Crane was slowly, deliberately telling him that Annie was to belong only to the young man who courted her in the traditional way. Sspo mi tá pi—Above Person—would disapprove of any man who broke the law. The Creator would not be pleased with such a union.

Red-Boy felt shame as the eyes of the two fathers met his. He lowered his head. He opened his mouth but could not speak. He turned away and saw not Annie, but The Judge, the Black Robe priest of whiteman justice. Then The Judge became The Raven and flew off into the lodge fire.

He felt her close by—his only true Sits-Besides-Him-Woman. Still, he could not see Annie. Finally, only her mournful eyes were touching his. He looked harder but could not find her. A terrible sorrow overcame him as he saw only his father and Running Crane.

Then Thomas was gesturing with his arms, his gray eye-pools deep, seeming to tell him about the Deer Child, yet also warning him about Annie—that lurking in the young girl's shadow are real but unseen dangers.

Now his father's words were clear. A comforting warmth returned, and the breath of Cold-Maker had vanished. Red-Boy was much younger now—he had come home.

>>>→ • ←<<<

Thomas was speaking to him.

"In the early days, your grandfather, Big Brave-Frank Mountain Chief, had another name, Big-Beaver Humor-Kotscea. He was the last of the great Piegan chiefs. He had four wives. Your mother is one of his three children now living.

"Red-Boy, your great-grandfather, Mountain Chief, had five wives. Mountain Chief believed whitemen to be savage and wicked. He was unafraid, walking over to a party of seven whitemen sent by the Big-knives, the soldiers, over the Backbone-of-the-World to locate the Piegans."

Then, Red-Boy's father was telling him how in the early days, Mountain Chief stole a powerful black horse from the Crow Indians. This horse was well known among the Blackfeet. Red-Boy knew the story of Mountain Chief's Black Horse. The Black Horse was special, brave and strong. So when the Piegan warriors had no name for their society, Mountain Chief gave them a name. The Black Horse Society.

$$\text{»»}\rightarrow \bullet \leftarrow \text{«««}$$

Peter awoke to banging, cursing. Two guards walked by, the shorter one shoving a small crumpled envelope through the bars, and exclaiming "Here, chief, you gotta' smoke signal." Snickering, the two sauntered off.

Peter rolled over and grabbed the crumpled envelope, ripping out its contents in an instant. His breathing came in heavy bursts. The letter was ghost-written, by whom he did not know.

*Christmas, 1923*
*Dear Red-Boy*

*I am writing you without the knowledge of my mother. I have not forgotten you. I miss you. But I cannot tell anyone what my heart really knows. I have been threatened by others that if I do this I will be sent away.*

*Now I have something to tell you. The man Victor Sanders he approaches me. I do not love him. I tell him to go away. He tells me that I will never see you again. Is this true?*

*Now I tell you something else. Red-Boy I cannot give up my life for you. My heart knows you but I cannot see you. I wish I could come to your prison but it is too far away for me to travel. I must take care of my sisters and mother and my father here. One of my sister's babies died last month. It is very hard.*

*Now I must tell you that your letters must stop coming to me. It is like you have gone down the ghost trail and I will not see you again. I am sorry.*

*Annie Running Crane."*

Peter stared at the words: "I will not see you again." Dizziness overtook him and he lay back, squeezing his eyes shut.

Peter read and reread the letter until he felt Coombs' hand tugging at him, telling him that the guards were ushering them to the mess hall and that he must go with the others and eat.

Coombs knew Peter's letter had brought bad news. Still, Coombs coaxed him down from his bunk, lowered his voice almost to a whisper. "Food is gonna make you feel a lot better. Let's go." He gently took his cellmate by the arm and pushed him out in front of the guard as the short line to the mess continued to grow.

Peter kept going over Annie's carefully-penciled letter. He would survive. He would return to her.

But again, the reality of hatred broke Peter's thoughts of redemption. Monroe stepped close and casually whispered his now familiar threat to Peter, "Krankk gonna get even for yer kicking my pretty face." Then he turned and grinned at Peter.

Peter, Coombs and Gunny joined Big Ed at one of the long wooden tables in the middle of the mess hall. Peter was pushed out to an end seat.

"Shit, how the hell's Peter gonna put on any weight eating this," swore Big Ed, spooning in watery soup. The others looked over and nodded.

Out of the corner of his eye, Peter saw Krankk staring at him from three tables over. Peter sat straighter and glared back out of hollow sockets, fierce dots, never blinking.

Seeing his enemy, now, was an awakening from the frightening and shameful images in his head. For there sat a huge, scalped whiteman with prairie dog holes for a nose. Peter smirked ever-so-slightly, never taking his eyes off Krankk. The situation had changed. The Medicine of his father, his grandfather, his great-grandfather, stilled his fear. Somewhere deep within, he knew he would rather die than cower before one who stood on small legs.

Krankk, his thick lips twisting into a vicious frown, slowly rose, holding his empty tray in front of him.

Peter glanced toward the guards at the other end of the mess hall. No one paid attention to what was unfolding.

For an instant Peter feared standing alone. But he was a Piegan. Son of a Chief, grandson of Big Brave-Frank Mountain Chief, and great-grandson of Mountain Chief. He would stand his ground.

Krankk strode to within five feet of the table. Peter's heart thumped primordial war drums. The huge man's head and bloodshot eyes held Peter's even stare.

Feigning a slip, a huge, burly arm hurled the metal tray like a discus, the edge slashed the Indian's left temple.

The crash of metal on bone brought an explosion of white hot light, throwing Peter Stabs-By-Mistake back into the foxhole, blinded by the intensity of the exploding shell.

>>>→ • ←<<<

Again in the stinking foxhole, he reached under him and felt the arm of his comrade. The arm came loose and he held it out, like the severed leg of a coyote, dripping blood. He heard himself scream. A thousand fragmentation shells exploded overhead. Trembling uncontrollably, flat on his back, covering his dead comrade, he lay stupefied by the resonating light and the whizzing "thunk thunk" from shrapnel splattering into the ground.

"Fill the goddamned sandbags!" someone barked above the screaming and shelling.

He scooped up earth, laced with pieces of human flesh, and filled bag after bag, pausing long enough to gag and retch. He felt a cold stinging in his right hand.

Then, it was quiet. He lay looking up at the dark night, a perimeter of shadowy, denuded trees piercing into the intense, now distant, flashes of light. Shadows bent and faded, transforming themselves into human forms. Darkened faces leaned over and peered down with questioning looks and furtive gestures, then blurred once more into trees whose branches were whipped about by Cold-Maker's most chilling wrath. Then, it was dark.

>>>→ • ←<<<

It was morning and Red-Boy saw Old Mountain Chief sitting on the ground.

Seated atop his favorite sorrel pony, Red-Boy saw himself smiling at the sleeping figure of his great-grandfather. The pony moved and Red-Boy was now standing in the middle of the camp and saw the Crees sneak in. Cree arrows and bullets came into the lodge where Old Mountain Chief slept, his gun and coat beside him. His wounded wife pulled him by the hair and he jumped up, hollered, grabbed his gun, bow and arrow and knife and rushed from the door as a Cree was coming in. Red-Boy saw Big Brave and Old Mountain Chief and the others shooting at the Cree, allowing the women to run into a corral for protection.

Left Hand was right behind Green Grass Bull. A Cree ran up to Left Hand, pointed his gun in Left Hand's face, but before he pulled the trigger, Green Grass Bull turned the gun aside. The bullet glanced from his head. Left Hand killed the Cree.

Then, the pony carrying Red-Boy moved again. Red-Boy saw his grand-father take a gray mare, a fast Buffalo horse, while other hunters butchered and skinned the Buffalo all around.

After talking to six old men who were skinning Buffalo and offering to give others half of the back fat, Big Brave-Mountain Chief and his pard-ner, Boss Ribs, bumped into each other as they chased after two young Buffalo bulls running over the hill. Red-Boy's grandfather, Big Brave, shot one arrow. But the big Buffalo bull running at top speed turned and hit Boss Ribs. Big Brave aimed another arrow and was about to snap it off when the bull stopped, turned again and charged. Big Brave was thrown from his startled horse.

Red-Boy stared as the bull stood over his grandfather, snorting and shak-ing his head from side to side and pawing the ground. The slobber foam was dripping on his face. Red-Boy looked into the bull's eyes; they were blue. Then Sun changed the bull's mind and he walked away. Big Brave, Mountain Chief sat up.

Red-Boy saw his grandfather's horse standing near, his guts hanging out. His belly had been ripped open by the bull's sharp horn.

Red-Boy felt a pain at his temple and cried. He tried to push the pain away by pushing in the horse guts. They came out again and the pain in his temple throbbed.

Big Brave, Mountain Chief tore his shirt in strips and tied the horse's guts up and led his horse toward camp. Red-Boy knew the horse would die. Red-Boy wanted to hide his eyes from the guts because they made the side of his head hurt.

Big Brave's older brothers saw him leading the horse and cried, "Buffalo hooked! Let's try to save her. We will sew her up."

The men threw the mare and pushed the guts back into the mare's belly and stitched her hide with horse-tail hair. The men then bound a tanned calf hide around her and a blanket. The mare shivered and puffed up.

Red-Boy felt himself sitting atop his bone saddle. But his heart was on the ground. He was ashamed of the pain in his head. He would stay out on the prairie and go to the little hill, and talk to Naa-tó 'si (Sun).

> *"Naa-tó 'si, take my words*
> *Let enemy charge*
> *Let me get killed*
> *Face battle, forget sorrow."*

Then, Red-Boy felt himself settle back into his saddle. His mouth was dry. Big Brave, Mountain Chief handed him a raw kidney.

Looking down, his grandfather's puffed gray mare had become the Black Horse beneath him. Red-Boy had become one with the Black Horse, who now reared and kicked his front hooves at the Sun. Big Brave gave the signal to charge against the invading Cree.

>>>→ • ←<<<

Peter slowly, gingerly, cracked open his swollen eye to the sharp light. He was on his back in the snowy-white prison infirmary, covered with starched-white sheets. An orderly dressed in white with greasy black hair, was arranging things on a white tray.

He turned his head. "Ouch!" The pain from the left side of his head spread across his forehead.

"Just settle down, Peter. There was a bad accident in the mess the other day. You've been out for quite awhile," stated the orderly in a somewhat condescending tone.

"Really hurts."

"Yeh, I know. We've given you tincture of opiates to control the pain. You'll be here for awhile."

"What happened?" Red-Boy blinked at the bright ceiling light.

"Seems that boss Krankk slipped and cracked you on the nut. Caught you with the edge of his tray."

"Slipped?" Red-Boy asked incredulously, trying to prop himself up. "Ouch! Ohhh!" He settled back. "He never slipped, man." Red-Boy stared over at the orderly.

Glancing over, the orderly shrugged. "You don't remember him walking over to the guard?"

Red-Boy stared and said nothing.

"Seems that slip cost Krankk some time in isolation. Word is that he's back out, though."

Comforted by the soft pillow, Peter carefully turned his swollen head. A window. He could see outside the prison walls. He drank in the lush sight of lovegrass outside.

He imagined himself with Annie, riding fast ponies onto the prairie, up hills and into a draw next to a stream. Then, the night fire and vividness of Annie's soft form, her lovely face, the fresh scent of her black hair next to him—visions which made Red-Boy's eyes sting. He shut his eyes and slept.

He struggled to come awake. Out, beyond the greenery, were cottonwood trees and tall prairie grass. He turned again to times-far-back, his ancestors and smiled. He remembered the dream, the Black Horse.

The dream of his ancestors brought him power.

The dark horse kicking high its hooves towards Naa-tó 'si, the Sun. The Black Horse with powerful hooves—his War Medicine. The gutted gray mare in the dream had been healed by Mountain Chief for Red-Boy, transformed to be his Black Horse War Medicine.

$$\text{»»→ • ←«}$$

The morning he was to be transferred back to his cell, he asked the orderly if he could take a small piece of silk and coloring powders—pencils, charcoal, crayons, paints—whatever would work its way into the silk.

"What for?" asked the greasy orderly. He beckoned to Warden Biddle, who happened to be standing in the hallway.

"To do some painting," Peter replied.

Warden Biddle looked at the Indian skeptically and frowned. He reminded the orderly that the inmate might merely use the silk to try and either hang himself or choke someone else.

"No. Just a small piece." He held up his hands to show the eighteen-inch measurement. "I want to make a painting to send to my father."

The warden flashed an amused smile at the look of earnestness on the Indian's face. Finally nodding, he instructed the Indian that he must work on the painting under the supervision of the trustee-librarian in the prison library when the others were exercising or working in the prison shops. Peter nodded, smiled and said he appreciated the favor.

Peter returned to his cell. Yet, this time, the fabric of his life behind bars was different.

Somewhere in the opiate-induced daze, he had remembered something his father and Oliver Sanders had told him to do. He had gained enough hope and would write to his father's whiteman friend, the Easterner, Christian Schuster. Perhaps the whiteman could untangle the wrong that had been done at the trial. Perhaps Christian Schuster could help get him home to Annie and his family.

Peter soon learned that the prison librarian—who the others jokingly referred to as Shake Spear—stuttered almost uncontrollably and read incessantly. He also wrote letters for the inmates. Shake Spear's thick eyeglasses made his dark, beady eyes appear button-sized. No one quite knew what criminal misfortune had befallen the fellow. Some rumored he was doing time for embezzlement. Yet, the intense little man seemed quietly intrigued with Peter's new project.

Each day, under the watchful eyes of his stuttering overseer, Peter began the long, slow and painstaking process of giving form on silk to the vision of his Power.

»»→ • ←«« 

One afternoon when Coombs returned to his cell from exercise, he found his cellmate seated cross-legged on the floor facing the toilet, arms outstretched on his knees.

Approaching, Coombs' eyes widened. Markings of red and black crossed over the Indian's face and down his cheeks where he had inscribed small circles. Each of Peter's hands rested palm-down on his still knees. The man wore no shoes. Glancing down, Coombs thought he saw hoof images on the bottom of both blackened feet.

"Jesus H. Christ, man, are you crazy!?" Coombs shimmied around to the front of Peter, next to the commode and squatted down in front of the Indian.

Peter's expression had become a curtain, hiding the Power revealed to him in the dream.

"You crazy bastard! You know, you damn near got killed by that son-of-a-bitch Krankk. Now he sees you like this, he sure as hell will poke your tight, sweet little Indian ass again."

Slowly, deliberately Red-Boy raised his eyes and met Coombs' stare.

"Now I will tell you something, Coombs. You take my talk and listen." The Indian's eyes were fierce, blazing black—penetrating right through and far away. "The tomahawk is raised by Red-Boy against the boss Krankk. My ancestors, my grandfather, my father and I are all Piegan warriors. It does not matter what you think. I will not die at the hands of this evil coward, because my Great Medicine protects me."

To Coombs, the Indian seemed mesmerized, a zombie. Perhaps the infirmary doctors had given him too many opiates. Or perhaps the Indian had moved in on Krankk's racket and stolen and hidden the drugs. Coombs glanced around the small cell, half expecting to find a broken vial.

Reaching out, Coombs tried to shake sense into the Indian. The Indian's hand shot out and blocked the approach with such blinding quickness that Coombs flinched and drew back, retreating to his bunk.

There, emblazoned on the Indian's palm, was the unmistakable image of a horse hoof.

Christian F. Schuster

# VIII

# The Dilettante - 1925

he hypnotic click-clacks and the gently swaying Pullman car brought heaviness to the man's eyelids. He glanced out the window at the snaking Connecticut River, sparkling in the fertile flood plain. This late spring of 1925, lush stands of oak-hickory hardwood forests framed the river's edge. The river's misty reflections submerged him into a world of childhood memories along this waterway, once the highway for Canadian Indians who floated timbers down this river to the towns along the Connecticut Valley.

"Coffee, sir," asked Sullivan, the black porter's baritone voice breaking through the haze. Blinking, Christian F. Schuster nodded and looked up.

"Yes, black coffee would be fine." The man slowly rubbed his tired eyes. The fifty-six-year-old New Englander had been up all night in Willimansett, giving last-minute instructions to his vice-president at the Holyoke Box and Lumber Company.

Sipping his coffee, Christian Schuster watched the river disappear behind them. White tufts of steam from the black-and-red-trimmed Mallet compound locomotive drifted past his window. The "iron horse." That's what his Blackfeet friends called it. Yet this late spring departure was no ordinary trip to Montana. All winter long, he had read and reread the letter in his hand, the contents of which had added to what he had learned of this tragedy over the past few years. Peter had been in Leavenworth Penitentiary, now, for three-and-a-half years. He took another sip of coffee, spilling some on his corduroy pants.

"Damn," he muttered, as he began the letter again.

*Leavenworth, Kansas*
*December 20th , 1924*
*Dear Friend*

*Your letter of the 11th instant was received on the night of the 14th in-*
*stant. My friend and the friend of my father, I regret that it is ever my*
*misfortune to write to you and others from a penitentiary.*

*I tell you, my friend, this was made possible by the machinations of a*
*conniving halfbreed Indian. But, since the Maker-of-all-things has or-*
*dained it to be so, what can any mortal do?*

*I thank you for the Tobacco, picture and the stamps you sent along*
*with your good letter. I have smoked some of the Tobacco, and I shall*
*enjoy many more dreamy moments filled with reminiscences of things*
*that were and of those that could have been.*

*Some day, I want to meet you in person again. I wish you and your*
*family a Merry Christmas and a Happy New Year. I am, with greet-*
*ings in friendship, your Indian friend. I shake your hand from my*
*heart.*

*Peter Stabs-By-Mistake*

The man's eyes narrowed and he frowned. From a distance, Christian F. Schuster might well have been mistaken for Teddy Roosevelt, but without a handle-bar mustache and thick spectacles. He took another sip of coffee and ran his fingers through his gray-streaked, black hair.

Peter Stabs-By-Mistake. Since receiving the first letter, he had regularly sent the young inmate letters and gifts, hoping to bolster his spirit, while explaining ways to get him released.

The young man's letter had probably been ghost-written by one of the more literate of the penitentiary's inmate "poets." Although Peter had attended boarding school, he could only read and write with difficulty—was not nearly so literate as to speak of "machinations" and "dreamy reminiscences."

From his leather-upholstered seat, he glanced up ahead at the concrete buttress supporting the trestle. The Boston & Albany railroad train was now crossing the Connecticut River from Springfield, Massachusetts. He knew exactly what Peter Stabs-By-Mistake meant by the question "What can any mortal do?"

Schuster knew the concrete and steel sarcophagus that was Leavenworth Penitentiary would kill the boy just as surely as tuberculosis and influenza had killed off hundreds of his tribe's people. If his spirit could not soar free of the concrete and barbed wire walls, then the guards and the inmates — most assuredly the white inmates — would prey upon him like a wounded badger.

He glanced out the window, as if to escape the starkness of the image of concrete imprisoning Peter.

Thomas, his mother, and all his other relations called him Red-Boy. There was no way any of them would ever be able to understand the punishing isolation that existed within the walls of Leavenworth.

He thought about isolation and contradictions; the Great War, then prison for the young Blackfeet. He thought, as well, about his own lesser contradictions; a prominent New England businessman on his way by rail to spend time with his friends, the Blackfeet, in Montana. He thought of things his mother had taught him, things he had discovered, expectations of his business associates and Holyoke society.

>>>→ • ←<<<

A beautiful black, flint weapon with a notched groove for binding the handle. His first stone tomahawk had a sharp, ground edge. At age seven, Chris had found the tomahawk on the bank of the Connecticut River after a spring freshet. Long before then, it had been buried in the earth.

The boy had run home to show his mother his "prize possession."

Chris's mother, a stout German-Bavarian immigrant, gently but consistently had taught her son to be respectful of the Indian children. Oftentimes handing him a bag of donuts, she would suggest that he take them to the Indian children whose fathers were on the log drive that was being pulled down the river by Brattleboro.

"If you get to know those Indian children, you will learn more about nature than you will ever learn in school," his mother told him. "Once all this land was theirs," she said. "Our soldiers drove them from their homes and hunted them like wild animals. Someday you will meet Indians and make them your friends. Then you will learn much more about the things that you like."

>>>→ • ←<<<

Christian Schuster grinned as he remembered telling his high school sweetheart, Marie, how he first became an entrepreneur at the age of ten years. His mother had encouraged him to earn money by selling muskrat skins. With his hard-earned money, he secretly purchased a muzzle-loading musket to hunt Buffalo, like the Indians did.

"What happened?" she had asked.

"Well, I snuck out of the house one morning and tried to shoot a real live Buffalo. The kick from the extra-heavy powder sent me flying back into sharp corn stubble and I threw up."

"Your mom must have grounded you for good," Marie chided.

"Oh, no. She just bathed me and rubbed some liniment on my bruises."

Later, Chris sheepishly owned up to Marie that he had surreptitiously scraped the lead pipes in his parents' basement thinner and thinner to make shot for his muzzle-loading musket.

Despite Chris's childhood eccentricities and peculiar penchant for emulating the Connecticut River Indians with his Buffalo hunts, Marie married him anyway. She decided that a man with a German-Bavarian mother who taught him to respect everyone, including Indians, must be special.

>>>→ • ←<<<

"Whaanngg!" The man was jolted out of his reverie by the high-pitched yowl-whistle of the passing locomotive. They were now traveling upland into the heavily forested Berkshire Hills of western Massachusetts, blanketed with eastern white and red pines, pitch pines and hemlocks. Fields dotted with white dogwoods and red rhododendrons, interlaced with moist, drooping ferns and filled with muskrat, rabbits and raccoons, all of which he had hunted as a boy. The entire area mirrored the Glacier National Parkland of the Blackfeet, where he loved to hunt and fish and live with his Pikuni friends.

He tucked the letter, which he had been holding for the past several hours, into the front pocket of his shirt. Tiny mist rivulets smeared down the pane of the half-opened Pullman window as he peered out.

There, off to the left of the tracks and back a-ways, fixed to a wall was a torn sign, "Pittsfield Welcomes Coolidge."

Chris remembered that this was the place where Teddy Roosevelt was nearly killed; a trolley car had slammed into his carriage during the President's September, 1902 New England tour.

Reaching over, he closed the window.

His friend, Calvin Coolidge, now occupied the White House. He chuckled at the incongruity of the lone, tattered campaign sign appearing suddenly in this isolated New England town. Coolidge would not have come; he would have sent Dawes, his running mate. Silent Cal disliked almost anything having to do with public campaigning, never really venturing forth anywhere in the '24 election.

The roots of Chris's familiarity with the President stemmed from the days when Coolidge served as mayor of Northampton. Yet his friend had grown more enigmatic after becoming President. Calvin had personally told him that he was "troubled by the plight of the American Indian," speaking vaguely of the time "when the Indians may become self-sustaining." Yet he never pressed for legislation to eliminate the rampant hunger and disease that had confronted Chris every summer when he traveled out West.

To Chris, the Indian Bureau was just another prison. Like Leavenworth, it encased his Pikuni friends — a post-war curtain woven of indifference and excuses, tattered with the holes of an insufficient budget, bureaucratic fumbling and corruption. Not a thread of compassion. With the issuance of fee patents to the Indians in 1918 came land fraud. Indian lands ended up in the possession of whites. What was even worse were the Bureau superintendents. Over the past fifteen years, three were dismissed from the Indian service; one was sent to the penitentiary and another left Browning after he was indicted.

Yet some in New England jabbed at Chris, calling him a "hypocrite," living on the East coast nine months out of the year amid wealth on a large estate, then late spring and summer living among the plains Indians. Others ridiculed him for coming out West.

They called it his New England "hobby interest" to assuage his guilt about being a rich whiteman. Their sarcasm was barely concealed — come to live among and "lift up their spirits," they would jab.

The Holyoker felt tired and uneasy. Life was strangely unsettled for his Blackfeet friends in a new way. He and Marie had discussed Peter's imprisonment and his own frustration at being unsure he could do anything to help. He remembered his wife good-naturedly chiding him, as she always did, for his "obsessive passion with the noble savages."

The New Englander's thoughts and worries began to run in circles until he grew weary, then drowsy. Finally, his worry drifted off as the hazy-green blur of the passing New England forests soothed his thoughts.

Rocking in the Pullman, he smiled, then winced, as he recalled the harsh sunburns and his mother's many ministrations and her stern lectures.

Undaunted by disastrous Buffalo hunts, young Chris did his best to be an Indian, a great hunter and scout. Days in the sun had seemed the logical way to becoming dark-skinned. Thankfully, the lad learned not to expose his total nakedness to the sun. Still, it had taken a particularly harsh experience and a visit to the doctor to teach him why Indians wore the breechclout.

>>>→ • ←<<<

That June morning back in 1881, he and his friend, Jack North, spotted a partly sunken birch-bark canoe floating downstream.

Wading out to the canoe and hauling it ashore, the boys made plans to mend it and paddle down-river to a tribe he knew as "King Philip's braves." He'd read about them in one of his school texts. A month passed while the boys patched the canoe with pine pitch and cloth until it was watertight. They made two paddles from driftwood. Finally, with a loaf of bread and a sack of potatoes, they started on their voyage. Having seen pictures of Indians kneeling while paddling their canoes, Chris and Jack assumed the position and bent to their paddles.

In the noon-day sun, they rounded a bend and spotted a little white wigwam on the shore.

The boys pitched forward as the canoe rose, tipped, and slid with a tearing sound, spiked on a sunken log hidden just below the surface of the water. Watching their waterlogged canoe slowly submerge and drift underwater down the stream, the boys slogged through the willows near the little wigwam. Smoke slowly curled from the top.

There, seated on a log next to the structure, was an Indian. A real Indian, not a circus Indian. The boys stood frozen, unsure of what might happen next. The man's dark face was pock-marked. He stood tall and straight, his long, braided hair swung forward over each shoulder. He still had the trace of a chuckle as he greeted the boys. "Little bad luck, huh?"

"Do you belong to the tribe downriver?" asked Chris.

"No. My people live far away in north country. They are Tobiques. I am called Bow Maker."

"Tobiques," repeated Chris. "Where do the Tobiques live?"

"Tobiques live where the Saint John River meets Tobique River up north." Seeing the eagerness in the faces of the two youngsters, the Indian saw an opportunity to turn the current situation to his advantage.

"I go sell baskets in the village. Wigwam is not safe alone."

The boys were more than happy to watch Bow Maker's wigwam each day while he went to the village. In return, the Indian helped the boys construct a river-worthy canoe along with two painted paddles.

All summer, the boys seized every opportunity to paddle or hike to Bow Maker's wigwam — their summer camp, they called it.

During those long days, Bow Maker showed the boys how to hammer and strip ash saplings, how to weave baskets with the strands and how to make watertight bowls from birch bark by sewing the seams with the small roots of hemlock, then pitching the joints. He taught them how he made feathered arrows.

One afternoon in August, Bow Maker unrolled a bundle which contained goose feathers, sinew, arrow shafts and a small bag of pitch. He stripped three feathers from the quills and cut them about six inches long. Then, he tightly wrapped the feathers with sinew at the notched end of the arrow. He spread spruce pitch over the wrapping and stuck the arrow into the ground while the melted pitch dried. Then he repeated the process. With a flint, he knapped two small points and bound them with sinew to the arrow shafts. He painted the shafts with a red powder paint which he moistened with his fingers. Bow Maker presented the finished arrows to the boys. Wide eyed, the young lads received the gifts, the most precious possessions they could imagine.

Bow Maker talked of his people. "Long ago, we were many. Now we are few, like deer. The deer and we are brothers. We are both afraid of whiteman," winking as he spoke. Bow Maker told the boys stories of the ways and cunning of animals and humorous tales of the tricks played by animals on each other and human beings.

By the end of the summer, the boys knew why the first birds came, why the stars are bright, why the leaves turn different colors. They knew how to use herbs and roots and the innermost bark of certain trees to make almost anything a person needed.

When the leaves started turning yellow and reddish, Bow Maker told the boys, "Now I go back to my people, they wait for me." Presenting the boys with the red-painted maple paddles, he told them that no harm would come to them if they came to visit the Tobiques. "My people, they will treat you good."

At the end of that magical summer, Chris turned twelve years old.

>>>→ • ←<<<

The motion of the Pullman car rocked his dreams this late spring after-noon in 1925. The staccato of the train wheels beneath became the drums of the summer of 1901 at the home of the Tobique, Bow Maker.

It took many years before Chris and his childhood friend Jack North —now dubbed Old Bug Grease —were able to make the trip to where the waters of the St. John River crash down into a chasm of rock, filled with ancient potholes.

Bug Grease, the intrepid canoe sailor, did so much scratching of his skeeter-ravaged face and neck that after weeks in the Allagash he looked as if he had been bitten by everything but a rattlesnake. Itching and scratching, Jack returned home before the two completed the journey down river to Bow Maker's Tobique village.

Rather than risk an unfriendly reception when he arrived, Chris decided to wait on the beach after learning that his friend from all those years ago had gone to a whiteman village to sell fish.

At sundown, a birch canoe with its single blade cut through the stream. A tall Indian stepped lightly to the shore and carried his canoe into the willows. Chris recognized Bow Maker.

Going to him and holding out his hand, Chris watched his eyes. Bow Maker's mind went back and a look of recognition crossed the Indian's eyes. With a broad smile, he grasped Chris's hand. "White brother, big man now. Come."

Chris followed Bow Maker to his father's wigwam. Inside were many oc-cupants seated on the earth—old men, women and several children who quickly crawled behind their mothers. All eyes were turned towards the whiteman in suspicion and mistrust.

"Always the Indian is like that. He only believes when he knows the naked heart," Bow Maker had once explained to Chris.

To the gathered occupants, Bow Maker now related that Chris was his long-ago young friend of the South Country. Trailing his words, Chris no-ticed a gradual softening in their eyes, and the stern faces relaxed and turned to the whiteman in welcome.

White Wolf, Bow Maker's father, shook Chris's hand and greeted him. "My boy, he say he invite you to visit us. He believe sometime you come. Now we see your face. We glad. We let no harm come to you."

Bow Maker asked about Chris's friend, Jack. Smiling, he wanted to know if Chris and his friend had taken other canoe voyages. Chris and Bow Maker told the people about the good times they had enjoyed at the little camp on the river shore twenty summers before.

Chris told them about his recent Allagash hunting trip with Old Bug Grease and how the chiggers had sent Jack home. Amused smiles and laughter took over.

When Bow Maker told how Chris's first canoe had sunk and of the disaster that appeared on the two boys' faces, the laughter spread. "That village you look for that time, maybe it Tobique. Now you find it."

"How you like to take traverse far up Tobique River to visit my friend, Little Beaver?" asked Bow Maker. "Little Beaver, he is my friend. We get plenty meat and salmon. We travel long trail. We make three camps before we see Little Beaver. He got good birch canoe. It not sink like your canoe." Chris joined in the laughter with Bow Maker and the others. "We use his canoe when we come down river."

Chris's heart raced. Just as he had when the offer to look after Bow Maker's wigwam was made, he told his friend he would meet Little Beaver and hunt with them. Bow Maker smiled and turned to his mother. "My mother, she speaks to you. She says, 'now we eat.' "

Mink Woman, Bow Maker's mother, handed them tin plates piled high with a feast of fresh salmon and set before each a cup of herb tea.

In a deep sleep that night in the Tobique village, a strange dream came to Chris.

In the dream, his tipi was set up on the shore facing Dawn Sun. Painted above the door was a little straight pine tree. A voice in the dream said, "Pine Tree is your brother. I have painted it on your tipi." Then, Chris saw a lean-to made of pine branches, a thick bed of brown needles, and he tasted again the sweet juice behind the inner bark.

When Morning Sun awoke them, he told Bow Maker about his dream. The Tobique was impressed and remained silent for a long time. "That was a powerful dream," he said. "It is good to have dream like that. Pine Tree, it stand straight, it never lean. I paint what you dream on your tipi. It bring you good luck."

With charcoal, Bow Maker carefully drew a Pine Tree over the door of Chris's tipi.

》》→ • ←《《

Chris awoke with a start, confronting, again, the real purpose of his trip to Montana this time. He needed to talk to those who knew how and why Red-Boy had been imprisoned.

To his Pikuni friends, Chris wanted to stand as a sturdy, tall Pine Tree. Yet, he knew not how or if his roots could work their way into the cracks of the Leavenworth crypt, revealing truth and, thereby, freeing Red-Boy.

Sullivan was ringing the small bell, announcing that dinner was about to be served in the dining car. The iron horse had just crossed the state line into New York, headed for Buffalo.

Chris took in the porter's easy, rolling gait. After years of trips out West, he had a friendly relationship with Sullivan and each year would catch up on the health and welfare of the members of his large family.

Sullivan's face and forearms bore dark, jagged scars. He had been injured rescuing his wounded first lieutenant during the Battle of Metz.

Chris had heard the story one evening, a few years back. Chris knew that this brave young veteran should have been given the Distinguished Service Cross. But the only acknowledgment was a Purple Heart and the privilege of holding a railroad porter's job and ignoring the assumptions of "Looks like that nigger's been in a hell'uva knife fight."

A light rain now streaked the windows. Darkening thunderheads hung low overhead and in the distance a shadowy, granulated, mist-like curtain of torrential rain fell on the hilly Berkshire country.

Dark and cold closed in and he thought again of Leavenworth Penitentiary.

A helpless, sinking feeling overcame Chris as he strode back to the dining car, feeling guilty, a privileged whiteman about to partake of a meal in comfort while Thomas's son, Red-Boy, sat in a concrete cell, put there by dark forces as real and elusive as the dark thunderclouds that now shrouded the train.

He sat in the diner car at a white linen-covered table, set with silver and china. He took a sip of water from the crystal goblet. Here, in the isolation of ease, the contradictions of his life dulled his appetite. Maybe he really was what others in New England saw him as—the hypocritical dilettante from Holyoke who pretended to know what was best for the "red man." Maybe he, too, was a fake who had led Thomas and Oliver Sanders to believe he could be of real assistance. He knew the stories of the whiteman driving the native people farther and farther back into the forest because he wanted all of the land for himself.

Wasn't he, with his factory and his home, a direct benefactor of that turn of events?

He wanted to do the right thing. Yet, what and how twisted into a knot in his stomach. Red-Boy, like so many of his Nation, would die of imprisonment, put there by laws and rules contrived and manipulated by whitemen like himself who had taken the land, filled it with their big, box houses and his box and lumber company, controlling it with their paper money and their paper justice.

Slowly, deliberately, the man got up and turned back towards his berth on the Pullman coach.

"Sir?" Sullivan cast a puzzled look at the man.

"Oh, Sullivan. I'm just not hungry now."

The porter watched Chris stiffly walk away from his meal, wondering what could possibly be troubling such a man.

Chris sank back into his berth and awaited the deep sleep that would untangle his knot and carry away the troubling thoughts.

Chris's first visit to the Blackfeet (Pikuni) (from left to right) Chief-Boy, Natosa, Cro-Feathers, Medicine-War-Bonnet, Curly Bear, Chris (Morning Eagle), Bear Head, Double-Runner. Behind sits Chris's first tipi Iroquio. Ka-neh-to-teh (He-leans-on-nobody).

# IX

# The Hunters

T he Berkshire Hills of Massachusetts, smothered with pine and hemlock, blended into stands of fir and beech oak, sugar maple and yellow birch, announced the approach of the Adirondack uplands of New York. Chris's mouth was dry. Perhaps a quick tipple might quench his thirst. Stretching and looking out, he spotted several urban-dwelling rock doves perched on a stump next to a rickety wire fence.

The New Englander strolled to the club car.

"Guess I'll have an Old Irish Whiskey," he quipped, winking at Sullivan. The porter was now euphemistically dubbing as "bartender." He eased himself into a seat at a linen-covered table for two in the plushy-upholstered club car.

"That'll make Mr. Volstead real mad, sir," the bartender grinned back. Prohibition meant that the stiffest drink to be had on the train after passage of the Volstead Act was "near beer," or vinegar and water, as Chris would joke.

Sipping his near beer, Chris allowed that at least it wasn't too early in the day to "drink" when that's all that was available. He studied the carved wood and silver embellishments accenting the curved walls and arched ceiling of the club car. Taking another sip, he again looked out the window.

There, in the fog, was the face of the girl. He strained to discern what was in her heart. Chris knew her parents but barely knew Annie Running Crane.

Then another face beckoned, and he was in the lodge of Thomas Stabs-By-Mistake.

"How's your whiskey, sir?"

"Well, Sullivan, it keeps the system clean, I guess." Sullivan chuckled. The two talked of summers past on this particular "route out West by rail to the plains." They often met in the club car early in the day where Chris religiously requested Old Irish Whiskey and Sullivan always prepared his favorite concoction of bitters, "with a twist of lemon," or near beer.

Sullivan went back to the bar and Chris was lost for a moment in the shadow of Red-Boy. Later, when Chris went back to his Pullman coach, "Old Irish Whiskey" washed him back to his earlier days.

The Tobique journey in 1901 to the village of Bow Maker was the first experience Chris had with an Indian who could not speak English. On that trip, he met the hunter, Little Beaver, who could not talk whiteman, and when they had hunted together they spoke only with signs. Still, they had killed a caribou bull.

Chris learned that the language of each tribe was different. Just the same, there was sign language. With slight variations it was universal.

Stretching back as the day wore on, Chris spotted black-eyed Susans, devil's paint brush, Queen Anne's lace and distant apple orchards. As the train and the sun moved deeper into the West, Chris's mind went back to the first hunt with Little Beaver, then forward to the first hunt with his Pikuni friends, with Peter Red-Boy and his father, Thomas. The Piegan hunting trek had taken them into Saint Mary River country in the fall of 1920. They rode horseback into the lush grasslands of the Saint Mary Valley, northeast of Two Medicine Lake.

$$\text{»»}\!\rightarrow\bullet\leftarrow\!\text{«««}$$

After one camp, they arrived at their favorite elk spot near the banks of the Saint Mary River. Thomas signed that Red-Boy would show Chris "plenty of elk tracks and holes where the four-legged little ones hide."

Next morning, a pot of boiled turnips was steaming and dried pemmican was set at each place. "Now we eat. Eat much," signed Thomas with a grin. "This time you and Red-Boy need strong food."

"Father says to 'fill up good,'" said Red-Boy. "Soon, I will take you where you will see tracks of elk. A big bull elk passed close to camp last night. He came down to drink from the river. All the elk come down to graze on the grass of the open hills."

Leaning forward with a wink, Thomas had whispered and signed, "Maybe so you have good shot and plenty of luck, then we not eat all the time turnips that I cook." Red-Boy and Chris laughed.

They took their 30-30 Winchester rifles and Chris followed Red-Boy into the thick stand of alder and cottonwood. Thomas remained in camp to hunt rabbit, "In case you warriors are not good shots this time."

Soon, they came upon freshly made tracks on an open hill. Pointing to a draw nearby, Red-Boy said, "They go that way."

The small elk herd had been feeding and traveling slowly. Red-Boy showed Chris the horn marks on two trees. A big bull had passed between them, up the steep draw. Following the tracks, they found fresh dung where the animal had bedded. Now and then they spotted hair on trees where the bark was rough.

Red-Boy, skilled and quiet, stepped over rotted, fallen timber and passed beneath low-hung branches. Now and then, Chris watched as Red-Boy crouched on a big moss-covered log, then rose slowly, silently to see what Chris could not see.

"S-s-s-s." The hiss could hardly be heard. It was a warning. Red-Boy stood motionless, seeing straight ahead into the forested draw. There, partly hidden among the trees stood the great bull, just his head and withers showing. He had neither scented nor seen them, but instinct had told him that danger was near. He had stopped feeding, frozen in his tracks. Slowly Red-Boy brought his rifle to his shoulder. Suddenly the bull's withers twitched and the animal moved.

Red-Boy had waited for Chris to shoot first.

"Wang! Wang!" spoke the two barrels nearly in unison. A crash! The four-legged forest creature vanished among the alder, cottonwood and dead timber. Chris thought they had missed.

Red-Boy sat down and motioned for Chris to do likewise. With soft whispers he said, "We will follow him now. He may travel far." Suddenly, he held up his hand, hearing sounds. "Wait. I think he will soon be sick. He will lie down and bleed a lot." The men followed the gut-shot elk several miles and saw where he had lain down and bled badly. His blood and tracks then led into a fresh clearing. The hunters came upon the animal at the far side. He was down. He would never see the sun again. The hunters dressed him out and with their united strength hung their kill on a big cottonwood sapling.

The trek back to camp took several hours, frequently interrupted with rest and talk. Red-Boy was curious about the New Englander. Chris found the young Indian quite knowledgeable about parts of the East coast he had traveled through with the Army.

Thomas was at work cooking dinner when the hunters returned.

"What? No rabbit to eat?" asked Red-Boy, grinning. He whispered to Chris that he had counted a coup on his father.

Smiling mischievously, Thomas turned and walked to the bank of the Saint Mary River. There, he held up two freshly caught trout. Walking a little further upstream, he pulled out a half-dozen submerged skinned rabbits for dinner.

After sundown, the threesome passed Thomas's medicine pipe four times, giving thanks. Before bedding down for a night's sleep, Thomas rubbed his back and signed, "Aaee. Lots of hard work catching those rabbits today." They all laughed.

Red-Boy and Chris sat on the ground beside the slow-burning camp fire, listening to the forest sounds carried by the night breeze.

"Are you planning on starting a family?" asked Chris.

"Maybe, when her parents approve," replied Red-Boy.

"There is someone, then?"

Red-Boy smiled and looked into the fire, poking the smoldering logs with a stick. Finally, looking over at Chris, the young man said, "Yes."

"Does she have a name?" asked Chris with a broad grin.

"Annie. Annie Running Crane."

"The daughter of Ted Running Crane?"

"Yes."

"Wonderful."

"She's very quiet, but you know, she's also very spirited," he said. Chris nodded.

"Wants the same things I do." Red-Boy paused, thoughtfully looking into the fire, then went on. "Better care for our sick people. She's been through much sickness herself. She's a real survivor though."

"She sounds like a very special young woman. You must love her a lot."

Red-Boy's smile opened even more and he slowly nodded.

>>>→ • ←<<<

Chris felt the gentle sway of the Pullman, pulled by the iron horse, returning him to his friends in Montana as it had many times before. Yet, this time Chris knew they trusted that he could uncover the truth about Red-Boy and would convince the whitemen with power to make the wrong right. The New Englander's closeness to Red-Boy and his father gave them hope that this white-man could break through the silence of those who knew the truth.

Certainly he knew his Pikuni friends were shrewd enough to have figured things out. They suspected and hoped Chris's friends were influential white-men politicians.

Yet the Holyoker felt unsure of his ability, unworthy of the faith they had in him. He remembered when the Pikuni were skeptical and distant, some even hostile at his presence, until they learned that he had nothing to do with the Federal Indian Bureau.

Chris knew whitemen friends with power who exhibited the same skepticism of Red-Boy's innocence and were reluctant to sponsor his release.

Reaching under his seat, he pulled out a worn brown-and-black-checkered suitcase. Opening it, he extracted a letter from the Piegan Elder, Curly Bear.

Chris had carefully read and reread the ghost-written letter after its unexpected arrival a few months earlier.

*Dear Brother—January, 1925*

*I hope this letter will find you in the best of health and hope that the All Mighty One will ever be your Guide and Strength and give you long life.*

*My wife is going to make you a dancing suit soon as we can get some skins.*

*Many of the little children have been sick with the measles. Some of the little children they have been sick for 19 days. There is much suffering for food.*

*Now I will tell you, my friend Bear Head went to the Agency for rations.*

*He was told by one Mr. Sanders that he would have to see Mr. Campbell the Agent first so we got no ration.*

*Now I am going to tell you my dear brother that you must come here now and speak with people who know what happened to Red Boy. His father Thomas Stabs By Mistake told me to ask for you to come and that you are a good man. You can do good things. I know you have a Piegan heart.*

*A Piegan heart will talk not with the tongue of a little child but of a powerful warrior. The people know what happened to Red Boy. They will be honest and tell the truth from the heart to you.*

*This is all I have to say,*

$X$

*Curly Bear.*

As he re-read Curly Bear's letter, the New Englander worried again that he might not be able to "do good things" for Red-Boy in an effort to be worthy of the confidence bestowed in him by this Blackfeet Elder. Chris folded the letter and checked off the pathways to justice he had already explored with those in power over the past several years, but to no avail. He shook his head. His friends were so patient before the wall of whiteman indifference and he wanted so much to reward their quiet, persevering ways and their faith in him.

Sun Dance camp, Browning, MT, July, 1900.  Photo courtesy of Sherburne Collection and William E. Farr.

# X

# Riding The Iron Horse

L ips pursed, eyes narrowed, he peered through pince-nez glasses. The man's demeanor bespoke matters far from the vistas of lush farmlands that rushed by. As the iron horse lumbered its way west this late May of 1925, the New Englander thumbed through letter after letter arrayed in front of him.

Christian Schuster was more than perplexed at the lack of interest displayed by Justice Department officials as well as Superintendent Frank Campbell and other Indian Bureau agents. He was angered and vexed at those in positions of authority—those who evidently had the ability to commute Peter Stabs-By-Mistake's sentence, but who seemed unimpressed by the evidence. And the evidence consisted mostly of statements gathered by those who had been present at the scene of the crime in Heart Butte, Montana back in May of 1921. Now, it was his turn to be suspicious. He had a gut feeling not all was as it had been presented to the court or to him.

He settled back and thought of how they were so suspicious of him when he first made his presence known at the Blackfeet Reservation, thinking him just another Federal Indian Bureau official.

Their sullen faces had relaxed when they realized, with time, that he was one who perhaps respected and liked them. He smiled as he saw them poking fun at his obsessive ways; this whiteman fidgeting with his strange metal letter machine—a typewriter—punctuating the night air with its strange clickety-clack staccato. He was forever fumbling with luggage which seemed so cumbersome and out of place to them. They smiled at his serious attempts to mimic elusive expressions which the Pikunis used to express emotion, awkwardly murdering expressions, such as "Unh" with "Ugh," not understanding the subtleties. He still felt their laughter. Yet rather than offending, they seemed to embrace him with their good-natured ways. With time, deeper bonds of friendship ripened, and he and his Piegan friends bound together with a chain of sharing and trust—a "chain that must not become rusty."

The New Englander weighed this trust against the half-answers and delays confronting him now. He wondered if the chain was rusting due to half-truths spoken by whitemen; or might it become rusted if he could not work to Red-Boy's advantage among the powerful whitemen?

Glancing at the papers in front of him, he focused on the wire he had sent to the attorney, A. A. Grorud, in Helena. He had retained Albert Grorud to proceed to the reservation to obtain affidavits to submit with Red-Boy's application for pardon to the attorney general. Grorud had obtained some affidavits and letters from the chaplain and warden at Leavenworth. These were to have been forwarded to Pardon Attorney Fry  months ago. Still, no word from the Department of Justice on the pardon application. Things seemed to be at a dead-end.

He mulled over the unexplained delays. Senator Thomas Walsh of Montana had promised he would take immediate action. Then he had backed away. The senator had become embroiled in the investigation of the Teapot Dome oil leasing scandal and was keeping a low profile. He suggested, instead, that Chris might have a better chance of securing a pardon if he went directly to his friend, Mr. Coolidge.

Next came the letter from attorney Grorud stating that Montana's federal judge could do nothing because he had not presided over the trial. Miggs, the Assistant United States Attorney for Montana, had promised Grorud that he would recommend a pardon. Yet nothing had been forthcoming from Miggs' office. Superintendent Frank Campbell had sat on the thing for several years, too. At first, he agreed to work for the young man's release, then used the excuse that his five-year industrial program for the Blackfeet Reservation—his pet Piegan Farming and Livestock Association—"requires my full attention." Christian Schuster didn't know what Grorud thought, but he knew better and despised Campbell's duplicity, having heard of his intense dislike for those who supported Peter's release. Campbell referred to all those on the reservation who opposed him on anything as "those damned Bolsheviks."

Pressing back against the Pullman seat and stretching his arms wide, he relaxed some. He was disgusted with Campbell and the other politicians. Yet even more, he was disgusted with himself for not having a politician's acumen necessary to get results.

His worry eased in the rhythmic click-clack of metal wheels on track, and his tired mind went back to the little Montana railroad station in the Judith Basin. There, the peaks towered into a sky that rose and spread until it stretched off to spaces far beyond the eye.

Years before, a journey to Judith Basin had brought him his first glimpse of the lush depths of the Piegan-Pikuni soul during an elk hunt. That's when he met the Pikuni named Áím mó níí si (Otter), and heeded Otter's advice to seek out Chief Boy.

That winter, Chris remembered, he had carefully packed up and sent Otter a bundle of warm clothing, explaining to him in a note that he hoped he would see the Indian's face at the time of the summer moon. In the pocket of a pair of trousers, Chris hid a silver dollar and closed the pocket with a large blanket safety pin.

The bundle was sent to Otter with instructions to deliver it to Chief Boy. Chris had thought that Chief Boy would thank him when he saw Chris's face.

»»→ • ←««

The following summer, Chris went in search of Otter and Chief Boy.

"Do you know Otter? Do you know Chief Boy?"

The Indian looked at the whiteman with the duffle bag and suitcase. "No."

"I look for his camp."

"Chief Boy, he camp over there, other side of creek. Come, I show you his camp."

Soon, the Indian stopped at the entrance of a big painted lodge. "Chief Boy lodge." A woman poked her head from the lodge door.

"What do you want?"

"I want to speak to Chief Boy."

"Chief Boy, he no here," the woman stated and turned.

"Tell Chief Boy that Otter is my friend. I know him. He is one of your people."

The woman quickly withdrew her head. Chris heard strange conversation from within. Poking her head out again, she exclaimed, "Chief Boy, he no want talk to you. Go 'way."

Chris figured that the Blackfeet were, indeed, unfriendly to strangers. He remembered the bundle he had sent to Otter.

"Tell Chief Boy I speak few words then I go away," Chris called out.

Again, Chris heard a muffled conversation within the lodge.

"Come," the woman said roughly as she held aside the door flap.

Stooping and entering the lodge, Chris stood awkwardly. A circle of powerfully built full-bloods—men, woman, children—all watched with suspicious, unfriendly eyes. They glared, giving a strong impression that they suspected he was about to steal their lands.

Chief Boy, wearing a red shirt, was sitting at the back of the lodge under his Medicine-Bundle.

"Uh, Otter told me about the Pikuni. He told me your name," Chris stammered, then gulped. The woman he had seen at the lodge-flap interpreted his words. Still, no one spoke. "I sent you a bundle. Did you get that bundle?"

"No, Chief Boy, he got no bundle," replied the woman.

"In that bundle were some clothes. You wear the red shirt now." Chris was confused.

"Chief Boy, he no want talk anymore. He want you go 'way."

The woman's bluntness hit him, a strong arm striking his chest. Then, he remembered the silver dollar. "Ask Chief Boy if he found a metal dollar in the pocket of the pants."

"Sa." The businessman from Holyoke knew by the tone of Chief Boy's voice that he said, "No."

Chris was annoyed now, but persisted. Reaching into his right pocket, he withdrew a safety pin and held it aloft. "That pocket where I hid the metal dollar was held with the brother of this pin."

Chief Boy's face changed instantly. At the sight of the pin, the Blackfeet chief drew from a buckskin bag the duplicate pin.

Chief Boy suddenly stood up, circled the lodge-fire, and grasped Chris's hand.

"Ó ki!" (Greetings). He signed to the whiteman to sit beside him on the old Buffalo robe under his Medicine-Bundle. He filled and lit his long-stemmed pipe. The pipe passed the circle four times in silence. There was a different look in everyone's eyes now, a softer look of friendliness. Chief Boy waited for Chris to speak, to tell him why Chris was there.

"I come from a far away country to visit the Pikuni. Otter invited me. My friend Otter is not here to say that my words are true. My tipi bundle is outside. I want to camp with your people. I would like to know about your customs.

That is all I want. I am your friend." Chris didn't understand what had happened, but he was eager to stay.

"So ka' pii" (Good). Chief Boy said a few words to the woman.

"He shakes hands with you," she relayed. "He is glad you come to camp with us. We set up your tipi now. We fix everything good. Little time, everything ready."

The tipi Chris had brought was set up close to the lodge of Chief Boy. As he pushed aside the door flap, Chris saw his bed was neatly made. A lighted candle sat in the center of the tipi, with his belongings carefully placed near his bed.

"You almost Pikuni now," grinned an old warrior. "Ki á nni a yi (tis so)". The other Elders chuckled.

That next morning, Chris awoke at dawn and saw seven lodges in a circle, all facing the sunrise. Smoke from the lodge fires rose straight towards the blue sky. Many dogs, each with a leg painted red, blue, yellow or green, sat blinking at the sun awaiting the scramble for the meatless bones. Ponies grazed on Buffalo grass and twitched at deer flies. Against the far-away, snow-capped peaks to where the waters of Two-Medicine-River rumbled by, giant evergreen firs surrounded the camp. Chris was told that here the Piegans and the Bloods had each raised Medicine Lodges at the same Sun Dance. Thereafter, the Piegans called the place Two Medicine Lodge.

Red Crow's woman approached and said, "Ki-áá-yo-to-kaan (Bear Head) and his woman, they come to visit you. They bring you food."

A powerful warrior, showing scars of many war parties, shook Chris's hand. Beside him stood his smiling woman, A-tso-tsi-ni. She handed Chris pemmican on a bark dish. She signed, "Eat, good."

Bear Head and his wife took Chris along many trails traveled by their Piegan ancestors. They told him of ancient battlefields and tribes with whom the Blackfeet had smoked the long-stemmed pipe. From them, Chris learned dances and games, customs, legends, myths and the true heart of the Pikuni.

That first Pikuni breakfast had been prepared by A-tso-tsi-ni. She brought stones and arranged a fire pit. In a short time, Indian bread, brown and crisp, was heaped on a flat rock and a kettle of coffee steamed in the coals.

Curly Bear and Ma-míí (Fish) came and shook his hand. Seeing Chris's tipi, Ma-míí began to sing and Curly Bear said, "Tipi, it Pikuni. Long ago we have tipi like that." Chris hoped his explanation made it through the translation. He told Curly Bear that he had brought to the Pikunis a duplicate of his first tipi which had been revealed to him by a dream in the far away Tobique country.

"So ka' pii, you got strong Medicine! Tipi with a Pine Tree over door, strong Medicine," proclaimed Curly Bear solemnly.

"What you say makes me happy…makes my heart glad," Chris answered, pressing his hands to his chest. "Since I was a boy, I have wanted to come to your country."

Bear Head then signed, "Now you come to visit us. Every 'moon-of-green-grass' (April) we see your face. My heart knows."

Others joined the circle: Stabs-By-Mistake, Double Runner, White Calf, Yellow Head, Red Plume, Leading Wolf, Medicine-War-Bonnet, Red Crow and a host of their relations.

To their great delight, the mistakes of the businessman from Holyoke in the etiquette of the Blackfeet were many. Chris's initial aversion to their apparent unconcern for Anglo cleanliness and his butchering of subtle Blackfeet expressions brought much laughter. Their laughter was a joyful embrace of the whiteman. They gently modeled the ways of the Pikuni in their own time, in their own manner. Still, the New Englander's impulsiveness and impatience to learn everything at once led to many amusing Old Ná pi prankster moments.

In turn, they learned that this Easterner cast a long shadow.

Yet, not all the people were so welcoming. Some found his intrusion offensive. Sometimes there were harsh, whispered words among others.

Later, Chris's mind would wander, seeking answers. Why did some seem boorish to others, to him? Was it the whiteman's liquor? Or just part of human nature?

Did the Elders see in Chris an influential whiteman who could do their bidding? He hoped not, but sometimes slept restlessly, turning dark thoughts over and over. Then day returned and with patience and laughter he was included in their daily lives. Perhaps their motives were not all that important.

>>>→ • ←<<<

Chris heard the drum as it summoned everyone. Bear Head announced the start of the Stick Game.

Camp fires lighted the area. Two rows of warriors, wrapped in bright-colored blankets, knelt opposite each other. Women and children formed a half-circle nearby. Bear Head and Chris stood and watched.

In front of each row of warriors lay two lodge poles on which the players drummed as they sang. Four hiding-bones, two marked with a thin, black band around the center, were used.

"Those bones are called Medicine-Bones." Bear Head explained. "The ten small pointed, carved sticks are counters."

Pointing to the bones, Bear Head told Chris that the actual game did not begin until one side held the four bones. To determine which side would hold the bones, each side chose a guesser and an expert at handling the bones.

"The experts are each given a white and a black-marked bone. The guessers win by guessing in which hand the opponent expert is holding the white bone."

Chris watched as the experts skillfully changed the white and black bones from hand to hand, their hands, arms and bodies in constant motion in front, in back, or under their robes. Bear Head explained that their actions imitated the particular animal which gave them power. The guesser then pointed forcefully to the hand which he thought held the white bone.

Bear Head announced that The Crazy Dog Society—the Blackfeet police—would challenge their tribal enemy, The Doves. The side holding the four bones selected two players, each given one of the white and black-marked bones. Two guessers on the opposite side watched carefully to see the hand holding the white bone. Every right guess was a point gained and the judge stuck a counting stick into the ground in front of the winning side. Sticks were won and lost until all ten were in front of the victors.

The game started with the drummers softly chanting the "Gamblers' Song of the Pikuni." It increased in volume, then gradually faded, alternately rising and falling in its own rhythm. The women added a minor tremulous note when the song reached a high pitch.

Bear Head's woman, A-tso-tsi-ni, alternately sang and made comic gestures at her husband and Chris.

The members of each society tried to distract their opponents by belittling their deeds with sarcastic or teasing remarks. They encouraged their own by drumming in unison on the lodge poles and by adding volume to the Gamblers' Song.

Ponies, blankets, moccasins and beaded buckskins were wagered. Some warriors were known to lose all they possessed. Many side bets were made, even among the women.

This night The Doves won.

The haunting melody of the Pikuni Gamblers' Song seemed fixed to the place. Year after year, Chris could never recall the melody when he returned to New England.

>>>→ • ←<<

Awakening from his past, Chris yawned and stretched his legs. He smiled at the porter.

"Dinner's 'bout ready to be served in the dining car, sir," the black man offered.

"Thank you, Sullivan." Chris returned the man's courtesy with a nod and a smile.

The ties of attachment and trust with his Pikuni friends were interwoven differently from the strings linking him with his New England colleagues, especially the politicians he knew. He was ashamed to be a whiteman when he, as well as his Pikuni friends, could see how loosely bound was the world of a white politician. Teapot Dome stood as a stark reminder of how easily whiteman laws could be manipulated and broken by the greedy—politicians or not—when gain was the prime mover. Forget compassion, especially for an outsider, especially one young Blackfeet convicted of rape.

His Pikuni friends lived in a patient world, a patience whitemen often dismissed as primitive and slow-witted. Perhaps an impatient judge or a rushed process was the reason for Red-Boy's conviction. Maybe, Red-Boy and his supporters believed truth would unfold to clarity in its own time, but time ran out.

Lingering doubts kept resurfacing for Chris. Something had gone very wrong at Red-Boy's trial. This "not knowing" drove the New Englander's curiosity and determination. Was it Red-Boy's lawyer? The court translator? The judge?

Reservation matters were, in their own way, just as complicated. There was sincerity from all the Pikuni he met—whether they liked him or not, you knew where you stood with each of them. There was genuine warmth from Curly Bear, Bear Head, and many others whom he had first befriended. But from those at or near the Indian Bureau center of control—Richard Sanders and his nephew Victor—there was a facade of sincerity that masked a secret heart devoted to self-interest. A kind of callowness fueled, he suspected, by greed and alcohol.

The same kind of commercial unsavoriness that made it easy, even understandable, for Superintendent Campbell to allow whiteman cattle to trespass and forage on grass-rich reservation lands while the fees disappeared and a blind eye was turned to the ubiquitous whiskey traders in Browning's speakeasies, whose lucrative business kept many reservation residents in a stupor.

These undercurrents of the dark side of the reservation—the "Agency Ring"—kept nagging at Chris. Behavior of Indian and Anglo alike in such dealings was not in keeping with the New Englander's ethic, the Pikuni sense of honor, the lessons of his mother, the teachings of Thomas Stabs-By-Mistake to his son. None of it reflected the magnificent composite image of the Indian chief etched into the U.S. nickel.

Perhaps it was nothing more than the betrayal of Blackfeet by Blackfeet, made easy by the blind eye of those on the powerful Tribal Council who felt threatened by Peter's agitation for the very things the council knew would never be approved by the whiteman's Indian Bureau.

Or was it Red-Boy himself? Other than the young man's protestations, the victim and none of the witnesses would say anything. A. A. Grorud had gotten literally nothing from the victim or her nervous girlfriends. It was as if the subject were taboo.

Was the young man really guilty of raping Annie Running Crane? The notion struck Chris as improbable but nevertheless a possibility he had to consider. Thomas had told him of Red-Boy's drinking when his son returned from the war. Had the young man really conquered the drink?

Shaking his head, he tried to rid himself of the questions and dead-ends and focus on possible solutions, or at least the next step.

Glacier Park, Montana, September 4, 1923

To Brother Christian.

"Because you are a true friend to us, the Pikuni tribe of the Blackfeet Confederacy, we are proud today to name you after one of our great warriors of long ago.

Apinakwi Pita- Morning Eagle-
Is the name we give you and make you one of us."

Morning Eagle's parfleche signed in picture writing given at the time of his adoption by Curly Bear.

# XI

# Morning Eagle
# (Aapinakoi Píítaa)

He awoke to the fleeting view of livestock and green farmlands. The central plains of Wisconsin stood in stark contrast with the flat, barren grasslands of Montana, where his mind continued to dwell.

The country's vast industrial and agricultural richness had bypassed Piegan country. The reason, Chris knew, lay first at the Blackfeet being pushed into the least fertile corner of their traditional lands, then at the door of the Indian Bureau, whose officials turned a deaf ear to the reality that made farming only marginally possible and cattle-raising not much better. The freezing hand of Snow-Maker limited the growing season and the four-walled shacks provided for the inhabitants were the perfect place to grow mostly sickness and death.

》》→ • ←《《

The stark reality of his friends' affliction had been visited upon him earlier one summer, when the Medicine-Pipe-Smoke ritual at Cut Bank had just ended. From sundown until sunup, that ancient Piegan ceremony had been observed until one by one the lodges faded from the creek bottom, as the owners pulled out for their homes.

Bear Head, his woman and Chris planned to make an early start the next morning. They were going to Heart Butte to set up their lodge and visit friends until the "moon-of-ripe-berries" (month of July) died.

Along the trail, they passed the bleached bones of Indian ponies. The ponies ate prairie grass wanted by whiteman sheep raisers. "Kill the ponies," was the order that came from Washington, D.C. Indian ownership was evidently not given a first thought, much less a second one.

Riders were seen coming toward them. As they neared the group, they saw Spopia (Turtle), his woman and young son. "Black Bull is on his robes. He is very sick," said Turtle.

"His friends and relations are camped with him on Little Badger Creek. We fear Black Bull will soon take the Wolf-Trail. I go now to find Heavy-Singer-For-Sick-People (doctor). I tell him to come quick and save Black Bull."

Chris's group was alarmed and hurried their horses. Everyone loved Black Bull, a warrior whom all people respected. The Sun was close to the edge-of-the-world when the group saw the little circle of lodges belonging to Wolf Plume, Turtle, Stabs-By-Mistake, Big Spring and Black Bull. No friends came to greet the party.

Approaching Wolf Plume, Bear Head signed, "Our hearts know. We meet Turtle." Faces were drawn in sorrow. Black Bull's sits-beside-him-woman led Chris to her man.

As Chris pressed the hand of his friend, Black Bull whispered: "My hand is weak, my friend. I see clouds hurry to the Great-Council. I sing for those who have gone before."

Slowly, the group filed into Wolf Plume's lodge and awaited his words: "Black Bull has been on his robes more than twenty sleeps. He suffer much. Many times we sent for whiteman doctor but he only came once. Now, Turtle, he try to find doctor. He tell doctor to come quick, that Black Bull going to die."

The waxing and waning supplication to Above-Person, mixed with the drums, bled out into the stillness of night as the group prayed for their brother until Sun had chased away the darkness.

At dawn, Chris met Red-Boy, the Piegan warrior of the Great War, the restless young man who, others had told him, angered some on the Tribal Council because of his constant demands of the Agency.

>>>→ • ←<<<

Red-Boy came to his father's lodge. "We fear Wolf Plume is going to stab himself. We know that he will do that if his younger brother Black Bull dies."

Looking directly at Chris, Red-Boy warned, "It is a custom of Pikuni to harm themselves when someone they love dies. We do not want Wolf Plume to do that. Now he is about to sing his own death song." Turning to the others, Red-Boy implored, "Please come to Wolf Plume's lodge. Talk to him. Tell him not to harm himself. He must not do that."

Red-Boy, Chris and the others went to the old chief's lodge. Wolf Plume leaned against his backrest, his eyes speaking misery and despair. He had not eaten for many days. The ashes of his lodge-fire were cold.

The Elders spoke in low tones to Wolf Plume.

Cutting-Nose-Woman, Wolf Plume's daughter, then interpreted Chris's words. "My brother, we have met in friendship for many good times. Now we meet again while our hearts cry with sorrow. Black Bull, your younger brother still lives. We ask Above-Person to come close, and to hear us while we pray for Black Bull. Only Above-Person knows if Black Bull will go to the Sand Hills."

Wolf Plume lowered his eyes, his head sinking low. Chris sat close. "Wolf Plume, you are a Pikuni warrior. All people love and respect you. Your children, grandchildren and relations love you. Now your heart is naked in sorrow. All our hearts are crying. But your face, the face of a chief, does not tell what you think in your heart." Chris stopped. Silent for a moment, he watched, then slowly he continued.

"I know that it is a custom to harm one's self when a loved one dies. Yet, Wolf Plume, I know you will not do that. You must not harm yourself. We all depend on you, Wolf Plume, to make our hearts strong if your younger brother goes the way of the Wolf-Trail."

There followed a long silence. Everyone waited. Finally, Wolf Plume raised his head, his eyes glistening with tears.

"The words you speak are straight," replied Wolf Plume. "That is the way I have talked to my people when their hearts were killed with sorrow. My heart is not a coward. But it cries for my younger brother. Younger brother lost his mother when he had seen but five winters. Never did a mean word come between us. All my relations and friends, they pray strong for Black Bull. We try to save him."

Wolf Plume was silent for a long time. Finally he spoke. "I will do no harm to myself. Ki á nni a yi." Wolf Plume's grief for one so close to his heart had brought about the desire to self-kill. Yet, since the Pikuni do not fear death, they love life more.

No Pikuni was held in greater respect than Wolf Plume, both by his own people and those of other tribes. Long ago he owned many ponies, blankets and robes, making him a rich man. But he gave all away to those who were poor and in need.

Later that evening, Red-Boy asked Chris to ride to Two Medicine Lodge, fifteen miles away, as a last hope of obtaining help for Black Bull. The doctor's whereabouts were not known at that village. The men took a short cut back to camp and had just forded Little Badger Creek when Red-Boy stopped.

"My heart speaks to me. It says, 'bad luck at camp.'"

Chris did not meet Red-Boy's eyes. He had felt a heaviness as they rode into the swale.

Urging their horses along, the men approached camp.

"Do you read anything, Red-Boy?" Chris asked.

"I see one sign. The sign tells that the door of Black Bull's lodge is open. Sun is going away. It is cold. Perhaps someone has hung a black bear hide for the door-flap and the door is closed. Then our brother still lives. Soon we know."

The door of Black Bull's lodge was open. He had gone the way of the Wolf-Trail—he would council no more. His woman was walking alone among the lodges wailing her song of misery, and calling his name over and over again.

That night the women tenderly wrapped the body of their brother in his robe. They entered the lodge-with-the-open-door and chanted their mournful cries.

Later, Red-Boy, Chris and his friends sat by a fire under the shadow of Pikuni mountains. The heart of Bear Head was heavy with sorrow. He faced the Place-of-Rising-Sun.

*"Great-Above-Person, I ask that you hear what I have to say*
*I ask for pity.*
*You gave us Sun that we might live*
*Sun is no longer warm.*

*The ground on which I pray is our land no more.*
*These many peaks were named for our ancient Chiefs*
*The names have all been changed.*
*Great-Above-Person, you gave us the prairies and the mountains.*
*Now the prairies and the mountains are no longer ours.*
*You gave us the Buffalo that we might have real meat*
*The Buffalo have gone to the Spirit-Land.*
*Great-Above-Person, you have made food for many mouths*
*Pity the Pikuni and give us food that we may live.*
*Pity all people and give them food so they will be strong.*
*Give the Pikuni a homeland where we may set up our lodges*
*and where there is food."*

>>>→ • ←<<<

The New Englander sat up in his Pullman car, overwhelmed again with
the power and sadness of that night. He thought of the conversation with
Red-Boy during their ride to Two Medicine Lodge. Chris had asked why had
there been no doctor to attend the dying Elder? What could be done?

>>>→ • ←<<<

They had ridden a long time without speaking. Reaching hilly country,
they slowed their mounts.

"It's the same for all our sick people," the young Indian finally remarked.
"Especially the little ones…and the Elders…the helpless ones." His voice
blew away with the wind. Chris nudged his horse closer.

"Why, even in the war, the sick ones in France got medicine."

"What branch of the service were you in?"

"Army…infantry."

"Why'd you enlist, Red-Boy?"

The young veteran stopped his horse and studied Chris for a moment
while the animals munched on bunchgrass.

"My people honor the land. And we have always had a warrior tradition.
It is an honor to serve our country and to protect our people and our land."
He tugged at the front brim of his black Carlsbad and prodded his horse on.

"Did you see much action?"

"Yeah, just before I left," he replied.

Chris rode with the young Indian in perplexed silence until they reached a flat, grassy meadow glistening under the full moon.

"Can you tell me what happened, Red-Boy?"

The young man said nothing. Chris thought he had prodded where he had no right to intrude.

"I'm sorry," he offered.

"It's okay. My little boy fell ill. Just a baby. I went to the Agency. No doctor, I was told. My boy died."

"Peter, do you and your wife have other children?" Chris asked hopefully.

"Baby's mother and me, we never married. I left right afterwards for the war. When I got back, she was gone."

They rode in silence for several more miles.

"Peter, what made you stay?"

"My family...relations. My friends. Couldn't believe my people were sufferin' even more after I returned. Wasn't right. Stayed to help."

"What did you do?"

"Pissed off the Superintendent and his cowards," he laughed. He pursed his lips and jabbed out with his fist in mock attack. "I guess I got angry and then I got drunk." Chris smiled. "Realized whiteman's liquor was a big part of the problem, though. Then I sobered up."

"How do you think you can change things, Peter?"

"I don't really know," Red-Boy answered. "Damned Agency's so corrupt. Even our own people who work for Campbell, especially some of the interpreters who like to play favors."

"Who do you mean?"

"Unh! Couple of the Sanders. Richard and his little coward nephew, Victor."

Sensing the young man's anger surfacing, Chris sought to lighten the conversation.

"Isn't there anyone you like? One of Running Crane's daughters, I think you told me?"

Red-Boy glanced over, nodded and returned Chris's smile.

"Yes, Annie. I've told you about her." He paused and smiled.

"Tell me, how did you meet her?"

"I knew Annie when I was younger. When I returned from the war, she came to visit me and we talked. Now, we talk about our people a lot. She's very smart, aaeee." They rode several more miles before Red-Boy returned to the conversation.

"My friend James and me, we try to take care of the sick Elders at our cabin at Heart Butte." His voice softened. "With Annie...the young girl I was telling you about...we do things to help our people. Bring food, clothes, shoes for the little ones. It's a lot of work." He paused and smiled. "She tells the sick little ones it's okay, they will get better. Just like she has survived. She is what inspires me. Keeps me goin'...keeps me believin' we're gonna survive by takin' care of each other."

Turning, the young man's eyes fully met those of the New Englander's, and the whiteman from the East caught his first glimpse into Red-Boy's heart.

»»→ • ←««

Sullivan was busy conversing at the front of the Pullman coach. Chris smiled broadly. The man returned the compliment.

Sullivan's father had a distinguished Civil War career, serving in the Fifty-Fourth Massachusetts under Robert Gould Shaw. Although his father had taken a rebel bullet, he had survived Battery Wagner.

It had not been lost on Chris when Sullivan related to him what good medical attention his father had received behind Union lines by the Sixth Medical Corps.

After Coolidge's State of the Union Address in 1924—when he appealed to Congress to appropriate millions of dollars to prevent the hideous crime of Negro lynching—Chris had spoken to his friend about the equally hideous treatment of Native people. From their days together in Northampton, Chris knew that Coolidge respected Chris's strong opinions about the country's treatment of Indians. So the president never expected any fawning expressions of friendly persuasion from the Holyoker. After a spell, Chris wrote the president a blunt reminder:

*"SPLENDID MR. PRESIDENT... WHAT ABOUT OUR INDIANS?*

*Many years ago there was born WOLVERINE. This creature is known by another name, THE INDIAN BUREAU...It will not allow the*

*public to go to the other side of the CURTAIN and see the true con-
dition of the Indian.*

*Why, because the public would find there INEFFICIENCY, UN-
TRUTHFULNESS AND DISHONESTY. They would find that some
of the AGENTS are charging the Indian NINE DOLLARS for one single Army blanket....That the Indian is obliged to purchase merchan-
dise from such merchants as the AGENT designates, although the
Indian could buy the same goods at a lower price elsewhere....That
monies belonging to the Indian were unjustly withheld....That Trachoma and T.B. was prevalent in nearly every family and without
proper medical care...That the condition of many Indians is worse
than SLAVERY...."*

Like Red-Boy, Chris had made enemies among the bureaucrats. He repeatedly urged Washington to look behind the curtain, learn the truth for
themselves. At times, he wondered what his friendship with Coolidge really
meant, seeing pictures of him wearing the red man's costumes and praising
the Committee of One Hundred. All public relations. With few exceptions did
he ever see his friend, the Great White Father, do more than briefly lift the
curtain.

Out on the prairie, after the train passed through Fargo, North Dakota,
rolling brown hills and rock formations drifted by — Spirit-Riders, Curly Bear
had called them.

»»→ • ←«««

"Friends, I have something to say," Chris began. "My words will be
good. Aaee." He paused, looking around to each in the group. He was
greeted with smiles.

"In the faraway country, where the Sun comes from, a man with a clean
heart lives in a big lodge. This man has been my friend for many Winters. He
speaks with a straight tongue. He will be my friend 'til we both take the Wolf-
Trail. Ah. I say to my friend, 'my Piegan brothers need meat.' My friend who
lives in the big lodge says, 'We will give the Piegans a Beef-Cow.' The heart of
my friend is good towards the Piegans."

Chris paused a long moment, studying their faces.

"The Beef-Cow that my friend gives you is now tied to a cottonwood tree at the creek. This Beef-Cow is now yours. That is all I have to say."

Red-Boy and the other men rolled up their leggings and took their shirts and moccasins off, rushing out of the lodge with their knives down to the creek, where two Indians on their ponies looked after the tethered animal.

Medicine-War-Bonnet took the ax but was so excited that his legs wobbled. The old man gave the ax to Bear Head, telling him to knock the cow down. Bear Head was as bad off as his old friend. So, after a lot of wobbling and jabbering, Red-Boy knocked the cow down for them. They all jumped on the critter while she was kicking. Medicine-War-Bonnet cut her throat. Bear Head cut her feet off, then cut her tongue out. Chris laughed, telling them to hurry or the cow would run away.

Chris took his friend Bear Head aside and asked "Are you not afraid that the cow will tell what cowards you two old Piegans are?" He winked at the old man. They laughed.

Knowing that at sundown there would be story-telling, Chris brought his bag of tobacco to Bear Head's lodge as the Sun sank behind Rising-Wolf-Mountain. The entire Pikuni band was there. "Ó ki, Ó ki, friend. Aaee," they bid greetings to Chris.

The old warriors, including Many-Tail-Feathers, who was one-hundred-and-seven-years old, counted coups—telling of their great acts of bravery when on the war path and on raids against the Crow and the Sioux.

All of the Elders and warriors spoke except Red-Boy. Grinning, the young man finally nodded at the whiteman.

Chris now had his turn.

"I have listened to Bear Head and my almost-father, Medicine-War-Bonnet. You speak of your brave deeds. You count many coups. You have told me about stealing many ponies from your enemies. So ka' pii, that is good." The whiteman paused and smiled at Bear Head, then winked at Red-Boy.

"But your white brother believes only what he sees with his own eyes. Ah! My eyes see very good today." Chris poked at the lodge-fire embers and gave Bear Head and Medicine-War-Bonnet a mock frown.

"Your white brother is sad...his heart is on the ground....I have seen with my eyes, today, that my Piegan brothers are cowards...I have heard my Piegan brothers talk with a tongue of the Chippewai....My brothers are brave? No...only Red-Boy, who did not speak of coups, was the warrior who knocked the Beef-Cow down."

The men were motionless, some—including Red-Boy—grinning with anticipation of the teasing that was about to come.

"When you speak to me of your brave hearts, you speak with a crooked tongue.... Today you were afraid to kill the beef-Beef-Cow...that is what I saw with my eyes....Ah..that is all that I have to say...."

»»→ • ←«««

A great, wholesome laugh erupted in the Pullman car, catching the attention of all around, including Sullivan.

"Something funny you see outside, sir?" asked Sullivan with a smile.

"No, Sullivan, just a thought I had of a funny time." Indeed, there had been much laughter and great teasing all around Bear Head's lodge-circle that evening.

Beneath the teasing, Chris had seen Red-Boy's mettle—his deep feelings for his sick and dying Elders, his mature presence of mind, even prescience. The young veteran had seen great suffering, yet knew the curative power of laughter. Chris was sure Red-Boy was incapable of breaking the spirit of another human being, let alone violating the sanctity of a woman.

As the iron horse puffed its way across the prairie hills, up toward the Missouri River and the Great Plains Plateau, Chris's eyes and mind rested on the now-darkened North Dakota hills, the distant black clouds.

The shadowy hills slowly prodded his vision into subconscious images reflecting perhaps the most important single event of his life, the one defining experience in the late summer of 1923 which, besides his friendship with the Tobique Indian, Bow Maker, had prompted this particular trip to Montana to investigate the imprisonment of a young Indian man.

»»→ • ←«««

"Pooh sa poot (Come). Curly Bear, he invites you smoke in his lodge," signed Bear Head, as he raised the door-skin of Chris's tipi.

Another council, Chris thought. To be asked to sit at their council was a sign of confidence. Strangely, though, Bear Head wore a solemn look. A Pikuni council had dignity and decorum. Those who achieved respect by worthwhile deeds had precedence. Still, at council, as at daily life, laughter was welcomed.

Chris grinned to himself when he thought of his close friend Curly Bear, well known for sporting his Woodrow Wilson campaign button and other metallic decorations whenever he wore the drab whiteman's clothes. "To make the whiteman's cloth more colorful," he joked. Over the years, the kindly expression on Curly Bear's face invariably drew Chris towards him.

Curly Bear greeted Chris and signed to him to sit at his left. Like most Pikuni, Curly Bear was broad-shouldered, tall and powerfully built.

In Curly Bear's hair this day was a single eagle feather below which hung his long braids over his chest. On the ground in front of the Old Chief lay his tobacco-board and stone pipe-with-a-straight-stem. In silence, he filled and lit the pipe. It passed the circle until, in silence, four pipes were smoked. When the pipe was emptied and laid aside, the words of the man-who-changes-the-talk spoke.

"Curly Bear, he has something to say to our almost-brother."

Curly Bear turned to look directly at Chris. The whiteman was surprised at his stern look, fearing he had brought offense somehow. Silence followed.

Glancing to his left, Chris noticed Thomas Stabs-By-Mistake sitting perfectly still. His troubled heart filled the lodge, his eyes seemed to look across at the native-tanned leather lodge liner which encircled Curly Bear's lodge.

Now, Chris knew why he had been summoned to the council. It had been almost three winters since Stabs-By-Mistake's son, Red-Boy, had been imprisoned. They expected that their New England friend could do something to right the wrong that had been done to his son.

Seated at the council circle, Chris felt such helpless anguish. Perhaps they thought he should have moved more swiftly to untangle the whiteman knot of injustice. Perhaps they thought he had not tried or did not care.

Although Piegan men were proud—slow to ask a whiteman for any favor—they were honest. They did not hide their grief or their disappointments.

"These people who you see with your eyes are many, they are all your friends," said Curly Bear slowly. "You came among us nearly a stranger, for we had only known of you through others. The Pikuni, they are slow in making friendships." Curly Bear paused and stared at Chris.

I have failed, Chris thought. There was now no mistaking the purpose of this council.

"You have lived among my people. You have smoked and eaten in our lodges. We have smoked and eaten in yours. We have watched you. The words that you spoke with your mouth at our councils, they were straight. It is the wish of my people to make you a brother Pikuni. We believe in you, we have decided to make you one of us."

Curly Bear firmly took Chris's now-trembling hand, looked directly into his eyes and said, "I now adopt you as my son. Tomorrow we will give you a name." His eyes spoke as sincerely as the words from his mouth.

A long silence fell over the group.

"Curly Bear, I have heard your words," Chris finally uttered, almost inaudibly. "My heart, it...it is speechless. I...I...am so glad that you are my almost-father." The New Englander paused, his voice cracking, almost choking on his words while the others watched and smiled at the whiteman's awkwardness. "I am very proud to be your son."

"Aa pi ná kosi (Tomorrow), we call your name. Tomorrow you all Pii ká ni (Pikuni)," were the greetings from the circle.

Curly Bear then took a parfleche from behind his robe and lay before Chris a white-beaded buckskin suit trimmed with many skins, a pair of moccasins, a War Bonnet decorated with many winter-killed weasel skins, leggings and a breech-clout. As he unwrapped each article, he told Chris its history. He untied the string of beads from his neck and the Eagle-Feather from his hair and handed them to the whiteman saying, "I give these to my son. They are very old. They come from Buffalo days. The Eagle-Feather, it brought good luck in many battles. Tomorrow, when we give you a name, you wear these clothes. Then you are all Pikuni."

When aa pi ná kosi (tomorrow) came, the sun was high in the blue. It was the fourth sleep of "leaves-turn-yellow-moon" (September)—Chris's birthday. How his Piegan brothers had known that was never revealed to Chris. Perhaps it was Curly Bear's powerful Medicine that had spoken.

"Almost-brother, they wait for you, they call you," said Chief Boy. "Now we give you a name."

"Pooh sa poot, Náá pi ko an na pí (Come. Whiteman friend)," said Bear Head, as he led Chris into his lodge.

"My man, he will dress you. He will paint your face. Soon you will dance. Soon I have a Piegan brother," said Bear Head's woman as she went out of the lodge. Quickly Chris's clothing was exchanged for the buckskins and War Bonnet, and Bear Head painted his face with red earth paint.

"Ki á nni a yi" (enough), he said.

Chris followed Bear Head, who was always his helper, to the lodge of Curly Bear. Words of greeting came from all. Chris's almost-father signed to him to sit beside him.

A live coal was lifted from the lodge-fire with a forked willow stick and placed on a little pile of fresh earth in front of Curly Bear. Upon the coal he placed sweet grass, and held his pipe in the sacred smoke to purify it. The pipe was then passed while the Pikuni group asked Above-Person to give long life and happiness to all.

After the pipe ceremony ended and the pipe was laid aside, the Medicine-Man prayed. Then, he painted Chris's forehead and drew bands around his wrists, as he continued to pray.

In turn, each one of the Pikuni group prayed for the whiteman. Bear Head prayed last:

> "Spirits of Earth, come close to me
> Spirits of Night, come close to me
> Above Spirits, come close to me
> I pray for my brother
> I want you to hear all that I have to say:
> I pray that he will see the green grass come many times
> I pray that he will be strong
> I pray that no sickness will come to him
> He is my brother, he is one of us."

The soft throbbing beat of drums called the group out onto the prairie. Chris was told to sit on a Buffalo robe within a great circle of warriors, women and children. Louder and louder the drum beat as painted warriors threw themselves into the rhythm of dances of times-far-back.

When the dancing ceased, Chris's Indian father stepped to the center of the circle and signed to the whiteman to stand beside him and face the place of the rising Sun. As Curly Bear placed his hand on Chris's shoulder, the other warriors gathered about the two men.

Chief Curly Bear solemnly and slowly repeated his statement of yesterday: "The Pikuni, they are slow in making friendships. This whiteman, he has lived among us. He has smoked and eaten in our lodges. We have smoked and eaten in his. We know that we can believe in him. Now, we give him a name."

Outside the circle, Medicine-War-Bonnet had been speaking quietly with Bear Head. Finally, Bear Head gave a nod and Medicine-War-Bonnet approached Curly Bear and whispered to him.

Medicine-War-Bonnet had suggested a name, as is the custom.

"I now give you the name of a Pikuni who was respected by all the people. Many winters back, he went on the Wolf-Trail (Milky Way) to the Shadow-Place-of-the-Buffalo.

His name I give you. It will bring you long life. It will give you power for good deeds.

It will bring you good luck. You will be strong until your body is nothing."

Then, after a long silence, Curly Bear, looking directly into the whiteman's eyes, spoke.

"We name you Aapinakoi Píítaa (Morning Eagle)."

Those were the words of Curly Bear as he turned Aapinakoi Píítaa toward the home of the Sun.

"So ka' pii! So ka' pii! (Good) Aapinakoi Píítaa," was the greeting of the Piegans as they shook Morning Eagle's hand and called him by name.

"Now we take you as a brother in the Si ki mio tá si ksi (the Black Horse Society)," said Stabs-By-Mistake, pointing to the handsome high-spirited black horse richly decorated with beaded buckskin trappings that Bear Head was leading into the circle.

"Si ki mi! Si ki mi!" (The Black Horse! The Black Horse!), chanted the warriors and was echoed by the women.

Feathers had been braided into his mane and tail. His glossy coat bore the protection of war paint. He was now a Medicine-Horse.

The beat of drums was the signal. The War Dance of the Black Horse lived again. Painted bodies of warriors swayed and darted with serpent-like motion. Eagle-feathered Coup-Sticks waived high. War Bonnets fluttered and tossed as the wearers threw their bodies with force and vigor into the steps of victorious battle.

"Dance, Aapinakoi Píítaa! Now you are one of us."

》》》—→ • ←—《《《

Before he returned to his Heavy-Water-Country (near the ocean), a parfleche was given to the man from the Place-of-Rising-Sun at the Crown of the Rockies (Glacier National Park). It read in part: "We make you one of us."

The parfleche was signed in picture writing by many of the full-bloods of the Pikuni tribe, including Curly Bear, Bear Head, Thomas-Stabs-By-Mistake and other respected Elders.

Thinking again of the adoption parfleche, Morning Eagle eased back into his seat. Throughout it all, Red-Boy's imprisonment kept returning in his mind. Yet not a word had been uttered to him about the young man's fate by any Pikuni. A generous and patient people.

The iron horse carrying Morning Eagle rolled through the eastern edge of Montana.

Children at Willow Creek School near Blackfeet Agency, 1907. Image No. 638.124, courtesy of Archives Special Collections, The University of Montana – Missoula.

# XII

# Half-Blood and
# a Tough Little Badger

"Now remember, Victor, this lawyer from Helena, this mister Grorud's not gonna learn nothin' different." The older man's mouth was firmly set. "Don't worry, Uncle Richard." His smug grin was met with the older man's steely-eyed look beneath short-cropped, black hair. His grin morphed into a stoic black look as billowing dust in the distance announced the approach of attorney-at-law Grorud in his big black Cadillac.

The sun, this summer day in 1924, had burnt through the thin cloud cover and shimmered over the parched flat reservation.

Twenty-two white-framed buildings of the Willow Creek Agency, including the large building housing the boarding school, dotted the prairie landscape just a stone's throw west of Browning. The faint stench of fresh horse manure from nearby stables and roadside accumulations permeated the two-story, pitched-roof Indian Bureau office.

The agency office, with its white portico, was surrounded by the scorched grassland and framed by the jagged Shining Mountains. Beneath a cloudless blue sky, smoke fluttered in the occasional gust of wind signaling that the annual Sun Dance encampments were underway.

For Victor Sanders, waiting in the stifling hot interior of the agency office with his uncle, Sun Dance encampments were the furthest thing from his mind. The young half-blood government interpreter presented an unflinching image standing ramrod straight, glaring out the window, a scene that would have made Calvin Coolidge take notice.

Richard Sanders took his place behind a small desk next to a coat rack, vacant except for his white Stetson. He fidgeted impatiently, squinting outside at the approaching Cadillac.

The older man had it figured that this Grorud had been sent by the New Englander—the whiteman-outsider the others called Morning Eagle—to trip up his nephew, Victor Sanders.

>>>→ • ←<<<

Truth be told, Richard Sanders had lots of things figured out all along. Money and influence were power and power meant status and control. It was as clear as that, and the ends pretty much always justified the means. Having no sons of his own, he felt a kinship stronger than uncle to nephew with Victor.

Richard's white father, an Agency employee, had run a lucrative side business as a whiskey trader. Nearly fifty years ago, he had finally succumbed to a whiskey-ravaged liver. His Piegan mother's first husband was the powerful Elder Fast Buffalo Horse, who died after Richard's half-brother, Oliver, was born. "Powerful" and "Elder" meant nothing to Richard and protected none of them from poverty. Fast Buffalo Horse's offspring and relations had always ignored Richard in favor of Oliver, despite Oliver having taken his stepfather's surname of Sanders. After their mother died, Oliver was treated by his blood relations with the same respect previously given his father.

Richard could see they were all fools. The only survival was to be had by ingratiating oneself to the agency whiteman and learning the whiteman's means of gaining control. The old values coveted by the Elders—patience, long suffering and careful adapting—were stupid and faded into the past. He learned to speak whiteman and waited.

The Indian schools took the children of the tribe and his brother took to Maxine Leggett, the white school teacher. Oliver never knew that Maxine was generous with her favors wherever the whiteman's liquor flowed. It was true that one of the brothers was the father of the boy child. Oliver, being the noble one, claimed the child and married Maxine. He named his son Victor Black Looks after his friend, Thomas Stabs-By-Mistake, said the baby's constant scowl reminded him of the name of the old warrior Black Looks. Black Looks had been a revered and well-known Blood warrior and Elder, but to Thomas and Victor's father, the name really reflected the child's look.

Marriage hardly slowed Maxine's thirst or her willingness to share her favors in exchange for the means of slaking it. For a time Richard believed Maxine to be a good school teacher, when she was sober, but a better informant when she was drunk. Through Maxine, Richard was able to enter the lucrative world of whiteman bootleggers. With his translating skills, Richard insinuated himself close to the flow of monies on the reservation and was rewarded by playing white Indian agents against the influential full and mixed bloods. The result was his pocketing money for getting Superintendent Campbell and others to look the other way while bootleggers did business in Browning and white cattle ranchers escaped the levy of grazing permits or trespass fees for their cattle feeding on Blackfeet grasslands.

It was a great set-up. Needless to say, his weak and trusting brother finally caught on to Maxine and gave up on their marriage. She and young Victor moved into a government house by the school.

Oliver remarried and had a daughter. Pretty and bright, Marilyn knew about and thought well of her big brother Victor, but Maxine shunned Oliver and the ways of those "half-witted savages" on the reservation.

Victor, too, was a bright boy, but lonely, and didn't really fit in. He fought with the boys his age and wasn't allowed much contact with the little half-sister he adored. The childless Richard noticed the boy and thought his influence might be appreciated and rewarded. This time it wasn't Maxine he wanted but the means for satiating his thirst for greater power and influence. He approved of how "white-trained" the boy was. This would be important. Also, the boy didn't look or act "too" Indian. He had the right kind of abilities, one who would not stand out in a crowd of agency whitemen.

The more Maxine was drunk, the more Victor hung around his "uncle" Richard. Now, with Richard's help, Victor Black Looks rose from subaltern to Campbell's right-hand man; a government interpreter with access to both Blackfeet Tribal Business Council politics and Indian Bureau plans for the reservation.

When Frank Campbell's Piegan Farming and Livestock Association seemed to catch on with the Blackfeet Elders in the early 1920's, Richard Sanders quickly pushed Campbell's five-year industrial program for the Blackfeet at each of the Blackfeet reservation communities. Victor attended every meeting with his uncle. He was seen modeling the serious demeanor and whiteman dress of his uncle.

Campbell's farming and cattle-raising ideas proved a mixed blessing. Many of the Elders supported the ideas but were hostile to Campbell's trade-off. Traditional ceremonies such as the annual Sun Dance must be given up in favor of raising summer crops. Later, the younger men did not take well to the superintendent's plans because they could not make a living. Poor farmland and harsh Montana winters killed Elders, children, crops and cattle alike.

Victor's plan was to gain a seat on the Tribal Council. Only then would he win the respect he coveted from his Blackfeet neighbors—those like Peter's family who had Piegan status.

For Victor, the symbol of reaching his goal was the destruction of his childhood foe—Peter, Red-Boy—now sitting in Leavenworth Penitentiary.

Richard Sanders had cunningly deflected earlier attempts to inquire into Peter's conviction. He had put them off with the assurances that Campbell, and even the Indian Commissioner in D.C., were "doing all they could do."

»»→ • ←««

Morning Eagle's attorney, Grorud, pulled up outside the Agency.

"Damned Morning Eagle…."

"Good afternoon," enjoined Mr. A.A. Grorud, Attorney at Law. "You must be Victor Sanders, the interpreter. I was told to contact you regarding the Peter Stabs-By-Mistake trial."

The tall, shaggy-haired man entered, holding a worn briefcase in his left hand. He was dressed in an ill-fitting pair of baggy brown pants. Dark perspiration pools stained the underarms of his white shirt. He pulled a pair of bifocals from his shirt pocket and carefully centered the eyeglasses on his oversized nose. Immediately reaching into his front pocket, he extracted a card and awkwardly held it out to Richard, who sat motionless.

"Afternoon, Mr. Grorud," replied Victor, who stood motionless, arms crossed. "Anything you want to know about Stabs-By-Mistake's case, just ask me," announced Victor, eyeing the attorney while reaching out to take his card. "This here's my Uncle Richard…Richard Sanders." The older Sanders, still seated, nodded almost imperceptibly.

"Yes, I've heard about you, Mr. Sanders, and your brother Oliver," the attorney added nervously. "Fine government interpreters."

Victor frowned, put off by the whiteman's overlooking him. An awkward silence followed.

"Well, yes, let's see. Christian—er, Morning Eagle, asked me to get up here and interview some of the main witnesses at the trial and get affidavits." Grorud was now rustling through his brown leather briefcase, pulling out papers, placing them on the small desk in front of the immobile Richard and digging back in for more.

"Ah, yes. Let's see. Well, of course, I will need to talk to the young woman. Annie, Annie Running Crane, is her name. Then I'd like to talk to some of her friends who were at the trial. Let's see … Louise Red Fox, a Miss Maggie Wolf Plume and Miss Mary Horn." Grorud glanced up over the top of his bifocals.

"Well, let's see now." Richard parroted the whiteman's display of lawyerly demeanor. "Louise, Maggie Wolf Plume and Mary Horn are away at Sun Dance ceremonies with their families." Richard Sanders paused, looking at Grorud's briefcase and then at the papers. "Would be really hard to locate them 'cause Sun Dance ceremonies are now held at different times in different places all over the reservation."

"I see. What about the Indian police officer, Peter White Man? I understand he was a material witness and saw the victim with the defendant."

"Yes," broke in Victor. "He and I both saw Mr. Stabs-By-Mistake taking foul liberties with the young woman. Mr. White Man is one of our best policemen. He will tell you exactly what we both saw because we were both there."

Taking off his bifocals, Grorud rested his briefcase on the small wooden desk next to his papers and turned towards Victor, examining the young man intently. "Why don't you just tell me what you saw then, Mr. Sanders?"

Victor quickly glanced at his uncle who was fixing a steely-eyed glare right through Grorud's spine. Richard nodded for his nephew to proceed.

"Annie's mother, Nellie Running Crane, was afraid harm would come to her daughter at the hands of Peter Stabs-By-Mistake. It was as simple as that. Peter White Man and me followed him and saw him on top of Annie and raping her. White Man arrested Peter and we took him to the sub-agency jail."

"So, can I go talk to Annie now, and her mother, too?" queried the attorney.

After a fleeting check with his uncle, Victor responded, "Yes … if you'd like ….We can go a short distance to their house. I will interpret for you." Richard stood and joined his nephew.

"Good, then. You can ride in my car."

>>→ • ←<<

The small shack stood on the right side of the rutted road, surrounded by tufts of brown prairie grass set in the brownish-yellow seascape of rolling hills. Here and there, other shanties or lodges were perched atop the vast, barren land.

The three men were greeted by several wide-eyed children who had never before seen such a black, metallic monster.

"Nellie Running Crane, I have come with Mr. Grorud from Helena, Montana," translated Richard while making the introductions.

Victor went immediately to a frail-looking young woman seated next to the grub box, feeding small strips of cow suet to a child.

"Mr. Grorud, here, is one of Morning Eagle's helpers and wishes to talk with your daughter, Annie Running Crane," continued Richard.

Nellie Running Crane, solemn faced, looked up at the mention of Morning Eagle and cracked a faint smile at Grorud. Richard then motioned for his nephew, Victor, to come translate.

Victor approached Nellie, interpreting English for the woman and the Pikuni dialect for Grorud, while listening to Nellie speak.

"If this whiteman is sent by Aapinakoi Piítaa, then he may speak to my daughter. She will tell him the truth." Nellie Running Crane spoke loud enough for Annie to hear.

The slender girl with long, braided hair rose and walked slowly over to her mother. Her eyes were black, darkened grapes set in crimson-rimmed sockets. Her sunken eyes looked intently at Black Looks, then darted to Grorud, then back to Black Looks.

Victor stood close to Annie, leaning into her as if ready to prompt her every word.

"Daughter, tell the man what happened to you here. What made Red-Boy go to prison."

Grorud noticed that the young woman was hesitant and trembling. She was obviously not well, maybe from consumption or malnutrition, he supposed.

>>>—→ • ←—<<<

A small but spirited child, Annie Running Crane had been born in the lodge of her parents at Badger Creek during the leaves-come-out-moon (May). The family eked out a living on a barren, hilly land allotment supplemented by government rations and whatever wildlife her father could trap or hunt. Muskrat and deer, when plentiful, provided a feast. The winters were usually long and severe. Then, the diet was sarvis berries, turnips or potatoes and whatever meat the family could scrounge.

Chronic undernourishment stunted the growth of most Indian children on the reservation. Annie was no exception.

Annie, Louise and Emma Running Crane, when young, began helping their mother under the watchful tutelage of their grandmother, Little Petrified Stone. They prepared meals from the rations received at the Willow Creek Agency: small morsels of meat, a half-pound of flour and some bacon, beans and small rations of tobacco and coffee.

Grandmother gave the three sisters charge of little Blue Paw, a nervous puppy who became permanently attached to Annie, the one who always fed the pint-sized dog food scraps.

The fall when Annie was seven, she and her grandmother spent a full afternoon making birch dolls—the simple dolls that had no eyes. Annie loved her first doll and named her "Little White Weasel." The doll became Annie's secret friend. She knew the doll would protect her other "baby dolls." Grandma had taught her and her sisters that the cute, winter white weasels are very fast and protective of their young. Later, Marilyn Deer Child and Louise showed Annie how to stuff the doll heads with grass and make their faces. The two older girls helped her make doll clothes from scraps of the precious blue and red trade cloth.

In the fall, Annie collected cottonwood leaves that she folded and tore into little tipis, all arranged in a circle. She imagined her tipis to be a great Sun Dance encampment of painted lodges where everyone wore brightly-colored deerskin and calico dresses, a place where there was lots of food and laughter.

Blue Paw always sat outside the little encampments, wagging her tail, patiently waiting for Annie to finish her Sun Dance for the day so the little puppy could follow her home.

When she was well, Annie and the other children played the one game that seemed to make them all laugh the most—crack-the-whip. While they all held hands, the leader would sing, "Skunk with no hair on the backbone" and then run, attempting to touch the last child in the whip. If successful, the last child would move to the front of the line. When Black Looks was the leader and Annie was at the end of the whip, she would duck and squeal to avoid Black Looks' outstretched hands; she always found his probing fingers annoying.

During Sun Dance encampments, all the boys would see who could throw the "sliding sticks" the farthest. If the encampment was near a river bank, soft, wet clay was molded into balls and fitted into the end of a long willow rod. Swinging the rod with the ball on the end, the pellet would fly through the air, hitting an opponent. Victor was a poor sport and always got angry when he was hit. Then he would cheat to get back at whoever was better at the game. Almost always, it was Red-Boy who bested Black Looks with a "bullet" on the buttocks and Black Looks who sought vengeance. Often Victor would leave the game and go away to sulk with Blue Paw nipping at his heels while the others laughed.

Snowy, wet winters meant a cold damp cabin. Although the family tried to maintain a warm fire, when left unattended or when Cold-Maker's breath was strong, smoke choked the hovel built on a small government land allotment at Heart Butte—not like before when Annie and her parents lived at Badger Creek. Annie coughed and coughed, her eyes were red and swollen. Her coughing grew worse when family rations ran low and the only food was sarvis berries and moldy flour. Then, Annie often vomited what little she ate.

Chief Running Crane could command some attention for his daughter from Indian Bureau officials. It was ironic, though. Traditionally, one became a chief by gaining the respect of others, by making sacrifices, including distributing one's wealth. A chief would give away his horses, clothing and food to the less fortunate. In so doing, a chief gained the immense respect without the material trappings a whiteman would expect an important dignitary to enjoy. Ted Running Crane was no exception. He gave freely of his time, his wisdom, and occasionally small portions of the family land allotment.

A doctor treated Annie only once. The child rallied, but then grew worse again. A few friends, Curly Bear and Thomas Stabs-By-Mistake, brought portions of a beef cow, deer and elk meat when they could.

For a time, Nellie and Annie stayed with Nellie's relatives at Willow Creek, to be closer to the doctor at Browning. Louise and Emma Running Crane stayed away from boarding school to help their father at Heart Butte with farming chores and to help their mother take care of their sister at Willow Creek.

After still another failed year, Ted Running Crane finally gave up farming at Heart Butte and moved to Willow Creek to build a small ramshackle clapboard house for his wife and sick daughter. There, he renewed his bid to survive as a small crop farmer.

Life had gone from sparse to desperate. Two years of summer drought had withered away the crops. No hay could be cut for winter livestock feed. The winter of 1918 was an endless tale of loss. Underfed cattle and horses died and nearly one-third of the young adults died of influenza.

Perhaps it was Nellie's over-protectiveness or the extra rations provided by family and friends, but somehow Annie survived.

Before the war, Annie often saw Peter Red-Boy and Marilyn Deer Child. They always helped deliver rations of sugar or flour or large hind-cuts of deer and elk meat, occasionally beef.

Annie thought of Red-Boy more as an older brother and Marilyn, who became Louise's close friend, as an almost-sister. When he saw her healthy and at play, Red-Boy laughingly referred to Annie as "that tough little badger."

About the time Annie was able to go back to boarding school, both Marilyn Deer Child and Peter Red-Boy were seldom around. Victor Sanders saw an opening.

The arrogant young man told Annie of his plans to prosper as a reservation cattleman, bragging about his purchase of Liberty Bonds during the war. Maybe Victor liked Annie, but for sure he liked the status he would gain by marrying into the Running Crane band. Traditionally, the Running Cranes had served as Blackfeet scouts. Ted Running Crane, a Piegan chief, as well as his father and relatives, were all very influential. One had been a prominent tribal judge, others noted reservation policemen.

At first skeptical of Victor, Annie's mother appreciated his ability to secure food rations and medical help. Victor Black Looks finally convinced Annie that he could "turn things around." He would follow in his uncle's footsteps by becoming a government interpreter and perhaps, later, a council member.

While Annie was at the boarding school at Cut Bank, her sister, Emma, married Nelson Bull Child. Nelson built a small log cabin at Heart Butte. Annie missed her home, but Victor was a frequent visitor and a welcome source of news about her family.

Victor's attention grew more demanding when Red-Boy returned from the war and began to spend time with "his" Annie. Red-Boy made Annie laugh. Victor pouted and plotted and encouraged Nellie to mistrust Red-Boy. Victor had not forgotten his childhood rivalry with Red-Boy or his mother Maxine's recipes for creating conflict.

Nellie dutifully warned her daughter that Red-Boy brought back ways of the world that would corrupt her daughter. What's more, Red-Boy might be infected with "foreign diseases." She took firm steps to protect Annie from seeing the veteran of the Great War, the decorated Piegan warrior of the American Expeditionary Force.

Yet Annie was enamored while Victor was incensed and jealous. Victor plotted and spied. Finally, when he saw Red-Boy with Annie, he told Nellie.

Soon after Peter Red-Boy was arrested by the Indian police, an urgent visit was made to Annie's sister, Emma Bull Child, by a small posse: an Indian agent, Victor and Richard Sanders and a policeman, Peter White Man. Emma was told that she must go off to boarding school, now.

"Why?" her husband Nelson asked incredulously.

"Because, Emma, you have been home too long and haven't had a proper education. The law requires that you get schooling," came the explanation from Richard. The Indian agent nodded his assent.

"I will do no such thing!" huffed Emma Bull Child indignantly, raising her head defiantly.

"If you do not, the police will take you away. Listen Nelson, if you or anyone else interferes, you will be jailed."

A struggle ensued, Emma screamed and Nelson lunged at the Indian police officer. Tackled and thrown to the ground, Nelson was bound, gagged and taken off to jail at Heart Butte for a week.

Emma was taken to a boarding school in Lawrence, Kansas. She was there nearly a full year before she was finally allowed to go home. Her release was due to the efforts of a whiteman she later knew as Morning Eagle. Pregnant when she was forced from her home, Emma returned home with her baby boy.

>>>→ • ←<<<

Annie never forgot the deadly calm in Victor's instructions to her before Red-Boy's trial, about the danger to her of the "whiteman's law" and the "proper" way to testify in the whiteman's court.

"You tell them what I have told to you! You understan'!"

"But my parents have told me that —"

"No!" Victor cut her off abruptly in mid–sentence, the palm of his hand thrust in front of her face.

Annie flinched. "Why do you tell me what to say?"

Black Looks glowered with impatience. "Do as I say or you will be sorry. Very sorry!"

The girls were all seated in a row on a shiny, hardwood bench outside the immense courtroom at the federal courthouse in Great Falls, Montana.

"You must do as I have said. The whiteman's court is different. If you do not tell the jury men what I say, the federal judge, he will be very angry with you." Victor spoke quietly but looked solemnly at each of the girls in turn.

Annie had seen the black-robed judge. His sharp, curt mannerisms frightened her.

"You take what I say. What I tell you, that is necessary for you to say to convict Stabs-By-Mistake," Victor Black Looks concluded in a harsh whisper, then beckoned to Nellie.

Annie's mother seemed to understand and added her admonishment to her daughter in her Pikuni tongue.

>>>—→ • ←—<<<

After the trial, Victor tried to woo Annie into marriage the traditional Blackfeet way. One evening, the young man presented two cayuse ponies to Ted Running Crane; but Victor's ugly voice in warning had never left Annie.

"No! You will not win me into marrying you!" The young woman stood her ground, nostrils flaring, dark eyes blazing. She hated Victor for his smug gloating as Red-Boy had been taken away. "Now you take your horses and go!"

Annie turned to her father, her breathing coming in excited bursts. "Father, I love another man, not this man. Black Looks, he is not a true warrior," she blurted, loud enough for her mother to hear.

Later, Nellie asked her daughter who the other young man was. When Annie told her, her mother wept softly. Her father sat silently by the cabin fire, rocking back and forth on his willow rest, letting his wife handle the girl.

As much as Annie feared for Red-Boy and wanted nothing to do with Victor, she was too frightened to tell anyone about the lies. She knew they would take her away to boarding school like they did Emma, or maybe she too would be sent to prison. What would happen to her family if she did not obey the whiteman's law as Victor had instructed? It was the whiteman law, the Agency that gave rations to her family. Without rations, they would all die. She dared not disobey.

Yet inside, she nursed the terrible arrow-wound she had inflicted with her lies. She loved her older, almost-brother Red-Boy and missed him desperately.

The longer she kept her secret festering, the sicker her heart became. With the passing of each moon and each winter, she grew more depressed and withdrawn. Nellie worried that her daughter's sickness would return. No one would be able to rescue Red-Boy.

Then one afternoon in late September, 1923, several weeks after Morning Eagle's adoption, Red-Boy's parents gave Annie Running Crane a most unusual introduction to the whiteman from the East.

»»→ • ←«

All of the Elders were there in Thomas Stabs-By-Mistake's lodge at Cut Bank, seated around the lodge fire—smoking the pipe filled with kinnikinnick.

"We have asked you here, Aapinakoi Píítaa," announced Curly Bear, "to honor you with the ancient Piegan ritual given to us by Ná pi."

Humbled by his friends' kindnesses, Morning Eagle lowered his head reverently. Behind him, Thomas flashed a quick grin which was returned by the others.

"You, our brother, will witness the transfer of the sacred 'skunk medicine bundle,'" intoned Curly Bear with exaggerated solemnity.

Annie and her friends, having heard about the meeting, stood at the flap of the lodge. They saw the winks and smiled. The Eelders' shared feast of beef cow, beans, potatoes and coffee had filled everyone's bellies and now it was time for Curly Bear to start the ceremony.

"Aaee, here is the mic-cisa-misoi" (stinkwood), Curly Bear whispered.

Glancing to make sure Thomas's wife would not notice, Curly Bear placed some alder "stink wood" into the lodge fire and looked back at Thomas.

Catching the grin, Thomas puffed his cheeks, contorted his wide mouth and showed his teeth. The stink wood caught fire.

"Burriiippp!" A long, muffled flap-bouncing rumble fart cut through the air from Thomas Stabs-By-Mistake, as if a hot Chinook wind had blown through.

A foul miasma immediately filled the lodge.

"You pig!" screamed his wife. "You are a disgrace to this family! Get out of my lodge! Now!" Every face in the circle froze, serious and solemn. The New Englander stopped breathing. Thomas rose silently and majestically and faced his wife.

"Woman, you will not talk to me in that tone. You will come here and sit down by my side."

Silently, slowly, the Elders began retreating past Annie and the other girls at the flap door. First Curly Bear, then Bear Head, followed by Tom Spotted-Eagle, then the others. Some held their noses. When the last one had left, Morning Eagle's face was pale and ashen and his lips were pursed tightly to-gether. He rose gingerly, glancing first at Thomas, then at his wife, as a wooden spoon flew through the air just as Thomas ducked. Morning Eagle's mouth dropped open as he rushed through the flap.

Annie, holding open the flap, yelled to Morning Eagle, "I think there's goin' to be a fight!"

From within the lodge, great yelling and commotion erupted with the throwing of objects, the sides of the lodge spasming as various pots, pans and pieces of wood struck the blanketed covering. The yelling grew louder. Thomas came running from the lodge holding his pipe above his head, his wife chasing him with a small, iron cooking pan.

"Oh no, this will not do!" cried the New Englander. With a horrified look, Morning Eagle stepped between the two quarreling spouses.

"Please stop! Please! Oh no, please stop!"

At that instant, Curly Bear, Spotted-Eagle, Bear Head and the others pounced on Morning Eagle, gingerly taking him to the ground and pummeling him with flattened hands, all exclaiming that he shouldn't interfere, that he had broken a sacred Blackfeet law and that he had committed a great sin.

"Oh my God, no!" croaked the anguished whiteman, as he was rolled onto his back.

Unexpectedly, he was now confronted with uproarish laughter. All the men were holding their stomachs, reeling and rolling on the ground, kicking and screaming over and over.

Once again, the Blackfeet earthy sense of humor, inspired by Old Man Ná pi legends, had claimed the unsuspecting Morning Eagle. Thomas Stabs-By-Mistake and the others had counted a coup.

Embarrassed, Morning Eagle got to his feet, dusted himself off, and smiled weakly, looking even more red-faced than before.

"What just happened? My God, can somebody tell me what just happened?"

Thomas and his wife were both seated in front of the lodge door hugging one another and crying with laughter.

Annie took the New Englander by the hand and led him away from the lodge.

"This is how families have their fun," she said softly in broken English. A smile crossed her lips. "Thomas and his wife are great tricksters". She paused now and looked up at him, her smile growing wider. "You should learn Ná pi's ways," she giggled.

Morning Eagle stood, silent and sheepish. "What did Ná pi just teach us?" the New Englander asked, finally giving the young girl a puzzled grin.

"Old Ná pi the trickster, he teaches us about good and bad spirits. Thomas and Curly Bear just showed you that our women are important; they take care of the lodges." She paused, lowering her eyes. "And the bad air inside too," she giggled.

That was how Annie first met with the New Englander, Morning Eagle.

Seeing Annie with the whiteman, Victor approached and, smiling broadly, offered to translate.

>>>→ • ←<<<

Victor Black Looks had Morning Eagle pegged as a "troublemaker," another outsider out to ruin his plans. After Uncle Richard had warned him, Victor summoned Nellie, Annie and the others to the Willow Creek Agency. They were not to change their story. They could never change the things they had said in the whiteman's courtroom "under oath." To do so would be "like breaking a sacred oath to Above-Person." That's a whiteman's crime. They would go to prison for "perjury." Not completely understood, the English words sufficiently frightened Nellie. She lectured the girls that what was said and done at Peter's trial could not be undone.

The warning accompanying the ominous sounds of the whiteman word, "perjury," was enough to seal the lips of the girls with fear. The government interpreter had learned well from his mother and his Uncle Richard.

He, and he alone, would control Red-Boy's fate as well as his own. He would win Annie's heart. Then, after he was chosen as a Tribal Council member, he would get the coward Red-Boy a pardon on his own terms. He would be a powerful hero and the guilty Red-Boy would be an outcast.

>>>→ • ←<<<

A long silence had fallen over the group inside the small Running Crane cabin, that sweltering summer afternoon in 1924. Here, too, Victor had translated Annie's words into meaning that served "the greater good."

"Mr. Grorud, Annie Running Crane doesn't speak too good English, so I'll translate for her and ask her to speak in her native tongue." Victor assumed his natural, authoritative government interpreter demeanor. A pleased, confident grin straightened Uncle Richard's dark moustache.

"All we were doin' was holdin' hands down at . . ." said the young woman, being suddenly cut off by her mother.

"All you were doin' was a crime. He never offered you or your father or me nothin'. No horses or nothin.'" Nellie, her hands on her hips, continued berating her daughter in Pikuni. "I told you I didn't want you near him, daughter! He was with whites too long in the war! He was destroyed by them!"

Perplexed at the outburst, Grorud turned to the interpreter.

"Mr. Sanders, what are they saying?" the lawyer asked.

"Well, Annie and her mother both said that Peter Stabs-By-Mistake committed a serious crime." Annie fixed a hard stare at Black Looks. Grorud assumed the hostile look was related to the violence of the recalled experience.

"But," Annie cried out in English, "tell him what happened!" Victor quickly turned and gestured to Nellie who ushered her daughter outside. Grorud, first startled, then perplexed, was silent. No one else spoke.

"Look, maybe the women are too upset to continue," remarked Grorud.

"Yes," added Richard convincingly.

"Okay," the lawyer's trial experience took hold. Often, going too far with a cross-examination only made matters worse.

"So, let's see if I got this right." Grorud consulted his notes, then turned to Victor as they left the Running Crane home.

"Peter and Annie were seen holding hands. They started arguing. A struggle ensued, and then Peter was on top of her with her dress up. Is that about it?"

Victor nodded solemnly, then slid a glance of satisfaction at his uncle.

Sham battle, 1899. Photo by Thomas Magee, courtesy of the Sherburne Collection and William E. Farr.

# XIII

# Counting Coup
# (I Naah Maah Ka Wa)

For Red-Boy, the melting away of Snow Maker's blanket from the recreation yard in December of 1924 ushered in yet another undefined season of gloom behind the immovable Wall and time. Red-Boy worked painstakingly at his project, the one activity that gave his life movement.

Despite, or maybe because of the pain in his war-wounded hand, continued work on his painting was elevated to an act of sacred sacrifice. First came the head, then, slowly, the black body appeared; the horse finally grew legs, then hooves. In time, the form was no longer riderless. The young Indian worked at his creation with color, vision and imagination. Still, he did not know who was riding atop the Medicine Horse. The rider had no face.

The painting remained in the prison library, supported on an easel, giving the librarian-curator Shake Spear an opportunity to offer sometimes whimsical, sometimes helpful suggestions.

Sometimes, color meant for the silken image was spirited away, back to Red-Boy's cell. His father had taught him the how and meaning of what was done with war paint in the long-ago-days.

At first, Coombs was perplexed. Then, he began to feel a bit edgy and decided to keep his distance from the young Indian, who was always seated cross-legged with his arms resting on his knees, facing the commode. Some Indian thing, he decided. After all, stuff like this was one way somebody could escape the insanity of the meaningless monotony that would suddenly make a man scream or strike out for no other purpose than to simply feel alive.

"Krankk," came Red-Boy's even, expressionless voice. Coombs glanced up from the paperback he was reading, thinking he misheard his cell mate.

"Krankk. That's his real name, Krankk?" Red-Boy was seated cross-legged, motionless, in front of the toilet, looking at the wall of the cramped cell.

"What?" Coombs seemed annoyed by the unexpected question. "Shit, man, don't you listen... didn't I tell you 'bout his name, for chrissakes?"

"Krankk. They call him that 'cause he's a grouch, aaee?"

Coombs flashed a crooked smile and chuckled. "'Cuz his name's K-r-a-n-k-k," he slowly spelled out. "Get it? K K K."

Red-Boy only nodded, his eyebrows knitted with a scowl. For Red-Boy, the only name for a thing using that sound with such frequency was the popular smoke of his people—kinnikinnick. Thinking his assailant was named after certain contraband he seemed to control within the walls, he asked, "Does his name mean that he controls the tobacco and cigarettes in here?"

Coombs let out a belly laugh and remarked sarcastically, "Hell no! Jesus, Peter, sometimes I think you're a real fuckin' zombie!"

Turning, Red-Boy scowled, then grinned when he realized Coombs was merely poking fun. "So, you gonna answer my question?"

"Well, Christ, Peter. Since you're always the last one to know, I'll tell ya." His sarcasm was softening. "In here, the three letters in the sonofabitch's name mean KKK." He paused. "Ku Klux Klan, my friend."

In the service, Red-Boy had heard a reference to the three letters meaning "The Klan." It always seemed to be directed at the coloreds.

"You remember...I told you the shithead is proud he's a Klansman. He even brags about why he's doin' time in here. Lynchin' and murderin' niggers. Hates all niggers." Red-Boy's eyes narrowed into a cloud of contempt. "Fact is, he hates all people of dark skin. To him, yer just another nigger!" Coombs forced on awkward laugh.

Bracing himself, now, with his left hand, the Indian rose slowly and stood still. Facing Coombs, he turned and sat on the edge of the commode. The young man set his jaw and fixed on Coombs a look so hard and fierce, Coombs believed his cellmate might crush his forehead through the cell wall without flinching. Veins in his neck stood taut as arrows in a quiver. Then, the Indian lowered his eyes, stood and lifted himself up to his bunk. He rolled softly back onto his pillow, stared at the ceiling and said nothing.

»»→ • ←««

For weeks, Coombs had been nagging his cell mate to get out and clean himself. Out of sheer stubbornness, the body odor and lice had been largely ignored by Red-Boy. Coombs was unaccustomed to this Indian's apparent nonchalance about hygiene, unaware of the customary Blackfeet pride taken in personal cleanliness: frequent bathing in streams, food prepared in the open and cooked over an open fire. Coombs had only known Red-Boy's stories of the sick children back home eating with unwashed hands, blow flies everywhere.

Red-Boy steeled himself for another week. His trips to the shower had never been alone, except for the past month. Things began taking a different turn.... Monroe and several others had begun showing up unannounced. The encounters had set Red-Boy on edge. Avoiding the showers, so he could concentrate more on his painting, seemed the logical choice.

Finally, Coombs' curses became so loud and vile that the cellblock guard ordered the Indian to "go shower immediately." Red-Boy glared at the guard with contempt.

"See ya in a bit," Coombs laughed. Red-Boy glanced back and walked towards the common shower.

The Indian strode past Monroe's cell.

"Hey, snatch!" Red-Boy didn't flinch but continued walking.

It had been over a year since Krankk had smashed the metal tray against the Indian's skull and there had been no further trouble from the cell boss. Rumor had it that he was satisfied he had cowed the Indian, making him "toe the line." Still, Red-Boy carried his nerves close to the surface on this walk.

"Hey, Pussy! Pussy! Pussy, com'ere!" He passed Krankk's coyotes.

Turning right, down a hallway and some twenty yards to a door on the left, he peered in. The showers were empty.

Red-Boy took a slow, deep breath, then strode past the concrete pillars to the adjacent wall where he undressed. He laid his clothes carefully on the dressing-stall bench and glanced back. No one. He walked back between the pillars to the shower heads.

Without a sound to warn him, his left arm was jerked and twisted up behind him. The startling, overpowering strength and pain took his breath. A sharp metal point was pressed under his chin. Red-Boy was clasped in an immense fist of muscles attached to a sweaty arm bulging with tattoos.

His feet left the floor in a dizzying swirl; his racing thoughts stopped dead as he was slammed against a wall.

The huge fist again twisted his arm. Red-Boy's shoulder blazed with fire. He felt the sting of the sharp steel shiv pressing into his neck under his chin.

"Yer my woman! Get down and let me feel your mouth, snatch!...You don't bend down for me and suck, I'll cut ya open now!"

Red-Boy moved slowly, complying with the beast's demands.

Slowly, the metallic point withdrew, the iron fist relaxed. Red-Boy, calm—his awareness heightened—heard only his heart, a drum beat, sure and steady. He turned and sat down on the bench and looked up into the glassy eyes and up the prairie-dog holes of the hairless one.

No one was present. Krankk would have his way.

With an iron grip dug into Red-Boy's shoulder, the Klansman's other hand held the jagged piece of metal to Red-Boy's neck.

"Bend and suck, ya little squaw fucker!"

The Medicine Black Horse ran in the shadow of a distant mist.

The Indian, lowering to do the cell boss's bidding, brushed the man's right shin with the index finger of his left hand—he counted coup.

"Aaiiieeee!!" Red-Boy's war cry filled the space and reverberated off the walls. His right arm, taut as an arrow, rigid as the front hoof of Medicine Black Horse, shot upward. The wild "elk-dog" reared on its hind legs, kicking high at the Sun, at the prairie-dog holes. The hoof of the Black Horse, in the base of his palm, slammed back the prairie-dog nose of the Klansman's descending head. In an instant, the nasal cartilage of the prairie-dog nose hit the nasal bone. The bone broke into the sinus cavity. The shattering frontal bone penetrated the giant Krankk's brain.

It was all in slow motion, the loud "Crack!" filled the space as the war cry died away. As the two-legged beast fell with life leaving him, the jagged shank ripped into Red–Boy's lower abdomen.

"Aaaah!!" Red-Boy screamed, grabbing at his stomach, only to see his hand bathed in blood which fell on the dead body of Krankk and mixed with the blood of his enemy.

"Unh! Unh!" Red-Boy grunted and squinted. He dropped to one knee, the room began to heave and lurch. The columns, the blood and Krankk's naked head began to twist into a vortex. Red-Boy felt his body being pulled into the blood-red swirl.

He saw Coombs and the others bending over him, their mouths agape and twisted, calling for help. No sound.

The horse was standing near, his belly ripped open by the bull's horn.

"Must get horse tail hair…sew up the belly. Stitch the belly with horse hair." Red-Boy called out, but his voice was silent.

He was being lifted—weightless—drifting further away, outside the shower room, past fixtures and pipes, off to the vastness of the yellow prairie. The horse was now carrying him. He peered down, looking for Annie.

He felt himself going home. Back in time where life moved, near his grandfather, Big Brave.

>>>→ • ←<<<

They were moving east to the Cypress Hills again. They came upon a Cree camp of seventy lodges with wagons and carts and travois. The Piegans went right at them, killing a lot of Crees. Later, he saw the Piegans raiding the enemy from Milk River to Fort Benton. Many horses were captured. After the killing of the Piegan Chief, Many Horses, by a Crow, and the killing of Piegans by Gros Ventre, another battle, a bigger battle, was near. During the thick of the fighting, a rider on a Black Horse rode behind the Piegan lines. His head was covered with a black blanket. The Gros Ventres, Crows and Sioux shot at the rider and his horse many times.

The rider and Black Horse were never hit. The enemy became alarmed. Their spirit broke, they turned and ran.

Then, Red-Boy and his grandfather were astride fast runners. His grandfather wore his War Bonnet and held his shield and spear. He had no gun. The Crees shot at Big Brave as he rode the whole length of the battle front, but he was not hit.

Then, Big Brave's father, Mountain Chief, charged the Crees in a big coulee near the river, then ran his horse back under full fire, back to his people. The people tried to hold Big Brave back from charging. But Mountain Chief turned his son loose.

Red-Boy saw his grandfather run and jump in an enemy trench, then fall and get up. He made for the coulee. Again, he was knocked to the ground by a shot. He thought blood was coming from his mouth, but when he wiped his mouth there was no blood. Big Brave took off his War Bonnet. There, on the sides and in the back, were broken feathers. Elk Horns saw him and helped him up. Big Brave was not hurt, but his head had been creased by a rifle ball.

Big Brave saw an old man, Sun Calf, a Blood Chief, and dragged him away from the shooting. The trilling of women and men was loud in praise of Big Brave-Mountain Chief's deeds in that battle, called by the Piegans

"Many Chiefs' Battle."

Dead and wounded enemy were everywhere, over the flat and in the coulee. Big Brave saw a Cree's horse stumble and fall. The Cree jumped up and made for Big Brave, taking arrows out of his quiver. He held his bow up but the sinew broke and he did not snap that arrow. The bow string was wet. The Cree then grabbed Big Brave's hair and pulled his head toward his as he reached for his knife. He held Big Brave's head and Red-Boy saw the long knife come close to his grandfather's head.

Then, he felt the knife sink into his own belly. Ah-e-e-e!!

But Big Brave-Mountain Chief's War Bonnet had saved him. It was wrapped around his breast. It had turned aside the knife.

Big Brave fell. The Cree, thinking he was killed, walked away. Big Brave took the knife, jumped up and grabbed the Cree's hair and stabbed him. He lay dead by his spear and quiver full of arrows wet from the river. Big Brave took the Cree's spear, quiver and rattle.

Big Brave-Mountain Chief was now among his people. He said "I pity the enemy. Let those who live go to their homes." Hundreds of dead Crees were lying on the prairie or floating in Cole Banks River. The battle ended.

Red-Boy felt overpowering pain again in his side and saw the gut-stabbed horse. Annie was near but he couldn't find her. He counted the dead Crees, floating in the swift waters of the river.

He closed his eyes in the weakness of the pain and thought he would awaken beside her.

He felt hot and sticky buried inside the belly of the gut-stabbed horse. He tried to move, to escape, to open his eyes. He had to find Annie.

>>>—→ • ←—<<<

Red-Boy gasped and opened his eyes. His heart pounded. All around him was whiteness.

Must be on the Ghost-Trail to the Sand Hills, he thought. His piercing and what the Elders had told him came back; once a warrior is pierced, Naa tó' si (the Sun) can take his life at any time. This was his destiny. He had entered the Ghost-Trail, the path of all those who had gone before.

Naa tó' si had, at last, delivered him now from the beast, Krankk.

A swarthy man's face floated above him.

"Peter. Peter Stabs-By-Mistake. Can you hear me?"

"Yes," the young Indian heard his own voice reply. His lower gut was on fire. Trying to lift his head, he saw stars.

"Whoa. No you don't. You rest," came the deep-soothing, male voice. "You're mighty lucky, Peter. You lost a lot of blood. The guy who cut you just missed killing you."

Carefully, he touched the pain. The sutures felt like a steel bear trap clamped tight over his abdomen. Sharp porcupine needles made every movement painful. He saw the Medicine Lodge-pole at the Heart Butte Sun Dance and felt the pain of his piercing. This new pain felt more remote. Still, it was paralyzing, burning and clawing at his gut.

"Am I hurt bad?" he asked in a whisper.

"Well, from the looks of things, we thought we lost you. Just rest now."

Leavenworth's only physician started to leave, then stopped and hesitated. Turning around and coming back, he asked, "By the way, when they found you in the shower, you were asking for horse hair. Did you lose something? A piece of clothing?"

Red-Boy looked up. He shook his head slowly, then closed his eyes and sank into the pain. Like his Sun Dance piercing, the pain burst forth in burning waves, letting him know he was alive.

He listened to his slow breathing. After awhile, he drifted off into a peaceful darkness.

>>>→ • ←<<<

Afraid to even ask about Krankk's whereabouts when he regained strength, Peter was visited one morning by prison officials, including the warden. They explained to him that he was lucky to be alive, a fact which seemed to baffle the whitemen surrounding his bedside. There were questions to answer. Men in suits asked questions about what happened. More questions. More stares. Still more questions and finally faint smiles and nods from the officials, explaining to him that it had all been so "unnecessary." They had been made "aware of the circumstances." This would not happen again.

The men in suits told him he had killed the prison boss but would be exonerated of any charge of murder because of Coombs and the others. His veteran friends had, indeed, "protected his backside." Coombs and the others had apparently seen the assault and the hand-to-hand kill maneuver that all veterans had carried back with them from the Great War.

Then, they told him he would be placed in The Hole. Completely exonerated and going to The Hole—a steel-walled, steel-floored isolation cubicle designed to house the most incorrigible inmates. He would go there, they informed him, "for your own protection" from Krankk's followers until they could be "transferred out."

"Why won't moving me to another cell block protect me?" he asked. "Because other cell block bosses, Krankk's allies, would seek revenge," they said. Still, their eyes seemed to tell what their tongues would hide.

He would be placed in "protective confinement," to waste away in The Hell Hole.

Red-Boy wondered if the prison officials hid their real intent. Did they want to protect him or to assure the other inmates that this Indian was being severely punished?

>>>→ • ←<<<

Many had been overcome by The Hot House, a name attached to Leavenworth by the inmates. During summer months, there was only one wall-mounted fan on the entire tier of cell Block B, blowing sluggishly foul air around in short, hot bursts, occasionally hitting one's sweating body like a concussion from a nearby mortar round.

Behind the steel trap-door of The Hole, there was no fan.

He remembered the relief he felt in the sweat lodge. The flap door would always be opened four different times to let out the steam and let in the exhilarating cool air. In The Hole, the sweat—on his forehead, over his chest, under his arms, between his legs—evaporated in the mind-numbing heat before it hit the steel floor. There were no cinder block paths to trace, no motion to distract him, no ray of light to define his mind from the world.

Time ceased.

The events of his mind were the only remaining reality. It was all like dream time, blurred, broken, strange. He would yell, screaming back at the sounds in his head, releasing a coil of choking inner rage, as if to communicate with unknown ghosts; but it was all pretend—the sounds coming back were echoes from inside himself.

Yet it was not pretend, because he was alive. He was semiconscious, disembodied, floating free, only to return when the heat or the guards pulled him back, back from the edge of sanity or insanity.

Once, after straining to hear the sounds, any sound, from without, he felt his heart beating out a distorted, uneven rhythm. He listened to his body. It was as it had been with Thomas and the Elders in the Medicine Sweat Lodge back home.

"A man does not feel with his mind." He heard his father's voice.

"Red-Boy, you must listen to your heart when you are in here. Feel with your heart. Your heart will tell you what to do."

After that, the bad spirit of alcohol had left his body for good.

Slowly, the terrible isolation, like the bad-spirited alcohol, left him. He listened as he felt the pounding of the life pulse throughout his body.

The black shadows in the corners of The Hole, in the edges of his mind, slowly transformed themselves and the long sleep with its dream overtook him.

»»→ • ←«««

Red-Boy looked around, struggling to make out the distant forms in the fescue grass. There, in the far distance, next to an old Otter-Medicine Lodge, stood the Black Horse.

Slowly, he walked toward his Spirit Power.

Strangely, the Medicine Horse was not moving as the Black Horse had in his vision. Somehow, it was different from the horse in his silk painting.

Red-Boy was startled, shaken. Had his Medicine Horse been killed when he struck this death coup on Krankk? Had his Spirit Power been gutted by the brute's metal shank?

The Black Horse spoke to him. "Pooh sa poot (Come over here)."

As Red-Boy approached, the Black Horse became blurred. He strained to see. His head grew hot. He leaned towards the Black Horse, his vision over-run with his fear.

Approaching still further, the Sun's light grew brighter. Red-Boy thought he saw two horses. The light grew white and more blinding. He threw his hands up and cried out, but there was only silence.

When he dropped his hands, the horse nearest to him spoke.

"Come over, Red-Boy."

The young Indian walked still closer.

There were two horses. Both mounts glittered with a silken white sheen. Large crimson spots bled into their flanks, underbellies and manes. The horses were no longer black.

Atop one horse sat his grandfather, Big Brave-Mountain Chief.

Holding the other by the halter was his father.

"Ó ki!" Red-Boy greeted. There was only silence.

Slowly, Thomas's hand reached out, beckoning him towards a distant lightness.

Again, Red-Boy called out and closed his eyes.

»»→ • ←«««

He awoke again in the smothering darkness. His eyes adjusted to the smooth sameness of the steel enclosure. He lay there on the floor and listened.

Slowly, his heartbeat moved to a calmer rhythm.

Then began the quiet ebb and flow that was his life: return to the darkness of The Hole, then back into his recurring dream. The seemingly eternal pattern of ascending to his vision, then awakening, erased all sense of The Outside.

Once, upon returning to the darkness, a sound began outside his head, beyond his voice. The grinding and clanking of steel doors grew closer. He saw guards standing before the weak light of the open steel door.

Sound and light and uninhibited movement—all were new again. He was alive. The world of Leavenworth seemed as open and fresh as the prairie and he was grateful.

Back in his cell with Coombs; back to familiar routines. Through it all, summer had passed into fall. The protection Red-Boy had so desperately wanted, before, was now his without asking. Coombs was boss again and Big Ed and Gunny were part of the pecking order—the "new racket" as Gunny called it.

The old boss's remaining minions seemed afraid of the gaunt, ghost-like Red Man who had killed the giant Krankk with a single blow.

Still, Red-Boy did not revel in the coup he had counted. He knew the Black Medicine Horse had been given to him for survival, a survival that only began with killing his enemy.

It was now time to finish the silk painting. This single work would again shape for him a life apart from the lives of the others, free from the walls that held him. His Medicine Horse had changed.

Since the Medicine Power given to him in the dream had been not destroyed but transformed, Red-Boy knew it was time to change the painting to complete his vision. Entering the library where he had last left the painting, he noticed that the painting and easel had been removed.

"Aaee, Shakes. Seen my paintin'?" Red-Boy gave the little librarian a broad smile, expecting one in return.

Seeing him enter, the trustee turned white, his head visibly shaking. He stared at the Indian but said nothing.

"Thought I was dead, huh," Red-Boy joked as he strode over to the desk, thinking Shake Spear was just having one of his shaking spells. "Did you keep it safe for me?" Red-Boy asked.

The librarian rose from his chair and with a jerk of his head, motioned to the far corner behind his desk and some shelves.

"I tried to Pa...P...Peter."

There, leaning against the wall, half-covered with paper debris and boxes, stood the collapsed and splintered frame. The silk had folded over on itself.

Red-Boy held it out to the light. The silk had been crudely slashed diagonally, ending just at the belly of the Black Horse. The cloth was stained a dirty brownish hue.

Holding the thing closer, Red-Boy caught the foul odor of human excrement.

"Who did this, Shakes?" The Indian's eyes were wet and blazing.

"Ssss...sor...rr...sorry, Pp...pet...ter, Peter." The tattooed librarian was clutching his desk for support. He looked at Red-Boy, then at the shredded silk, with sadness and fear in his watery, pale eyes.

"Who...Shakes? Who did this?" Red-Boy's fierce look set the trustee back against his desk.

"M...ma...monn...Mon...Monroe, Monroe," he finally blurted out.

"You seen him do it?"

The librarian gave a nervous, jerking nod. "D...d...didn'...ssee...me, th, th...though." Somehow the quick undersized trustee had hid like a fox and caught sight of Monroe.

Shake Spear cast a wry smile, then beamed at Red-Boy. "Ta...th...they, ta, ta, transferred hi...hi...him out."

Red-Boy nodded and grinned back.

"Man, for a little badger, you sure got big balls, aaee." They both laughed.

Red-Boy understood. Shake Spear's snitching on Monroe might have cost him his life.

Red-Boy was impressed with his librarian friend. He seemed timid and harmless on the outside. Perhaps, Shake Spear's racket was as influential as Krankk's had been, at least with the prison officials.

>>>→ • ←<<<

Shake Spear came through again for Red-Boy and a new silk canvas and easel appeared. Coombs informed him the librarian-turned-quartermaster had gone straight to Warden Biddle himself.

Peter Red-Boy, once again, took to his task of creating anew the vision of his Medicine Power. Slowly, Red-Boy recreated his vision day after day in the prison library while the others worked in the prison shops or took exercise. He painted at other times, if the guards gave the nod. As his painting emerged, he thought of home and the lodge of his father and mother, the Sun Dance, the stick games, and most of all of Annie, laughing.

One night, while walking leisurely in the prison yard, a "good time" privilege he had earned, he looked for the North Star—the Star-That-Never-Moves—and imagined a celestial connection with his family and Annie. Perhaps, even his long-ago Deer Child. He remembered drawing his blanket closely around his shoulders as he sat in the chilly night with his father and the others around the lodge-fire at Cut Bank. Rides-at-the-Door had turned to him and said, "It is about the Star-That-Never-Moves that I will speak."

>>>→ • ←<<<

Pointing off to the north sky, he began his story.

"In the much long-ago-time, before that Star was in the night sky, there lived a Pikuni woman in a skin lodge with her two boy children. The woman's man was a strong and good warrior. His coups were many."

Rides-at-the-Door told how the Pikuni woman's warrior had been killed while on a raid against the enemy, how the oldest boy, Never Laughs, who had seen eight winters when his father died, was the provider for the family, furnishing meat and hides for their lodge.

"'My mother,' said Never Laughs one day, 'for many winters I have been a boy. When the last Night-Sun died, then I was a man. Now I go to the North Country. When I return, I will be like my warrior father and you will be proud of me.' The mother begged her boy not to go. But the boy was determined; he mounted his pony and rode away to North Country.

"Sun had traveled across the blue four times. Never Laughs came to a creek that was swift and deep. He saw Ki áá yo (bear) in the willows on the opposite side. A great Buffalo was drinking at the stream.

"'Powerful friend, pity me. Take me across the stream so that I can kill Ki áá yo.'

"'I will take you across the stream,' said the Buffalo, 'but you will not kill Ki áá yo. I am your friend and I know that you seek a powerful Medicine. You will find what you are looking for. You will become the greatest chief of all the Piegans, but you must do what I say.'

"Clinging to the hair on the Buffalo's hump, the boy was carried across the stream. When they arrived at a great rock, the Buffalo said, 'Stay at this side of the rock where Sun is warm. Stay there four sleeps. Drink no water, eat no food. After Sun dies four times, Dream-Maker will come. You must do what he tells you. If you do these things, you will become a great chief and people will talk about you for as many winters as there are leaves on the trees of the forest.'

"After Sun died four times, Dream-Maker came and said to the young Piegan, 'Get up from your robe. Look at the Road-to-Spirit-Land (Milky Way). Take an arrow from your quiver. Shoot that arrow to the North sky. Then shoot three more arrows there. When you shoot the fourth arrow, grasp the arrow with your hands as it leaves the bow. That arrow will carry you to a far-away-country where you will look down on all your people. You will then become the greatest chief of all the Piegans.'

"Each day when Sun had gone to sleep, the mother had gone to the hill-top and cried with her head under her robe. She prayed to Sun, Night Light and Morning Star. She asked them to send her boy back to her, but the boy never came back.

"One night, the mother saw a bright new Star, one she had never seen be-fore. For many winters, the mother went each night alone to the hilltop and prayed to that Star for pity. The woman lived to be very, very old. Time came when her hand was weak. She sang for those-who-had-gone-before. Soon, she too would go on that trail alone and never turn back.

"Dream-Person came and said, 'Piegan woman, each night for many winters past, you have looked with your eyes at the Star-That-Never-Moves. That star is your boy. Your boy, he never died. He is the Never-Moving-Star, the North Star. He has brought long life to you.'"

>>>→ • ←<<<

Red-Boy fixated on the Star above and away from the concrete walls. Rides-at-the-Door's story warmed Red-Boy's heart and gave him hope. He, too, was the same never-moving-person that the young Piegan had become.

In The Hole, Dream-Person had fully revealed to him his powerful Medicine. He too, with his powerful Medicine, would shine down.

"Coombs, I'm goin' to write a letter to Annie tonight," announced the young Indian as he returned from his star watch.

"Peter, you just never give up, do you!" Shifting from his reclining position, Coombs reached for his pad and pencil and handed them to his cellmate.

"It's only goin' to make yer paintin' hand start hurtin' again," he said. "Then, the inside of yer damned head," he joked. "'Sides, she's probably married another guy by now...without even telling you. Jesus, man! Happens all the time in here. Makes men go crazy. Seen men kill over their women turning sour on 'em."

Red-Boy frowned.

*Feb. 7, 1925*
*Leavenworth Prison*
*To Annie Running Crane,*

*Annie I write to you this letter after looking at the Star-that-never-moves. My heart for you never moves. Please look at the North Star and you will see me. I will look at it with you. We can see each other with the Star. When I come out of here I must tell you now that I want you to be my woman. My only true sits-beside-him-woman. Our hearts are the same.*

*Please write to me as soon as you get this letter. When can you come? I am worthy of you Annie. I have survived many bad things in here and I know that I can be your husband and a good provider when I get out.*

*Now I must tell you one more final thing. I have found my true Medicine Power. It was revealed to me in a dream. In here I am painting my Medicine in a picture. Each day I work on it I think of you and my family. Please tell your mother and father that my thoughts for you are pure and I never meant you any harm. You have a good family and I have a good family.*

*Your heart is with me forever.*

*Red-Boy*

Later, while working on his silk painting in the prison library, Red-Boy handed the sealed letter, addressed to James Vielle, to a burly guard on duty. He asked the guard if he would please give the letter to Warden Biddle for delivery. Red-Boy figured his old friend would see that the letter got to Annie. The guard grinned, nodded and took the letter.

That evening, as usual, he sat cross-legged on the floor, facing the toilet and the cinder block wall. Red-Boy stared at the crisscrossing fibers of rock and concrete that formed what he now saw as the paths between Cut Bank and Heart Butte and Browning—passageways of his life beneath the Shiny Mountains, the strands that wove together the very fabric of his soul.

Morning Eagle's third tipi. The Pikuni paint his lodge with sacred paint and the ceremony takes four day. Mountain Chief transfers his Otter Medicine to Morning Eagle. He tells Morning Eagle that Morning Eagle's Indian relations say that Morning Eagle should take their prayers in his heart, for Morning Eagle of their clan; the Doves and Black-Horse Societies. (From a photo postcard.)

# XIV

# The Otter Medicine Tipi and Black Looks

Curly Bear and Thomas Stabs-By-Mistake were the first to approach at sunrise. "Aapinakoi Píítaa, brother," said Thomas. "Your eyes see the faces of your friends and brothers. Our words are solid like Mother Earth. I speak for my people. We have been thinking a long time about what we are to do." The Piegan Chief paused and looked directly at Morning Eagle, unsmiling.

It was October, 1924—the time of "leaves-falling-moon"—a year after Morning Eagle's adoption. Morning Eagle wondered if a disappointed Thomas would tell him he had decided that the New Englander could do nothing, after all, to obtain his son's release.

Stabs-By-Mistake slowly looked around, then back at his friend.

"We have decided to transfer the Otter Medicine Tipi to you. The Medicine Paint, Prayers, Songs, Buffalo-Stones, Medicine Pipe and all that belong to the first Otter Medicine Tipi go with it. Your friends and brothers will help me with the sacred ceremony. The ceremony will last four sleeps."

Morning Eagle just sat, blindsided by this announcement of a decision he was completely unable to comprehend. He could not believe what he was hearing.

"The first tipi was made of the hides of many Buffalo," said Curly Bear. "When the hides became nothing, then the owner of the Otter Medicine made another tipi. All tipis disappear, but the Medicine that belongs to the tipi never dies. The Otter Medicine is very old. It came to my grandfather's grandfather in two dreams. It has always belonged to my relations. Aapinakoi Píítaa, my brother, you have counseled many times in the Otter Medicine Tipi."

Curly Bear continued, "Now I call for help. I call your friends and brothers to help me with the sacred ceremony. I call for help from the Spirit of the

Woman who found the first Iniskim (the Sacred Buffalo Stone). Buffalo Body, he is a Medicine Man. He will pray for us. He will paint our bodies with Sacred Paint that we may be pure, then we can prepare the tipi. We will paint the tipi design with paint from the earth. On the fourth sleep the tipi will belong to you with all its Sacred Medicine."

"Now, my brother," announced Thomas Stabs-By-Mistake, "when the painting of the tipi is finished, I will teach you the songs and prayers that belong to it. After the tipi belongs to you, then you must take good care of it. You must never dance in that tipi. You must never play games in it. All talk in that tipi must be with a straight tongue. It is sacred. See that no harm comes to your Medicine. Ki á nni a yi." (Enough).

"Otter Medicine came to my far-back relations through dreams," continued Stabs-By-Mistake. "It came from the water. In the early days when the Piegans were camping along Elk River (Yellowstone), a boy was drowned. The boy's father, he stayed at the place after the camp had moved. He prayed much for his boy to come back and threw bundles into the river. The bundles, they were presents to Under-Water-Person. The man hoped that Under-Water-Person would pity him and return his boy to him.

"Under-Water-Person then called out to the boy, 'Come.' The boy came.

" 'Now,' said Under-Water-Person, 'I give you back to your father. Tell him the words that I speak. Tell your father that the Otter is his Medicine. Tell him that his Medicine comes from the water, it is very powerful. Tell him that he will have good health. Tell your father that long life will come to him.'

"When the boy came back to his father, he told the words that Under-Water-Person spoke." Thomas slowly nodded at Morning Eagle and the others.

"Ki á nni a yi!" (That's it) said Mountain Chief. "Thomas, you never forget the dreams." Then he nodded for Thomas to finish the story.

"In the early days the Piegans had a great piss kan (Buffalo jump) where they chased the Buffalo over a cliff into a corral and killed them with bow and arrow. My grandfather's grandfather had a dream while sleeping near the piss kan. In his dream, a very small boy came to him and said, 'Come to my tipi at the bottom of the cliff.'

"Once there, the little boy showed my grandfather's grandfather the paintings on his tipi and told him: 'All the circles around the bottom of the tipi are the stars. They are reflected in the water. The points above the circles are the mountains. The red at the top of the tipi is the clouds. The yellow paint between the clouds and the mountains is the muddy water when the great flood was here. The eight Otters are in the muddy water. They live there. The throat, heart and kidneys are all marked. They are red. The Bunch Stars and the Seven Stars are painted on the smoke flaps. They are powerful. The tanned Otter Skin that hangs from the lodge-pole has bells around its neck. The bells are the ripples of the water. The Otter Skin, it is a flag that has great power. Make a tipi like this one. It is very powerful. It comes from the water. The Otter Medicine is strong. The Butterfly is the Bringer-of-Dreams. It is painted high up on the back of the tipi. It means that you will have many dreams about your tipi. It is the Dream-Person that has much power and truth.'

"Then the boy taught him the songs that go with the Otter Medicine Tipi.

"When my grandfather's grandfather awoke," continued Stabs-By-Mistake, "he invited all the men to come to his lodge. He told them his dream. He said to the men, 'Now, I will paint a new tipi. My dreams gave me the Otter Medicine. The power of the Otter Medicine is strong.' Ki á nni a yi." (Enough).

Four days later, the painting of Morning Eagle's Otter Tipi was finished. The painting bones and frayed twig paint brushes were laid aside and the pegs were drawn from the stretched canvas. Heads bowed in prayer as the women raised the Great Medicine Tipi. Sun smiled down upon the group and songs of gladness came from the rising hearts of Morning Eagle's brothers and sisters.

This Dream-Tipi, like those of far-back-days, stood out against the western sky. Painted curtains were hung, willow backrests put in place. Robes and blankets were spread and all of Morning Eagle's belongings were neatly placed. A fire was kindled within the circle of stones for the burning of sweetgrass.

Morning Eagle was seated on his painted Buffalo robe beneath his Medicine Bundle awaiting the gathering. Soon, Stabs-By-Mistake, Curly Bear and Bear Head, along with Morning Eagle's other Piegan friends—Big Brave-Mountain Chief, Buffalo Body, the medicine man who prayed for them, Wolf Plume, Natose, Spotted Eagle, Swims Under, Big Spring, Turtle, Red Bird Tail, Runs-Through-the-Enemy, Day Rider, Black Horse Rider, Walks-With-Head, and Shoots Each Other—entered the lodge, each taking his place according to rank or age.

Four times the Medicine Pipe was smoked in the ceremony of prayer. All heads were bowed as Stabs-By-Mistake prayed:

> *"First-Medicine-Woman, who first found Iniskim.*
> *We want to pray to you.*
> *The Pikuni, they know all about you;*

*You have brought long life to many people.*
*We ask you to bring good health to our brother:*
*To take away all trouble from him and give him long life.*
*Naa tó' si, Iniskim, listen to our words;*
*Our hearts speak these words.*
*The Otter Medicine knows."*

A deep stillness fell over the group. Then Mountain Chief spoke.

"Now, I will tell Aapinakoi Píítaa more. The owner of this Otter Medicine Tipi, he will have a long life. His Tipi will stay with him. That is good. Everybody will want the owner's long life. It is very great. All his undertakings will be successful."

Taking a buckskin bag from under his robe, the old blind chief of the Pikuni, Mountain Chief, reached for Morning Eagle's hand and spoke, "These Buffalo Stones, these Iniskim, I found in the long-ago-times. I have kept them safe. They are powerful Medicine. They bring good fortune. They belong to your painted Tipi. I give them to you so that you will live a good life in the future as a result of this gift."

Then, Mountain Chief slowly held out a wooden board lying at his side.

"Now, I give you my Tobacco-Board. It has traveled much. I made that Tobacco-Board. I used it only during ceremonies that meant much. A man uses only four Tobacco-Boards during his lifetime. So, I give you this, my last Tobacco-Board, Apinakoi Píítaa. It belongs to your Medicine Tipi because I am your relation."

"Now, brother," said Stabs-By-Mistake, "I give you the Medicine Pipe that belongs to your Tipi. Its Medicine and Power go with it. All those who you now see with your eyes have prayed for you. They want you to have a long life. They want no trouble to come to your heart. We give you this parfleche. The names on it tell the Otter Medicine Tipi belongs to you."

»»—→ • ←—«««

As he sat in his Pullman coach this late spring day in 1925, the memory of wood smoke cleared from his mind, and Morning Eagle thought the Otter Medicine Tipi might provide a key for unlocking the truth. He would give those who testified at Red-Boy's trial the right to enter the Otter Medicine Tipi, a sacred gathering place. If they knew and believed that he now had the powerful Medicine, then the truth might at last be known.

Yet, as he looked out at the expanse of eastern Montana's bracken prairie land, he remembered the words of Stabs-By-Mistake. It is sacred. He wondered if the younger ones would take the Otter Medicine Tipi seriously.

The scant new testimony uncovered by Grorud during the previous summer seemed more revealing for what it did not disclose than for what it did. Witnesses had apparently been unavailable, being away at Sun Dance ceremonies. Grorud had told him about the fear written into the face of the young victim, Annie, and the commanding presence of the government interpreters, Richard Sanders and his nephew, Victor. Annie was not allowed to talk to Grorud in English, speaking, instead, through the interpreter who had also been a primary government witness. Victor Sanders was a conduit through which everything flowed. Always hovering close by was his Uncle Richard.

Morning Eagle had written to his adoptive father, Curly Bear, of his suspicions. Curly Bear's ghost-written reply assured Morning Eagle that Oliver, James Vielle, Nellie, Annie and hopefully the others would come to talk with him this summer.

Something about Victor's name struck Morning Eagle just then. He tried to remember what Grorud had told him about this peculiar half-blood, the son of a white, alcoholic schoolteacher and a quiet Piegan Elder. Something had been told about the man's face—his looks.

That was it! Victor Sanders' Indian name. Yes, Oliver Sanders had told the Helena, Montana, attorney that he had given his half-blood son the Indian name Black Looks. His namesake was the revered Blood Indian who lived with the North Piegans and Bloods in Alberta and who owned the sacred Bear-Medicine-Knife. Surely, the namesake of such a man would be honorable, not disgrace his family and the reputation of the one after whom he was named.

The others had taken Morning Eagle to meet this powerful Blood Elder years before.

The hot Montana sun glared through the Pullman windows, casting diamond glints off the silver work on the walls and faceted glass ornaments.

Out of the vastness of the Great Plains, already baking in the sun, the raised Otter Medicine Tipi and Black Looks' knife—the Bear-Medicine-Knife—came together in the New Englander's mind.

>>>→ • ←<<<

It had been sundown of the last day of the Sun Dance Medicine Lodge ceremony. Morning Eagle had just returned from the lodge of Stabs-By-

Mistake after talking with Ni nai stá ko — Mountain Chief — who had told him about the Bear-Medicine-Knife of Black Looks. It was a knife of great power that was regarded with respect and even fear. Mountain Chief suggested that Bear Head and his woman, A-tso-tsi-ni, take him north to the Blood country to meet Black Looks.

"Ai yi!" exclaimed Bear Head. "Your words, they make us happy. We want to see our relations."

"Yes, some of our relations, they are very old. They are glad to see us," echoed A-tso-tsi-ni.

His eyes shining, Bear Head explained, "I know the owner of the Bear-Medicine-Knife. He lives among our relations. I will ask a favor of him. I will ask him to unwrap the Bear Medicine Bundle. Then, your eyes will see Bear-Knife. This I will do for you."

After journeying many miles and crossing the Canadian border, they finally spotted the Blood camp on the bench land. Two riders came toward them and circled many times on their fast ponies, looking for tribal signs while trying to make out their intention.

Bear Head signaled, "Friend. Same blood." They followed the two riders to their camp.

Dog Child, Calf Robe and Sikkumapi greeted the three. Dog Child's woman had set up a tipi for the group and a steaming kettle hung on the tripod.

That night after visitors had left the lodge and the three were alone with Sikkumapi, they requested he go with them to the lodge of Black Looks to smoke with him. By doing so, he would know that they were about to ask a favor.

"Black Looks will grant the favor that you will ask," said Sikkumapi. "He is my friend. He will tell us how the Bear-Medicine-Knife came to him. Come brothers."

A Night-Bird-With-Ears-Far-Apart (owl) was talking to a coyote as the group crossed the circle to the lodge of Black Looks. Slow, deliberate greetings were exchanged and the long-stem-pipe-of-straight-talk was smoked. A long silence followed, after which the object of the visit was made known.

"The whiteman, Apinakoi Píítaa, he has been one of us for many winters," said Sikkumapi. "Mountain Chief, he told him about the Bear-Knife. Now he has come to your country. He sees your face. You are the owner of that knife. He would like you to tell him how that knife came to you. Aapinakoi Píítaa, he ask you that favor."

The Blood warrior sat long in silence before replying.

"What you ask, I will tell. I will tell how the Bear-Medicine-Knife came to me. First we go and see One Spot. He is very old. We fear he will never see green grass come again. One Spot, he knows the names of all the owners until the knife passed to me. All the words that he speaks will be straight."

>>>→ • ←<<<

From the slowly-swaying Pullman, the setting sun had exploded into a huge crimson ball, with frayed scarlet ribbons settling across the western sky. Its disappearance brought a night curtain and black thunderclouds over the Rockies. Daggers of lightning ripped and flashed over the darkening plains, taking his mind back.

One Spot was on his robes when Black Looks and the group entered his lodge. His arm was weak, but his smile grew wider as they entered.

"My moons are few. I am like a little child," said the feeble old warrior, who had seen more than ninety winters.

After everyone was settled on the ground near One Spot, he began.

"That knife is very, very old. The enemies that it killed, they are too many to count. Nobody knows how it came to the first owner. Many times an owner gave more than fifty ponies and ten robes or blankets to possess it. It has great power. It has always brought protection to the owner. All the owners but Black Looks, they have gone to the Sand-Hills."

The old warrior stopped and was silent for a long time. It was as if he were again seeing each of the owners of the knife.

Finally, One Spot continued. "Now I will tell you their names." His eyes looked far away as he recalled the names: "First owner, Kills Many Enemies; next owner, Calf Coat; third owner, White Quill; fourth owner, Cross Bow; fifth owner, Long Horn; last owner before Black Looks, Lazy Young Man. That is all I have to say." He closed his eyes. His visit to the scenes of long-ago seemed to have exhausted his strength.

Morning Eagle reached over and pressed the old warrior's hand to show his gratitude.

The group returned to the lodge of Black Looks, where he continued the story.

"Now," said Black Looks, "I will tell my white brother the terrible way that Lazy Young Man gave me the Bear-Medicine-Knife:

"Lazy Young Man, he took his drum and sang many songs. He taught me those songs. They were songs of the Bear-Knife. Then he took the knife from the sheath and danced on the prairie. Then Lazy Young Man, he painted me like a Bear and said to me, 'Now you are a Bear. I am going to throw the knife at you. Grab the knife just like a Bear would.'

"So, I danced like a Bear, and when Lazy Young Man threw the knife at my breast, I caught it with both hands and was not cut. 'Now,' I thought, 'the Bear-Knife is mine.' But my friend said, 'No.'

"Lazy Young Man, he grabbed me and threw me into a bunch of rose and bullberry bushes. Those bushes have long thorns, and I felt scratched and cut all over my body. Then my friend, he said to me, 'You are brave, you must dance again like a Bear.' So I jumped out of the bullberry bushes. After I danced, my friend, he came and struck my back two heavy blows with the flat blade of the knife.

"Then my friend told me, 'When you want meat, when you want protection, the Medicine of the Bear-Knife will bring you those things. The Medicine of the Bear-Knife is very strong. It is so strong that all people are afraid of it—Take It.'

"Now you know the true story of the Bear-Medicine-Knife. That is all I have to say," said Black Looks, the Blood who lived many sleeps to the north of the reservation at Cut Bank.

Slowly Black Looks unwrapped the Medicine-Bundle of the Bear-Knife.

Before Morning Eagle lay a huge knife, the blade of which was twelve inches long. The handle was made from the lower jaw bone of a grizzly bear with the two long teeth serving as guards at the lower end of the handle. The sheath was made from Buffalo hide, and attached to it were ornaments of power.

»»→ • ←«««

Sullivan was gently prodding him, poking him awake. Yawning, Morning Eagle asked, "Are we there yet?"

"No sir. Supper time."

"Ah, thank you Sullivan." The sky had now transformed itself into a deep, dark blanket, wrapping itself around the landscape and the Pullman. "Gee, it must be later than I thought."

"Yes sir. Just want you to know the supper car is almost closed," Sullivan explained gently. "You've been sleeping a long time, sir. Must be good dreams, huh," he chuckled.

"Thank you, Sullivan. Yes, I've been thinking of my Pikuni friends and my Otter Medicine Tipi," Morning Eagle explained.

"Otter … medicine … tipi," the tall man slowly pronounced the words as if trying to understand their significance.

"If you have time, I'll tell you about it over dinner, okay?" grinned Morning Eagle. "My trip to the Pikunis this summer requires me to uncover a secret."

"What's that, sir?"

"Well, a young Pikuni man is serving time at Leavenworth prison for a crime he did not commit, I think. There were many who testified against him at his trial, saying he raped a Blackfeet girl. But they were coerced, I suspect. Their fear has made them first lie, then remain silent...afraid to talk about what actually happened."

Morning Eagle paused as he entered the dining room car. The place was empty. Sullivan had already arranged a place setting for Morning Eagle at his favorite table.

"Seems there may have been something of a conspiracy," remarked the New Englander.

"How do you mean, sir?" asked Sullivan.

"It's a shame, but the government interpreter at the trial, who says he saw the young Indian man assault the girl, may not have told the truth. What is worse, his given Indian name is Black Looks."

Sullivan instantly froze, his face revealing nothing of what he might be thinking.

Sensing something wrong, Morning Eagle immediately shook his head.

"No, Sullivan, what is wrong with the man is not his skin color or the name. Black Looks is the name of a revered Blood warrior up in Canada. This warrior possesses very powerful Medicine. He owns the Bear-Medicine-Knife, which makes him very respected. But the young interpreter at the trial, Victor Black Looks, seems to have no powerful Medicine like his Blood name-sake. I fear he has a dishonest heart and has resorted to trickery."

The porter relaxed but said nothing.

"But how to prove the young man was untruthful," continued Morning Eagle. "That's the problem, my good man."

"Sir, what about the otter...tipi?"

"Well, Sullivan, that may be the key, for that is the powerful Medicine that my Pikuni friends gave to me when they made me one of them." Morning Eagle took a slow sip of water and set the glass down gently as Sullivan came forward with a plate of roast beef, mashed potatoes and green beans.

"My Otter Medicine Tipi may just help me find the truth," the whiteman nodded to stalwart Mr. Sullivan.

Heart Butte (background), (left) Morning Eagle's Otter Medicine Tipi, (right) Bear Head's Tipi.

# XV

# A Visit to
# Morning Eagle's Lodge

The squeaking brakes of the iron horse spooked the half-dozen crows beside the rail line running through Cut Bank. The Pullman slowly glided by the small wooden station platform, dark-skinned faces peering at the windows, a few strange, some painted and bedecked in feathered finery. Perhaps the few white "tourists" might make use of the train's brief stop to purchase "authentic Indian souvenirs" and trinkets. Such commodities were hawked here and down at East Glacier Lodge by those in the shadows of a disappearing culture, clinging to survive on a less than meager existence.

Wearing a blue flannel shirt, buckskin leggings and moccasins, Morning Eagle alighted from the Pullman to the accompaniment of the chuff-chuffing, spasmodic gasps and groans and metallic clank-stomp of the tethered iron horse. The coal-black beast was impatiently hissing and spewing forth great clouds of steam from beneath its rounded iron "hooves." In tow was a large carrying case for his typewriter, a leather parfleche and two bulging, frayed tan suitcases, each wrapped with a leather belt.

He had told Grorud to stay in Helena. He, Morning Eagle, would attempt to talk to the girl and her mother and the others who had been present at Peter Stabs-By-Mistake's trial.

"Aaee, pretty fat saddle bags you got there," joked the stout Indian as he reached for the suitcases. The Indian's braided, still mostly black hair belied his seventy-five years. The lines and crows' feet told of much wisdom acquired through a long, hard existence.

"Curly Bear! It's good to see your face again!" exclaimed Morning Eagle as he patted the shoulder of his adopted father. "And your Woodrow Wilson button!" he added with a chuckle. "I always knew you were a good

Democrat." They all knew the Elder wore the president's campaign button out of gratitude for the unconditional pardon Wilson had given to Curly Bear's friend, Sspopii—Turtle—in 1914. The revered Blood Elder had spent thirty-four years in confinement, wrongfully accused of murdering a whiteman.

"After every snow, it's always good to see your face, Aapinakoi Píítaa. But your saddle bags always weigh as heavy as the iron horse," reminded Curly Bear. The others laughed.

"Thomas, it's good to see your face. Is the Otter Medicine Tipi ready?"

"Yes, Aapinakoi Píítaa. But you won't have a place to sleep with all these whitemen comforts you brought." They all smiled.

Morning Eagle's old friend Bear Head, a burly Elder, was there with Wolf Plume, a short, wide-faced, full-blood Piegan who had seen more than sixty winters.

As the men greeted Morning Eagle, sometimes they spoke by sign, but more often in their Pikuni tongue, which their friend had come to understand rather well over the years.

The five men began the trek to Stabs-By-Mistake's lodge.

"Your friend Grorud came," said Curly Bear. "Didn't seem to speak to Nellie Running Crane's heart. Oliver's son was there." There was a long pause before Curly Bear added, "Maybe he translates into whiteman words and does not tell what the Pikuni tongue says." Morning Eagle nodded.

Wolf Plume spoke, "Everyone I talk to thinks Red-Boy never dishonored Annie Running Crane."

"Aapinakoi Píítaa, do you have a plan?" asked Bear Head. "You need powerful Medicine," he offered in broken English, walking slightly behind the others.

As the men reached the side of a grassy knoll following the descending road, Morning Eagle recognized the designs on his Otter Medicine Tipi. It stood next to Bear Head's tipi. Further along, tucked into a slight draw next to Cut Bank Creek, stood the lodge of Stabs-By-Mistake.

Continuing to walk, Curly Bear added, "Bear Head speaks with a straight tongue, Aapinakoi Píítaa. It's like the story of the wolf and the coyote," he grinned, glancing at the others. The New Englander grinned too.

Stopping to stretch, Morning Eagle turned to the others and said, "Curly Bear, tell us about the wolf and the coyote."

With a sly smile, Chief Curly Bear sat on the ground, the others joined him and he began his story.

"A Wolf sees a Coyote following a she-Badger. The Wolf believes that there is 'somethin' up', so he follows them way up a mountain. The Wolf slyly creeps up near the Badger, who he sees lying on her back.

"The Wolf watches and soon the Coyote comes along and gets on top of the Badger. After watchin' them for quite a while, the wolf sees the Badger very slowly scratch the dirt with the nail of one little finger and the Wolf sees the Coyote's tail, which is standing up straight, move slowly to and fro. This is the end of my story."

Morning Eagle was perplexed.

"I don't get it. I'm sorry."

The others were laughing while Curly Bear was holding his sides.

"My son, Red-Boy, he called Annie his tough little badger," Thomas broke in, a wistful smile on his face.

"There was no coyote lyin' on top of the badger at Red-Boy's trial, Aapinakoi Píítaa," laughed Bear Head. Thomas Stabs-By-Mistake was nodding his agreement.

"No one saw Red-Boy on top of Annie ever," explained Chief Curly Bear, getting up. The group continued their slow trek to Morning Eagle's lodge.

"I have talked with James Vielle. He was Peter's good friend and was with him and Annie," explained Thomas.

"Can I talk with him?"

"More than that, Aapinakoi Píítaa. Vielle has also talked with Oliver Sanders. He tells me that Oliver speaks to him with a straight tongue."

"Very good," replied Morning Eagle. "When can I talk to Oliver?"

"They are coming up to your lodge in two sleeps," Thomas told him.

"Very good! Now what about the others?"

"I have spoken to Annie's father, Ted Running Crane," replied Curly Bear. "Wolf Plume and I spoke with him. You must go and speak with him soon. He will talk to you."

"What about Annie and her friends?"

"You must speak with Running Crane first," signed Wolf Plume. The others offered no further explanation.

Slowly, the group made its way to the Otter Medicine Tipi of Morning Eagle and were greeted by Thomas's sits-beside-him-woman, Steals-In-The-Daytime-Woman.

That evening, after a feast of sarvis berries, back fat, pemmican and coffee, the men sat around the lodge-fire inside Morning Eagle's lodge and had many smokes of kinnikinnick from Chief Curly Bear's pipe.

The next morning brought more families and friends for greetings to the Otter Medicine Tipi. The wait for Oliver Sanders and James Vielle had begun.

When sundown had come and was greeted by a second sunrise, then mid-day, Morning Eagle grew concerned, expressing worry to Stabs-By-Mistake and Curly Bear that Oliver and James might not show. Looking at Thomas, Curly Bear smiled.

"Aapinakoi Piítaa," Thomas began, "Curly Bear has told you many times that here you are on Blackfeet time." Morning Eagle smiled and shook his head, the men chuckled.

"But you said two sleeps," insisted Morning Eagle.

"Well maybe Vielle had a really long first sleep," Curly Bear teased. Thomas and the old chief both put a hand on their friend's shoulder. Curly Bear said, "It's always James, the younger one, who sleeps the longer sleep after the Sun comes up." Curly Bear winked at Thomas. "That's why we call him Drags-Behind, aaeee." They all smiled. Morning Eagle understood.

Just before sundown, two horsemen rode up over the rise overlooking Morning Eagle's lodge. The others were preparing to play the stick game next to Bear Head's lodge, so the two riders approached almost unnoticed.

"Aaee...Good to see ya', Oliver," greeted Stabs-By-Mistake. The heavy-set Elder Piegan nodded. "And you too Vielle," added Thomas. The gaunt, twenty-eight-year-old horseman grinned when he saw the game that was about to begin. "Yer just in time to join in." Thomas gestured to the group of men seated next to Bear Head's lodge.

The New Englander was more eager to "get down to business," anxious to know more about what the men would say. Thomas, however, seemed to be in no hurry. James went to join the game.

Then, he remembered the first time he witnessed the Stick Game, the wandering melody and timbre of the Gambler's Song. Perhaps, like the unhurried paths of the Montana creeks and rivers, it was just the Pikuni way.

"Good," replied Oliver. "The long ride with my young pardner has got us in the mood for some fancy gamblin.'"

The men laughed as Oliver and James Vielle seated themselves opposite Curly Bear and the others. Morning Eagle sat next to Wolf Plume and Bear Head. Curly Bear's outstretched fists hid the two bones.

Morning Eagle was chosen to hide the bones in Curly Bear's hands. While his teammates sang and beat the lodgepole with short clubs, Curly Bear, mouth set tight, face solemn, swayed to the singing of the women and the thump of the drums. The elder chief moved his hands to and fro, now in front, now behind his back, passing the bones from hand to hand. When he stopped, the guessing began.

At last, Curly Bear's side had nine of the ten willow sticks needed to win.

The singing stopped, the beating paused. Curly Bear held out his weathered hands, fists clenched tightly. Oliver was to guess for the opposing side. There was discussion and several arguments punctuated with short "unh, unhs." Then, a consensus reached, Oliver pointed to Curly Bear's left palm. Curly Bear opened it slowly, turned it upright and grinned. There, in his strong calloused palm, was the losing bone.

Loud, explosive protests came from Oliver's line as Curly Bear and the others rolled back, shouting and kicking with excitement at having won. This evening the stakes could be higher than a few horses, robes and guns.

"Curly Bear, what are the stakes in your fancy gamblin' game?" asked Oliver.

"The stakes are high, Sanders!" Curly Bear paused, then looked solemnly over at Wolf Plume and Bear Head. He quickly winked at Thomas. "Oliver, you and James Vielle must meet tomorrow morning in the Otter Medicine Tipi and speak with straight tongues to Aapinakoi Píítaa."

Oliver and James feigned reluctance, then grinned and looked over at Morning Eagle. Everyone laughed and nodded. Morning Eagle nodded back at the two men as they clasped hands with Curly Bear.

Once again, everything happened here in its own way, in its own time.

»»→ • ←«« 

The revered Blood Chief Red Crow joined the men for a special morning meal of Buffalo boss ribs at Stabs-By-Mistake's lodge. Red Crow had brought the gift of boss ribs down from Canada, where small herds of Buffalo still survived. After finishing their feast and paying their respects to Red Crow, Oliver Sanders and James Vielle prepared to meet with Morning Eagle. A stiff wind had turned the cloudy morning sky into a clear, blue blanket.

Thomas's pipe was passed around four times. Morning Eagle then returned to his Otter Medicine Tipi. Reclining on his willow-rest, Morning Eagle rubbed his stomach, the anxiety over his role as finder of truth creating an almost palpable knot that burrowed like a prairie dog into his gut.

"Thump, thump, thump." Morning Eagle counted the blows on the side of his lodge, hearing Oliver call out, "We have brought kinnikinnick from Stabs-By-Mistake."

"Come in." James bent low, entered and Oliver followed. The two men sat in front of the slowly burning lodge-fire and Oliver removed kinnikinnick from the leather pouch he had brought along.

Morning Eagle's Medicine pipe was passed four times, then laid aside. He leaned back against his willow-rest and took a deep calming breath. Off to the side was perched his metal contraption, the Royal typewriter.

"I know it is difficult for you to come and talk straight about what happened more than four winters ago, Oliver. I know your son, Victor, might be angry with you for coming here."

Oliver Red-Bird-Tail Sanders fixed a long steady eye on Morning Eagle.

"I have now seen sixty-six winters, I think, and I am an old man, Aapinakoi Píítaa. I feel my strength getting weaker with each snow." He poked a stick into the embers of the lodge-fire. "Soon, I will be taking the trail of those who have gone before." He set the stick aside and a long minute passed before he spoke again. "But before I do, I must make things speak the truth."

"For many snows, I have worked with the whiteman's Indian Bureau as a translator. My brother Richard has done the same. But Richard and I follow different paths. Victor, my son, he is closer to his uncle. I had hoped that Victor would follow in my steps." As he shook his head, his long braids swayed and rolled over his protruding stomach. "Now, I know my son has done a great wrong." He shook his head again, remaining silent.

"Unh!" he finally uttered with a short, explosive burst. "My son, he tells me that he wants to sit on the Tribal Council. He says that when he sits on the council he will see that Peter is released." He resumed stabbing at the white-hot embers. "I see through my son's actions, not his words. I tell him that I do not care to look twice at a two-faced man." The old man scowled, continued nodding and poking with the stick but said no more.

"Red-Bird-Tail knows and I know that Red-Boy is honorable with women," said James Vielle. "We know this because when Marilyn Deer Child got with child, Red-Boy was good to her. Stayed with her and provided for her. I helped out."

"Yes," broke in Oliver. "What James says is true." Morning Eagle leaned forward. "Deer Child works in the White Father's city. She writes to me and tells me about Washington, D.C."

"When did you last see your daughter, Oliver?" questioned Morning Eagle.

"Not for many winters. Not since the beginning of the Great War when Peter left." The old man glanced down. "That's when Deer Child's baby died.

But Thomas Stabs-By-Mistake and me, we have always been at peace." A long silence followed. The only sound was the warm chinook wind rustling the canvas lodge.

"Now, I will tell you something about the whiteman's trial of Red-Boy at Great Falls."

"You were there in September of 1921, acting as an interpreter, yes?" asked Morning Eagle.

"Yes. Interpreter. But the judge, he asked Richard to interpret for Nellie, Louise Red Fox, Maggie Wolf Plume and Mary Horn. They were all witnesses against Red-Boy." Oliver leaned intently towards Morning Eagle.

"Was your son, Victor, there too?"

"Yes."

"What did Victor do?" asked Morning Eagle.

Oliver Sanders lowered his head and stared hard at the flickering embers. He began rocking back and forth in intense contemplation. Raising his head, the beleaguered father now looked fully at Morning Eagle.

"Yes. Victor, he spoke to these witnesses," Oliver began slowly. "The young girls, they asked him many questions. I fear he told them what to say. I told none of them what to say. When they were each called to the witness stand, my brother Richard interpreted for the judge and the men of the jury. I was not chosen to interpret, so I did not stay when they spoke to the jury. But later, I came to see Red-Boy. He told me the witnesses had looked at Victor and lied. He said Victor had sat where his eyes could meet the girls when they spoke. The next day, I came back to the courtroom and I too noticed the girls. They were very nervous and frightened and looked often at Victor. They spoke very low when asked questions. They had never been in the whiteman's court before."

The old Indian paused, resting his chin on his hand. "I am very certain that each of these girls had been told what they should say. Their talk was not natural. Morning Eagle, that is all I have to say." Oliver Red-Bird-Tail lowered his head, again, and continued rocking back and forth, fixing a distant gaze at the embers.

"Thank you, Oliver. I have always known you to be a decent and honest man." Pausing thoughtfully, Morning Eagle turned towards James Vielle. "Were you at Red-Boy's trial?"

"No, Aapinakoi Píítaa. I was not told about the trial, ever." The lanky Indian stood up to fetch another poking stick from the corner near the fire logs. "The problem is with the girls. They must speak without fear or they will not speak with a straight tongue to you. Or maybe, if they speak with a straight tongue now, they will be frightened later on and change what they say."

"How do you mean?"

James glanced over at Oliver, who nodded his assent for the young man to continue. "Because Victor, he has frightened the girls. He still talks to them. Sees them at the agency offices. Even follows them sometimes."

"Were you with Red-Boy when Victor and the Indian police found him with Annie?"

"Yes."

Morning Eagle slowly nodded.

"Before you tell me what you saw, I must do something." The whiteman arose from his willow cushion and put paper into the black machine. The two Indians watched. Staccato sounds filled the lodge as the New Englander poked away at the machine-of-many-fingers. Then, the clicking stopped.

James Vielle stood and bent over the typewriter. "Makes whiteman's writing in black painting." He smiled back at Oliver, who nodded. "The younger ones have seen these work at the boarding school. Many of the Elders have not. Will it type Pikuni words?"

"The machine only types the English letters that I push here," explained Morning Eagle. He turned the platen. Out of the machine rolled an "Affidavit" that Morning Eagle had typed for Oliver Sanders to sign. He handed the piece of paper to Oliver, then put a fat cottonwood log atop the coals of the lodge-fire. Seating himself again on his willow-rest, he continued. "Now, James, tell me what you saw with Red-Boy on that day back in 1921."

The young Indian looked into the now-flaming lodge-fire and thought for a moment.

"In the late afternoon, Red-Boy and me were ridin' a short distance from Annie. Then Red-Boy got off his horse and walked to where Annie was standin'. When he got to her, they walked a few steps away from where I was. I saw them talkin' there together. I saw them jus talkin' and holdin' hands. There was no loud screams or loud talk or any noise or nothin'. He was never on top of Annie." The lanky, young Indian paused, thoughtfully stoking the lodge-fire. He then looked directly at Morning Eagle.

"After Red-Boy and Annie was together for a few minutes, Red-Boy, he came back to where I was and got back on his horse. We both rode to our friend's place. It's 'bout half-a-mile away from where we seen Annie. When we left Annie, she was walkin' back towards her place. Aapinakoi Piitaa, that is all I saw and heard. I never seen Red-Boy hit or harm Annie or get on top of her."

"Thank you, James. You, too, speak with a straight tongue. Now I want you to look and listen for a minute." Morning Eagle returned to the Royal typewriter. Again, a staccato of clickety-clacks rattled from the machine-of-many-fingers. When Morning Eagle was finished, he laid another typed "Affidavit" in front of James Vielle and resumed his seat in front of the lodge-fire.

"Oliver, if you would like to read what I have typed to James and to yourself and if you agree with what I have typed on the machine, I will ask you and James to sign the statements. I will witness them." Oliver and James both nodded and Oliver read aloud while Morning Eagle stoked the fire.

After they signed, Oliver carefully handed the papers back to Morning Eagle. The New Englander explained that he would forward the papers to attorney Grorud in Helena, the one who had been up to the reservation the previous summer.

"Now, I must go and talk to Ted Running Crane and the girls," explained Morning Eagle.

Without warning, Oliver held up a hand. With a stern look, the interpreter firmly uttered, "Don't. That would be unwise."

A shocked look erased whatever momentary pleasure Morning Eagle had experienced in obtaining his first two affidavits.

"But Thomas and the others told me that it would be wise to talk straight with Running Crane."

"I have seen him before coming up here," replied Oliver.

"He is not at Cut Bank?"

"No. That is what made my journey longer." The old interpreter knew that Morning Eagle was not understanding. "The words spoken between Thomas and Running Crane are friendly. But not so between Thomas and Nellie. Nellie, she knew what happened between Red-Boy and my daughter Marilyn Deer Child. She heard lies about how Red-Boy behaved so she disliked Red-Boy. But more than that, she had resolved that her daughter should not marry. She was afraid that having children would kill Annie."

Red-Boy's friend, James Vielle, sat with eyes fixed on Oliver. The government interpreter spoke softly now.

Oliver stabbed at the embers with Vielle's poking stick. "But I spoke with Running Crane and Nellie. They understand my heart. They know I am here with you, Aapinakoi Píítaa."

Finally laying the stick down, Oliver Red-Bird-Tail said gently, "There is no need for you to go see them. They will come here and bring their family."

Morning Eagle's mouth dropped open. A broad smile wrapped around his face as he held out both hands to Red-Bird-Tail.

"You have convinced them to come up to the Sun Dance ceremony here at Cut Bank later this summer, yes?"

The interpreter grinned and nodded. "Yes, Aapinakoi Píítaa. And I say this to you now. You are much respected here. You have many friends. Ted Running Crane and the others know that your Otter Medicine Tipi is strong Medicine. I told them that you have visited the Great White Father's lodge often and that you have powerful Medicine. I have told them all of these things and they have agreed to come here for the celebration."

Reaching for his Medicine Pipe, Morning Eagle filled it again. The three men passed the pipe. Later, Morning Eagle prepared coffee over the lodge-fire.

Lodge-fire embers burned low and Morning Eagle, alone now, settled down on his willow cot. He wondered, what must Oliver have told Running Crane? What if the young women, or Nellie, were skeptical of the power of his tipi? Shadowy images traveled around in circles as the smoke from the lodge-fire drifted lazily up through the smoke-hole, past the ear poles at the top of his Otter Medicine Tipi.

Then other thoughts that were furthest back drifted in the smoke. He dreamt of his Tobique friend, Bow Maker. He dreamt of the nearness he felt to the old Blood Warrior Black Looks and his ancestors when his hands had touched the blade of the powerful Bear-Medicine-Knife.

»»→ • ←«««

Here, in the summer of 1925, small crop farmers like Ted Running Crane could not afford to spend the traditional weeks, even months, away from tending their crops. The shorter, more numerous Sun Dance ceremonies in-stituted by Superintendent Campbell worked for men like Running Crane, al-though Campbell's constant reference to the Sun Dances as "heathen rituals" was just one more reason to dislike the man and the Bureau.

This summer was unusual. Running Crane and his family, their relations and friends trekked some twenty-five miles northeast by horse and wagon from Willow Creek to Cut Bank to attend the ceremony there, instead of the one held much closer at Browning. James Vielle had come back to tend the vegetable garden and crops while Ted and his family were gone to Cut Bank.

Chief Running Crane was a proud man, still angry at the way his daugh-ter Emma had been stolen from her family. He knew how humiliated and powerless his son-in-law, Nelson Bull Child, had felt at the hands of the Indian police and Bureau officials. Running Crane had thought the Bureau officials were his friends. They seemed to have raised the tomahawk against his family for no reason. It was more than a dozen sleeps after James Vielle and Oliver arrived before James Drags-Behind bid his goodbyes and rode off toward Willow Creek. Three weeks to the day later, Running Crane's family made their way into Cut Bank.

The arrival of the little group from Willow Creek marked the beginning of the Sun Dance ceremony, which had been postponed to await the arrival of Running Crane.

This particular year, Thomas's sits-beside-him-woman was chosen to serve as Medicine Woman in the Sun Dance. Only a virtuous woman could be chosen to play this leading role. By tradition, an older woman who had remained strong in times of crisis would be chosen. Through the months of Cold Maker's wrath, Steals-In-The-Daytime-Woman had made a vow of fasting at the Sun Dance.

All of the Piegans from the surrounding area, as well as Blood relatives and Siksika (Northern Blackfeet) relations and friends from across the border in southern Alberta, had assembled in the ceremonial lodge circle. On each of four days the Medicine Woman, Steals-In-The-Daytime-Woman, weakened from days of purification fasting, led a travois carrying the Sun Dance bundle around the Cut Bank lodge circle. On the fourth day, the Medicine Woman's procession arrived at the site selected by the tribe to raise the Medicine Lodge. Thomas and a male instructor, wise in the ritual, purified themselves on each day in a sweat lodge made by the Black Horse Society from one-hundred willows.

The fifth day ushered in the complicated ritual of transferring the valuable natoas bundle to Thomas's wife in the Medicine Woman's own lodge. The bundle, containing sacred garments and accessories to be worn by the Medicine Woman, was transferred from Curly Bear's sits-beside-him-woman. She had acted as Medicine Woman the previous year.

In the late afternoon of the fifth day, when the intricate natoas bundle transfer was completed, the Medicine Woman's procession wound its way out from the Medicine Woman's lodge around and back through the unfinished Medicine Lodge. Young girls and women in poor health, or ones wishing to receive the blessings of the sacred Medicine Woman, came forward.

Each year, the Sun-Lodge consisted of a large center pole cut from a tall cottonwood, forked near the top. Fastened to the center pole were presents of moccasins, blankets and old clothing, gifts to the Sun and Moon. This year, nine cottonwood posts were connected by stringers laid in the forks, one for each band of the tribe which had been responsible for erecting the lodge.

Shortly before sunset, the ceremony climaxed with the raising of the Sun-Medicine Lodge. First, they raised the center pole. The center pole had to be raised completely without mishap, or the Medicine Woman would be deemed less virtuous than she was proclaimed to be—a bad omen. Then, the rafters were bound together with hide thongs and, finally, the sides of the lodge were covered with green cottonwood boughs.

This year, Steals-In-The-Daytime-Woman was proclaimed a completely virtuous woman.

Notably present was Victor Black Looks, watching and waiting to see if this year there would be a piercing. The "piercing" was now conducted surreptitiously by young men who vowed to give sacrifice for a life spared in the Sun Dance of their tribe.

This tradition was particularly loathsome to Victor, who understood cunning but not bravery, greed but not gratitude. Victor had seen and reported several in the past, for which Campbell had rewarded him.

This year, none of the young men sent Victor Black Looks racing back to the sub-agency with stories to tell.

»»—→ • ←—«««

Throughout the Sun Dance ceremony, the Otter Medicine Tipi of Morning Eagle became the special gathering place for Oliver Red-Bird-Tail, Ted Running Crane and others. Emma Bull Child was there with her husband and three children. Annie's friends, Louise Red Fox, Maggie Wolf Plume and Mary Horn had also come with their families.

After the Medicine Pipe was passed four times, Morning Eagle approached Chief Running Crane with a request to speak with Nellie. The two entered the Otter Medicine Tipi one evening as other Pikuni families sang and danced in the waning days of the celebration. Oliver Sanders stood quietly by the lodge flap.

To Morning Eagle, Ted Running Crane looked like the Indian on the US minted nickel. He watched and listened but said little. He seated himself opposite Morning Eagle and next to his wife Nellie, whose eyes were lowered. Oliver Sanders, the interpreter, slowly entered and sat next to the host.

"My daughter and I cannot speak with you as one voice on the matter of Peter Stabs-By-Mistake," stated Nellie through the interpreter. "My daughter and I have had differences in the past. Sometimes, she has chosen to go different paths than I have instructed for her. But I love my daughter. I worry that if she does not stay close to her family, her health will leave her."

"I understand," replied Morning Eagle. "You are a virtuous and good woman, Nellie Running Crane, and you speak with a straight tongue. Please tell me what is in your heart." He nodded to Oliver to resume translating.

"Aapinakoi Píítaa, we trust you as a friend and as one of our people. Your Otter Medicine Tipi has great power. We believe you have great power and can help us. We believe that you talk with a straight tongue to the white Indian Bureau and you tell them of our suffering, of our hunger and sickness." Then she stopped. She lowered her eyes again and said nothing. Everyone waited.

"Now I will tell you something about my daughter Annie and Peter Stabs-By-Mistake." The woman stopped again and looked over at her husband, then looked down again. This was obviously not a task she had chosen, but one she felt compelled to finish.

"The day it happened, it was several hours before the sun went down. We were all stayin' with my husband's relatives at our old home at Heart Butte for a time. Mary Horn came to our place and told me that Peter Red-Boy was with Annie and that they was holdin' hands. I did not want my daughter seein' Red-Boy. I got very angry and ran down the road towards the school house. After I went a short distance, I saw my daughter alone, walking toward home. I was very angry and made Annie go with me to the Heart Butte sub-agency. When I got to the sub-agency, I saw Victor Sanders and Peter White Man. I asked these men to stop Peter from meetin' and seein' my daughter. Victor Sanders, he say to me that he would go after Peter Stabs-By-Mistake." Nellie stopped, again, as if searching for something inside of herself. No one spoke.

"Now I will tell you this. At that time, I did not believe any whiteman's crime of rape had been committed on Annie. I did not go to the sub-agency to cause any whiteman's crime to be brought against Peter Stabs-By-Mistake. I only went to get their help to see if they could stop Peter from meetin' and seein' my daughter." She paused again. "I know about Peter Red-Boy and Marilyn Deer Child. I was worried when Red-Boy started seein' Annie. My daughter, she has been sick and I don't know if childbirth would be good for her. But I was not angry because he committed rape on Annie. I was angry because they told me that Red-Boy and Annie was holdin' hands." Nellie raised her eyes, meeting those of Morning Eagle.

"I understand," he said.

"You see, it is our custom. No lover of an Indian girl can touch her hands without the parents giving their approval." She looked over at her husband who nodded his assent. "I had great anger when I knew my daughter was holdin' hands with Peter Red-Boy. I had not given my approval. I was afraid for Annie and I wanted Red-Boy punished." Nellie again grew silent for a long moment. Morning Eagle noticed her lips moving in soft, deliberate whispers.

"Now I will say this to you, Morning Eagle. His crime of holdin' hands against our ancient custom cannot mean that he must go away forever. This is all I have to say."

"You are a good and virtuous woman, Nellie Running Crane. The powerful Otter Medicine of my tipi will protect you. I say to you now that when I leave this place after every visit and go back to my home at the place-where-the-sun-first-rises, I tell those in power how strong and honest you are and how worthy the Pikuni people are of being called American citizens and being treated as the equal of all American citizens."

The New Englander paused, glancing over at his metallic gadget perched on his two suitcases. "You must help me now and bring your daughter and her friends to speak with me. But first, I must go to the machine-of-many-fingers and make whiteman's writing in black paint. I will show you the paper when it is finished, when you return."

Curious about how the machine worked, Nellie stared at the typewriter, then turned to accept a nod from her husband, who beckoned her to summon the others. Slowly she retreated from the lodge, watching and listening to the clickety-clack of the metal contraption. Ted Running Crane stared with dignified intensity at Morning Eagle's fingers as they clipped along the tops of the keys.

Softly, silently, Nellie went to the lodge of Spotted Eagle and summoned her daughters, Annie and Emma Bull Child, and their friends, Louise Red Fox, Maggie Wolf Plume and Mary Horn, to come quickly to see the clickety-clack machine with metal fingers which painted the whiteman's language in black letters.

For the five young women, Morning Eagle represented a kind of curious enigma, a whiteman who had been brought in and made one of them and given powerful, traditional Medicine. For the Pikunis, who were distrustful of outsiders, especially whites, the giving ceremony of transferring the Otter Medicine Tipi represented a singular act of trust by the Elders. The young women wondered who this man could be to receive such honor.

Morning Eagle's lodge was outlined against sunset over the Backbone-of-the-World—the central core of its halo a glowing red, bleeding into scarlet purple fissures and melting into the shallow gray of nightfall. The lodge fire gave the Otter Medicine Tipi an eerie translucence, all in all, an impressive sight to the young women. Approaching closer, they heard the letter cipher. At first, mistaking this for the sound of coup sticks or snake rattles, they hesitated, not daring to enter a private Sun Dance ceremony still taking place.

Nellie quietly explained it was a machine-of-many-fingers which painted letters of black paint on white paper. Having been to boarding school, the girls understood. Annie, Emma and their friends hesitated, taking in the lodge lines and decorations signifying the power and sanctity of the lodge they were about to enter.

Nellie struck several blows at the lodge door announcing their presence. Running Crane carefully opened the flap and beckoned them to enter.

Glancing up from his typewriter, Morning Eagle beheld Annie, a very thin, young Indian woman with strength and determination in her eyes. Her braids hung down past her thin chest. With her head again lowered, she seated herself opposite her mother.

Beside Annie sat Emma Bull Child. Emma's cheeks were less sallow and her fuller figure bore witness that she was healthier than her sister.

The other young women slipped awkwardly past the lodge-flap door as Running Crane returned to his place beside Nellie. The girls glanced around furtively, noticed Oliver Sanders sitting next to Morning Eagle, then stood mute, eyes lowered.

Annie and her mother sat cross-legged, their eyes equally determined, fixed upon one another as if transfixed by a terrible dread. Not a sound was uttered.

Several blows broke the silence. Morning Eagle beckoned for the lodge-flap to be opened. Wolf Plume nearly bumped into his granddaughter, Maggie Wolf Plume, as he entered the now rather crowded lodge.

"Aapinakoi Píítaa, you are holding council in the powerful Medicine Tipi," announced the elder in his Pikuni tongue. "I see my granddaughter and her friends found a place to hide from the Medicine Lodge feast." Wolf Plume's gentle introduction seemed to break the ice.

"Thank you for coming, Wolf Plume," remarked Morning Eagle. "I wanted to speak with your granddaughter, Annie Running Crane, and her friends about Red-Boy's trial." Wolf Plume nodded his assent.

Emma Bull Child suddenly spoke, her now familiar fierce eyes flashing. "It was also a trial for me! They came, those men, and took me away to boarding school before Red-Boy's trial!"

Before he spoke, Morning Eagle wondered how Ted Running Crane managed in a home seemingly filled with fierce-willed women.

"Emma, when you were taken away to boarding school, how many winters had you seen?" queried Morning Eagle.

Emma looked at her father.

"Eighteen, no, nineteen winters by our count," remarked Ted Running Crane in a low, deliberate voice. Nellie nodded in agreement.

"And you were not at the trial, Emma?"

"No."

Morning Eagle looked long at Annie Running Crane, her frail frame straight and determined, her bony knees protruding as she sat cross-legged by the lodge fire. "Annie, how many winters had you seen when you were at Red-Boy's trial?"

"By our count, at least twenty... maybe twenty-one winters," interjected Running Crane. "Nellie and I may have lost a year for Annie when she was younger with the illness." Annie nodded her agreement.

"I am told that in the whiteman's court it was said that Annie was fourteen years old," said Morning Eagle to the entire group.

"No!" replied Annie firmly. Then silence.

"What happened?" asked Morning Eagle.

"Black Looks, he told my mother to say fourteen years in the whiteman's language." She stared at Oliver who glanced down at the fire. "He said the whiteman counts the years a different way than we count our time—our winters."

"My son did not speak to you with a straight tongue," said Oliver softly. "He hid the truth from you, Annie, and I am sorry," he offered. "I was not in the court when Nellie spoke of Annie's age." The interpreter looked searchingly, first at Annie, then at Nellie. Annie held his look, then nodded acceptance of his words.

"When I was with Red-Boy in the "leaves-come-out-moon" (May), he only touched my hand. And after this, he got on his horse and rode away. My mother, she was mad at me for being with Red-Boy." She paused, her spine sagged a little.

Then, again sitting straight, steeling herself. "We did so much together. He talked about his times in the war. He told me the good things that he wanted to do for our people. We went together to take blankets and food to our old, to the children."

Annie looked long at Nellie and her father with imploring, moist eyes, and in that same sad, passionate voice, continued.

"Father, Mother, it is true that I love Red-Boy and I fully wanted to marry him in the church. But I argued so much with you then about being with Red-Boy and you threatened me. That's why I never told you of the times we spent together."

"Annie," her mother started to say, silenced in mid-sentence by Running Crane's firm, outstretched hand.

"My daughter, say what is the truth to Aapinakoi Píítaa," Chief Running Crane quietly directed.

Glancing back at the three young women standing by the lodge door with the Elder Wolf Plume, Annie continued. "We left the school house at Heart Butte sub-agency 'bout four o'clock. Maggie Wolf Plume and Louise, they were walkin' way ahead and Mary and I were behind them. We walked awhile and saw Red-Boy and James Vielle riding toward us. Mary walked on, but I stood and waited for them. They stopped...Red-Boy got off his horse and came to me. James just sat on his horse and waited for Red-Boy." She paused briefly. "At Red-Boy's trial, I said that they were both ridin' on the same horse." She paused a long moment. "And that James Vielle could not be found anywhere."

"Why did you say that?" asked Morning Eagle, with a puzzled look.

"Victor told me to say that. I don't know why." Annie turned again to her friends and they nodded.

Suddenly, Morning Eagle understood Victor's clever ploy. He wondered if Uncle Richard might have helped conjure it up. How best to blunt the testimony of Red-Boy's best material witness—perhaps his only chance for an acquittal? Put them both on the same horse so that Vielle becomes an accessory to the crime of rape, whisking the perpetrator from the scene of the crime on his own horse.

Annie's voice, now soft and unsure, brought Morning Eagle back to the task at hand.

"Then, after Red-Boy's trial, Victor and I, we argued." The young woman's shoulders slumped, her head was trembling.

"What's wrong, Annie?" asked Morning Eagle. "You are safe with us here. Everyone, your parents, everyone knows this," he said gently.

As if with all her might, the young woman straightened and lifted her chin. Yet her voice trembled some. "He, Victor, told me if I told what really happened after the trial, that he would tell the Superintendent. The Superintendent would tell the judge that I lied at Red-Boy's trial. He told me I would be taken away for the whiteman's crime of . . ." she hesitated, looking over at Morning Eagle.

"Perjury? He told you he would report you for committing the crime of lying in court—perjury?"

"Yes."

"Annie, look at me now," gently commanded Morning Eagle. "I speak from my heart and I speak the truth. You have nothing to fear. Please tell me what happened." Morning Eagle waited. Running Crane nodded to his daughter.

"Red-Boy got off his horse and came over to me. When he came over to me, my friends who were with me ran on to where my parents were stayin'. Red-Boy and I stood there talkin'. James was just sittin' on his horse." Annie's eyes moistened and she looked first into the fire and then at her mother.

"I miss him still. I am not afraid to tell you. We met at places in Heart Butte. We went places together." Her back was straight and her voice sure. "Red-Boy never abused me. He was always worryin' 'bout me." She paused, wiping her eyes.

"Anyway, that day at Heart Butte, Red-Boy and I talked. I left for home and he went back to where James was holding his horse. Before I got home, my mother, she came runnin' at me. She was very angry. She took me to the sub-agency, where we met Victor Sanders and Peter White Man, the Indian policeman." Annie stopped and looked searchingly at her mother. Nellie lowered her eyes. No one spoke. Finally, Annie Running Crane continued.

"At the sub-agency, my mother told Victor Black Looks that she wanted him to stop Red-Boy from payin' attention to me. Black Looks, he said to me and my mother that Red-Boy had committed a very serious wrong and told me to say and tell that Red-Boy had committed rape upon me." She lowered her eyes and shook her head. The sadness had again swamped her courage and determination.

Morning Eagle's eyes narrowed as he asked, "Did Victor threaten you, Annie?"

Haltingly, softly, cautiously, the young woman continued. "He told me that if I do not say Red-Boy had committed rape on me that I will get into serious trouble. The judge, he will be very mad; I will be sent away from my family, sent away worse and longer than Emma had been. I feared that I would never see my family or that harm might also come to them if I do not do what Black Looks said." She looked again into Morning Eagle's eyes and, nodding, added: "His Uncle Richard, he is very powerful."

"Annie, will you tell me what happened when you were at the trial."

"I was very nervous. And I was very afraid. Victor Sanders was sittin' right there. I didn't want to tell the things Victor told me to say, but I didn't want to get into trouble with the judge and be taken away. I had never been in any whiteman's court before in my life. So I told to the judge what Victor had said. Then I felt very sad."

"What about after the trial, Annie? Did Victor talk to you then?"

"He brought horses to my father's house and he tried to court me." Annie's friends broke into nervous giggles. "Wanted me to marry him in the church. The whiteman's church. I had bad feelings about everything that had happened. I told him to go away."

Ted Running Crane, grinning slightly, exchanged nods with Oliver. Then Nellie spoke:

"Victor helped me when Annie was sick. Then Victor helped me because I was afraid Peter Red-Boy was abusin' my Annie. But then I heard from my daughter that Victor told her that if she changed what she said in court, that she would go to prison. That was not good to do."

Wolf Plume, coming closer to the lodge-fire, now had his say. "My granddaughter told me that Victor Black Looks talked to the girls and told them what to say in the whiteman's court. He threatened them that if they told the truth about what they saw with their eyes, they would go to prison. After, he told them they would go to prison if the judge learned that they spoke falsely in the whiteman's court."

Morning Eagle shook his head sadly. "These were all lies. The whiteman's court does not send witnesses to prison. Victor's father is an honorable man and has come forward here tonight in my Otter Medicine Tipi and has spoken with a straight tongue." He turned to the three girls still standing near the lodge-flap door. "You are all very brave to have come, and now I ask you girls to speak as your friend Annie has spoken, to speak with a straight tongue and tell me what you saw that day when Red-Boy was with Annie."

The girls hesitated. Finally, Maggie Wolf Plume stepped forward and stood by her grandfather, who nodded at her to speak.

"Yes, what Annie has said, she speaks the truth. We learned later that the two men on the horses were Red-Boy and James Vielle. When we first saw the man get off the horse and come close to where Annie was standin', we were far ahead and became frightened. We thought some stranger would do harm to our friend Annie and so we ran to Nellie's home." Maggie Wolf Plume looked over at Nellie Running Crane who nodded slowly at the young woman. "Mary Horn soon came and told Nellie that it was Red-Boy who was out by the road touchin' Annie. Nellie started to run in that direction.

We did not know that Peter Red-Boy and Annie, that they was together, that they was together many times."

"Did anyone tell you what to say at Red-Boy's trial?" asked Morning Eagle.

"Victor Black Looks, he told us to say that our friend Annie was fourteen of the whiteman's years. That is not true, but we were afraid. His Uncle Richard, he is very powerful. We had never been to a whiteman's court before and Victor, he told us that fourteen of the whiteman's years was the same as our counted winters."

Morning Eagle shook his head and gave Oliver a sad look. He could see the shame the man carried because of the deeds of his son.

Oliver Red-Bird-Tail returned Morning Eagle's nod, slowly stood and faced each one inside of the lodge.

"Many times my son has brought dishonor upon my family. My deeds and the deeds of my daughter, far away in the whiteman's Washington D.C., we have tried always to do what's good for our people and to bring honor to our family." Oliver stopped, placing his hands to his mouth in prayerful contemplation.

"For many, many winters I have been an interpreter for my Pikuni people, giving the true meaning of our language into the whiteman's English. My brother Richard was translator at Peter Red-Boy's trial. I now see that my brother and my only son abused this sacred trust as government interpreters. My family has been dishonored by my brother. My heart is full of shame for my son. My heart is good towards you, Running Crane and Nellie and your family and all my Pikuni friends, here. And to you, Aapinakoi Píítaa."

Only the lodge fire made a sound. The silent looks inside gave away the tenderness each felt for Oliver, for one another and for Peter Stabs-By-Mistake and his family.

The quiet was broken by the deep, rasping cough of Annie Running Crane. Her mother accompanied her outside, away from the heat of the lodge-fire and the smoke.

Low voices continued inside the Otter Medicine Tipi, followed by the clickety-clack of the machine-with-many-fingers, as it rolled out page after page of letter drawings telling what had been told this night within the sacred Otter Medicine Tipi. The pages would carry their talk to attorney Grorud in Helena, the messages then sent on to the Great White Father's

Lodge in Washington, D.C.

Walking a short distance away from the Otter Medicine Tipi, Nellie and her daughter stood together beneath the Never-Moving (North) Star and the Seven Brothers (The Big Dipper).

Now, Nellie carefully draped a woolen blanket over her daughter as they sat on the ground. Annie lay back in her mother's arms and gazed up at the bright Never-Moving Star. Tears filled her eyes.

"Mother...Red-Boy sees me," she said softly.

Nellie looked down at her daughter for a long moment, puzzled.

"Red-Boy has heard me speak the truth to Aapinakoi Píítaa, Mother. He is smiling."

»»»→ • ←«««

Two silent figures, perched on their mounts, watched from the shadows. Black Looks stared at Nellie and her daughter and remembered how he had been humiliated by Annie when he brought her the presents of horses, pemmican and beaded ornaments. His jaw tightened at the memory of her and her friends' treatment of him, a government interpreter, a trusted assistant to Superintendent Campbell.

Black Looks glanced over at his Uncle Richard, whose face was hidden beneath the deep shadow of his Stetson.

Old wounds of humiliation and rejection would be avenged. He vowed he would somehow right the stinging loss of what he wanted—the loss of Annie, the status of the Running Cranes, all stolen from him by his enemy. An enemy of such cunning that even four years after his imprisonment, he still held Annie's heart.

Old Agency on Badger Creek, 1898. Image No. 638.109, courtesy of Archives & Special Collections, the Universe of Montana – Missoula

# XVI

# Crooked Tongues
# Rust the Chain

The late afternoon sun of the first big "snow-moon-of-winter," (November), lit the prairie grass in the fall of 1925. It cast long shadows of the three horsemen cantering toward the lone sub-agency office at Browning. The wind whipped the grass, yanked at their coats and leggings. The men crouched lower over their mounts and held their broad-brimmed hats.

The warmth of the potbelly stove inside the white clapboard building of the Bureau agency rendered the weather irrelevant to the waiting Frank Campbell. He and Victor Sanders had been discussing the upcoming Tribal Council elections to be held during the "moon-of-the-first-warm-wind," the yearly Chinook wind that blew from the south every December.

The Blackfeet Tribal Council was composed of more than a dozen members from the various communities on the reservation. On paper, council members regulated the police force and supervised protection of wildlife and Blackfeet traditions. The Elders knew better. Mostly, the council was a rubber stamp for whatever the Bureau wanted.

Not surprisingly, the slate of council candidates consisted mostly of younger half-bloods, successful tribal cattlemen or farmers eager to promote whiteman ventures for their own gain, and all encouraged by Campbell and the Indian Bureau.

Thomas Stabs-By-Mistake, Big Brave-Mountain Chief and other Elders viewed such goings-on with, at minimum, mistrust. Charges had been made that inherited lands, allotments and leasing income from whiteman grazing privileges had been squandered or, at best, mismanaged. Requests for an accounting of fees supposedly collected for thousands of trespassing cattle and sheep had repeatedly gone unanswered.

Even worse, the Indian Bureau had spent hundreds of thousands of dollars of tribal funds on irrigation and farming projects—projects destined to fail in Montana's harsh climate. Haying seemed the only productive enterprise, in a good year. In a not-so-good year, families existed on the meager rations handed out as Campbell saw fit. Those who supported his plan ate while the land itself died, unable to support even the livestock that could supplement an agency diet.

Victor Sanders, the newly declared Tribal Council candidate, sat with his feet on Campbell's desk, confidently telling how he would promote Campbell's Five-Year Plan once elected.

A horse whinnied, then another. Campbell went to the window to check. The two men exchanged nods and Victor Black Looks retired to the next room.

Campbell watched. The nearly-blind Big Brave-Frank Mountain Chief, sat still atop his sorrel mount as it was led by Thomas Stabs-By-Mistake, who had already tethered his horse under the overhang at the side of the building. Big Brave slowly dismounted. His two gray braids swung over his chest as he unbuttoned his gray wool overcoat.

With them was Oliver Sanders. The horses, now all tethered, were eager at the trough as the men approached the door.

Ignoring Oliver, Campbell beckoned to Thomas and Mountain Chief to come in. Oliver waited until after Mountain Chief and Thomas had followed the whiteman inside.

The Superintendent offered "hot java," then settled behind his large desk and began his usual small talk about the weather.

"Looks like the coming Chinook might clear some grazing land," offered Campbell. The men knew that the Chinook breath would, at best, provide such a brief period of grazing that it was of little use in the growth or survival of the cattle.

Mountain Chief turned to Oliver and spoke in a low, even tone.

"Mr. Campbell," Oliver began, "Mountain Chief has talked to others who have seen the brands and markings of whiteman cattle and sheep on the reservation. They want to know if you've asked for trespass fees."

Campbell made no attempt to conceal his disdain for the Indian translator. It was Oliver who had complained to Senator Wheeler of tribal suspicions that Campbell was taking wool profits from Indian sheep while running his own sheep on the reservation and allowing the Park Saddle Company to trespass on reservation lands at no charge.

"Oliver, you can read Inspector Blair's report," came the Superintendent's icy reply. "He has fully investigated these matters and found nothing wrong."

Oliver held Campbell's gaze until Campbell looked away. Then, he translated Campbell's remarks for Mountain Chief.

"Unh!" came Mountain Chief's short retort.

Briefly, Oliver explained to Campbell. "These men know the whiteman's written offerings … his reports … don't change the reality of what is occurring on their land." Oliver sat back now and continued.

"Mr. Campbell, we came because you had somethin' to tell us." The men did not expect to be put up at the sub-agency accommodations overnight and were anxious to return to their lodges.

"Well, to tell you the truth, I have a proposition to make to you, Frank." Campbell, in the manner of a whiteman who wanted something for nothing, spoke directly to the old chief using his Christian name.

The old chief studied Campbell intently, then spoke.

"Mountain Chief was my father. He gave me the name Big Brave-Mountain Chief," translated Oliver.

Annoyed with the whole situation, the superintendent apologized, "I'm sorry." Then, trying again, he said, "Mountain Chief, I know Peter Stabs-By-Mistake is your grandson. We at the Indian Bureau have been contacted by certain people who have asked that Peter be pardoned for his crime and we want to do what we can to help."

"My grandson, he make no whiteman's crime." The old chief glared at Campbell.

"Who are these men who approached you," interjected Oliver.

"The man you call Morning Eagle has talked to me. Then there was a representative of Morning Eagle here from Helena asking questions." He furrowed his brow. "There could have been others. My memory does not recall."

"What does my grandson's freedom mean to you?"

"Well, the reason I asked you here is to tell you that if you and your family and your followers vote for the candidates that the Bureau supports for Tribal Council, then I'm sure we can all work together to free Peter." Oliver again translated.

Mountain Chief looked away and studied his son-in-law's face. Thomas returned the old man's look and nodded. He was more than skeptical. He knew that Black Looks was a candidate for council. "Is one of your men Victor Sanders?" asked Big Brave.

"He is, and as an official interpreter he would be in a position to assist greatly in freeing Peter."

In Pikuni, Oliver discussed with the others the superintendent's proposition.

Abruptly, the old chief stood.

"We go now," announced Mountain Chief in his very best English.

Looking to Oliver, Campbell seemed perplexed.

"Big Brave does not make decisions in one night. He does not make a decision like this until he has talked to our people."

Turning, the three men left. Oliver pushed open the door to the agency back room; he felt no need to enter or even look inside. Then he slowly turned to leave. "We will let you know soon enough. We go now."

Campbell walked to the window and watched them ride away. Rain had begun to softly pelt the window. Black Looks entered the room. Together they watched as their visitors tucked their hats low and broke into an easy gallop into the blowing rain.

"Well?" asked Black Looks.

"We'll see. We'll see," the Superintendent repeated, a slow crooked smile crossing his face. "Go home now, Victor."

$$\text{»»}\longrightarrow \bullet \longleftarrow \text{«««}$$

The lone horse tethered at the sub-agency was unhitched and the rider, huddled against the rain, started out in the opposite direction. He would know soon enough. Now, he would go see his mother and whet his thirst. Maxine always kept a stash of "whiteman's water" at her place. Where she got it was her business, he really didn't care. Maxine had a cunning that had helped her to survive. She had it figured correctly that the whiteman's water was the catalyst that enabled the whiteman to graze his livestock on Indian land without paying fees. Black Looks knew that those Indians who still held allotment lands would be offered free bootleg; soon after, whitemen's cattle would graze their land. No questions asked; no fees paid. Just let the Agency handle it. She and Uncle Richard had told him the same would work for his election.

As he approached his mother's neatly-shingled clapboard house, the rain had moved on and moonlight highlighted the cabin. The place was dark.

He entered and called out. There was no answer. He lit a candle and glanced around at the disarray of bottles on the wooden floor. Half-eaten pork and beans dried on a rickety wooden table. The dense, bitter-sweet odor of stale hops filled the place.

In the back corner of the cabin was a small bedroom. There, Victor Sanders beheld a long familiar scene, his mother drooling on her pillow—out for another night.

He bent low to make sure she was breathing, then retrieved the other pillow from her bed and a woolen blanket that had slipped to the floor. He would sleep and wait for her to sleep it off. He needed to talk with her.

A half-empty bottle sat on the cigarette-burned coffee table. He smiled and took several high-arching gulps and was soothed by the burning sensation all the way down his throat.

Like a sore tooth, Campbell's conversation with the old chief and his son had chafed his nerves. He tried to console himself. If this plan didn't work, at least whiteman's water would keep his pockets full.

He took several more swigs from the bottle and blew out the candle. His thoughts flowed listlessly, his eyes played with the shadows as he lay down on the soiled pillow. Slowly, unevenly, he felt his body drifting off as the wind outside whistled over the expanse of the prairie and his ambition.

(left to right) Chief Boy, Bear Head, Swims Under, Turtle (the Piegan, not Sspopíi), Mami (Mamíí; Fish).

# XVII

# The Backbone-of-the-World

"Damnit, Yessup! Judy, get over there and tell Yessup to bring that sonofabitch's file in here, will ya!" barked Miggs. The man's short hair stood at attention. "Jesus, I asked for the damn thing half-an-hour-ago!" The Assistant U.S. Attorney was in high temper this early June morning in 1926.

The short, wiry, nervous New Yorker had graduated from Columbia Law School and had been appointed by President Harding's people to his post in Helena, Montana. His resentment of landing in this "infernal hick town" was made clear to all who passed his way by a steady stream of sarcasm, colorful invectives and caustic remarks at or about the paperwork and office staff. All those around did what they could to stifle whatever deadly mood swings the little Irishman might exhibit on any particular morning. Failing that, they did what they could to stay out of his way.

"Mr. Yessup will be right in with the file, sir." The slight, middle-aged secretary, Judy, spoke just above a whisper.

"Tweek...tweek...clang!" The black-and-silver-guilded ceiling fan wobbled and reverberated as it rotated.

"Blast it all to hell! How many times have I told you to get those idiots in maintenance off their asses and up here to fix this contraption before it kills me."

"Yes sir," came the quiet reply. "Right away, Mr. Miggs." The little woman scampered away. This was one of those stay-out-of-his-way kind of days.

Bright enough to graduate in the top third of his law school class, he had worked hard for Harding's election and deserved better than exile to Montana as a reward.

"Squeek...squeek...twang."

"Dammit," he muttered and shook his head. That contrivance they call a fan not only destroyed his concentration, but it did nothing to keep his office cool, and nobody in maintenance seemed to care one whit. That's the way things always went for Miggs. Everyone around him was either stupid, too damn lazy to get anything done or running a goddamned racket, and his thankless job was to get to the bottom of it.

His drive to get to the bottom of things earned Miggs over a ninety percent conviction rate during his tenure, a fact he made sure everyone knew.

Miggs' chief social outlet was Saturday nights, when he enjoyed poker and bourbon with R. W. "Clyde" Pomeroy, a New York transplant, and his cronies. An investor-speculator with close ties to a Texas oil company, Pomeroy and his cohorts were immersed in the ongoing oil exploration game being played out on the eastern edge of the Blackfeet Reservation. Each week, Miggs was privy to all of the oil leasing intrigues, including any Tribal Council interference with leasing ventures in the "eastern region." Miggs had it figured that his investment with "Clever Clyde" would prove very lucrative.

Aside from his poker nights, the only other consolation for Montana's unmarried Assistant U.S. Attorney was his growing assortment of political memorabilia—campaign literature and buttons dating as far back as "Tippecanoe and Tyler, too." It afforded him even greater bragging rights. Everyone in the office was forced to listen to him gloat over his "conquests." His prized possession—the "Lincoln-Hamlin" button—he kept hidden in a small case in his safe, only to be displayed after a particularly satisfying conviction.

Ruminating on his collectibles soothed him. So did gazing at the bluish-gray mountains framed against a near cloudless sky by the large window in his office. In the distance, white-capped glaciered mountains touched stringy clouds; slanting morning sunlight highlighted the deep rocky shadows. Thin stands of pine on the hills descended to thick evergreen forests right up to the outposts of Helena's prospering rooftop cityscape, built by crooks, railroad financiers and miners-come-West.

This expansive view of the Blackfeet Backbone-of-the-World—the jagged, overthrusting Rockies-reminded him of the less impressive Adirondack and Appalachian Mountains, places his father had taken him when he was a boy.

Early on, the youngster knew the world had turned against his father—indeed his whole family—when a corrupt Tammany Hall politico had eliminated the outspoken Irishman's city job. Then his father succumbed to influenza.

Miggs became obsessed with expanding his dead father's collection of political memorabilia. Dickering and beating down dealers and collectors became his passion. He would add to his father's legacy, no matter what the cost.

Yet here, this bright morning, he had to deal with that interminable son-of-a-bitch Senator Thomas J. Walsh, "that little piss-ant Democrat senator from Montana" who seemed to delight in embarrassing Miggs. Part of Miggs' domain of drudgery was prosecuting criminal violations on Indian Tribal Lands. As usual, that goddamned senator had his staff nosing around again, making inquiries.

Just this morning, the "piss-ant senator" was actually putting pressure on him, had wanted to talk to him, about some damned Indian. Something about the pardon attorney, James A. Fry, and a Blackfoot serving time for rape down at Leavenworth.

"Yessup, it's about goddamned time! You got that file on Peter, Stabs-what's-his-name?"

"Sorry, sir. Yes sir, right here." His nervous young assistant bustled toward Miggs with a brown manila folder, torn and wrinkled at the edges. Between Yessup and his boss, a sloppy plug of tobacco hit the lip of a wide-mouthed copper spittoon. Miggs wiped his mouth with the back of his hand, then reached for the folder. Yessup flinched.

"U.S. versus Peter-Stabs-By-Mistake, yeah this is the one. See this package I got from Mr. Fry yesterday, Yessup?"

The nervous and more than slightly repulsed assistant replied, "Yes, sir," his head nodding like a woodpecker. At times, Yessup felt like a sycophant. It wasn't so much that Yessup was meek as it was that Assistant U.S. Attorney Miggs intimidated him, just like he did every other Justice staffer.

"You know, I've been waiting for that damn Injun's criminal file all morning long. You know why?" Without pausing for a response, he pounced, "Because that goddamned Walsh feels sorry for this renegade Injun' at Leavenworth! I can smell it!"

"Sorry, sir."

"You say that one more time, dammit, and I'll throw your head out that window!" Miggs managed to shout, point and demand as he looked at the file. "Get over there Yessup. Sit down and listen to me, dammit!"

"Yes, sir." Yessup sat before Miggs' oversized oak desk, his throne.

"Shee-it!" he muttered to himself as he leafed through the criminal trial file of Peter-Stabs-By-Mistake and the separate stack of affidavits and pleas

Fry had sent.

"Listen to this! Here's this drunken Injun, Peter-Stabs-By-Mistake, who poked some squaw on the reservation and wants a pardon. He deserves the name." Miggs exploded with a gut laugh. Yessup followed with a slightly forced laugh.

Since his boss was laughing, Yessup finally spoke. "Seems the Indian is Blackfeet, a Piegan."

"Jesus, I know he's a fuckin' pagan, for chrissakes, Yessup! All these Indians do is drink bootleg and screw. Shit, they're the walking zombies of Montana."

Yessup fixed a brief, hard eye at his boss, then settled back in his chair and tried again.

"No, boss, he's P-i-e-g-a-n." Yessup's attempt at clarification was met with Miggs' icy stare, the same stare he used when cross-examining a petty bootlegger. "A Blackfeet Pikuni, boss...same thing," the assistant meekly offered.

"I don't give a shit if he's pickiunish or a black pagan!" dismissed Miggs with a wave. "The bastard belongs in prison, but now our wonderful pardon attorney is beating down my door. Walsh has gotta be behind this. For some reason, he wants Fry to investigate the whole goddamned mess of a trial that happened five years ago!" Miggs paused, wondering whose racket was gumming up somebody else's racket.

"Yessup, how'd you like to go open the door for Walsh when he comes barging in here with his stinking Havana cigars, telling me how to do my goddamned job?"

"No, sir," replied Yessup, respectfully shaking his head.

"Goddamn right!" Miggs pushed his leather chair back, swiveled to his right, glanced out at the Rockies, then back at Yessup, his beady eyes blazing, "Well, hell, let's get cracking, then. Did you actually read through the stupid file?"

Yessup obviously paused too long. Hands on his hips, Miggs barked, "Well?"

"Sorry sir...er sorry. Sir, there was no trial, sir. Just a plea of guilty after the state rested its case...er, I should say, after the victim started to testify."

"Humm. Any physical evidence of the rape?" Miggs slowly eased himself back into his chair and relit his cannon-shaped cigar.

"None in the file, sir."

With a slightly perplexed look, Miggs leaned forward and looked intently at Yessup. "You mean you didn't even see any goddamned semen stains in the file?" Miggs' head snapped back as he roared out a loud guffaw at his own sarcastic attempt at humor. Yessup waited. Miggs leafed through the file without paying attention and barked, "Which prosecuting attorney handled the thing for the government?" as if trying to prove his assistant did not know what was there.

"O'Donnell, sir."

"And what did O'Donnell have to say?"

"Well, I called him and he said a few things that surprised me."

"Such as?"

"Well, he thought the judge's sentence was excessive." Yessup paused. "Told me he thought we should recommend clemency."

"Bullshit! That one's another goddamned little pinstriped shithead runnin' god-only-knows what kind of scam." The boss swiveled towards the window. He paused. "Well, I'll be dipped in shit! O'Donnell's probably the one put Walsh up to ride my ass...to open up this can of worms."

O'Donnell, now the pinstriped Democratic congressman from Montana, seemed to have an inside track on what was going on at the reservation. He would go on and on about conditions, the damage caused by trespassing cattle and bootleg alcohol. Miggs had never set foot on an Indian reservation except when he had to confer with Superintendent Frank C. Campbell and other Bureau officials, and that was plenty as far as he was concerned. O'Donnell and Senator Walsh were always pestering him to go more often.

What the hell was O'Donnell doing, questioning the judgment of the federal sentencing judge? What kind of crap was that for a former prosecutor? What the hell were he and Walsh up to? he mused.

"That O'Donnell's nothing but a goddamned four-flushing phony!"

"What's a four...."

"The sonofabitch is so goddamned phony, you have to flush four times just to get rid of all the bullshit!" Miggs leaned back and looked up at the now-stationary ceiling fan.

"I smell something fishy, Yessup. All I see from the stuff Fry sent me is a bunch of sham affidavits from a bunch of squaws saying what a mistake the whole thing was." Rotating forward, he was now actually reading each affidavit and flipping the file pages back and forth.

Suddenly, he stopped and held up one affidavit.

"So...this guy...calls himself Morning Eagle...is the one pushing for the Indian's release." The little prosecutor glared at his assistant, thoughtfully twisted the cigar in his mouth. "Ah ha...I'll bet he's in thick with Walsh and O'Donnell. Damn it! I smell O'Donnell and Walsh spread all over this file like shit!" Suddenly jerking to a ramrod-upright position, Miggs announced, "I think this Eagle guy has gone to those little shit-heads O'Donnell and Walsh and they're trying to screw us and embarrass the whole goddamned administration!"

Yessup looked perplexed. "How do you mean, sir?"

"Oh for chrissakes! Pull your head out of your ass! If you're gonna work in this office, man, you have to be savvy. We have to protect our asses!"

"Sorry, sir, uh...." Yessup paused. "But how's this Blackfeet's case going to ruin Mr. Coolidge's...."

"Listen!" barked Miggs, spreading his spindly arms wide. "Remember Coolidge's Committee of 100? That Committee issued a report on the BIA back in '23. Remember? Then the goddamned Indians began agitating to review the president's Indian policies, so now we're saddled with the blasted Meriam Commission. Lewis Meriam and his boys are supposed to review these tangled Indian trust accounts and recommend how to clear up all the bureaucratic and accounting screw-ups. 'Course the Justice Department wants the report to be favorable to Mr. Coolidge's administration and the president's handling of Indian affairs and trust funds."

"Is the investigation going badly, then, sir?"

"Yessup, if we investigate this thing, I have to do one of two things. Either I have to recommend a lousy, rotten pardon for the Indian, which makes us all look like a Klan lynch mob that railroaded criminal convictions on reservation land. How do you think that'd look when the Meriam Commission comes knocking on our door?" The little boss slowly leaned back, scowled at the ceiling fan, then bolted upright to finish his thought.

"Or, we can do nothing. But if we do nothing, then that phony Eagle guy will have O'Donnell and Walsh on our asses all over again." Miggs leaned sideways and shot another wad into the spittoon. Yessup swallowed and looked away.

"So what are you going to do, boss?"

"What I'm going to do, Yessup, is send you out there to talk to these goddamned pickiunish pagans and see if we can find out what really happened out there. You understand? And find out who this asshole Eagle guy is. Then, we're gonna shuffle papers and blow smoke to see how best to cover our asses and protect the administration."

"Boss, excuse me. I gotta go to the restroom."

≫⟩⟩→ • ←⟨⟨≪

Miggs gave the retreating Yessup an incredulous look.

The long drive north from Helena to Great Falls, then west through Cut Bank and Browning, was a relief for Yessup. As he motored across the rolling grass plains towards Glacier National Park and the Blackfeet Indian Reservation, the shadow of his boss grew less harsh.

Yessup had visited Congressman Miles O'Donnell in Great Falls the previous day. Without any physical evidence linking Peter Stabs-By-Mistake to the victim, O'Donnell reached the same conclusion that Yessup had when he read the transcript of the trial. The government had relied exclusively on translated testimony provided by a government interpreter and material witness, Victor Sanders.

Yessup and O'Donnell were particularly troubled that the judge had allowed Richard Sanders, a relative of a witness for the government, to serve as official court translator at the trial.

Peter Stabs-By-Mistake had pled guilty before the victim, Annie Running Crane, had finished testifying. Was that because he was guilty or because the cards were simply stacked too high against him?

Hoping to interview Victor Sanders, Yessup asked Congressman O'Donnell to request a meeting with Campbell and the young man.

Yessup motored his Model-T into the woebegone town of Browning and parked in front of the sub-agency office. The building, a single-story, run-down wooden structure with a pitched shingle roof, needed paint.

Briefcase in hand, Yessup walked in expecting to meet the two men. Instead, he was ushered into the superintendent's office, where two vacant chairs and Superintendent Campbell stood, but no Victor Sanders.

"Good morning. And how is the U.S. Attorney's office holding up in Helena?" asked Campbell. The six-foot superintendent towered over Yessup. Like Yessup, the man looked a bit overdressed for the surroundings, sporting a white shirt, silk tie, gray vest and black suit.

Others had remarked that Campbell's tenure at the reservation, about five years, had been nothing short of stellar—no corruption scandals. He'd been given high marks from the Harding and Coolidge administrations. Indeed, General Scott, who had visited the reservation in August of 1922, had remarked that Campbell "has awakened the spirit of the Blackfeet people."

"Oh, we're holding our own." replied Yessup matter-of-factly. He glanced around, hoping to find Sanders close by. "I've come a long way to keep the boss happy ya know," joked Yessup.

Yessup had, indeed, come far, having grown up a mixed-blood, one-quarter Blackfeet, with relations and ancestors who were Cree, Assiniboine and Anglo. Raised in Helena, the slightly olive-skinned young man had never lived more than a summer with his native relatives. He'd been lucky that a scholarship had paid his way to college. Hard work every summer had seen him through law school at the University of Washington in Seattle. He clerked for a firm in Helena before taking the bar examination. Then he landed the intern job with the U.S. Attorney's office as an investigator.

The seemingly timid assistant had goals and plans. Never letting on about his heritage, he knew more than Miggs gave him credit for, much more. But he also aspired to be in Miggs' shoes—an Assistant U.S. Attorney. He needed to understand the case and do the right thing. Still, he needed most of all, for now, to stay on Miggs' good side.

Yessup paid attention. He knew that underneath the surface of glowing reports of home canning, needlework and beadwork, many Blackfeet were disdainful of Campbell's program and performance.

"I guess he sent you up here to discuss Stabs-By-Mistake's conviction, huh?" Campbell retorted.

"Yeah. I guess one of the material witnesses was Victor Sanders, who acts as your interpreter. There was also an Indian police officer named Peter White Man."

"Good," came the superintendent's smooth response. Again, Yessup looked around, expecting to see either Sanders or White Man enter.

"Can I talk to these witnesses?"

"Well, Peter White Man's no longer around."

"What about Mr. Sanders?"

"Oh, he is very busy for me right now. He's over in Cut Bank, talking to some of the older tribal members." Campbell waited for Yessup to turn his way, again. "Sanders is also running for Tribal Business Council and has been spending a lot of time out of the office." Yessup was more than annoyed by this obvious bullshit runaround. He bought time to think by asking:

"Well, can you tell me, Mr. Campbell, what you know of what happened here five years ago down at Heart Butte? Did either of these two men tell you they had witnessed Peter Stabs-By-Mistake violate the victim, Annie Running Crane? After all, you did testify at the trial."

Campbell turned to the yellowish, barren landscape outside. A long silence followed.

As well-oiled as his hair, the superintendent summarized, "Well, the two men indicated they saw Annie Running Crane violated by this Indian and they fully interviewed other witnesses who were present."

"That's interesting. But you see, Mr. Campbell, there seems to be a problem reconciling that with what these young women, Miss Running Crane and her friends, are saying now. Victor Sanders talked to each of them before the trial, right?"

"That's right," said Campbell firmly. "You have to understand that this Peter Stabs-By-Mistake was a real troublemaker over here. Like I testified to at the trial, everyone was afraid of him, especially the girls. He was violent, made threats."

"Oh?"

"Yes, he and his other cohorts."

"How do you mean?"

"Well, Peter and his friends agitated things at the community meetings. They threatened me and my staff when things didn't go their way. Peter even tried to ruin the work of my Farming and Livestock Association, especially among the full-bloods. You know, the full-bloods support my programs. Everybody but Peter and his bunch can see how good it is."

"How exactly did Peter and the others cause you trouble?" asked Yessup.

"Well, every year, for a full month in the summer, the Blackfeet would gather for their tribal Sun Dance encampment. Of course, this encampment would take place right when the crops and livestock needed tending in early summer, so it had to change."

"I see," remarked the investigator. Yessup already knew all this, but let Campbell continue.

"Thomas Stabs-By-Mistake is a tribal chief and doesn't want to give up the old ways, at all. His son, Peter, got really angry at our agency for trying to make a legitimate compromise about the amount of time taken up by the Sun Dance ritual. Again, Peter and his bunch made trouble and scared folks with their threats." Yessup already knew Campbell had angered everyone when he tried to eliminate the Sun Dance altogether.

"After Peter was sent off to Leavenworth, I was able to work out a satisfactory compromise with the tribal elders. The Sun Dance is now held at different times and locations on the reservation and lasts only a week. The crops get tended and the people get to do whatever it is they do at their Sun Dance gathering." Yessup knew that the older and middle-aged full-bloods had sacrificed sharing the ritual with their families by leaving younger members to look after the crops. It was not right; the Sun Dance was for families. The celebrations of tribal unity and worship were as fragmented as the half-baked plans of the Indian Bureau.

"It's clear the older full-bloods really like raising their own crops," said the Superintendent confidently.

"Excuse me, Mr. Campbell, but could you tell me again what this has to do with Peter's conviction for rape?"

"Sure. He made himself very unpopular trying to agitate against everything...the elders, what our agency was trying to do for these folks. He just plain disrupted things quite a bit." Campbell paused again, glancing out the window, trying to appear thoughtful. "Why, he even threatened to burn down one of our agency offices. A lot of the Indians, here, not only didn't trust him, they were afraid of him."

"I am still a little bit confused, sir."

"Well," interrupted Campbell, "he was like a lot of the veterans, a known womanizer and boozer, to boot." Campbell was now nodding his head, as if this gesture would somehow affirm the young Indian's guilt. "Really thought he was special... caused a lot of trouble. Why, there was talk that he got Oliver Sanders' daughter Marilyn pregnant. The baby died and Stabs-By-Mistake ran off to France."

"How do you know all of this?"

"Everyone around here knew it. In case you don't know, I have good law enforcement here on the reservation. And trusted informants."

"Who are your informants, sir?"

Campbell stared suspiciously at the little man before he finally answered. "Well, Victor Sanders, for one. Victor's uncle, Richard Sanders, and the Indian police here on the reservation."

"Where is Oliver Sanders' daughter now?" Yessup asked.

"Oh I think she's back East somewhere...got a government job."

"So, where can I find these other people...take statements?" queried the investigator.

"Well, it's hard to tell, hard to run them down. Damn hard to do on the reservation. The police, here, are always out on patrol, trying to catch bootleggers or puttin' to rest some quarrel. And, of course, Victor Sanders is very busy right now." Campbell stood and stepped to the door, signaling that the meeting was now over. Walking past Yessup, he gave him a side glance. He held the door. His smile never reached his eyes.

"Good luck to you on this thing. I think you're gonna find, though, that this Peter Stabs-By-Mistake fellow was a real bad apple."

Yessup nodded politely. Campbell had no interest in the validity of this case. He was busy with his own agenda. Still, drinking had always been a big problem on the reservation, destroying lives and families, prompting criminal activity, including prostitution and rape.

Okay, so maybe Peter Stabs-By-Mistake was an Indian who drank and made trouble, but apparently just for the Agency. Yessup suspected there was more to the young veteran's troublemaking than random drunken rages. Life for no one on the reservation existed as portrayed in the velvet picture of the beautiful Indian girl that hung in the Justice Building back in Helena. Yessup knew. He looked around and saw reflected in the faces his Cree uncle's tired face and the squalor surrounding the lives of his distant cousins. He had seen all that before the current budget cuts, which now meant even less in food and medical services. He had seen the devastation and chaos that the epidemic of the past decade had brought to Native people. The influenza and harsh winters had mercilessly killed cattle, crops and people. Campbell could say what he wanted, but Yessup knew.

Back in the car, the young assistant went over how Miggs had figured the situation. The US attorney's office was placed between the demands of Senator Walsh and Miggs' own determination to protect the administration from being embarrassed by the release of a young Indian who may or may not be a troublemaker as well as "guilty as hell."

The young lawyer had his doubts but wasn't about to rock the boat. Miggs' job, and therefore his too, was to keep the water calm. "Keep cool with Coolidge." Yessup smiled at that, but within himself he thought, at what expense? For now, he would just dig a little deeper beneath Frank Campbell's smooth talk.

>>>→ • ←<<<

There had been no way to find the men he wanted to talk to. He was sure Campbell had seen to that, no matter what he might have said to O'Donnell.

On the drive back to Helena, Yessup recalled how out-of-place, how embarrassed, he felt in the reservation community, dressed in a gray flannel suit and maroon silk tie, the sweat making his white shirt stick to his back and chest. Oliver Sanders had chuckled when the two men had made their way to pay respects to Chief Thomas Stabs-By-Mistake.

"So you're the investigator, huh?"

"Yes sir. And you're Victor's father?" queried the investigator.

"Aaee." Oliver studied Yessup closely. "For a mixed-blood, you sure look uncomfortable."

Maybe it was a suggestion that the surprised Yessup remove his tie, or at least loosen it a bit, before they entered the cramped quarters of Thomas's lodge. Slackening his tie, Yessup went on.

"Seems Mr. Campbell likes your son. He mentioned that your son and his uncle keep him pretty informed about things. Didn't mention you as bein' part of his informant team, though."

"His team don't concern me," came the curt reply.

Having correctly identified a rift, the young investigator acknowledged Oliver's earlier remark about how it was always easy for one native to recognize another, no matter how mixed or diluted the bloodlines.

Several gaunt palominos were feeding leisurely from a wooden trough as the two men walked the last quarter mile to Thomas's lodge. The air smelled fresh and clean, save for the occasional whiff of horse manure and hay.

"Well, Mr. Sanders, I fear you're right about how I'm dressed." Yessup shook his head and smiled at the older man. "But, you wear a white shirt and tie when you work for Mr. Miggs."

Oliver nodded and grinned. "Well, you look very 'white' and official."

"Supposed to match whiteman's justice, I guess," replied Yessup. Both men laughed.

Their laughter seemed to cause a stirring from within the lodge. An older woman with long, dark grayish hair poked her head from the lodge door and asked, "Whach'ya want, Oliver?"

"We want to speak with Chief Thomas Stabs-By-Mistake," Sanders replied.

"Chief Thomas...he's not here." The woman shook her head.

Oliver translated. "Tell Thomas that Mr. Yessup here is my friend. I know him. Part of his blood is of our people."

The woman came out of the lodge door and studied Yessup carefully. He felt even more conspicuous and foolish in his flannel suit, black shoes, white shirt and, at least, loosened tie. Looking over at Sanders, he smiled.

"We could have used this man to keep the crows away from our crops this spring." Oliver Sanders and the woman chuckled. Even without translation, Yessup knew the joke was on him. The amused look vanished and she frowned as she spoke again to Oliver Sanders.

"Yessup, Thomas's woman thinks you're from the Federal Indian Bureau. She says Thomas wants nothing to do with you."

"Tell Thomas's sits-beside-him-woman that I am not from the Indian Bureau, that I come from Helena, from the whiteman's Justice Department to investigate her son's conviction." Oliver translated.

The woman now ducked inside the lodge and dropped the flap. Yessup heard low conversation from within. When she poked her head from the lodge, she did not look at Yessup, but spoke to Oliver.

"Chief Thomas, he does not want to talk to you. Go 'way, we don't want you."

"This doesn't look too good," Oliver said and motioned for Yessup to step back a bit. "Let me talk to her for a minute."

Oliver approached the woman. "Steals-In-The-Daytime, tell Stabs-By-Mistake that I have recently spoken with Aapinakoi Píítaa at Heart Butte and he has asked us to come speak with your man."

Again, she turned, stooped, then disappeared back into the lodge. Yessup heard more urgent, muffled conversation.

"Come," the woman said, as she opened the lodge-flap.

Oliver signaled Yessup to follow and, bending low, entered first. No seat was offered either man. Yessup hung back, standing by the lodge-flap.

Despite the heat, a lodge fire illuminated the large tipi. A War Bonnet of black-tipped eagle feathers hung from a lodge pole. A wooden-pole tripod holding a large brass kettle straddled the circular fire pit surrounded with stones. Fragrant kinnikinnick and dried meat hung from cross poles. Willow backrests, trimmed with red and dark blue-black trade cloth, stood at the head and foot of each robe-covered bed.

Looking around, Yessup knew that the Spirit of Long-Ago-Days sang inside this lodge.

Under his Medicine-Bundle sat Chief Stabs-By-Mistake on his Buffalo Robe. In front of him lay his tobacco board and long-stemmed smoking pipe. On his right and on his left sat seven powerfully built full-blood men.

Suspicious, unfriendly eyes watched. Yessup swallowed hard, fearing these men considered him their enemy, no doubt come to steal their lands. Yessup was impressed by the united presence of strength and manhood, of culture and intelligence.

Yessup knew who he was and the barrier he must cross. Looking directly at Stabs-By-Mistake, he said, "Oliver Sanders told me about you, that you are a Piegan Chief. He told me that you are the father of Peter Stabs-By-Mistake." Yessup stopped and glanced at Oliver, who slowly, carefully translated his words.

Stabs-By-Mistake responded with a sullen, suspicious look at Yessup.

Yessup understood. "Chief Stabs-By-Mistake, we come at the request of Morning Eagle to talk with you about your son." Oliver followed up Yessup's words in Pikuni.

Suddenly, Thomas Stabs-By-Mistake uttered a prolonged "Unh," with an upward inflection.

Oliver turned to explain, "He's being sarcastic and doesn't quite believe what we say."

Then came an explosive, short and very loud "Unh!" from the chief.

"Thomas is protesting. He will not talk anymore. He wants us to go."

Yessup was disappointed and perplexed by the man's reaction.

Returning to Yessup's car, Oliver Sanders suggested they travel to Heart Butte and meet Morning Eagle with the victim's mother, Nellie Running Crane. Sanders thought Yessup might make more progress if Morning Eagle were present.

"Who is this Morning Eagle?" asked Yessup.

"He is one of us," replied Oliver Sanders.

»»→ • ←««

By the time they parked in front of the ramshackle clapboard house with tar paper roof in Heart Butte, Yessup had ditched his suit for a cotton shirt and corduroy trousers fetched from his duffle bag in the rumble seat. Perhaps Yessup would have better luck interviewing Morning Eagle and Nellie in more casual attire. For sure, he would be more comfortable.

Dust swirled around them as they approached the door of the clapboard shack. A man in a red-flannel shirt with rawhide leggings and moccasins opened the door. For an Indian, Yessup was taken aback by the man's mustache and skin that was lighter than his own. Yet Sanders had said this man was "one of us."

"Welcome, my Pikuni friend," said the flannel shirt to Oliver Sanders. Yessup was even more perplexed when he heard the red-flannel shirt speak perfect east-coast English. "We told Thomas Stabs-By-Mistake you sent us up to talk with him," replied Oliver. "He sent us away."

With a dismissive gesture of his hand, the red shirt replied, "I knew he would. Stabs-By-Mistake does not trust the tongue of strangers, especially white strangers." The red shirt was now looking directly at Yessup with a gentle smile. "Come on in." Yessup was really confused now. If I'm white, then what's he? he mused.

The men entered and were greeted by a stout woman in worn calico blouse and a long, faded blue trade cloth skirt. Her long braids rested on large, flaccid breasts, her arms were crossed. It was stifling hot and dusty. Oliver motioned for Yessup to sit in a chair to the left of the entrance.

Behind Nellie sat a young mother with an open sore on her face. She was seated on a cow skin, nursing her baby. Yessup, noticing the grub box near the door, peeked inside; some rancid sow belly, traces of woolly mold, wormy grain. Two other children sat on the ground, each with a bit of cow suet.

Oliver spoke softly to Yessup in English. "Cow suet is good, but it does not agree with the children. They are never strong, they are always sick."

"What do they do for food?" asked Yessup.

"Well, if the father spends time with the crops, he has little or no time to kill gophers and rabbits for food. Since no one else in the family is here, they must have gone hunting, I guess." Yessup gulped and tried not to shame the women by looking at them with pity.

"This is Annie Running Crane's mother, Nellie, and her daughter Emma and children," introduced Oliver.

"Is Annie here?" asked the investigator, knowing he was being as abrupt and rude as a whiteman.

"No," came the red shirt's answer. "She's away trying to get food with her father."

Yessup was anxious to find out what Nellie's role had been in Peter's trial and asked Sanders to question Nellie regarding her daughter's rape charge. Oliver spoke the Pikuni dialect and gestured to Nellie. She continued to stand in front of the men, her arms folded in front of her, eyes downcast, totally mute.

He had been wrong to just ask, like that. He knew better and now he had ruined his chance to get straight talk from Nellie Running Crane. Yessup was angry with himself. He might as well have kept on that damned white shirt and suit.

Finally, the red shirt did the talking, explaining that Nellie Running Crane never intended to accuse Stabs-By-Mistake of the whiteman's crime of rape. She was angry that Peter had committed an old Blackfeet tribal crime of holding hands with Annie. Nellie was then told that this tribal crime was the equivalent of the whiteman's crime of rape.

Yessup furrowed his brow. "Who on earth told her that?"

"Victor Sanders," nodded red shirt.

Oliver, with an awkward, strained look, motioned for the men to step outside.

"Mr. Yessup, I know that Red-Boy has a good heart because he was here with Marilyn, my only daughter, during a very hard time. Then he went off to France." The red shirt nodded his assent. "I really miss my daughter," said Oliver with obvious pride. "But she's okay now."

"Where is your daughter now?" Yessup asked.

"In Washington D.C. with the Department of Justice." He paused, thought a moment, glanced up, then continued. "I guess she's working in the Department of Justice with the man that Morning Eagle, here, wrote to… about Peter being in prison."

Yessup's jaw tensed and he feared his boss might be right. It looked like Justice was gonna be in a bigger pickle than anyone had realized. "So, how can we get Nellie to tell us anything?"

"She won't talk now because she's afraid," replied Oliver.

"Why is she afraid?" asked Yessup.

"She's afraid that she would get into bigger trouble if she didn't tell the story like she was told to tell at the trial," replied the red shirt.

"Well, can we get her to tell me in her own words?"

"She already has," replied Morning Eagle. "She signed affidavits that have been sent back to D.C. Your boss may even have them."

Now the thing was truly perplexing to Yessup. He had seen Peter's criminal trial file, and Miggs had mentioned the more recent affidavits. Yet Miggs had kept the affidavits to himself, for his eyes only, neglecting to pass on this critical information to Yessup. Part of Miggs' paranoia, he supposed.

"Where can I find your son, Victor?" queried Yessup.

"Who knows. He's out campaignin' 'round the reservation for Tribal Council," replied his father almost apologetically. "My pride in him is not there," he said and shook his head.

"Yeah, he is known as Campbell's 'man,'" asserted the red shirt. "You know, we've been complaining about Mr. Campbell. He's ignored and twisted the true state of the suffering and poverty that you see around here." The red shirt paused, looking directly at Oliver.

"Lots of bitterness between us and Campbell."

Yessup had heard that Campbell called those he considered too pushy "those damned Bolsheviks."

"A lot of us really spoke out when he threatened to take away our Sun Dance rights for the sake of the whiteman's way," stated Oliver. "Campbell finally gave a little bit. But a lot of the people are scared. Scared even to talk, especially to any whiteman from the Indian Office."

Yessup looked down. He had certainly looked and acted like a fool whiteman, another bureaucrat from the Indian Office. Still, the people trusted red shirt, who obviously was anything but full-blooded Blackfeet.

"Victor has promised to see to it that Mr. Campbell will get Peter Red-Boy freed if Victor is elected to the Tribal Council," asserted Oliver. Oliver kicked the dirt with his right foot. "But that's not the right way. I am not happy in my heart about what my son is doing but he is a grown man and on his own."

Knowing there was much he did not understand, and even less he was going to learn from the Running Cranes, Yessup suggested that they bid their goodbyes to Nellie Running Crane. Entering the shack, again, Yessup bowed to the older woman.

Suddenly, the young mother seated on the ground cried out, "Aieee!"

Yessup flinched. "What's the matter?"

"She has a breast infection and needs a doctor," replied the red shirt. "It's been three days now since we sent for a doctor, but no doctor comes."

"Great pain for my daughter," Nellie Running Crane remarked solemnly. A long silence followed.

Motoring over the dusty, rutted road, Yessup asked, "Was the daughter at the trial?"

"No," replied Sanders. "She was sent away to boarding school after the incident but before the trial."

Yet another piece of a still senseless puzzle, thought Yessup.

All the way back to Helena, Yessup kept seeing the pain and anguish on the face of that young mother trying to nurse her baby and feed her hungry children a piece of cow suet.

Yessup was eager to scrutinize Peter's file. All of it this time. How old had Annie really been at the time of the crime? What other information about this case was sitting on Miggs' desk?

»»→ • ←««

Back in an already sticking white shirt, Yessup rushed to Miggs' office the following Monday. His armpits dripped and he felt scarecrow-hollow inside his flannel suit, strangled by his silk tie. The notes he carried stuck to his sweaty palms.

Miggs was ensconced behind his desk, his Irish-green bow tie perfectly straight. The fastidious little boss was reclining in his chair, slowly puffing away on his cigar. He was proud that just the day before he had outsmarted another rookie collector to obtain a coveted "Lincoln-Johnson" campaign button. The prize now rested within the small confines of his safe. Ignoring Yessup as he entered the room, the little man, seemingly calm, was yodeling "O"-shaped smoke signals that drifted up to be cut away by the ceiling fan.

"Squeek...ting...ping...dang!"

Suddenly, with one swift, jerking motion, Miggs—cigar clenched firmly between his teeth—let fly a thick rubber band. The elastic object bounced off the center of the fan, was caught by a fan blade and went flying across the room.

"Dammit! Get in here NOW!"

Yessup flinched. So much for calm, he thought. Yet this particular summons was directed at the little woman pushing past Yessup to stand before her boss, trembling.

Tilting his head sideways, Miggs implored, with pained sarcasm, "Would you pll-eee-ase, for the umpteenth time, tell those numbskulls to get off their dead asses and fix this goddamned fan?!"

"Certainly Mr. Miggs. I'll run down there myself right now."

Watching the flustered secretary scutter off, Yessup understood. Miggs was as out of place here as he, Yessup, had been on the reservation. Miggs thought himself too good to be stuck way out in Montana deprived of certain creature comforts, cheated out of an exalted position. Today, the poor secretary and the ceiling fan bore the brunt of it all.

"Well, what did you find out there, Yessup?"

"The people I talked to sir," Yessup paused. "Well, it's rather complicated." He cleared his throat and consulted his notes. "Campbell says Peter Stabs-By-Mistake is a known trouble-maker who drinks, is violent, and not to be trusted around women. Seems to have a bit of a history there, too, from what I hear." He glanced up at his boss.

"But on the other hand, Peter is very well-liked and popular with the full-bloods. The people think he is a good man who works only for the benefit of his people. I tried to talk to Peter's father as well as to the victim's mother but they wouldn't talk to me." He lowered his voice and did not look his boss in the eye. "Seems they don't like white men, especially strangers."

"Now, I did talk to a government interpreter who, although not the interpreter at the trial, was there part of the time and he thinks Peter is innocent of the crime. This is where it gets complicated." He again consulted his notes. "This interpreter is the father of one of the witnesses, but he's also the father of a girl Peter supposedly got pregnant before the war."

"Did he now?" Miggs sat up and leaned forward. "Did you talk to her, or to the son?"

"Well, no. The son, Victor Sanders, who was a witness, is running for Tribal Council and is all over the reservation drumming up votes. His father, Oliver, is not pleased with his son and suspects Victor might have been involved in getting the victim and the other witnesses to lie. But here is the really interesting part. I couldn't talk to the daughter 'cause she's off the reservation. Works in D.C., Department of Justice, her father says."

Miggs dropped his cigar in his lap, then did a little chair dance recovering the thing and brushing away the hot coals. Bodily harm avoided, he leaned forward, and, as if he feared the answer, asked Yessup. "What did you say her first name is?"

"Well, I didn't say, but her name is . . ." He consulted another page of his notes. "Marilyn, Marilyn Sanders."

"Oh, good God!" Miggs closed his eyes and moved his lips slowly together as if massaging something inside his mouth. He leaned back in his chair. Then, he shot a bullet-wad of tobacco into the spittoon and began to laugh almost hysterically.

He swiveled back to face Yessup. "Goddamn it, I knew those sons-a-bitches were trying to set me up! I'm gonna get that goddamned Fry for this, that phony little silver-stockinged Brahmin!"

Unnerved, Yessup didn't ask about the witnesses' statements that Miggs had not shown him.

"Boss, there is just this one other thing," Yessup offered almost apologetically. Miggs' face slowly started to redden again. "This Victor Sanders, known as Campbell's 'man', has promised everyone that if he is elected to the Tribal Council, he will get Peter released."

"Who told you all this crap?"

"Oliver Sanders and that other fellow, name's Morning Eagle. I don't know how he fits in. He's not an Indian; he's pale and speaks very good English."

"Where the hell is this Morning Eagle's nest, did they tell you?"

"Don't really know, but he speaks Pikuni and the people seem to trust him, from what he said. The people talk to him."

"Didn't I tell you? Another goddamned agitator!" Miggs was nearly frothing now.

"He said the victim, her mom and others had signed affidavits, which I guess he sent back to D.C." Yessup wanted to see those documents but was not about to make a direct request.

"Well, goddamnit, no one is going to see anyone's phony statements! You know why, Yessup?" Without waiting for an answer, Miggs barged on. "Because, while you were trying to guess who this Morning Bird is, I found out! He's another bastard, dilettante, maverick Democrat out of New England, out to screw us and make the administration look bad. He probably made up the statements, then had those ignorant Indians sign 'em."

Yessup bristled but quietly asked, "But you said you wanted me to investigate this?"

"No, dammit, you don't listen to me! I said I wanted you to go up there and 'talk to a few people'. Not investigate the whole goddamn department. So, you went and talked to a few people and that's where this thing is going to stop. Right here, and right now!"

"But, boss...."

Jabbing his stubby index finger on his desk, Miggs glared at his impertinent assistant. "Right here, right now, we're gonna put a lid on this whole goddamn thing! I tell you, no matter what I do with that depraved Indian, I'll be playing into the hands of that sonofabitch Walsh, and whatever his scam is. We gotta clip the wings of this bird from New England before he makes a fucking laughingstock of Coolidge's Indian policy. You told me, yourself, that this renegade Indian and his old man and this bird fellow are a bunch of goddamned agitators."

Miggs settled back, slowly blew out a waft of smoke, swiveled his chair toward the window and nodded slowly. "What I'm going to do, Yessup, is let this Sanders fellow who's running for Tribal Council, and Superintendent Campbell, handle the whole damned matter. Why, your investigation proves this is the perfect solution."

"How so, boss?"

"Jesus, Yessup! Don't you ever listen?" Miggs swiveled back and glared at his subordinate.

"If I let these two assholes handle the matter, we'll be alright. If Victor Sanders is defeated for Tribal Council, fine. The Indian will stay locked up at Leavenworth. If he gets elected, then they can do whatever the hell they want and it won't have anything to do with this office. Besides, I'm damn sure Campbell will keep the lid on. No way in hell can I let some drunken Indian who raped a squaw get out of prison! It'd be all over the goddamned newspapers that Coolidge is soft on Prohibition. Then that holier-than-thou Meriam Commission will make a mockery of us. Hell, they'd nibble us to death like a goddamn swarm of red ants!"

From this as with so many previous exchanges, Yessup gleaned that Miggs' smarts went deeper than just his conviction rate and his litany of clever, colorful invectives. The quick-witted little boss had honed a sharp political instinct that served him and the power brokers around him well.

As if to calm and reassure himself, Yessup's pugnacious boss leaned back in his chair and took a long breath. Then he began his final summation.

"If this Victor Sanders gets himself elected, I can shift the blame to Campbell if he pushes too hard for the Indian's release." Glaring out the window, as if addressing a jury, the Assistant U.S. Attorney came to his closing statement. "We are not going to have any repercussions. This shithead is not going to be sprung so he can rape another squaw or, God forbid, one of our white women. We're gonna toe the line for the administration."

Swiveling back at Yessup, Miggs asked, "Don't you have somethin' to do, now? Take a piss maybe?" He roared with laughter.

Yessup, with the sight of sickness and hunger again in his mind's eye, rose to leave. "No sir. Just have lots of work to do."

Blackfeet visit Chris and camp at Titan's Pier, South Hadley, Massachusetts. Facing front, left to right: Chr (wearing hat), Red-Boy (wearing war bonnet), Marie (Chris' wife) and Thomas Stabs-By-Mistake.

# XVIII

# The Place-of-Rising-Sun at Heavy-Water-Country
## – Summer 1926 –

"Damn. Damn, damn, damn!" James Fry muttered, then appeared suddenly at the doorway, uncharacteristically glowering up and down the hall as if looking for help. Seeing her, he stopped short. A flinch of self-consciousness overcame the pardon attorney, which Marilyn Sanders thought amusing. She smiled, sensing her arrival had caught him off guard.

"Oh, I'm terribly sorry, Marilyn. Please excuse me," he apologized in his ever-so-polite, smooth Boston brogue.

Her smile widened. Whatever he may have wanted was forgotten as the soft chime of his desk clock beckoned him back to his office.

He smiled wistfully, returned to his desk and frowned again at the letter he had received from Yessup.

Why hadn't Miggs, himself, written instead of his underling? He had been dismayed when the letter first crossed his desk. It was like trying to dispose of a boomerang. His letter to the Holyoker and his instructions to Miggs should have put the thing to rest, but here it was, back on his desk!

"Damn," he muttered as he leaned forward on his elbows, burying his face in his hands. The headache that had been with him all morning was throbbing.

Slowly he got up, crossed the hardwood floor and softly closed the door to his office. He peered out his large window at the passing cars and people on Vermont Avenue below. The Office of the Pardon Attorney was housed in one of more than a half dozen Justice Department buildings — a large Victorian-era edifice several blocks from Pennsylvania Avenue's southside and Murder Bay. The neighborhood was regarded by many as an eyesore. Still, the lush greenery of the cherry and magnolia trees lining the sidewalks seemed a refreshing escape from the tangle inside his head. He sighed, then rocked on his heels.

If he did nothing about the young Indian's pardon request, the president's political enemies, even the prominent trouble-making Holyoker, might propose some kind of "corrupt racket" between Victor Sanders, the opportunist, and his Washington, D.C. "connection," a sister who just happened to work for the pardon attorney. He could see the yellow-dog headlines.

Of course, the proper, the ethical thing to do, was to investigate the matter fully and openly. Doing so would undoubtedly prove embarrassing to many and, no doubt, dangerous.

If he were to open the matter up quickly, would it all just blow over? But then, this was an election year and doing anything could produce enough scandal, for long enough, to influence the outcome. The riddle of what he should do — thrust upon him from two worlds — carved deeper furrows in his forehead.

His thoughts drifted to something more pleasant. Seeing Marilyn's smiling face earlier pleased him. He had become deeply attracted to the young woman; he wanted her close to him. The thought of her leaving him was almost unthinkable. But, given her connection to the Indian case, he really should transfer her. But he would miss her so . . .

James A. Fry, pardon attorney, tried to minimize the damage political opponents could wreak. Still, the former attorney general had been skewered by the Teapot Dome scandal, accused of criminal activities by Montana's Senator Wheeler. Now, Senator Walsh had been dragged into the investigation. The Montana crowd could be pretty damn nasty. How would it look if the spotlight swung to his office?

Yet, Coolidge had been true to his name, keeping cool and distancing himself from the corruption. He, too, would be cool. He was not about to give Coolidge's Democrat foes an opening to charge Coolidge's new Attorney General, John G. Sargent — his own boss — with obstruction of justice or influence peddling.

He returned to his desk. Nervously tapping a pencil, he wondered how to keep Marilyn aboard and ethically investigate the matter. What could, or would, Marilyn be able to tell him about all this?

An idea emerged; he would simply talk to Marilyn. Thoughts of her demurely seated across from him quickened his pulse. He couldn't ask her straight out, like he asked her to take a letter. No, he'd need to befriend her, coax it out of her....

He knew he would just get more nervous if he thought too long about what to do. He straightened himself in his pants, made sure his shirt was properly tucked in. Then he walked purposefully from the room as if he were about to launch a minor skirmish.

She liked her window desk. He enjoyed it too; the light accentuated her beautiful neck. As always, he longed to touch her lightly-bronzed skin, the soft curve of her shoulders tapering to her well-defined waist. He watched her type away, her back facing him. Suddenly, his mouth was dry.

"Er-uh, Marilyn ah, would you...could you please step into my office for a moment?"

"Certainly, Mr. Fry," came her obedient reply as she swiveled gracefully to face him.

Walking swiftly back to his office, Fry felt embarrassed by his thoughts and guilty about his motives.

Taking her accustomed chair in front of Fry's desk, she sat down, crossing her legs, pad and pencil poised and ready.

Suddenly, his mind went blank and his eyes quickly searched the room.

"Marilyn, you, ah, did remember to rewind my clock?"

"Yes, Mr. Fry." She paused, then smiled. "For sure, I promise." They both laughed. Oh God, he thought, his palms were wet; here goes.

"Well, Marilyn, I, er-uh, was wondering if er-uh-uh —"

"Yes, Mr. Fry?"

"— if you would be so disposed Saturday evening, to ah-er-uh, to uh-uh —"

"Yes?" Marilyn Sanders was touched to see James A. Fry, the dignified, patrician pardon attorney, awkward and vulnerable, trying to broach a social topic.

"Er-uh-uh, would you be agreeable to having dinner...with me...Saturday night...tomorrow night? Perhaps?" Fry sat staring at her, face flushed.

Marilyn smiled sweetly, nodded, and gave her answer with a demure "Yes." She paused, noticing how wide Fry's eyes had gotten. Although she fancied him a handsome enough man, he now looked perfectly comical. "I would love to," she continued. "Where would you like to have dinner?" There followed an awkward silence as she noticed the man's Adam's apple bobbing up and down.

"How about that er-uh...little Italian restaurant. You know...the one down the street from your apartment? In Georgetown?" It surprised her that Fry knew the whereabouts of her apartment.

"Oh, I think that's nice," she exclaimed, getting up.

"Would seven o'clock be okay?" He paused. "For me to come by?"

"That's perfect," she replied with a smile. "I better get back to work, now," she said, her smile growing wider. Leaving, she kept his office door open.

Most of the rest of the day was a complete blur for Fry. He sat transfixed, going over and over again his conversation with Marilyn Sanders. Her reaction. Her every movement. He felt himself completely consumed by this young woman.

Finally, he decided he had to get back to work. He closed his door and attempted to do what he could to utilize the small space still left in his mind.

Compared to the other attractive women he had dated, he could feel her beauty overcome his Brahmin conceit. She must have many suitors. He was flattered by the suddenness of her acceptance.

Still, he felt guilty about his real reason for asking her in the first place. It was business. Just business. The politics forced him into reaching out to this young woman for help. But then again, whatever his reason for asking, she was lovely and he was looking forward to being with her.

The thoughts kept chewing at him; the pile of work on his desk went unnoticed.

He had to cancel his dinner date. She would be shocked and offended if he tried to pump her for information. He just couldn't do that to her. She would resent him and ruin any real chance he might have with her.

He would cancel his date and transfer her out of Justice. No conflict of interest; he could serve "the higher purpose." Still, he wanted to do neither, despite his Brahmin pride and sense of propriety.

By the time he finished weighing his costs and rewards, Marilyn was gone for the day.

>>>→ • ←<<<

Marilyn's mind was occupied with James Fry's invitation as she took the trolley to her flat in Georgetown.

She had presented just such a situation recently to her friends. Rosa Diabo, who worked at the Smithsonian, saw no harm in accepting if he asked. Ruth Muskrat had been skeptical.

"He pretends he's busy, you know," Marilyn laughed. "But he looks at me sometimes like..." she broke off.

"Like what?" asked Ruth. Rosa slowly refilled Marilyn's glass with several hefty ounces of green créme de menthe, a supply her Mohawk relations in Canada always kept replenished.

"You know...in a strange, yearning kind of way." She took a sip. "I just know he's interested. My father would say, 'Daughter, his eyes betray what his heart knows.'"

"Or maybe," Rosa nodded and paused, then leaned closer, "just womanly intuition."

Ruth frowned. "So you want to go out with him, then?"

Marilyn nodded tentatively.

"But you're not sure?" Ruth's question suggested the answer: No.

Marilyn shrugged and looked down. "What do you think?"

"Well, I certainly think it won't hurt. He won't bite you for heaven's sake." Rosa chuckled.

"Well, not bite, but..." Marilyn went on uncertainly. "He's a lot older. And from Boston, went to Harvard...smart...not my type at all."

"Ah. Your intuition is telling you 'No.'" Smiling, satisfied, Ruth Muskrat looked searchingly at her young friend for a long moment.

Marilyn sipped from her glass. "Well, the girls at work have told me he's the most isolated, well-behaved guy at Justice."

"Now, Marilyn, you know it's always dangerous to date your boss," replied Ruth. "I don't think it's a good idea at all."

"But Fry's a different sort." Marilyn paused, slowly shaking her head. "I don't know. He's definitely not a womanizer. No one has ever seen him on the outside...no parties, or even glimpsed him with a woman. Maybe he's too shy to date."

"Girl, my spies over at the Smithsonian tell me you're right. He's just shy and a little snobbish. I think you're safe." Rosa winked, catching the glint of a smile in Marilyn's eyes. "Isolated, probably lonely...harmless."

"I don't know about harmless," interjected Ruth. "His people are of a different kind than we are, Marilyn."

"You mean because he's Anglo?" Rosa was surprised that Ruth Muskrat would delineate "his people" from "their people."

"Not any Anglo, Rosa. Fry is from Boston, Brahmin relations. Do you think his parents would approve of their son dating a Native woman?"

"Well, you got me there, girl."

"I wonder what his family is like," said Marilyn.

"You're not from their highbrow, phony social station in life, my dear. But there is one thing...one catch we haven't thought of," continued Rosa. "For all his parents know, you could be European royalty."

They all laughed. Ruth Muskrat added, "For all you know, darling boy might show you off as this beautiful Spanish princess."

»»→ • ←«

Marilyn was sure that she knew now why her boss sometimes behaved in strange ways. She caught him staring at her in a soft, imploring way. His eyes betrayed a loneliness. Yet, she was certain his eyes spoke of feelings for her. There was a chance he, too, missed having a physical relationship, making him as vulnerable as she was.

She had felt such loneliness and confusion for a long time after Peter left for the war.

She wondered how it would be sleeping with a whiteman, a man who had been married, a man from Harvard. Would it be different? Or would she enjoy sleeping with him because he was sexually experienced?

Marilyn stood up to clear her head of such thoughts.

Then it hit her.

This was about Red-Boy's pardon request. The file had not been in her office for dictation. She had not filed the thing away. It had to be on his desk. He had discovered something that had prompted him to ask her to dinner.

Ruth Muskrat had been right. This was not a good idea.

The mere thought of the two of them—she and Red-Boy—caused her to sink down into an old wellspring of sadness. Sadness she had been so certain she had left behind her.

Lost in old memories, Marilyn took a deep breath as she stepped off the trolley. She was now far away from the heartbreak, here next to the Atlantic Ocean, watching the sun rise every morning. Safe again within her circle. She was always the first proud one, ahead of all her people, to see the sun come up each morning.

»»→ • ←«

The little red-awning Italian restaurant on the corner overlooked the Potomac. The perfect spot this June evening for a couple, a table on the cobblestones just outside. Spring filled the capital city with dogwood and magnolia, interlaced with a rainbow of azaleas. Blossoms provided added cover for mockingbirds, whose singing accompanied the hum of the ubiquitous cicadas.

Her boss was conservative in gray tweed pants, dark shoes and a blue short-sleeved shirt. His shirt revealed arms and a chest more powerfully built than she had imagined. He appeared younger to her here, away from the office. Without his glasses, she could see his dark brown eyes. His strong chin and combed-back dark hair gave him features similar to her male relations. She liked the flecks of grey hair at his temples and even the small area of male-pattern baldness made him look distinguished.

His companion wore a stylish dress that stopped with a flare just above her knees. Her carefully bobbed coal-black hair framed a pretty, round face. Full smiling lips were moist with dark red lipstick.

The waiter quietly strolled to their table and took their order. He brought each of them a cold near beer.

The warm breeze from the Potomac seemed to ease his tension as Fry began asking questions about her life in D.C. Marilyn liked how the breeze teased little strands of hair covering his patch of baldness as he leaned towards her.

"That's a very pretty dress. You seem to have quite an artistic bent," he offered.

"I attend Corcoran School of Art in the evenings." she told him.

"Do you paint or draw?"

"Silk paintings mostly," she replied.

The drinks plus Gershwin's *Rhapsody in Blue*" playing inside the restaurant settled Fry's nerves.

"Do you have time to read much?" he asked.

"Yes, I like to read, fiction mostly." She paused, taking a thoughtful sip.

"Have you read anything by Sinclair Lewis?"

"Sure," she smiled knowingly. "I'm a fan of his. *Main Street* and *Babbitt.*"

"Read them both, too. I liked Hemingway's *The Sun Also Rises* better, though."

Marilyn was not surprised by Fry's preference. It fit. Ruth Muskrat and Rosa had talked about the story. The man shared a lonely kind of emptiness with the "Lost Generation" depicted in the novel Yet here, more importantly, he seemed interested in her.

"What made you come to work for Justice?" she asked.

"Kind of a family tradition, I guess," Fry replied matter-of-factly. "Family just expected it. My father, being an attorney, and the family's Republican party connections…." Fry paused, took a sip. Marilyn's smile touched him. He went on. "Father went to Harvard. So I did. The family way, I guess." Fry's remark might have been egotistical, but what Marilyn heard was apologetic, even wistful.

"Were you in the war?"

Fry looked away, out at the river, reminding himself that he had tried very hard to hide his occasional respiratory distress from the mustard gas. "Yes," he replied turning and looking down at his half-empty glass. Uncharacteristically, he took a high arching swig, setting the glass down gently, and looked away again.

"I'm sorry," the young woman offered, then was quiet, expecting more from him.

"I don't talk about it much." He paused, then looked over at Marilyn.

"You've probably noticed I sometimes have occasional tremors," he said, grinning sheepishly at her. The young woman nodded. "Mustard gas poisoning. But I was lucky." Fry paused for a long moment. "My wife wasn't though."

The young woman drew back, her eyes wide, looking intently at the older man, wondering how her boss's wife had died in the war.

"Was your wife overseas?" Marilyn asked softly. "Was she with you in France?"

"Oh, no…I'm sorry. She died from the influenza back here in the States while I was overseas." The pardon attorney's mouth was now open and sagging. The boss she thought was merely vulnerable was now completely untangled in front of her.

She slowly reached out her hand to rest on his.

"Thanks, Marilyn. It's okay." Her hand felt warm and reassuring and he didn't pull away.

The waiter appeared with their meals. He then lit a red candle on the table.

The candlelight cast a warm glow over Marilyn's smooth arms and neck. The young woman's appearance, as always, drew him, but now it was more than lust or fantasy. Her simple directness, her beauty without artifice, revealed a very special young woman, somehow guileless but wise, thoughts both attractive and challenging. They finished their candlelit meal in silence at the table on the cobblestones in front of the restaurant overlooking the Potomac

River. Like the music, time with Marilyn played out in a lovely slow melody for Fry. The pardon attorney had completely forgotten about Yessup's letter and Peter Stabs-By-Mistake.

"Why don't we go for a walk," he offered, as he paid the waiter, leaving a generous tip, paying tribute for the time, the place, the evening with Marilyn.

"A walk will be good," she replied. "I often walked or ran after eating back home."

"Tell me again, where is home?" James Fry asked, momentarily forgetting he knew—knew where she came from, knew who she was related to, knew why he had asked her to dinner.

She was quiet for a long time and Fry thought that she had not heard him. But maybe her thoughts were elsewhere....

"Montana," she said with a softness almost lost in the rustling of the cherry trees. She knew he already knew.

Like a cold slap, he was back to the reality of Yessup's letter. The reality of the evening's agenda.

The spell was broken and now he must tell her the truth, what he had learned, why he was going to have to transfer her to another department. But he didn't want to, not yet. It would keep a while longer. Why spoil the pleasure of the evening.

They walked on but stopped talking, or maybe he stopped listening. He couldn't put it off. He tried to swallow but couldn't. His breathing came in shallow gasps. Without a thought of how he was going to tell her, he began.

"Um, I have a confession to make, Marilyn. Forgive me, but it has to do with work. I am quite embarrassed to talk about it."

"What's the matter, Mr. Fry?" She looked guarded, suspecting it had to do with Peter's file but saying, "Is it about my work?"

"Oh no, no. You work's fine, really wonderful in fact...and, call me Jim, please," the pardon attorney offered with a weak smile.

"Okay," she laughed. "Jim." Fry's nervous stomach was now turning with the realization that his young secretary's expectation of a pleasant social evening was about to end in disaster. He tried again, and swallowed hard. His lips seemed to stick together.

"Well, you remember that investigation I asked Miggs in Montana to do on that young Indian fellow who asked for the pardon? Peter Stabs-By-Mistake?" Without waiting for an answer, he continued. "I got a letter from Miggs' office telling me that one of the government's witnesses in that case, a

Victor Sanders, is related to you. He's your brother, half-brother, I under-stand?" He turned to study her expression and found the young woman walk-ing beside him with her head held high, as though she hadn't heard him.

"Why didn't you tell me?" he finally prodded, perplexed and a bit an-noyed by her calm when he was a wreck just asking the question.

She stopped and looked at him. For an instant Fry feared she might turn on her heels, leaving him there embarrassed and alone.

"Why don't we sit over here," she pointed to a park bench beneath a gas light. For a long moment, she sat quietly, looking away. She shrugged a little and said, "I just didn't think it mattered that much."

"Well, I can understand that, Marilyn," he offered, relieved she wasn't angry and wanting to reassure her. Now he had to say the hard part out loud. Such talk was unseemly. No gentlemen would ever say this, but he looked away and went on.

"But the investigation revealed that you bore a child by Peter Stabs-By-Mistake." Afraid to look at her, he said nothing more.

Finally, she turned her body and looked fully at him. When he met her eyes, they were full of barely-checked tears. Like him, she too held secrets more tender than words could reveal. Yet he was too far into it now to stop, so he gently pushed on.

"Can you tell me about it, Marilyn?"

"It's a very private matter. Peter and I happened a long time ago. The baby died…Peter left for the war. I left my past and my people. I thought maybe Peter had been killed. I heard nothing about him until Victor wrote about the trial."

Trying to back away from her very private pain, he asked her about her home, her people. She told him that she had been raised by a Piegan father, Oliver Sanders, a fine, well-respected man and that her mother, a Gros Ven-tre woman, had died before she came East.

They resumed walking, watching the Potomac flow silently and flat to the Atlantic Ocean.

Fry tried to explain how her working in his office might lead to embar-rassing charges of corruption and influence peddling if Peter were to be given a grant of clemency.

"Then I can just transfer to another agency," she suggested.

"Well, it isn't that easy," he scowled.

Marilyn cast her boss a perplexed look, then softly smiled to herself; he looked like a little boy pouting because he didn't get his way. She wondered what her boss was thinking.

The night breeze turned chilly as Fry suggested they return to Marilyn's flat.

Expecting to be thanked for the evening and sent on his way, the man was pleasantly surprised to be invited in for coffee.

The place was cozy with bright objects from home. He saw her paintings, her quilt and bead work. She explained how she had learned these crafts mostly from her grandmother. He looked a long time at the silk painting above the couch. He marveled at her sensitive touch; she possessed a skill he had not imagined.

He watched Marilyn open a bottom drawer and retrieve a letter. "This is the last letter I received from my almost-brother, Victor." She handed it to him.

"Almost-brother?"

"Because he's my half-brother," she explained.

The pardon attorney carefully studied the letter. When he finished, Marilyn explained how his mother, Maxine, had abused alcohol and had ruined any hope that her half-brother, Victor, could ever be trusted. He was a product of his white mother's self-centered, conniving ways.

Fry listened thoughtfully, but when she opened up about her family, his attention began to wander. Sensing he was no longer listening, she stopped. He gently took hold of her hands.

"Marilyn, I need your help. This is a delicate situation and I think you can help us."

"How?" She sipped her coffee and shook her head. "I won't contact Peter, if that's what you want."

"Was that because he's guilty?" Fry wondered.

"No, I believe he is innocent. He stood by me when I had the baby and supported us." She was silent for a long minute. "No one knew how good he was. He stayed with us...tried to do everything he could. Then, after the baby died, he went to France." She shook her head sadly, folded and refolded her dish towel. "You have no idea what living out there was like. The Peter I knew was a kind, gentle man. If he raped this girl, then the war must have changed him." Marilyn's sympathy for the man surprised Fry.

"Well, what I want you to do is to write your father and ask him what he saw and heard at Peter's trial. I believe he can help clarify the conflicting stories. You've told me that you miss your father very much. That he is a good man. Can you write to him and ask him to help, tell us what he knows?"

Marilyn remained silent, her eyes lowered. Finally she answered.

"Yes, I guess I can do that." She couldn't believe Oliver would have been taken in by Victor's deceptions. Still, her father, who had always been an honest, decent man, often did not believe that others did not speak with a straight tongue.

"Thank you, Marilyn. I think I should probably go now. Your coffee was awfully good." He paused, looking over and winking at her. "I really enjoyed being with you this evening. I'm sorry I had to talk work and invade your privacy. I know this is not an easy situation." He smiled as he got up from the couch.

She accompanied him to the door.

He turned. "Well, I guess this is goodnight. Thank you, Marilyn."

She leaned forward and kissed him softly on the cheek. "Thank you," she whispered.

"You're very sweet," he replied with a smile as he moved out into the hallway, hearing the soft click of her door close behind him.

»»→ • ←««

It had been several weeks since Marilyn had posted the letter to her father. She didn't write to him very frequently and had started her letter at least a dozen times. She wasn't sure if Oliver would even reply. If he didn't, she was pretty sure Jim Fry would be disappointed.

Still, their evening led her to believe he was safe. She would take the risk and let him into her circle, for he too had been willing to share his thoughts with her, as well as listening to hers. This important man treated her like she too had importance, significance.

One Friday evening they took in Charlie Chaplin's *The Gold Rush*. They spent most of the night in her flat debating the pros and cons of Manifest Destiny. Fry could only see how the transcontinental railroad had been "the greatest single advancement for the country since the Civil War."

Marilyn's point of view was how the whiteman's iron horse implanted across the prairie had meant the loss of the Buffalo and the disappearance of her people's lands as gold miners, ranchers and politicians claimed it for themselves. She wished Ruth Muskrat could teach him how blind he was to the damage done by Manifest Destiny. His white, ethnocentric, upper-class background easily dismissed her argument as clearly parochial, even backward. Still, her passion and lucidity attracted him.

For Marilyn, caught up in the depths of her sentiment, his lack of interest in the history and plight of her people went unnoticed. The certainty and smoothness with which James Fry patiently articulated his ideas and depth of learning, coupled with the status of his accent, nearly swept Marilyn away.

Dinner and a film were the usual dates, sometimes blending into relaxing, sometimes spirited conversation back at her flat. That was before the evening they saw Cecil B. DeMille's *The Ten Commandments*. It started on the walk back.

"Have you read the Bible?" asked the pardon attorney.

The young woman scowled. "They tried to teach it at the boarding schools we had to attend." She looked lost in thought until they reached her place.

Once there, she excused herself. "Be right back." Watching her sudden retreat, he felt awkward and tried to busy himself with a book, Fitzgerald's *The Great Gatsby.*

As her eyes adjusted inside the dark bathroom, vague outlines of the young Red-Boy grew out of the shadows. He sat across from her in their small new classroom in Cut Bank. What a miracle it had seemed after the decrepit school at Willow Creek had been destroyed by fire, ridding them of the stagnant water flooding in the basement and the smell of dead mice and decaying, rotting vegetable matter floating in the fetid stink.

Discipline at Cut Bank was stern and unrelenting, lessons rigid; first the Pledge of Allegiance, then a pupil recitation from the Bible, followed by ciphering or numbers, then recitation from the English reader. Lunch and recesses were withheld for the slightest of offenses. No child was allowed to converse in the Pikuni tongue or to utter another child's Pikuni name.

>>→ • ←<<

The teacher was standing over the twelve-year-old Red-Boy, hands on hips. "Peter, your turn to recite today's lesson from the Bible." The boy trembled.

Marilyn knew reciting from the book of the black robes from the whiteman's church would offend his father and the Elders, those who had taught him the true ways of Sspo mi tá pi—Above-Person—and the lessons of Ná pi, the trickster. To recite out loud in front of the others would be to openly disrespect his parents.

"No," came the youngster's soft-spoken answer.

"What did you say to me, young man!?" The veins in her neck were like rawhide cords. The boy's head was bent.

"I can't…" Marilyn flinched, hearing the "Thwack!" of the teacher's ruler as it struck his shoulders, his back.

All the children had sat frozen in their seats. She had covered her ears against the stoic whimpers and moans. She'd never heard these sounds before. Her parents, her people had never counted coups on children. To punish a child this way would surely break the child's spirit.

Looking up at herself in the darkened bathroom mirror as she washed her hands, Marilyn remembered another day when Red-Boy was told to recite the meaning of Christmas. He stood in front, mute. When prodded, he remained silent. Again, the teacher brought out her ruler.

The boy began explaining in a halting manner the Christ story of the Blackfeet—the star-legend of Pá yi, whose Blackfeet mother was Feather Woman and whose father was Morning Star (Venus). Born in the sky as Star Boy, he came to Earth and lived in poverty among the Blackfeet. Called Scarface (Pá yi), he was ridiculed until, through his bravery, he reached the home of the Sun, where his scar was removed.

The teacher interrupted and tried correcting the boy, attempting to get him focused on the nativity in Bethlehem. Then she again went for the ruler. Red-Boy, in defiance, completed the story in the Pikuni tongue.

Pá yi was sent back to Earth by the Sun God to instruct the Blackfeet in Sun worship. Having brought forth the Sun Dance celebration, Pá yi returned to his Sun home and became young Morning Star or Star Boy (Jupiter).

Yanked by his ear, Red Boy was dragged, wincing, from the class. Then the awful onslaught…"Thwack!……thwack!"

Marilyn remembered the huge red welts on the boy's hands and arms and face, others on the back of his neck.

Chief Stabs-By-Mistake and a delegation of Elders, including Big Brave-Mountain Chief and Curly Bear, were warned not to interfere with school, or allotments and rations would be cut.

That was what Marilyn knew of the Bible.

>>>→ • ←<<<

She rinsed her face and prepared to return to the pardon attorney. How could she ever make him understand? But he might understand; after all, he was well-educated and seemed compassionate, in an awkward sort of way. She tried hard to push away memories of Red-Boy. Back in the living room, Fry stood and smiled at her as he searched her face. "Everything okay, Marilyn?"

Her smile was reassuring as she joined him on the couch.

"Oh, I just needed to freshen up, Jim. Everything's fine, the food and everything." She paused and looked directly at him. "I hope you weren't upset...what I said about the whiteman's boarding schools."

"Not a'tall, Marilyn." He winked affectionately, trying to lift the mood. "I see you've been reading Fitzgerald. Now there's a guy who's really down on greed and striving for wealth." Marilyn nodded and shrugged. Fry tried another topic. "Would you tell me about your schooling as a child?" Fry arranged his face and raised his eyebrows into a look of interest. "Please?"

The young woman watched his face as she gathered her thoughts.

"Well, we could not speak our own tongue or talk about our cultural or religious ceremonies. If we did, the ruler or birch whip was brought out."

"Were you ever disciplined?" he asked.

She raised her finger. "Only once. I tried to explain how, even though we used a different name, we all worshiped the same Creator." Fry's brow furrowed and he shook his head. "They did not understand we do not pray to the Sun. We pray to only one Creator—Beyond-Sun-Person—and that what we think of as our Sacred Church is what white people named the Sun Dance."

"Tell me about the Sun Dance."

"The Sun Dance gathering is our most sacred religious ceremony. Once a year many, many wagons loaded with lodges and families wind their way to the foothills and form a great circle on the Sun Dance ground where the lodges are quickly put up by the women. There are many campfires and everybody is hungry. So we cook a lot of beef and feast. Then we raise our Sun-Lodge, our Medicine Lodge, around a tall Center Pole. The Medicine Lodge is like a Church, a place to give thanks to the Creator, to Beyond-Sun-Person."

Marilyn stood and retrieved a long-stemmed pipe from the top drawer of her dresser.

"This Pipe-with-the-long-stem belongs to my father. He gave it to me when I left. When my relations pray in the Medicine Lodge, the Pipe is made pure with the smoke of Sweetgrass. The Pipe is pointed at the Sun, because Beyond-Sun-Person lives far beyond. We call the Sun 'Naa tó' si'...the giver of life to all living things."

Marilyn handed Fry the Pipe and watched him slowly finger the smooth stone bowl.

"After the Pipe is pointed straight at Naa tó' si, the Sun, it is pointed to Earth. The stone bowl of the Pipe represents Earth, because Beyond-Sun-Person gave us Earth for our home. The wooden Pipe stem represents all living things on Earth which the Creator has given to us. The Pipe smoke represents our prayers rising up to the Creator asking help for our families and relations, for good health, long life and for guidance to live right. And that is how we pray in our Medicine Lodge."

"That's very interesting. Thank you, Marilyn." Marilyn took the Pipe and returned it to her dresser.

"Since I left, Father wrote that Superintendent Campbell has tried to do away with our Sun Dance. He did not succeed, but the ceremony is much shorter now," she said, her voice trailing off.

"Tell me more about your beyond-person," he asked, confident that her spiritual teachings were beneath his protestant Brahmin orthodoxy.

"Well, the Creator is 'Naa to yi ta pi,' which means Beyond-Sun-Person or Sspo mi tá pi, 'Above-Person'. Beyond-Sun-Person is all Powerful. He made Naa tó' si, the Sun, and the Moon, which we call 'Ko' komíki'somm.' And He made Morning-Star, which we call 'Aa pi só wooh ta.' He made the grass grow and the Buffalo for our food and the Earth on which we live." Spreading her arms, Marilyn's voice softened. "He made all that we see with our eyes and all that we hear with our ears."

Sensing that either her boss was confused by the Pikuni expressions or simply not following her, Marilyn stopped, sat back down and smiled, waiting for his response.

Catching his own inattention, he smiled back and asked, "Do other tribes believe the same as you do?"

"Well, I can tell you what my mother, Crow Woman, told me about being a Gros Ventre. Some of her family were Chippewa. Basically, the stories are the same, but they call their Creator Manitou."

Again, the distant look in Fry's eyes; Marilyn thought he might still be a bit confused. Despite that, his gentle questioning and seeming interest made her feel accepted somehow, or at least safe.

As if suddenly reminded of something, Marilyn jumped up.

"Before I tell you more, I must treat you to something," she said mischievously, glancing back over her shoulder. Her boss's distant look evaporated in the glow of her small flirtation. From her kitchen cupboard, she retrieved a small bottle of Imperial Gin and two small glasses. A gift from Rosa. The pardon attorney was enchanted by the young woman's audacity. He was the only one amongst his colleagues at Justice who didn't know where every speakeasy in D.C. was. Now, here he was with ready access to every conceivable type of liquor brought down from Canada. Of course, for "private use" only. That euphemism kept one conveniently out of reach of the Volstead Act. Yes, imbibing a little gin with Marilyn would be a very nice "private use." He smiled broadly at her and raised his brows.

Not much was said until she refilled his glass and she finished her second small sip.

"Now I will tell you what my mother taught me about Manitou," said Marilyn Deer Child. Assuming he wanted to understand.

"In times-way-back, Manitou made the world, then he made the Indians. At first, the Indians were not strong. Manitou decided to give them stronger bodies and better minds, so he made the Indians like that. Now Bad-Under-Ground-Spirit was watching and he was jealous. He made evil thoughts come to the minds of the Indians. He told them to steal and to kill and to do much evil. Manitou found this out and he told them not to do evil, that it was bad and if they continued they would be punished." Deer Child paused, glancing at the older man's neutral expression.

"Then Manitou told his children that they would be poor and hungry, but if they followed his teachings, they would be happy in their hearts and would not suffer because he would give them food and tell them how to live. Then Manitou told them to build each year a Worship-Lodge and pray in this Worship-Lodge to be strong, brave and have clean hearts. If they did this, he would protect them and give them long life. Then he told them how to build this Lodge. That is why we build it with cottonwood." She took another small sip of her Imperial Gin.

Leaning back with a sigh, Fry took a swallow of gin and looked almost wistful. "Do your people, your mother's people, believe each person has a soul?"

"Well, the black robes, the priests, taught my mother that Manitou had later told the Chippewa and all the other tribes that He would give each person a soul that would be with him until death. The black robes said Manitou had sent one Person to teach our people many things and that the black robes would tell us his words. From then on, we did not need to ask or tell Manitou anything because He would already know what was in our hearts. Good-Spirit would come to us every night and will teach us the words of this Person...how to live, how to get food and robes. This Person would ask Water-Spirit to sprinkle water on the Earth so the grass and food would grow.'"

"Did God tell your people that there would be life after death?"

With each swallow of Imperial Gin, James Fry looked as if he had wandered to some far back time. His eyes were shiny. Maybe it was the gin, but maybe he was being pulled back to a long-ago sadness of loss, that intimate place they knew in each other.

Marilyn didn't know what he really wanted when he asked, so she took the question at face value.

"The black robes told Mother and Mother told me that Manitou said, 'I will put a Spirit called Big-Spirit aside to meet your soul after you die. First, there will be a Glory-trail from the Earth to the powerful Big-Spirit, then there will be two trails leading from this Glory-trail. At the fork will be another Spirit with much power. He will know all that you have done while on Earth. If you have done much wrong and your heart was bad and if you did not believe in Manitou, then Spirit-at-the-fork will make you take the trail where there is suffering and no happiness.'"

They were both quiet. Marilyn was caught again between her mother's soft voice and the harsh loneliness of the boarding school. And Fry, just lost. Quiet with his empty glass, his mind now far away from this little flat in Georgetown.

Softly, Marilyn finally spoke hesitantly, "Thank you for listening Jim. I have never really spoken this way to a whiteman before." Her eyes, too, were a bit shiny.

Fry looked directly at her now, as he reached out and took her soft hands in his. She looked down at her lap.

His heart was suddenly pounding and his mouth felt dry.

"Marilyn?"

"Yes?" she looked up meeting his eyes.

Without a thought, he toyed with her beautiful shiny hair. Then, his lips were on hers, and he was embracing her. Her lips were cool and tasted of gin and lipstick, her mouth was warm and her tongue met his. She returned his embrace, pulling him closer.

He dropped soft kisses below her ears, down her neck. She lifted her chin. The heat and weight of her breasts pressed into his chest. He slid his hand between them, his thumb brushing across her erect nipples.

What on earth was he doing? He had to draw away while he still could.

"Oh no," she softly sighed, as he moved back.

"I'm sorry." His voice sounded strange; he was sure he was being more gallant than sorry.

She offered her hand and whispered, "Come."

His arousal still not under control, he was afraid to take the hand she offered. Yet, having her back in his arms seemed to be his only thought.

She drew down the Murphy bed and switched off the room light. Only the soft street lamps and the moon illuminated the room and one another.

"Come," she whispered.

He meant to ask if she was sure, but instead just nodded and followed her.

The darkness hid his undressing. She didn't watch him but stood at her dresser and removed her bracelet, her earrings. Finally, she was letting go of the last link with love, long gone.

From beneath the sheets, he watched as she slowly undid her dress, letting it fall to the floor. Then, there she stood, soft full breasts, the dark apex at the top of smooth legs.

He drew a steadying breath. If he had ever felt any hesitation, it had now vanished.

Without a sound, she came to him. He lay on his side, propped up on his elbow.

She smelled of soap and gin and pressed her body to his. She searched his eyes in the dark. He kissed her, then hesitated.

He felt her smile. Then she shifted her weight and guided him into her. His decision to be gentle left him the moment she moved.

$$\text{»»→ • ←««}$$

Still quiet, but completely spent, he slept. She lay beside him, listening until his breathing turned slow.

She softly slid from the bed, slipped into a light robe and went to the kitchen. After searching to the far reaches of a top cupboard, she retrieved the small bundle of special herbs and made herself a cup of the tea. Not tasty, but comforting. She would not again endure the pain and fear of another child.

Finishing the tea, she went to the bathroom and douched, a lesson passed on by Rosa. This evening might not have been the best idea, but neither did it seem too bad.

She listened to the clock tick and let what was left of the gin slowly gentle her mind.

As if already dreaming, she lay next to him and wondered if the gin or her own feelings had prompted their lovemaking. With his hand under his cheek as he slept, he seemed even more vulnerable. Perhaps it was this feature alone that had attracted her—a need of his that she could fulfill.

Sleep did not come. The soft ticking of the clock matched her heartbeat. She decided she had been listening only to self-flattery. Crow Woman had warned her; the protective pathway for an Indian girl was not to sleep with a whiteman unless married to him, otherwise she would be shunned. Maybe that was true, but her mother was gone to the Sand Hills and Marilyn was a very long way from home.

She yawned and wanted to sleep but could not relax here next to her sleeping boss.

This educated, widowed man had certainly not been with very many women in a while. Even to her limited experience, his coupling seemed awkward and over very quickly. Not at all like it had been with Red-Boy. She regretted the comparison, even resented it. Yet, there it was. But why not. Red-Boy had been her first, and he was of her people. She had been drawn to a reassuring kind of strength he had, as if he were her almost-brother. She remembered how they had shared secret horseback rides to remote, tall grasslands. Maybe their physical coupling had not been all that different. Maybe it was just her feelings, knowing that his affection stayed with her afterwards. Or maybe she just remembered it that way. Whatever it was, it was lost long ago.

Perhaps she had thought she could recapture it again with Jim Fry. Yet the Imperial Gin had only relaxed her inhibitions and now, with it all washed away, she was thinking of Red-Boy.

Alone on a kitchen chair, listening to the relentless ticking of the clock, the pleasant interlude had become a parade of ghost people; people and things she had pushed away, she now yearned to grasp.

She rested her head on the table and finally darkness began to melt away. The Place-of-Rising-Sun at Heavy-Water-Country was soon at hand.

When the older man awoke, she silently, dutifully prepared a breakfast of bannock bread, sausage and fruit. He was affectionate, but their silences were long and awkward. Each made perfunctory remarks about objects in the room, the food or activities outside the window. For a long time after the pardon attorney left, Marilyn watched the smooth Potomac River flow by and the carefully costumed older women with their parasols on the arms of nat-tily-dressed men in wing tips and derby hats or boaters. Occasionally, a Model-T or a Hertz Yellow Cab whizzed by, and horse-drawn carriages rolled along with young couples inside, animatedly talking or laughing.

She felt older than her twenty-seven years. And empty. An emptiness and bitterness like a chill wind. And she was lonely. She wondered what was left for her in D.C. She wondered if Oliver would write to her.

She intended to think about the night with Jim Fry. But her mind went back to the Sun Dance celebration. She and Red-Boy had met the wagon load of beef rumbling along the dusty road. The Indian Bureau had loaded meat on a manure wagon. The meat bounced through the dust and heat covered only by blow flies. Red-Boy had angrily confronted the agents and scraped quantities of stable manure from between the broken planks of the wagon body.

Deer Child's jaw clenched. She raised her head defiantly, remembering the bulletin circulated by the Commissioner of Indian Affairs proclaiming that "all the Indians are Happy and Contented."

Coolidge's Commission never knew about, or at least never mentioned, the things Deer Child and Red-Boy had seen. Ruth Muskrat Bronson was right; nothing would come from the Commission because they had all been picked by the whiteman's Indian Bureau.

She looked below and saw the postman leaving her building.

»»—→ • ←—«««

*"Deer Child — May 1926*

*Daughter my heart rises that you have written to me. When I got your letter I know that Naa tó' si sees and hears everything. So many win-ters have passed. After every snow I ask the Sun to give you long life. When you left the sun shone with no heat for many winters. But my heart is always good towards you daughter.*

*My hand is weak with your almost-brother Victor. He does not show me his heart. He sometimes talks with the tongue of a child, especially now. He runs for the tribal council and tells everyone that he will free Peter Stabs-By-Mistake if he is chosen. But my eyes tell what his tongue would hide. He hates Peter the father of your first born. Now I must tell you something else daughter. Peter's woman is Annie Run-*

*ning Crane even as Peter is behind the prison. But to Annie Victor is a
dog-face. I know this because I have spoken with her.*

*Now daughter I tell you something else. After Peter's trial I talked to
Annie Running Crane. Annie she was frightened. The judge had
asked your Uncle Richard to put the words of Nellie Running Crane,
Louise Red Fox, Maggie Wolf Plume and Mary Horn into English.
But I know Richard's words did not tell what really happened. The
women they were all very scared from the thunder clouds pressing
down on them. They did not know the whiteman's court practices. I
fear these women spoke as they were told to do when they went before the judge and jury men to speak. I know that your almost-
brother told them what to say.*

*Now I tell you something else Deer Child. I believe in my heart that
Peter should not be in prison. I do not believe that Peter committed the
whiteman's crime of rape. It is good that you are where you are. You
can do much good for Peter. Please tell Mr. Fry that what I say is the
truth. Daughter I speak with a straight tongue.*

*I pray that you my daughter may see the young grass and that the
Great and Merciful Spirit protects you. I am now 67 winters and am
old. I wish to see you my daughter before I walk the ghost trail.*

*Red-Bird-Tail Meenk-Swarlsis"*

Marilyn Deer Child wiped tears with the back of her hand and carefully
placed the penciled, hand-written letter on her kitchen table. Oliver's pen-
manship seemed less firm than she remembered, some of the circles a little
jagged, the lines a little crooked.

Now, the tired young Pikuni woman who had come East to get away felt
a jagged tearing at her heart. Her almost-brother may have committed perjury and coerced others to lie at Peter's trial. She could not bear the shame of
her almost-brother. Her father wanted her to know the truth and to do the
honorable thing.

She remembered Red-Boy's devotion to her and their child. His angry
defiance in the face of agency cruelty and injustice. She respected him. And,
in a special place deep within her circle, she still loved him for his strength.

She quietly asked Sspo mi tá pi (Above Person) to bring Red-Boy the power of fire from the Sun and to let the long vision of the night stars guide him now through this dark time of injustice.

She would obey her father whom she loved and missed above all else, knowing she would never face shame by honoring her father's counsel. She would give her father's letter to her boss.

Slowly, the tears slid down onto her father's letter, smudging the pencil lines, leaving holes where the lines had once been smooth and circular around her guarded circle.

Shrine convention, July 27, 1923, Washington D.C. (left to right: unidentified, unidentified, White Quiver, Cha Reevis, Levi Burd, Bird Rattler, boy, and Victor J. Evans, with Two Guns White Calf on far right). Delegation prompted by criticism from Robert Hamilton and James Willard Schultz that Blackfeet were starving under Superintendent Campbell's leadership. Photo courtesy of William E. Farr.

# XIX

# Don't Look Twice
# At A Two-Faced Man

The very thought of one agency of the government—the Indian Agency—being forced to take a position opposite another agency over whether or not to free a federal inmate vexed Fry. The March 1926 letter from the New Englander kept needling him. And why was Marilyn's relative, this Victor Sanders, so interested in freeing Stabs-By-Mistake when he testified that he had seen him commit the rape?

Things would have been different if only the Holyoker hadn't requested Justice to investigate the whole thing. It certainly could embarrass the Indian Agency and it wouldn't do for Justice to second-guess the Indian Bureau. He had hoped that leaving it up to Miggs out in Montana was far enough removed from D.C. not to trip things up for the administration. Still, he felt uneasy about the Holyoker's telling him that he knew Blackfeet Indians of "good standing."

In the middle of it all there were Fry's feelings for Marilyn.

How could he manage this potential minefield of bureaucratic embarrassment and not lose "his precious Marilyn"?

Fry felt doomed. He would lose Marilyn's treasured presence because of his duty to avoid the appearance of impropriety. To further justice. To correct wrongs that probably had been done.

He supposed he was glad that Yessup had confided in him. It was good that he knew about the connection between Marilyn and the man responsible for Stabs-By-Mistake's incarceration.

Yet, there it was again. Why did Marilyn's half-brother, Victor Sanders, now claim that he would work for Stabs-By-Mistake's release?

>>>—→ • ←—<<<

Marilyn Deer Child went over and over the words in Oliver's letter: "Please tell Mr. Fry that what I say is the truth…you can do much good for Peter…Daughter I speak with a straight tongue."

The young woman had honored her father's wish by giving her boss the letter.

She was worried about Oliver; he seemed sad and frail in the letter. Should she tell James Fry that she wanted to take leave from her job to go home? She wanted to see her father, to judge the situation for herself.

But maybe leaving suddenly might be taken as an offense. She didn't know how Fry might react. He often overwhelmed her with his attention while remaining aloof and disinterested. She wasn't sure how much she really liked him, but she did remain curious about their relationship and his world.

She decided to ask Fry if he would like to take a vacation trip to Montana, where she could show him her home and land.

"Why would someone want to go out there when Boston is a helluva lot more interesting," he remarked dismissively.

They argued. Afterwards he apologized and told her he wanted to make love. She chided him, making it clear again that she would not have sex after the first time without protection. Having to be reminded, Fry felt chagrined and left in a huff.

Inwardly, he knew there was no way a real and lasting relationship with Marilyn was possible. What could he tell his parents? His mother would think Marilyn a mere "kneeduster," just another "skirt" she considered not suitable to keep company with her son. Knowing his mother's ability to spew biting sarcasm with a curt remark or simply a raised eyebrow, he thought it would be cruel to expose Marilyn to her. His father would simply stare at the beautiful young woman and give his son a knowing wink. No, he would not be taking Marilyn home to meet the family.

Confident that he could win her over, his ego soon recovered from her rejection of physical intimacy.

The next day, he agreed that perhaps a vacation to Montana would do them both good. Pleased, she asked if he would also take her to Boston. He gently deflected her entreaties, telling her he had to travel up to Boston that weekend for "boring" family business with his father, the lawyer. She gracefully relented.

After all, she had been invited to a Smithsonian art exhibit by Ruth Muskrat and several of her friends from Mount Holyoke College.

The embers in the living room fireplace were turning gray when James A. Fry entered. The wall clock chimed once, then resumed its meticulous ticking.

He retrieved the wrinkled letter from his pocket and squinted at the lettering.

"Please tell what I say is the truth," read the missive.

"The truth," he chuckled to himself, knowing that he held the solution to his problem in his hands.

He had grown up an only child in this immense Victorian-Gothic home in the Back Bay. All his life, he had heeded his Brahmin father's advice. Overcame adversity, honored duty, served the higher purpose. What was some uncomfortable "truth" when held up next to such lofty values?

Now back home, away from D.C. and the lesser frivolities of life, he felt justified in his superiority.

He read the letter one last time, then served the higher purpose—to protect the administration in an election year. Why even an Indian could understand how remaining behind bars served a more useful purpose.

Letting go, the letter floated listlessly into the fire.

The right thing, he thought, as he watched the paper curl and shrivel, flare then disintegrate into dark wisps.

>>>—→ • ←—<<<

Having graduated from Mount Holyoke, Ruth Muskrat Bronson was now a Bureau of Indian Affairs teacher. As their friendship deepened, Deer Child spent long hours listening to the Cherokee woman recount her teaching experiences and problems with reservation social work for the YWCA. In turn, Marilyn recounted her boarding school days and problems with disease and malnutrition for those who weren't enrolled in school.

Then, during that summer of 1926, the possibility of a new and different life began to emerge for Marilyn. At Ruth Muskrat's suggestion, she had enrolled in classes at Corcoran School of Art. Now her art work assumed a greater purpose-an outlet for her inner feelings.

One evening Ruth Muskrat and Rosa Diabo went with Marilyn to a Summer Arts Festival sponsored by the Smithsonian. Ruth Muskrat, in her traditional Cherokee Indian princess costume, was introduced to the crowd by the Dean of the Art School. Ruth then introduced the guest speaker, author Gertrude Bonnin, Zitkala-sa. Deer Child had read several of the Sioux writer's short stories and knew that Gertrude had uncovered oil lease fraud and corruption while serving as an investigator for the Indian Rights Association.

Gertrude spoke eloquently of the need for Native people to express themselves through art or writing or music, to address the abuses, including the genocide of Native cultures. Deer Child was delighted to align herself with women like Gertrude Bonnin and Ruth Muskrat, Indian women who were standing up and demanding rights, taking action, "coming out of our own Dark Ages and into the light of a New Renaissance." Marilyn was inspired.

After the speech but before Ruth could introduce the two women, Gertrude commented, "The beadwork in your blouse. Piegan I think. Or maybe Blood."

"Yes, It's Piegan," Marilyn beamed, impressed with the depth of the author's knowledge.

"Have you been in school here long?"

"No, not too long. I've been here in D.C. six, seven years from the reservation in Browning, Montana. I just go to school evenings."

"Well, let's go get a cup of java, okay?" suggested Gertrude Bonnin, beckoning to Ruth and the others to come along.

Astonished to be invited, Marilyn simply blurted, "Okay!"

"Since you know my name, what's yours?"

"Deer Child. Marilyn, Deer Child Sanders."

"Are you planning on returning to the reservation?" asked the Sioux woman.

"I don't know," Marilyn answered, glancing down.

"I've been talking to Marilyn about the idea of teaching," broke in Ruth. "I'm planning a career teaching with the BIA and think Deer Child would be good at that." Marilyn returned Ruth's smile.

"Yes, I think that's great," added Gertrude."

≫⟫→ • ←⟪≪

"Yessup, get the hell in here! Get in here right now!" Miggs was planted in his large leather chair behind his vast oak wood desk. His cigar was lit.

Jesus. The boss is in fine fettle this morning, thought Yessup. He grew ever wearier of his boss's little episodes of paranoia. As always, when shrouded in these moods, the little Irishman seemed addicted to his foul habit of smoke-eating—nervously chewing snuff and puffing on a cigar. All the yelling, spitting and cigar-waving mostly just made him want to pee.

"What is it now, sir?" He tried not to sound too annoyed.

"Son-of-a-bitch!" shouted the little lawman. "Yessup, goddamn it, man, sit down!"

Hands trembling, Yessup knew his boss had finally discovered that he had written to the pardon attorney in D.C.

In his head he had it all worked out, what he would tell his red-faced boss. He would tell him how the U.S. Pardon Attorney was savvy enough to keep the lid on. Especially since he had the blood relative of a material witness working in his own office.

Yessup, still rehearsing his defense, nearly missed Miggs' steely eyes fixed to his own. Yessup stopped breathing. His mind raced. What the hell did he really know about the workings of Washington politics. About this Fry. About Miggs' command. This was it. He swallowed hard. Hell, he was about to get the ax.

"You know what I found out?" The boss was glowering at him.

"Something I . . ."

"That piss-ant Walsh got to Frank Campbell! A real circuitous sono-fabitch—from top to bottom and sideways! Didn't think he'd really stoop so low. Christ, now Campbell's spreading word all over the goddamn Blackfoot Reservation that after the council elections he's really gonna spring that Injun bastard down at Leavenworth. You know, the one I sent you up to the reservation about, a while ago."

"Stabs-By-Mistake."

"God-damn it, stabs-me-in-the-ass f'chrissakes!" The little boss bounded from his chair, both hands perched on his desk as if ready to leap at Yessup.

"And you know what their secret weapon is?" Before Yessup could flinch or utter a vowel, Miggs blurted, "Booze! Damned Democrats in congress have been bitchin' at the administration for being soft on Prohibition. God-damned hypocrites!" He pounded the top of his desk with his fist and abruptly sat down.

"Those Democrats bitch about Prohibition not being enforced while they drink more booze than Al Capone could ever piss away in his bathtub. Then while they bitch and drink, they run bootleg all over the place...min-ers, cattlemen, even on the goddamned reservation. Causin' all kinds of shit. So, stabs-in-the-face got liquored up, screwed a girl, got sent to Leavenworth.

So Walsh gets Campbell to free stabs-in-the-ass, then turns around and ambushes the Indian Bureau and accuses the administration of being soft on bootleggers, not keepin' em behind bars, for chrissakes!"

"I guess that makes sense, sir" Yessup had heard it all before and was mostly relieved it was Senator Walsh and not him who was the target of his boss's wrath.

"You know what I think, Yessup?" This time, Yessup knew what his boss was going to say. "Don't get mad. Get even."

The Assistant U.S. Attorney swiveled his chair, shot a plug of tobacco the size of a paperweight at the cuspidor, and grinned with satisfaction at his assistant. Nodding, satisfied, he swiveled back to his desk, folded his hands contentedly on top of the files in front of him, picked up his cigar and squinted his eyes.

"Yep, I'm gonna get even with Walsh—that little Democrat worm. I'm gonna shove Stabs-By-Mistake up his ass!" Taking another puff from his cigar, he glared at his subordinate. "Then that sonofabitch will never be able to sit again!" he bellowed, throwing his head back and barking out a loud guffaw, followed by an even louder coughing.

Yessup waited for the other shoe to drop. He didn't have long to wait.

"Yessup, you're my man. You're gonna help me clean the shit out of that god-damned reservation."

Oh, Jesus, thought Yessup, suddenly realizing he needed to use the restroom.

"What do I have to do now, boss?"

"You GET to go up to the reservation to that little shithouse agency and tell Superintendent Frank Campbell that his Indian rapist will NOT, I repeat, will NOT, be released from Leavenworth under any circumstances under my watch! Is that clear?"

"Yes sir." Yessup's need to urinate increased.

"And, you will give Superintendent Campbell my words the very second you get to Browning, by God! You tell him he has been over-ridden by the fucking Justice Department in Washington, D.C. Is that clear?"

Yessup was out of his chair and half-way across the room, muttering over his shoulder that he would get on it right away, not to worry.

"Wait! There is one other little detail I forgot to mention."

Yessup feared his bladder might just find an outlet down his pant leg, but he turned to face his boss.

"You know what that savage little bastard did at Leavenworth?"

"What?" Yessup was not sure what Miggs was talking about.

"Sonofabitch killed a man down there. A white man, for chrissakes! Really swell, don't you think?"

"How did you find out?" queried his underling, momentarily distracted from the squeezing of his bladder.

"How! That's what the goddamned taxpayers pay me for!" Miggs paused and sat down. "Warden at Leavenworth told us." He pursed his lips and cocked his head. "So, listen to me, dammit! The only thing people are really gonna care about is that an Indian killed a white man in prison. There's no goddamned way I'm gonna help Campbell make Peter stabs-what's-her-name a free Injun.'"

Miggs was winding down now and had reached his usual dénouement of pacing and muttering. "Campbell needs to understand that any games being played up there with the tribal elections are gonna stay up there. Campbell needs to put a lid on the whole damned pardon deal. And I don't give a shit who promises to free the little bastard if he gets elected to their Tribal Council." Yessup pretended to listen, waiting for his boss to run down. "I don't care what he promises those pagans —"

"Piegans, sir," Yessup corrected, quietly.

"Goddamn it, don't interrupt me! I don't care if he promises to make Geronimo head of the Indian Bureau! It ain't gonna happen as long as it's on my watch and Calvin Coolidge is president! You got that?!"

"Understood, boss."

It was a close call, Yessup groaned with relief, feeling the tension released from his urinary tract.

Burial grounds at Old Agency. Photo by Thomas McGee, Courtesy of the Sherburne Collection and William E. Fa

# XX

# The Ghost-Trail
# to the Sand Hills

urning from the easel, Red-Boy noticed that his bookish friend had come to give his creation a look-see. "La...l...l...looks la...like y'....ya....yur g...going to ch...ch....chanaange y....yer pa'...pa' paintttinning," the bony, diminutive trustee-librarian stuttered out.

"Aaee. Got some new ideas. New visions," Red-Boy added.

The black horse was now mostly gray. The lone rider wore leggings and a breech-clout. Red-Boy was Sun Painting the horse and rider with the sun colors from his Dream Vision in The Hole.

The white eagle-feather bonnet, two-dozen upright feathers inserted in a folded rawhide headband, worn by the Blackfeet leaders—his grandfather Big Brave-Mountain Chief and great-grandfather Mountain Chief—stood out majestically on the lone rider. The headband was decorated with red flannel and brass discs and pendants of white weasel skin.

His war-wounded right hand had learned to mix and rub the paint textures and hues with soft, steady, sometimes flourishing strokes. Remembering the colorful embroidery on his mother's blue trade cloth dresses, he added those colors to the landscape and the rider, strokes and stitches of light and dark blue, dark red and deep yellow, white and black.

He pictured Annie while he painted, her delicate feet tucked into soft-soled moccasins of elk skin; Annie, his precious sits-beside-him-woman, in her elk-skin dress. He could picture the narrow band of trade beads on the neck opening, with broader bands circling her delicate shoulders. A still broader band covered the yoke on both front and back. At Sun Dance encampments, she added beaded or brass pendants to her hair and ears.

Her elk-skin dress hung straight, but still it reminded him of Deer Child's antelope garment, held at her waist by a broad belt of beaded rawhide, fastened with buckskin ties.

He carefully painted the colors of the warrior as he continued to envision the colors and beauty of Annie. His right painting hand seemed more steady, more skilled with the delicate artistry.

Day after day Red-Boy painted. Unexpected privileges were extended to him once he was out of The Hole. He had all the paint he wanted, was given extra time in the library and was allowed to let his hair grow. He imagined the rider on the horse as having the same hair. He and his Sun-Painted warrior both wore braids.

"To honor my ancestors," Red-Boy explained one day to Shake Spear. The librarian had noticed that the braids in the painting mirrored those of Red-Boy, carefully tied with rawhide draws at the ends.

The prison guards checked on Red-Boy and the progress of the painting, sometimes commenting but usually content to watch the inmate artist work with a kind of stoic aloofness. The Indian's face emerged bit-by-bit onto the canvas.

At mess with Big Ed, Gunny and the other veterans, they talked about the Great War; Red-Boy mostly listened. The horror and heroism he had been part of no longer defined him as a warrior. He had moved on. No one need explain to him the new horrors that had confronted him on the reservation, or the new heroism of those few who defied the corrupt "Agency Ring."

Red-Boy tried not to obsess about why he had been put in this place, but sometimes a cold, whirlwind rage swept through him. In time, even the coiled, poisonous touch of Krankk passed through him, nothing more than freezing wind passed over rippling water.

One evening, Red-Boy and a few others were given extra time in the exercise yard. As he followed the misty ribbon of the Milky Way, he thought of Annie and wondered if she ever still looked at the Never-Moving-Star (North Star) with him. The night sky was clear and clustered with stars.

He wondered if Black Looks had won Annie's heart, after all these years.

Later, lying in his bunk, he traced vague star patterns on the concrete and stone ceiling until he drifted off.

》》→ • ←《《

In sleep, he was back in his parents' lodge; his father was telling him the story of the Seven Brothers.

"In times-far-back, when our dogs instead of the Elk-Dogs, the horses, hauled the skin tipis and food when camps were moved, Medicine-Bear was a Piegan warrior who had seven sons. The oldest was given the name Máá ka yi naa, Chest Man. He was a great hunter and did many brave deeds. He was strong like a young Buffalo Bull.

"The seven brothers went into the bush, hunting. They did not know of the death of their mother. After eight days, they came back to camp. The big camp had moved. Their eyes saw only one lodge. It was their father's lodge. It was empty. All their belongings had been burned. They saw the head of their mother on the ground near their lodge. They knew that their mother had been killed. They never knew that the Great Bear, the owner of a bad and powerful Medicine, had transferred his Medicine to their mother and had given her an evil mind.

"The head spoke: 'Your Father and all our people have gone away, but we will live here in our lodge just the same.'

"Chest Man had brought in a great deer hide. It was on the ground near the head of his mother. The head spoke again: 'I am going to tan this hide. I am going to make Chest Man a buckskin jacket. Don't look at me while I am working...I don't want any one of you to look. While I am tanning this hide, I will have no pity.'

"The seven brothers hid in their lodge. They heard their mother chipping the hide. Chest Man was curious. 'I am going to see what our mother is doing.' The other six said, 'No, don't look out.'

"The boy was bound to see. He looked out and saw the head rolling back and forth.

"'I told you not to look, Chest Man,' said the head.

"In great fear, the seven boys ran out of the lodge. They ran fast; they were afraid. Right away, the head started rolling after them. Faster and faster they ran. Chest Man had a bow and four arrows.

"'We are going to get away,' said Chest Man and he shot an arrow far off. Where the arrow fell, they stood. It was a Medicine-Arrow. The arrow carried them there. Now we have escaped, they thought. But the head followed and came near. Chest Man shot other arrows until all four had been shot. The head still chased them. It was then only a skull.

"Every time the brothers believed they had escaped, they heard the cry of the skull: 'Chest Man, I'm going to kill you.'

"At last the fifth brother reached into a pool and took a handful of water. He threw it behind him, and it became Heavy-Water (ocean). The skull came to the Heavy-Water. It rolled back and forth calling for a helper. It dared not go into the water. It would sink. Came a little Water Spider and spoke to the skull. 'I will be your helper. I will make you a Water Spider so you can run on the water.' The Spider Helper did this, and the skull ran fast on the Heavy-Water. Then a Loon rose from under the water. The Loon ate the Skull-Spider.

"The Skull did not come again. The seven brothers were saved.

"The seven brothers came to a great forest. They were tired.

"Chest Man spoke: 'Brothers, we are saved. Let us sit on the branch of that big tree.' The tree and a strong branch had the shape of a dipper. Chest Man said to his brothers, 'We will never see our people again. We are lost.'"

"Now," said Thomas Stabs-By-Mistake, the teller of the dream story, "I will tell you how the Great Dipper, which we call The Seven Brothers, came into the sky, Red-Boy."

"Chest Man said to his brother, 'Let us decide what we will call ourselves.' The brothers agreed to this.

"'No,' said the brothers, to becoming the Ground, the Trees, the Water, the Buffalo, and the Mountains."

In the dream, the sixth brother had nothing to say. Red-Boy tried to open his mouth but nothing came out.

"Chest Man was the only one who had been given a name. A dream had come to him he announced. He was the Medicine Man of the seven brothers. 'Brothers,' he said, 'Let us be Stars.' The brothers agreed to this. They decided to be stars.

"Chest Man sat on the end of a branch. He took from his hair an Eagle Plume. 'I am going to blow this Eagle Plume,' he said. 'Close your eyes.' The brothers did as he said. Chest Man blew on the Eagle Plume.

"'Look,' he said. The seven brothers saw themselves far up in the sky. They were sitting as they did on the limb of the great tree—like a dipper.

"'Now,' said Chest Man, 'All the people will look at us when Sun is hidden. We will tell them where the directions are. They will call us the Seven Brothers. The Night-Clock-of-the-Sky — That-Which-Tells-of-Passing-Time.'"

>>>—→ • ←—<<<

He awoke to the pealing of the 5:30 a.m. bell, and stared at the concrete ceiling in his barred cell. He stretched, relieved to be on earth among the living.

"Out of bed! C'mon you shitheads! Get ready for breakfast!" The guards cursed, the groans, swearing and bodily sounds filling the cell block as the men slowly prepared themselves for yet another day of a formless, directionless existence.

To delay this reality, Red-Boy thought of Annie, only this time he thought of Annie and her mother. There had always been the conflict with Nellie, put off by the young warrior-veteran "troublemaker." His reputation for drinking. A Piegan and a veteran — like all the other Indian veterans, polluted by booze and the same army. Polluted by the same Army that had so brutalized their people during the past sixty winters.

A hundred times a day, Annie's beauty flowed back to him. The few times that Annie had dressed and left after their lovemaking, Red-Boy had sensed that Nellie would eventually know. If only Nellie could have seen his heart.

Then he saw not Annie, but Deer Child. The last time he saw her, her face — how she had held herself to him. They shared that; the shining inner beauty he saw in Deer Child, he saw again in Annie. The sameness surprised him. He had thought them very different from one another.

At day's end, Red-Boy would grow restless. He tossed after lights-out. Sometimes tears welled in the corners of his eyes as he thought of the infant son he had sired, then lost.

Turning on his side one evening, Red-Boy remembered when James Vielle, drunk, had staggered back to their log cabin and told him that the baby lay buried in a small plot close to where Deer Child's mother, Crow Woman, and his great-grandfather, Mountain Chief, had met the Ghost-Trail.

>>>—→ • ←—<<<

"Hey, Peter, what's been eatin' you, man?" asked Big Ed, the brawny veteran, at mess one morning. "Besides the damned lice and fleas?"

Gunny, noticing Peter Red-Boy's glumness, chimed in. "Jeez, man, you're in good with everyone around here. What more do ya' want?" The nervous little inmate blinked once or twice, then added, "Ya' want another Krankk for a block mate?" Everyone laughed.

For the first time at the mention of the brutal ex-boss, they detected the hint of a grin creep up the sides of the Indian's mouth.

"Hell, no! Another Krankk would foul up my whole operation in here," joked Red-Boy.

"Sure as hell would," said Gunny.

"You and Coombs got it made," laughed Gunny, poking at the new cell boss.

Indeed, Coombs, the oldest of the veteran inmates at Leavenworth, was once again the acknowledged boss in cell Block B. He was now known mostly as "Mr. B" or simply called "The Vet."

Coombs was again the man to go to for tobacco, pills from the pharmacy, pictures of nude women and the other "contraband" and services traded in a protection racket as old and hard-baked as the cinder block walls of Leavenworth itself.

Now that Coombs was cell boss, he feigned being too busy to write Red-Boy's letters. The cell boss delegated that task to Red-Boy's librarian friend Shake Spear, whose most lucrative racket, Red-Boy discovered, was his ability to create articulate jailhouse "petitions" and other assorted "legal documents," not to mention flowery correspondence which he traded for tobacco.

One hot, humid afternoon as the men were taking exercise, Red-Boy grew impatient with the bitching and moaning banter of his sweating veteran friends. "You are all cowards, everyone of you guys!" Red-Boy stood motionless, facing them off with an uncharacteristically broad grin. He was met with curious looks and sullen curses.

"Fuck you, chief! You never sweat."

"You guys don't know what sweat is," said Stabs-By-Mistake. "None of you guys ever been in a Sweat Lodge." His look of superiority cowed their mood.

"What the hell's a Sweat Lodge?" asked Big Ed, whose dark-armpitted shirt and soaked back signaled that he was perspiring buckets more than anyone else.

"I practically grew up in a Sweat Lodge, you cowards. Sit down and I'll tell you 'bout it." Slowly, a few of the men sat on the ground, others leaned against the wall near where Red-Boy was sitting cross-legged.

"When you want to ask another Pikuni for a favor, you first put up a Sweat Lodge. It's made of a round willow frame covered with skins. They're pretty big, 'bout four feet high and six feet across. Get it." He paused, looking around at the uninterested inmates sitting nearby.

"Then ya dig a hole in the center of the Sweat Lodge and fill it with hot rocks. Before you go in, you fill yer mouth with water. Then, once in, you squirt the water on the hot rocks. Boy, that steam is hot, makes sweat drip from yer body." He chuckled at the others' blank stares. "Good clean sweat...purifies the body, aaee."

"Purifies the body? Hell, I'd pass out," scowled Big Ed.

"Aaee," answered Red-Boy. "No, the steam, it cleans out the body. The spirit. It is a sacred religious ceremony."

"Jesus, you wouldn't find me goin' to your church," offered Coombs. "My chin would be on the ground in that damn thing. I'd be chokin', tryin' to breathe. If I said anything spiritual, it would be Christ's name. If I seen anything spiritual, it would be because I saw stars and passed out." They all laughed.

"Unh!" came Red-Boy's loud retort. "You are all cowards, you whitemen! My father, the Piegan Chief, he gave me my name. Red-Boy. From a Sweat Lodge ceremony many winters ago."

"Red-Boy's yer real name...not an alias, huh?" Gunny's question was accompanied by an amused look. "Guess all that damned sweat-lodge heat must'a turned you beet red!"

"No, you coward! That is how fathers give an Indian name to their sons." Red-Boy folded his arms and frowned at Gunny and the others.

"God, if I went into one of them sweat chambers for more than a minute, I wouldn't pass on anything. I'd just pass out from heat stroke," offered Big Ed. "I'd have no name to be given to me 'cause I'd be dead like one of them hot rocks!"

Gunny and the others were now making crude remarks and laughing so hard they forgot the humidity.

"So, did all that sweat down in The Hole clean out yur body?" inquired Gunny. Red-Boy shrugged nonchalantly, signifying gently but firmly that the sweats he'd endured with his father after the war were much more significant.

"What the hell happens to you in there while yer sweating?" Coombs asked.

"Can't tell ya. It's sacred. But when the water hits the hot rocks, the steam sucks your breath out. You want to pass out. But you don't."

"What d'ya do to keep from dyin'?" Big Ed wanted to know. The others, too, remained interested in the ritual.

"Well, I can tell ya that the sweat really purified me. Got me off drinkin' real good. My head would pound and pound like a drum. Then the heat from the steam would almost force me to the ground. I'd grab the ground, handfuls of dirt and all, and kinda hold on. At the end when the cool air hit me, I felt really good. Felt like I was purified. No more poundin' in my head, no more drinkin'."

"Why didn't you keep drinkin'?" asked Big Ed

"Didn't want to. The sweats felt better, I guess. Gets into your blood like booze does, only it feels fresh. Better."

Gunny pointed at Red-Boy's chest. "So that's how ya got those goddamned ugly scars on yer chest?" he laughed. "Someone in there throw a hot rock at ya' when you weren't payin' attenchun' to yer religion?" They all laughed. "Or did some fuckin' Bosch soldier stab you over there?"

"No, you cowards," answered Red-Boy with a grin. "These are from my first Sun Dance piercing." Coombs and the others stared, waiting for an explanation.

Red-Boy explained how the religious "piercing" was his way, an Indian veteran's way, of giving thanks to the Sun for keeping him alive during the Great War. How the pain of the skewers ripping through his flesh, as he sun danced, brought him closer to the Great-Unseen-Above-One "who protects us all."

He liked telling the others that the practice was outlawed; yet here was a way, a Pikuni Way, that made the young man feel proud. The others listened, intrigued by the appeal of Red-Boy's "illegal rite-of-passage" ceremony.

"Time to return! Git in line, you shitheads!" barked the guards, breaking the levity. Yet the men felt good, having seen the Indian veteran finally lighten up and talk to them.

The following week, Red-Boy's gloom returned, casting a shadow over the exercise yard. Coombs walked over to his friend.

"What did you say that Victor Sanders' Indian name was?" he asked.

"Black Looks. That's his name," replied Red-Boy.

"Jesus, Peter. They should'a given you that name too," joked Coombs.

The others joined in on the teasing. Red-Boy felt his face get hot, then remembered how fond his own people were of teasing.

"All right, you cowardly calves in a Buffalo corral." The men in the yard stopped, wondering if the Indian meant to fight.

"What are ya talkin' 'bout?" asked Gunny. Then he noticed the corners of the Indian's mouth sporting the hint of a grin.

"This place. When I am out here in the yard and look at that wall with the guard tower, I see the Piss kan, the Buffalo jump. I see the high cliff near Two-Medicine Creek. At the bottom of that cliff is where my people butchered the Buffalo for food and clothing in times far back, near Two-Medicine-Lodge. The Buffalo corral at the foot of the cliff was a place bigger than this yard and made with logs. My people, they built it with much strength. The Buffalo were powerful." Looking around at the stone and brick walls, Red-Boy muttered, "Maybe they think you cowards are powerful too. Look at these walls, they are like the Piss kan." The others laughed.

"I don't want no buffalo food in my piss can." The others continued laughing at Gunny's remark.

"You fuckin' cowards don't know anything! The Piss kan was made with big logs of cottonwood. In the Buffalo days, my father told me we Piegans hunted the Buffalo far out on the prairie. Our horses pulled all our things on platforms called travois. Many times, we traveled till our lodge poles used for the travois were worn short. Many times we came upon the enemy. When Buffalo were plenty, we used the Piss kan. Then hides were many and we could store much dried meat and pemmican." He paused, looking around the yard as if gauging the number of Buffalo to fill it. "Want me to tell you how we drove the Buffalo into the Piss kan?"

"You're gonna tell us how your old relatives drove a bunch of Buffalo into a big piss can?" joked Gunny.

"Yes, you will see what cowards you are. Now listen to my talk. Two rows of piled rocks and willows stretched far out on the prairie from the edge of the cliff. The Buffalo came within the arms of rock, and as they got closer to the cliff they bunched closer together. Way out on the prairie, they are as far apart as a rifle ball will carry. Behind each pile of rocks and willows, a trench was made. In each trench one of our warriors would hide. Out on the prairies, there were bands of Buffalo. One of our hunters would ride out from a coulee with a bright-colored blanket over his shoulders. He would dismount and move about in a strange way."

"Is that because the warrior was pissing in his can?" queried Gunny. The laughter was uproarious.

"Gunny," Coombs shot back, amidst ever more guffaws. "Of all us fuckin' veterans, you should be the first to know we all pissed in the trenches in France. 'Cept you, you pissed either in your pants or in your helmet!"

Now Red-Boy was laughing. He waited patiently for his comrades to come to their senses.

"Okay, now listen to my talk carefully, you cowards. The Buffalo, they would be curious. They would follow the warrior with the blanket over his shoulders. Slowly he would lead them into the opening between the rock piles. As soon as the Buffalo had passed the outpost, the warriors who hid behind the rock piles and the willows rose up and frightened the Buffalo. The willows would sway and wave and frighten the Buffalo forward over the broken cliff and down into the Piss kan. Fat cows would be slaughtered to supply meat for the winter. Bulls, calves, and cows, the animals still alive which they did not need, were turned loose."

Red-Boy paused as if expecting more crude levity.

"A-hyi—that was the time when the hearts of my Pikuni Elders were glad. Then they had plenty of warm robes. Sun shone with much heat in their lodges. This is what my father told me about the Buffalo corral." Red-Boy looked around at each of the inmates who remained silent.

Finally, it was Gunny who shook his head, looked around at the small yard and high walls before he spoke. "At least some of them animals were let loose."

"Have hope, you cowards. Maybe, like the Buffalo corral, the guards will let some of us they don't butcher go loose." Red-Boy laughed.

"Fat chance, unless we figure a way to break out," muttered the cell boss.

"Huh...jus' as simple as catchin' the prison express through that gate over there," came Gunny's sarcastic remark.

The mood was somber as the guards barked, "git in line!"

That evening happened to be the Fourth of July dinner mess. The inmates were served a special meal of chicken, mashed potatoes and stringy green beans with patriotically-decorated red, white and blue mugs of weak coffee.

The men were quiet. Red-Boy, having finally stripped the meat off of a drum stick, held the bone up in his right hand.

"Coombs, let me have that chicken stick on yer plate."

"Jesus, chief! I didn't know you were hungry 'nough to eat the bones too." The others laughed.

"Give me yer damned chicken bone and I will tell you somethin' now."

"Okay," replied Coombs, feigning cowardice while gingerly handing over the bone.

A bone in each upright fist, Red-Boy announced, "Next time we go into the yard, I'm gonna teach you veteran cowards some fancy gamblin'."

"What?" replied the cell boss. "I'm the only one around here who gets to do the fancy gambling!" Coombs glared at his cell mate.

"We'll see you get your cut," replied Red-Boy, smiling. "My people call it the Stick Game. The stakes are plenty high. Want to play?"

Coombs glanced furtively at the others who were all grinning now, nodding their assent.

For the next weeks and months, the men on cell Block B, following Red-Boy's careful tutelage, played the Stick Game in the exercise yard under the watchful, if puzzled, gaze of the prison guards.

Coombs was the hider of the chicken bones for the team known as "The Vets." Red-Boy was the hider of the bones for "The Chiefs." The marked bone was tied with a small piece of white string spirited away from the prison laundry. The stakes in the fancy gambling Stick Game became high, indeed. The befuddled guards never knew that when the noise was loudest—when

Red-Boy's side won the twelve stones—his group won the coveted stash of objects d'art, the gaudy girly pictures created by Big Ed, the best of Coombs' artistic minions.

The howls arising from Red-Boy's side when they were the losers meant that the tobacco sent to Red-Boy by his father and Morning Eagle was to be forfeited.

To the guards, the group of men playing this strange game resembled an innocent game of hide-and-seek. The seriousness of "turf wars" resolved by the Stick Game was totally lost upon the guards. Their perplexed looks and furtive mutterings telegraphed to the inmates suspicions that could never be confirmed.

>>—→ • ←—<<

The agonizingly slow time within The Hot House became more benign, simply because of the camaraderie. Time began to move again. Red-Boy grew accustomed to watching the Night-Clock-of-the-Sky (Big Dipper) change position around the Never-Moving (North) Star.

The silk fastened to the easel began taking on more of his vision, purifying his powerful Medicine Dream.

He worked meticulously and slowly each day, guided from within by the things he held sacred: Annie and his love for her borne from the ashes of the Great War, the stories his father had given to him, the love for his people, and his boarding school learning. This bridge helped him cling to what little hope he had when he read the frequent letters from his father's friend, Morning Eagle, the whiteman he had ridden with so long ago to fetch a doctor for a dying Pikuni Elder.

The New Englander's letters spoke of a passion for scouting and the whiteman's plans to create a Boy Scout troop on the reservation. With these letters, Red-Boy began to trace faint outlines of a project he and Annie might undertake, together, for the children.

More than once, after work on his silk painting in the library, Red-Boy dictated a letter to Morning Eagle, which Shake Spear willingly took down in exchange for a hefty plug of tobacco. He also awaited the day when he would talk with the lawman from Helena. Morning Eagle had written that the man whose name was Grorud would come. That fall of 1925, he finally received a brief letter from Grorud telling him that he would visit Leavenworth early the next year.

Red-Boy tried to ignore the passage of time, the nearness or distance of Grorud's visit. The joking and fancy gambling carried him on.

Most of all, there was his picture painting—the Sun Painting. The chief was now atop his horse. He wore the trappings of a great warrior. Still, the warrior had no face.

Yet, with each night beneath the Seven Brothers (Big Dipper) and in front of his evolving vision, Red-Boy knew his Ghost-Trail led from the tomb of Leavenworth into life, into his Sun Painting.

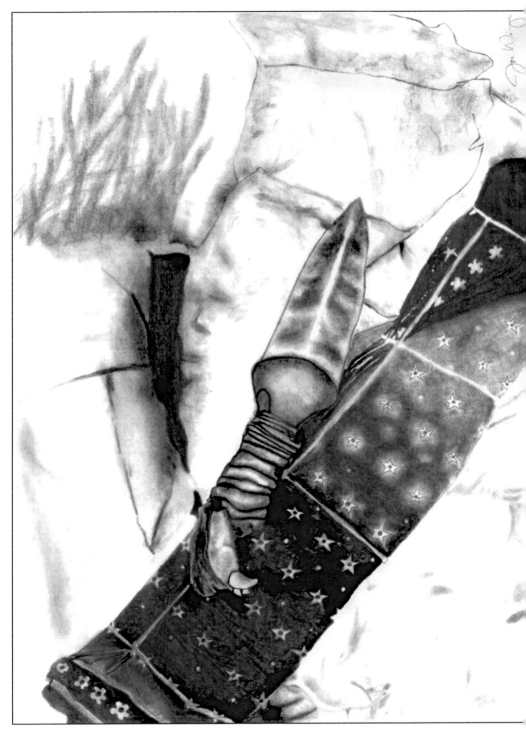

Drawing of Bear-Medicine-Knife, courtesy of Joseph Wagner.

# XXI

# The Bear-Medicine-Knife

I t was the time-of-the-moon-when-leaves-turn-yellow—September, 1925—in Cut Bank. Smoke climbed lazily from the scattered clapboard cabins and lodges, only to be fluttered away by the coming fall breeze. Scattered groups of cattle munched on short bluebunch wheatgrass and green needlegrass. Closer to the wooden shacks, partially harvested rows of corn danced in the chilly, fall breeze.

The talk among the few Piegan cattlemen was about hope that this Indian Summer would continue to ward off the hand of Snow-Maker and allow for more grazing time. The Elders, especially the Medicine Men, remained skeptical as usual.

Within the lodge of Thomas Stabs-By-Mistake was their friend Morning Eagle. Thomas and Morning Eagle sat comfortably at the lodge fire while Thomas's sits-beside-him-woman dug potatoes and picked the few remaining beans and ears of corn in her garden. Wolf Plume and Bear Head had joined the two men around the lodge fire.

Carefully, the Medicine Pipe was passed before Thomas spoke.

Setting the Medicine Pipe on the Buffalo robe in front of him, Thomas fixed his eyes on Morning Eagle and spoke to the whiteman slowly.

"Aapinakoi Píítaa, my Medicine tells me that the Great Chief of your Country, who whitemen call the President, is known by many to be an honorable man."

"My friend, the Great-Chief, is a man I know," said Morning Eagle. "I have visited his lodge and spoken with him. I have told him about our sickness and our troubles here, Poch-Si-Simaki. Also, after the Great Medicine Lodge was raised at the Sun Dance celebration, I sent the talk of Annie Running Crane and her mother and the others back to the Great-Chief's men."

Morning Eagle glanced over at Wolf Plume who was poking the embers with a short willow stick. "Now, I will tell you something else," Morning Eagle continued. "As we speak here, now, those who speak with the Great-Chief are looking at Red-Boy's trial. They will look at everything and then speak to the Great-Chief about Red-Boy's freedom."

Morning Eagle knew that, unwittingly, he might not be speaking to his friends with a straight tongue. Nothing had come from earlier attempts through Montana's senators, or from any of the others, to bring the matter to the attention of officials at the Department of Justice or even to the Assistant U.S. Attorney in Helena, Montana. He hoped that Grorud had done his best and had sent the affidavits on to Attorney General Sargent.

"My Medicine tells me that this new Great-Chief will not speak with a crooked tongue," said Thomas, solemnly giving Morning Eagle a slow, deliberate nod. Looking directly at Morning Eagle, he continued, "My Medicine tells me the Great-Unseen-Above-One will help the Pikuni in their sufferings. Above-Person will tell the Great-Chief of the Country what to do about my people and about my son, Red-Boy. That is all I have to say."

Behind it all, the New Englander's apprehension had been steadily growing; he was irritated at having heard nothing from Grorud and at being unable to get through to Assistant U.S. Attorney Miggs in Helena. Maybe he would pay Miggs a visit himself.

With each letter and the passage of days, weeks and months, hope was elusive, if not entirely dashed against what seemed to be very rocky political shores. Morning Eagle tried not to reveal his misgivings to the three men seated with him at the lodge-fire.

The lodge-flap drew back. Thomas's sits-beside-him-woman entered, holding her dress out with two hands, bucketing a load of emaciated, yellow-white corn, a few green beans and half-a-dozen potatoes. Turning, she opened the lid of the grub box and slid the edibles inside, closing it gently. Walking to the back of the lodge, she retrieved a big handful of dried cherries from a wooden bowl, which she brought over and carefully slid into Thomas's outstretched, cupped hands.

A twinkle came to the eyes of Wolf Plume and Bear Head. They were all about to embark on a night-of-many-laughs, a welcome diversion from the more serious thoughts at hand.

"Aaee, Aapinakoi Píítaa, let's see if you have the cunning of an old warrior," Thomas said, handing him several cherries. Morning Eagle, relying on his New England upbringing, trying to anticipate the appropriate way to display good manners, tasted the dried cherries and carefully tossed the pits into the lodge fire. Stabs-By-Mistake, Wolf Plume and Bear Head watched intently, displaying no emotion.

"Friends, these are very good cherries," thanked Morning Eagle, nodding his appreciation.

After handing Wolf Plume and Bear Head several cherries, Thomas put a handful of the fruit into his own mouth. There followed the tooth-crushing sound of crunching from each of the men. Stabs-By-Mistake looked at Morning Eagle with a sly, determined grin, then swallowed the cherries, crushed pits and all.

"Many times you see how we eat cherries. Sometime you come and live with the Piegans all the time, then you eat cherries like we do. When our children are very young, we teach them to have strong teeth. Three-Moons was a very old man, still he ate cherries like that. Everybody, they know about Three-Moons. Three-Moons, he gave my son, Red-Boy, his name."

"Aapinakoi Píítaa, we must cure you of whiteman-teeth that cannot chew cherry stones," signed Wolf Plume. The three Indians chuckled.

"Plenty times I see Aapinakoi Píítaa eat soft marrow and dried-meat," teased Bear Head. "But his teeth, they big cowards. They never bite cherry stone." They all laughed, again, while Morning Eagle shrugged.

Perhaps, his three friends were giving him a subtle, if not-so-direct hint. Morning Eagle needed to develop a toughness, especially when using his mouth, perhaps toughness of jaw when taking Red-Boy's case to the Easterners at the Great-Chief's lodge.

"I will try very hard not to be a coward," laughed Morning Eagle. "When I return to my lodge in the East, I will have my sits-beside-him-woman bring me cherries and I will eat them whole." The image of his proper New England wife, Marie, seeing him crunch down on ripe cherries, pits and all, made him laugh even more.

He would try his best to eat the whole of the cherries.

≫⟫→ • ←⟪≪

South Hadley was a quiet Massachusetts town on the eastern bank of the placid Connecticut River. Not too far south from Northampton, where his friend Calvin Coolidge had staked his political beginnings, stood Christian Schuster's chestnut log house at Titan's Pier, his sixteen-acre estate at river's edge, on the southern end of South Hadley. Titan's Pier was a steep, heavily forested spit of land jutting into the Connecticut, forming a deep cove upriver. The log cabin had been built in the early nineteen-hundreds by the New Englander with the help of Canadian Indians who floated timbers down the Connecticut River.

The cabin was an immense two-story structure at the front end, with a large stonework fireplace in the middle. The bottom floor extended out in the back. The windows were comfortably gabled.

Much time and effort had been put into building intricate stone pathways using local volcanic rock. Not a stone's throw from the log house stood an Indian artifact museum. A spreading, lush green euonymus tree, large hemlock, birch and oak trees, having escaped cutting and high winds, surrounded the cabin.

At the river's edge were numerous high-ledged outcroppings, providing scenic panoramas of the Connecticut River and Mt. Tom in the distance. The north side of the property included extensive frontage along the upriver Russell Cove, a former river channel containing habitat for water fowl and marsh birds.

It was a bright, sunny New England afternoon in 1926. The spring breeze off the river through the old hemlock limbs reached Chris in his comfortable, cane-seat rocker, reading through a sheaf of papers on his front porch. The cool shade of the trees took the slight humidity off his mind. Sunlight cascaded through the shadowed branches.

Instead of his usual tweed business suit, the Holyoke businessman was outfitted casually in a flannel shirt and slacks. His wife, Marie, sat next to him and crocheted. Every now and then she refilled the teapot on the small wooden table between the two. Reflecting her own flair for color, Marie wore a long red silk dress with green, orange, yellow and gold interlacing flower patterns at the top. A black belt accentuated her svelte middle-aged figure. She wore her slightly graying hair back in a neat bun.

Glancing over at her husband, she noticed the deepened lines on his forehead as he reached for his tea.

"Dear, you've been obsessing now for days…months…over that young fellow. You know you've done everything you can for Peter. Sometimes you just can't fight City Hall," she remarked with an air of resignation.

"Wish I could have done something sooner, dammit."

"Now, honey, you know you can't solve everything. You told me yourself that the girl and her mother didn't open up to you till last summer."

"Yah. They were all under the thumb of that fellow, Victor Sanders. But it still doesn't make sense, Marie," concluded her husband.

"What doesn't make sense?"

"The whole damn thing. In March, I wrote to Attorney General Sargent." He paused, taking a thoughtful sip of tea. "I specifically told him how that Richard Sanders fellow was trying to curry favor by promising to seek Peter's release if they'd elect his nephew, Victor, to the Tribal Council. I saw the dark shadows of those men—Victor and Richard Sanders—trying to advance their careers at the expense of this innocent man and their own people." He paused, again, to take another sip of tea. "I told Sargent I wanted the matter investigated."

"Well, did they investigate?"

"I don't know. I haven't been able to get answers from Senator Wheeler from Montana, and Grorud hasn't heard from Senator Walsh. He did say that Miggs, the Assistant U.S. Attorney, would investigate the Bureau's role in Peter's conviction." Setting down his tea cup, he pushed back in his chair, taking a deep breath.

"Jeez, now Grorud tells me he thinks Miggs is inclined to take Campbell's side of the story. Seems the Blackfeet Tribal Council was making noise like they wanted to pass a resolution this spring asking for the young Indian's pardon. I guess that really made Campbell mad as hell. But I don't understand why Justice hasn't done anything. Are they just sitting on the whole thing? Hell, maybe I am just as bad as they are, sitting back here doing nothing!"

"Now, honey, you've never been one to just lay down and quit. I know you better than that." She smiled softly. He smiled back. "Didn't you tell me you wrote Calvin a year or so ago?"

"I sure did. Just about two years ago, to be exact. But it wasn't about Peter Stabs-By-Mistake. It was about the horrible conditions on the reservation. I was trying to get Calvin's attention so they'd send some doctors up there. Got a really cold letter back from Charles Burk, the damned Indian Commissioner, who sent me some propaganda and the usual line of crap from the Interior Department... 'We shall investigate and do everything possible to correct faulty conditions, if existing.'" The New Englander made no attempt to hide his sarcasm.

"What's so damned strange is this Victor Sanders. He was instrumental in sending Peter to Leavenworth. And now he says he'll work to free Peter if he's elected to a spot on the Tribal Council. I just can't figure out what that's all about." He paused, looking intently at his wife.

They both sat for a moment in silence, listening to the breeze softly rustling the tall hemlocks and oaks.

"I don't know who or why, but something's fishy. The Tribal Council acts like it wants to pass resolutions and Campbell and Miggs just sit on their fat asses and do nothing!" His face reddened, again, as he drew his lips into a tight, straight line.

Marie rested her crocheting on her lap and took a sip of tea. Leaning toward her husband with an affectionate, but earnest, smile she said, "Well, Dear, you know this might be the year to get people to move."

"What do you mean ?"

"Well, Bill Butler is running for re-election."

Her husband's scowl turned to a broad smile as he realized his Marie had dropped just the right name. His savvy wife was at least half the reason he had navigated business so well in Massachusetts waters.

Senator William M. Butler of Massachusetts, the Republican National Chairman, was in a tight race for his political life. He was also a close friend of the president.

"Well, yeah, he's practically the only one I haven't written to," he said. But, as Republican Party Chairman, I doubt he would welcome hearing from me. Besides he's so damned busy, I'd never even stand a chance of hearing from him."

"Perhaps. But why don't you call on his friend, Art Chapin, and talk to him? He might have some influence or might suggest something."

Once again, Marie's read on the situation was flawless. Her husband knew of Chapin's effectiveness from their mutual business and legal dealings. Besides, he and Art Chapin had been fraternity brothers.

"Jeez, Marie, why didn't I think of that?" he replied with a sheepish grin.

"That's why you married me," she laughed. She gave him a peck on the cheek as she went inside for more tea.

$$\text{»»} \rightarrow \bullet \leftarrow \text{«««}$$

A week later, Chris sat at his large oak desk. The walls of his study were festooned with brightly woven Navajo rugs, several large photographs of mostly Blackfeet or Navajo gatherings of Elders, a quiver with three arrows and a large bow. His Pikuni adoption parfleche with the colorful signature drawings of his friends held the place of honor above his desk.

Shelves held peace pipes, arrowheads, and an occasional tomahawk. Indian arrowheads were embedded in the log wall closest to his desk.

Fixing a pensive look, he began composing a letter.

*Holyoke, Mass.*
*May 27, 1926*
*Dear Red-Boy,*

*I will ride the iron horse out to see my Pikuni brothers who are all thinking about you and have you in their heart. Know younger brother you are a Pikuni, your heart is strong. Your heart is powerful like the heart of your father. You are honest and straight. So you must have patience my brother. Five winters is a long time. Those winters will soon fade away.*

*I write many letters to friends in Washington, D.C. and I write to Attorney General John D. Sargent. I send them papers that I got from the straight talk in my Otter Medicine Tipi from Annie and Nellie Running Crane and the others who know that you did not commit the crime of rape. And I asked them to give you a free pardon right away.*

*The prayers came for your father and mother when they asked Sun Power for pity. That is good. Our medicine is strong. So brother, my heart tells me that you will be free from that cloud and all people will be proud of you because you live like a man and a Pikuni.*

*You told me about your plan my brother. I have thought much about what you told me. So my heart speaks to you straight. I have told you about the Boy Scouts and our plans to bring our young Indian brothers into the Boy Scouts circle. I will take the iron horse to the Rocky Boy Tribal Council this summer and tell them about the Boy Scouts. The young Chippeways and Crees are anxious to trade bows, arrows and quivers for money so they can pay their dues. I want to see the Boy Scout movement among the Indian boys become as great mountains in the west and am glad you have told me of your interest. The Indian Scouts will be known as the Little Buffaloes.*

*There is something more I want to say. Now you are like a young Buffalo Bull that is wounded with an arrow. Soon you will pull that arrow out and the wound will get well. Then you will be free and strong. Then you will be able to care for the Little Buffaloes.*

*Now, there is something more I want to say about the whiteman's law. It is a wheel of justice which turns very slowly. I know that the passage of time goes slowly and causes you to give up hope. Do not give up hope. Please know that I will not stop working on this for you. I found out that it will be good to get some more papers. I will get the papers and write to you again. Soon I will try to get you free. I will do all I can.*

*Now, I speak some words that you must never forget. Be very careful in all things that you do and words that you speak because they are watching you. You are an honored Piegan Warrior.*

*Read this letter many times. That is all I have to say to you. I shake your hand from my heart.*

*Morning Eagle*

Chris re-read his letter, squinting and thinking as he did so. It was a long shot. He remembered another long shot when he and Marie had traveled down to Washington, D.C., during the fall of 1924. Then, he had paid a visit to Calvin Coolidge to remind him that people must know the true condition of the Indian on the other side of the curtain put down by the Indian Bureau. The two old friends had reminisced about the president's mayoral days in Northampton and the Holyoker's activities with the Boy Scouts and collecting Connecticut valley Indian artifacts.

Timing. It was something his wife understood so well. The timing must be right for a long shot to stand a chance. It hadn't always been so on his White House visits. Maybe the timing would be better this year.

Folding the letter to Red-Boy, he leaned back in his soft leather chair and recalled his recent conversation with Arthur Chapin.

"Write the letter to Butler," Chapin had suggested, explaining that he was scheduled to meet with his "boss" within the next several weeks for a political fund-raiser. The GOP National Chairman was busy, but Chapin was confident that he would get his ear. Word had it that Butler was due in Washington, D.C. for a strategy meeting with Coolidge for the upcoming off-year elections.

Still, he didn't relish the thought. Butler's politics were too far misaligned from his own.

He wondered what Butler might want in return. Quid pro quo.

He retrieved his favorite pen from his desk and leaned back. The ornate pen, a birthday gift from Marie, was long and silvery, with a gaudy ivory covering at the upper end. His mind drifted as he slowly rolled the pen with his fingers. A cool breeze blew off the Connecticut River.

》》→ • ←《《

Seated inside his Otter Medicine Tipi, he sensed someone beckoning.

Wolf Plume and Big Brave were calling for help from the Spirit of the Woman who found the first Iniskim—the Sacred Buffalo Stone.

Buffalo Body, the Sacred Man, was praying and painting his body so that Morning Eagle could be pure, so that he could touch his tipi decorated with paint from the earth.

Chief Curly Bear sat close, singing the songs of the Otter Medicine Tipi, telling of old men walking eastward towards the home of the Sun.

When the singing died away, he looked—Curly Bear was gone.

Smoke from the sweetgrass drew Morning Eagle closer to Lazy-Young-Man, who was clutching the gleaming-white Bear-Medicine-Knife. He handed the knife—the twelve-inch, gleaming blade rising from the Grizzly Bear handle—to Black Looks, the revered Blood warrior.

Then the Otter Medicine Tipi lifted away and he stood naked in the presence of Black Looks, who raised the knife at Morning Eagle. Suddenly, the old warrior was transfigured into Thomas Stabs-By-Mistake.

"Grab the knife!" Thomas demanded.

The gleaming twelve-inch blade and bear-tusk handle of the knife tumbled end-over-end towards his chest.

"Grab the knife…like the Bear would! Take it!!"

》》→ • ←《《

The New Englander awoke with a startled gasp and recoil-jerk of his legs, nearly pitching himself over backwards out of his leather chair.

In his hand, he was clutching his silver and ivory pen. His knuckles were white.

The only sound was his heartbeat and the ticking of the grandfather clock.

Slowly leaning forward, Chris took a deep breath and began composing a short note to his friend Arthur Chapin:

*Holyoke, Mass.*
*May 27, 1926*
*Honorable Arthur B. Chapin*
*50 State Street,*
*Boston, Mass.*

*Dear Brother Chapin:*

*Enclosed is a copy of the letter to Senator Butler as suggested. I am sure that you told me to address this letter to Senator Butler. I have great confidence in him and with your valuable suggestions and influence, I know something can be accomplished.*

*Sincerely yours,*

Now, for the letter to the GOP National Chairman. It couldn't hurt to connect with one of the president's men. Plus, his business connections might feed into Senator Butler's political interest. After all, in Massachusetts in 1926, it really didn't matter if you were Republican or Democrat; it was whether or not you supported Coolidge and prosperity. The Holyoker was a supporter and Marie had reassured him that Senator Butler knew that.

Pulling the desk lamp closer, Chris began composing in his most polished New England prose style.

*Holyoke, Mass.*
*May 27, 1926*
*Honorable William M. Butler*
*Senate Office Building*
*Washington, D.C.*

*My Dear Senator:*

*Without going into a mass of evidence and correspondence, I wish to bring to your attention the fact that an Indian Boy, Peter Stabs-By-Mistake is serving a twenty year sentence in the Leavenworth Penitentiary for a crime of which he is entirely innocent.*

*In 1923, while visiting some of my Blackfeet Indian friends, it was common talk on the reservation that this boy was imprisoned through false evidence. I was asked by the boy's father, a pure blood Blackfeet of good character and high standing, to investigate the case. I did so during several past summers, finding the boy highly spoken of by many of the old people as well as the young. After hearing so much in the boy's favor, I personally interviewed the witnesses in this case in July of 1925, and each and every one of the witnesses stated, "that the Boy was Innocent of any crime." That they would all like to see him free. That the false evidence was given through lack of knowledge of the English language and threats. That several times previously these witnesses had made statements to this effect in efforts to obtain a pardon but such statements were sidetracked. In July of 1925 I wired to Attorney A.A. Grorud of Helena, Montana, to take the written affidavits I obtained from the witnesses and to proceed with application for pardon. He did so and these affidavits together with letters from members in good standing of the Blackfeet Nation and other individuals who speak highly of the boy's standing and character, were attached to the application for pardon. These are now in the hands of the pardon attorney in Washington.*

*Attorney Grorud and I have taken this matter up through Senator Thomas J. Walsh, but Senator Walsh is a very busy man and directly my chances are slim for obtaining his influence. Therefore I come to you by advice of some of your friends and others who know of your sterling qualities. I believe that Senator Walsh would gladly work with you in the furthering of justice.*

*Personally, I am after nothing except to bring happiness again into the hearts of the boy's old parents, and aiding the boy to secure his well deserved freedom. I have been advised to take this matter up through legal channels with other individuals and attorneys but nearly everyone with whom I have presented the facts of this case has advised me to come to you.*

*I wish to state further that should this boy be pardoned, my friendship for him will not end there, for I will help him to obtain an education, that he may become a self supporting citizen. The letters which I regularly receive from him warrant this.*

*Any further information which you may wish, I will gladly furnish.*

*Sincerely yours,*

Chris Schuster cast a knowing smile at his penultimate paragraph, for he knew Red-Boy to be far more "educated" and "self-supporting" than others with whom he had crossed paths.

He glanced out the window at his favorite old hemlock. The branches seemed to be waving and clapping in the late spring breeze as if applauding Morning Eagle for firmly biting down, chewing and swallowing the pits and all.

Two Guns White Calf.

# XXII

# The Great-Chief's Straight Tongue

This hot, sticky afternoon in July of 1926, the GOP Chairman was in a race for his political life. He found the President in the East Room of the White House. As was his custom, Mr. Coolidge was perfunctorily shaking hands with countless visitors—tourists as well as the more polished habitués standing in a line that began outside the front lobby.

The East or Blue Room was ornately furnished with a crystal candle chandelier and gold-frescoed paintings of James Monroe and Dolly Madison hanging at either end of the room. The place was uncharacteristically alive with well-wishers eager to make small talk with the famous man from Northampton, Massachusetts.

Senator William Butler watched his boss shake each man's hand briefly but vigorously while gently taking the hand and sometimes bowing slightly at the waist to the ladies. His reception smiles were reserved but genuine. The two large floor fans in the room made the air almost bearable.

The last of the Jeffersonian presidents, thought Butler, as he watched the man work the long queue of visitors, unpretentious, plain-spoken, even good-natured. Not a "big city lawyer." This was a fine, modest lawyer from Massachusetts who had been cut from the fabric of Abraham Lincoln. Butler knew that Coolidge, like Lincoln, had felt uncomfortable making a case for a client where the evidence seemed at odds.

Bill Butler had been told that the Northampton firm that had hired Coolidge had done so because Calvin made everyone laugh—"a very funny man." Indeed his sense of humor had been legendary.

Yet that was before the death of his son in 1924. That probably helped to explain why the President now always appeared reserved, rigid.

Nonetheless, the President had long political coattails which were not given gladly, even if some Republicans frantically reached out and grabbed at them. Everyone seemed to have confidence in the man, simply because everyone knew he did his best to do right. He kept his word even if it was not what others wanted him to do and he might not do what others thought he ought to do.

Coolidge never forgot a good turn. Back when he was governor during the Boston police strike, disaster had been avoided when, at Butler's request, he had called out the militia to take charge of the police affairs of Boston.

Butler had promoted Coolidge's agenda at the 1924 convention in Cleveland. He kept the Republican Party united and Coolidge had given him high marks for how he managed the campaign, which meant Coolidge was seldom obliged to speak at the dedication of a monument or before a religious gathering.

Butler smiled at his friend, who was wearing his dark pinstriped suit, white shirt and plain red tie. His bright red hair, tinged with gray, was carefully combed back from his high forehead.

Everything about the man was true and thin, careful and nondescript; nondescript except for the hair and the piercing gaze of his pale-blue eyes.

Beneath his greeting demeanor, displayed at times such as now, he was a fierce and tenacious fighter for what he thought was right.

He was a public official who had been reluctant for a political career. A man whose detractors, even the Irish Democrats, would do anything for him — even give him their vote.

For Butler, here stood the living embodiment of a political contradiction. A President staunchly desirous of focusing the country's roaring energy into business through tax cuts. A President who contrasted enigmatically with the country's racy, escapist mood.

The GOP National Chairman was anxious to get some time with the President for the matter at hand, his close re-election campaign against favored-son David Walsh, one-time governor of Massachusetts. The former governor was one of many Democrats with whom Coolidge had obtained successful conciliations. It was like running against the old power clique from Boston. Perhaps the President would discreetly pull strings and exact favors in Butler's race. He didn't know how or in what way the president might help, but he knew he needed to talk with The Boss today.

Butler had seen the First Lady leave the reception a few minutes earlier. He knew the President would feel less comfortable without his gracious and spirited spouse and hostess and this 'meet and greet' would soon end.

The President caught sight of Butler and smiled, beckoning him to come meet a couple from Vermont.

"Bill, I'd like you to meet Dr. and Mrs. Thomas Eldridge from upstate Vermont. Good friends of my mother and father. Real pleased to have you here. This is my good friend Senator Butler of Massachusetts."

Nodding, Butler shook hands and smiled. "Pleased to meet you. It's always nice to have the President's supporters come in person and visit the White House."

"I must confess, Senator Butler has visited me today on a rather mundane mission," the President announced, his face cracking the hint of a forced smile. "We must discuss party strategy for the upcoming elections."

The Vermont couple nodded and smiled.

"I must apologize to you both and to this room full of wonderful people who've come over this afternoon."

Turning, the President motioned to a military orderly standing by the door. The orderly promptly and snappily announced above the din that the President would be adjourning the afternoon public reception and that complimentary pens would be available on the way out of the White House.

Waving again and shaking a few more hands, the President and Butler quietly left by a side door and down the hallway towards the President's office in the West Wing.

More electric fans pumping stagnant air greeted the two men as they entered the Oval Office.

When the Party chairman met his boss, the banter usually started with family news being shared, settling lastly on Grace, the vivacious First Lady. For Butler, the axiom that opposites attract applied to the President and First Lady "in spades." Grace Coolidge exuded a ready sense of humor and was talkative at public gatherings or private dinners.

After a general discussion of congressional and senate races that should be funded by the Republican National Party, leaving out all races south of the Mason-Dixon Line, the topic turned to the Massachusetts face-off.

"Well, I see that our former Democrat governor in Massachusetts is giving you a run for your life, isn't he?"

"That's no consolation coming from you, Mr. President," Butler laughed. "You know, he's got his henchmen in Boston and up and down the coast all sewed up. I don't stand a chance against that damned urban Democrat machine."

As the chairman elaborated, the President seemed mildly distracted. Finally Butler noticed the President's attention focused over his shoulder. He turned and saw Frank Stearns, Coolidge's closest political adviser, advance man and friend from their Amherst College days, standing in the door.

"C'mon in Frank," invited the President with a warm smile.

Like Butler, Stearns was part of the "Massachusetts Gang," Coolidge's inner clique. He was a short, heavy-set man with a ruddy complexion, silver-white hair and a penchant for elevator shoes. But the gang admired the little bull-dog. Coolidge's shadow had, for years, spent long days with the President, beginning when Coolidge was mayor and continued with Stearns' office in the West Wing.

"Bill, here, thinks he's going to have a problem with our Democrat friend up in our old stomping grounds." The President and Stearns both chuckled as Stearns dropped into the chair next to Butler.

"Listen, Bill," Stearns offered in his usual gruff voice. "You and I are a couple of old pros. What you need is help from the Connecticut valley; from all those little towns from Springfield to Northampton, all the way up." Stearns smiled as he drew the familiar map in the air.

"Yes, but how do I get the vote?"

"Business. Big business," interjected Coolidge with a sly smile.

The chairman slowly leaned back and starred at the ceiling for a long moment.

"That reminds me," Butler finally said. "My staffers gave me a letter from that Holyoke businessman, Christian...."

"C.F. Schuster," the President broke in. "Know him well." The President was nodding and smiling now. "A bit eccentric at times, but solid nevertheless. He's outspoken. Doesn't mince words when it comes to the Indian Bureau," the President chuckled. "But the man's got good business sense. I like that."

"You think he'll help me?" Before the President could answer, Butler continued, "Seems the fellow wants to get a pardon for an Indian at Leavenworth."

Coolidge's eyes narrowed and his once-pleasant smile instantly dropped, his mouth becoming a straight line.

"Yes, he's quite opinionated on Indian issues. An interesting man," offered the President. "Knew him from my days in Northampton. Came to see us after I was elected. Met him and his wife over in the Blue Room." The President nodded. "Eccentric but solid."

"Well, I'm not sure that's what I need. Some eccentric businessman supporting my campaign. Jesus."

"Well, wait a minute, Bill," Stearns offered. "This man's a fighter."

"Yes," interjected the President. "Let me tell you a story, Bill. Seems that after a spring freshet one year a long while back, Christian found pieces of pottery along the bank of a brook flowing into the Connecticut River near Hockanum. He sifted a large section of the earth out." The President paused, as if again seeing Christian at work on the riverbank. "Do you know it took him two years of sifting and labor to piece together the little bits of pottery he found? The man's determined." He paused again, looking directly at Butler with his blue eyes. "The final result was a perfect example of some really old Indian pottery. Its value is priceless." The President leaned back triumphantly.

"Think having him support my campaign would do any good, Mr. President?"

The President leaned forward, his blue eyes locking on his party chairman. "Bill, listen. This is a prominent New England businessman. He is a persistent, honest, tenacious man. These are good qualities to have on your side." The chairman nodded; the President nodded back.

"Well, maybe he will help as payback for my putting forward the Indian inmate case he's so interested in."

"What you got in mind?" asked Stearns bluntly.

"You might be on to something, Bill," offered the President.

"Well, it's a rather delicate situation, Mr. President. It seems that the Indian boy was given a twenty-year sentence for rape under very suspicious circumstances. I mean the whole thing may have been a misunderstanding."

"How do you mean?" said the former Massachusetts lawyer, expressing a keener interest, now.

"Well, it seems that all of the trial testimony was translated and there were some Indian Bureau officials related to the witnesses who may have been overly involved at the trial."

"I see," said the President, shifting and glancing out the window with narrowed eyes. "You know, Bill, I'm being pressured to fund another commission to review Indian policies. They want us to audit the execution of treaty obligations, review trust accounts, look into abuses. Could be a bit sensitive in an election year," Coolidge concluded. "What else does this inmate have going for him, Bill?"

"Well, seems he's a veteran. A Blackfoot Indian who enlisted and fought at the Argonne."

Nodding, the President then asked, "What are the negatives?"

The chairman paused another long moment before answering. "Seems Peter Stabs-By-Mistake killed a Klansman in prison in self-defense."

The words stunned the President.

"Say what? Peter who?"

"Stabs-By-Mistake, Mr. President."

"Good Lord."

"He killed a Klansman in Leavenworth. Was put in solitary for a time. My staffers spoke with the prison warden, and the prison chaplain, and they got good reports, though. Seems there were witnesses. The Klansman was making him do an unnatural act."

Calvin Coolidge squirmed and stood up. "All right, I've heard enough." He reached to ring a bell, as if calling time out. The President's secretary soon appeared at the door of the oval office. "Barbara, would you kindly summon somebody over here who's handling a pardon request for Peter . . ." the President broke off. "What's his name, Bill?"

"Peter Stabs-By-Mistake," replied the senator.

The young woman's mouth broke into an amused smile.

"Mr. President, would you like to use the telephone outside to make the call?" she asked politely.

"No! You know I don't make calls of this nature. Not private enough."

This remark, by the obviously annoyed President, amused William Butler and Frank Stearns. They chuckled, admiring their friend's obstinate New England insistence for preserving privacy, while expressing a contemptuous disdain for such modern amenities as the telephone.

"Very good, Mr. President. I'll summon someone from the pardon attorney's office right away," the secretary replied with a slight sigh.

"Thank you."

"You mentioned this committee that's being formed," asked Butler. "I think I heard of it—that fellow Lewis Meriam. Isn't the Rockefeller Foundation funding the deal?"

"Yes." interjected Stearns. "But I don't want the committee making any recommendations before the elections."

The President remained silent.

William Butler wondered what the President thought. The timing on the Indian's pardon request seemed awkward. Pardoning an Indian convicted of rape could be politically dangerous in an election year. But, as the President's GOP Chairman, he might as well give the pardon request some preliminary attention. He just might need the Holyoker's help come election time.

Yet Butler had seen the letter. Others, including Thomas Walsh from Montana, had become interested but had backed away, done nothing. Perhaps the Holyoker was a liability, no matter whether you were Democrat or Republican.

"Well, Mr. President, I'll talk to this Schuster fellow and tell him I've discussed the matter with you," offered the chairman.

"You do that, Bill," said the President, now returning a polite smile. Butler knew that was his cue; the meeting was adjourned. "Must have my afternoon tea with Grace, Bill. I'll look into this for you when the file gets over here, okay?"

Getting up, Senator Butler thanked The Boss, bid him a good afternoon. "I'll be back in town in a week or so to discuss some interesting Republican congressional races out West."

"No you don't," instructed Coolidge. "We're not staying in this heat another day. I'll see you up at my father's place in Vermont, okay?"

"I'll look forward to it, Mr. President. We all need to get out of this heat."

With a nod, Senator Butler closed the door to the oval office and wondered what the President would do with that file. His musing was momentarily forgotten by the sudden greeting of the sprightly Grace Coolidge, breezing her way in with a tray of tea for the President.

As she entered her husband's inner sanctum, the First Lady smiled broadly at Frank Stearns, snappily on his way out, charged with an errand.

"Oh, hello Frank. Aren't you staying for tea?"

"Can't Grace. Have to scoot over to Justice." Even Frank Stearns knew that Calvin Coolidge preferred to take tea alone in the afternoon with his wife.

"Another slow day, dear?" Before her husband could answer, she asked, "Are the fans working okay?"

"Very slow. And boring." He paused, then added, "In answer to both your questions." The First Lady smiled then sat down to pour. Grace Coolidge's husband fell silent for a long moment. Then he announced, rather cryptically, "After all, before all of this, I was a lawyer from Northampton in private practice. I represented the common folk, didn't I Grace?"

Perplexed, the First Lady waited then finally asked, "What brought that on, Calvin?" She smiled as she served tea in delicate china cups from an antique table between the two chairs they always used for afternoon tea.

"Well, Chairman Bill just handed me an interesting legal problem to solve, my dear," he stated rather matter-of-factly, leaning back into his upholstered chair. "Seems that a young Indian by the name of Stabs-By-Mistake may have been mistakenly sentenced to a twenty-year term in Leavenworth for rape. Then it seems he killed one of those Klansmen who threatened him in prison."

"Jesus, Mary and Joseph!" exclaimed the First Lady. "What will Wild Bill want you to do next? Is your buddy Frank in on this little caper, too?"

Coolidge smiled, uplifted by his wife's casual openness.

"Well, actually, Grace, Bill's in a tough race with our ex-Governor up there at home. And there's a very interesting Holyoke businessman who might just be able to pull out the votes for him in the central and western part of the state. I told our 'Wild Bill' that I'd look into the request." He smiled softly at his wife. "Of course, I'm not going to do anything rash. You know that." He nodded reassuringly at her. "I sent Frank over to have a chat with Commissioner Burke at Indian Affairs to get to the bottom of a little mess they have over there."

Just then, one-half hour after he had instructed her to summon the pardon attorney, the President's secretary appeared at the door of the oval office with an obviously very nervous James A. Fry in tow. Seeing the twosome, Calvin and Grace Coolidge stood and introduced themselves.

"I am so glad to meet you, Mr. President and Grace... er, uh, Mrs. Coolidge," came the pardon attorney's awkward correction.

Sensing that this well-educated young man was flustered, the President held out a hand, offering him to come forward with the file. "It's been a very slow day, Mr. Fry. I guess I can spend a few minutes with one of your pardon requests, if you don't mind."

"Certainly, Mr. President."

Taking the file from his pardon attorney, the President remarked, "How are things over at Justice, these days? Must be lots of pardon requests coming in, seeing as we have an election coming up." The President chuckled, hoping a show of humor would relax the young man. The President wondered if the pardon attorney intended to remain in D.C. and endure this hot summer humidity.

"Yes, Mr. President, we're keeping pretty busy over there." Sensing an opening, the pardon attorney went on, "Is there anything you would like to know about this particular case involving Mr. Stabs-By-Mistake?" The pardon attorney mumbled the name.

The President sensed embarrassment from Fry at the Indian's name.

"No, Mr. Fry, that'll be all for now. If I need anything, I'll certainly let you know. Thank you."

Turning, the dismissed subordinate marched out of the oval office, the President's secretary leading the way, all the while thinking to himself that this briefest of encounters with the Chief Executive could have been far more of a feather in his cap had it not been for the request to bring Stabs-By-Mistake's file. Even the Indian's name was an embarrassment.

Obviously, the President was on to something very grim and it involved him. Perhaps even Marilyn. Sweat trickled down his forehead. Anger broke into muttered curses at Miggs as the pardon attorney hurried through the gate of the White House compound. No way to stifle the thing now. Obviously, the upstart little Assistant U.S. Attorney in Helena had been too busy handling whatever he considered to be more important matters.

Then he remembered Yessup's letter. The anger turned to disgust with himself for not having sat on the thing or ignoring it entirely that first day when the Indian's petition crossed his desk, way back when Marilyn had taken down his letter to the Holyoker.

The thought of the repercussions, of his harboring an affair with a young woman who had been intimate with an Indian seeking a pardon, made his gut ache. His father would never forgive him for losing his job, for disgracing his family. He resented ever having hired Marilyn.

Back in the Oval Office, the President set the manila file on his desk and resumed afternoon tea with the First Lady, preoccupied with more important concerns.

They talked of plans to visit his father's farm at Plymouth Notch in Vermont.

Swims Under in front of Morning Eagle's (Chris's) lodge.

# XXIII

# I Shake Your Hand
# From My Heart

"...s...sa...s....s....s'ee ta...ta...tuoo...h...ha...ha . . ."

"Horses," finished Peter Red-Boy for Shake Spear. The tattooed trustee-librarian had, by now, become Red-Boy's close friend, one of very few of his inmate friends who was not a veteran.

"Ye...yes!" exclaimed the bespectacled librarian. He liked to sit behind Red-Boy and watch the artist at work. He rarely said much, which suited his friend just fine.

"Aaee. Two horses makes for more company," joked Red-Boy.

The Indian had traded innumerable plugs of tobacco and assorted crude sketches for the flowery letters the little literary poet laureate had composed and sent for Red-Boy to Thomas Stabs-By-Mistake, Morning Eagle, Annie and attorney A. A. Grorud.

The arrival of Grorud's second letter again encouraged Red-Boy. The lawyer had first written that he'd be arriving early that year. Red-Boy had read and reread the lawyer's letter until the paper was worn through. This second letter spoke vaguely of doings about his pardon request back in D.C. and again promised a visit to the penitentiary "no later than May."

It was now June of 1926. Still, the lawyer from Helena had not come. Red-Boy received Morning Eagle's letter dated May 27th, temporarily lifting his spirits. But then the doubts came back and Red-Boy threw the letters away and again abandoned any hope he held within his pierced chest.

Chest Man became Red-Boy's diversion—Chest Man, the Medicine Man of the Seven Brothers in the night sky. The scars on Red-Boy's chest and his gut told him the only truth he knew for sure; he was still alive. Yet, he knew that having once been pierced at the Sun Dance, the Sun could, at any time, forever, take him from his people. He still watched his back. December 4, 1926, would mark the fifth year behind The Hot House walls at Leavenworth, years that had melted the crimson red gash made by Krankk across Red-Boy's belly. It had healed into a half-arrow, inclined towards his right hip, as if deflected by a war shield.

The original darkness of the Black Medicine Horse in the first silken painting was gone. After his Dream Vision in The Hole, he knew the color of the Black Medicine Horse in his Medicine Dream- the power protecting him from Krankk- must be hidden within himself forever.

Black-brown outlines of the new horse and rider had appeared. Their bodies blended together with orange, bleeding into rosy pinks, smudged here and there with brownish hues. The head of the rider-chief, highlighted with a brilliant white eagle feather bonnet, stared far into the distance. The sun-tinted prairie grass seemed almost fluorescent.

From behind the first horse, a second riderless horse was led by a black-braided warrior whose arm was pointed ahead to where the chief looked.

True to his dream quest in The Hole, Red-Boy's silk War Shield now reflected the vision Red-Boy held within his mind.

Mountain Chief, the great Piegan leader, and his son Big Brave-Mountain Chief had counted many coups, coups that had played across his dream time and had been carried onto the silk.

In the Sun Painting, his grandfather Big Brave stands and gestures into the distance for a purpose only Red-Boy knew—the escape from the blighted existence inside The Wall. For Big Brave, it was some far-away enemy camp, where Red-Boy counts coup and takes many horses. It is early in the morning at the beginning of a day's trip. Old Mountain Chief, seated on the companion horse, has spotted an eagle. A fierce War-Pita, a Morning Eagle. The silk War Shield appeared exactly as it should for Red-Boy—his ancestral destiny leading to a distant promise of freedom.

The Elders had taught Red-Boy that it was the tradition among great and revered Blackfeet warriors to transfer their powerful Medicine War Shield to a beneficiary worthy of safeguarding the coveted Medicine.

For Red-Boy, Peter Stabs-By-Mistake, the silken War Shield Sun Painting transported him to the outside world; it was a kind of Medicine Bundle he prayed might be ceremoniously opened, if only less than an eternity from now.

The four walls of Leavenworth had become the four sides of the Earth. The stone pillar guard towers straddling the east wall's gate marked his beginning.

The Sun Painting was the portal through which his sentence…or his life…would end.

Losing himself in the painting is all that gave him hope, counting the days until he was eligible for parole on August 3, 1928. Yet it seemed unlikely to Red-Boy that parole would ever be granted. He had heard from Shake Spear, Coombs and the others that it was often denied for rape offenders. Almost never granted for murderers. Even though it had been in self-defense, he had killed a man.

Again, he had decided the image was finished, only to change his mind and continue drawing and mixing colors, waxing and waning with the thought of leaving it and then going back, finally letting it stand.

Stretched onto a crude wooden frame and fastened to the wall beside his bunk, the War Shield offered an imaginary path away from counting the endless pebbles along the cinder block trail until, finally, with his twenty-year sentence reduced for good conduct, his confinement might be extinguished on that certain day, May 9, 1935. But what then? It was a day too distant to comprehend in any real way.

Annie's face, the dreamlike presence of her haunting dark eyes and soft hair, her touch, brought his dream's eye closer to his hope. For Red-Boy, that date — May, 1935 — was the end of the same eternity that Big Brave pointed to in the distance on the silk painting.

There the Indian sat, staring at Old Mountain Chief atop his mount on the War Shield hung from the wall in the tiny cinder block cell inside the immense concrete and steel confines of The Hot House, atop the lonely rolling prairie lands of Leavenworth, Kansas in the summer of 1926.

>>>→ • ←<<<

Far from the Hot House, Cold-Maker's freezing claw had unmercifully ripped through the reservation the previous winter. Oliver's letter finally arrived in early June, announcing that Chief Curly Bear had taken ill and died during the time when "grass-begins-to-grow" (April). At once, the stricken Holyoker boarded the iron horse to Cut Bank.

Grief held Morning Eagle in the grip of dark foreboding; apparitions spread from within, smothering all preoccupation with Red-Boy's release.

Occasionally, angry pangs of reality pierced through. When the Crown of the Rockies loomed, he harkened back thirty-one years. Then, Chiefs White Calf and Curly Bear, faced with sickness and starvation on the reservation, had negotiated the sale of Glacier National Park for a paltry sum. The U.S. Government had yet to pay the tribe. The Easterner bristled at his government's coldness with a disdain far harsher than any bitterness he held towards Cold-Maker.

Perhaps it was better for Curly Bear to have fallen asleep. Oliver's letter told of the elder being buried in the ground atop a remote hill overlooking Chief Mountain and the prairie grasslands he loved so much.

Upon Morning Eagle's arrival, Bear Head explained to his friend how Curly Bear had been prepared for his journey to the Sand Hills. Close to his body rested those articles Curly Bear had treasured most and would need for his journey: his Medicine Pipe and pipe bag, his War Shield, and his favorite heart symbol fastened to his watch chain. He lay on his elk robe covered with pictographs of his lifetime coups and accomplishments. He was dressed in his sacred weasel suit. On his head, he wore his straight-up headdress; his feet were covered with fully-beaded white moccasins.

Buried with Curly Bear, at his dying request, were the letters and presents Morning Eagle had sent to him over the years.

Morning Eagle withdrew to Chief Mountain with Bear Head and Oliver. There the three men fasted for several days. The second night, Bear Head gently encouraged Morning Eagle by recounting the words of sympathy and encouragement Morning Eagle had spoken to Wolf Plume when Wolf Plume grieved for his dying younger brother, Black Bull.

Back within his Otter Medicine Tipi, Morning Eagle opened his heart to Mountain Chief and the others —how he and Curly Bear had planned for Curly Bear to visit Morning Eagle's lodge back East. How he longed to share this kind and honest man's wisdom with his New England Boy Scout troops, and perhaps with those in Washington, D.C. who would listen to his appeal for Red-Boy's release.

When he had finished, a long, thoughtful silence settled over the little gathering. Then Mountain Chief spoke.

"Always a Piegan Warrior has a strong heart. Remember, Aapinakoi Píítaa…you are one of us."

Now, Morning Eagle listened as each, in turn, spoke of the gifts Morning Eagle possessed and of the chain which bound them all together. He was the holder of the Otter Tipi—a Sacred Medicine Lodge transferred to him by a revered leader who had feared no other man and with whom Morning Eagle would be forever united by a bond that would never rust.

A clearness of vision came through, a stronger sense of purpose.

No longer would the New Englander brook any weak excuses or interference from whiteman bureaucrats and politicians, those who Morning Eagle knew were bent upon weaving the quest for Red-Boy's freedom into a cynical illusion.

>>>→ • ←<<<

"Well, did you tell Campbell what I told you?" asked Miggs.

"Yes, sir," replied Yessup, seated in front of his boss's desk. It was a sweltering hot July afternoon.

"And?"

"He told me not to worry. Seems his plan is to keep the lid on the whole Stabs-By-Mistake issue, too."

"Swell," puffed the little Irishman. "Now you're startin' to learn — "

Sensing his boss was perhaps in an uncommonly good mood, Yessup leaned forward. He noted an unfamiliar, round metallic object on his boss's desk. "Got yourself a nice collectible there, sir," he congratulated.

"Yessup, I'll let you in . . . yesterday I weaseled this mint "Grant" button from this moron at a Helena pawnshop for next to nothing. Can you believe that?"

"Squeak, twang, ding, dang!" chimed the broken overhead fan.

Spotting the little bespectacled secretary at the door, Miggs bellowed, "Dammit, Judy! Will you get those idiots in maintenance up here to fix this damned fan?" With that, Miggs unleashed one of his thick rubber bands at the lopsided mechanical annoyance. "Either that, or put the contraption out of its misery!"

Flinching, the woman nervously replied, "Yes, sir. Right away." Turning, she caught herself and returned to the doorway. Screwing up all her courage, Judy reminded her boss, "Sir, the men were here yesterday at noon to fix your fan while you were out." She flinched again at Miggs' intimidating glare, only to catch herself one final time to make the forgotten introductions-the reason she had ventured down to Miggs' office in the first place. Turning, she ushered the two gentlemen into Miggs' office.

"Some gentlemen to see you, sir. Mr. Grorud and a gentleman from back East. About an Indian matter, sir. They say it's very important."

That late spring and summer of 1926 had been a busy one for Morning Eagle. Yessup had visited with Morning Eagle and Oliver that summer, just after Marie had forwarded James Fry's letter to Montana informing her husband of Miggs' investigation. That letter had finally prompted Morning Eagle to travel to Helena in late July to confer with attorney A. A. Grorud.

"Are you from the Meriam Commission?" barked the red-faced Miggs at the neatly-suited Easterner standing in the doorway.

"No sir. Name's Schuster. You know my attorney, Al Grorud." Miggs nodded. "Pikuni folks on the reservation call me by my given Blackfeet name, Aapinakoi Píítaa."

"Ahp-in' who?"

"Morning Eagle is the Anglo translation."

"Yes, we met a few weeks ago," acknowledged Yessup, standing to greet the visitors. He then quickly turned to meet his boss's glassy-eyed stare. "You remember, sir, when you first sent me up to see Superintendent Campbell. Remember?"

Ignoring his little subordinate, Miggs asked the Easterner, "What brings you way over here?"

"Well, the pardon attorney in D.C., Mr. Fry, sent me a letter last month saying you were in charge of investigating a rape conviction of Peter Stabs-By-Mistake. I am here on behalf of Peter and his family."

"I see. Yes. Mr. Yessup here is looking into the matter for us."

Waiting for a reply from Yessup, but hearing nothing, the Easterner continued.

"Mr. Miggs, I may have to return to Massachusetts to attend to my business earlier than usual this summer. But you know, if I ran my business back East by avoiding problems and tough questions from my employees and customers, I'd lose my business pretty fast, don't you think?" The Assistant US Attorney gave him a wary look.

"Folks on the reservation know this young man was falsely accused," continued Morning Eagle. "They and I have been asking some tough, hard questions, sir."

"Were you an eyewitness?" asked Miggs with barely concealed sarcasm.

"No, but last summer I took affidavits from the eyewitnesses and the victim, Annie Running Crane. I spoke with her mother. They all swear that Peter did nothing to the young woman." The New Englander fixed Miggs with a steady eye. "I forwarded the affidavits to Mr. Grorud, here."

"That's right," offered Grorud. "I sent the original affidavits on to the pardon attorney's office by insured mail, to make sure they didn't get lost."

"Have you seen those affidavits Mr. Fry sent to you, Mr. Miggs?" The Holyoker did not take his eyes off the Assistant US Attorney.

"Listen, Mr. Morning...Eagle. I don't need to be cross-examined by you as to whether we're doing our job here. I told you we're looking into Mr. Stabs...we understand the Indian situation very well up there, sir."

"Is that so?" replied the Easterner. "When you people actually read those sworn affidavits you're supposed to have in your possession, you'll understand the Indian situation even better."

"Now look here, sir! You aren't even aware that the Indian murdered another inmate at Leavenworth. We will handle this situation without any interference, okay?"

The New Englander's eyes narrowed as he approached the front of Miggs' desk and leaned forward.

"Understand this, sir. Peter killed a white Klansman in self-defense. The warden told me the Klansman was forcing the Indian to perform an unnatural act. You or I would have killed the beast, too!"

Miggs' crimson red face was shaking with rage. Utterly unhinged, the little lawman's bow tie was bobbing violently on his Adam's apple.

"Now you listen! Get . . .!"

The Holyoker's arm shot out as if to block the lawman's insult. "We can find our way out, sir. I wasn't born yesterday. I can see you are a very busy man with lots of nothing to do."

Turning to Yessup, then glaring back at Miggs, Morning Eagle asked, "Mr. Yessup, have you ever spotted a WOLVERINE?"

Before Yessup could do more than cover his smile, Morning Eagle was at the door. "Good day, gentlemen," he announced.

>>>→ • ←<<<

Chris Schuster had returned in early August to Holyoke — still consumed with thoughts of Curly Bear and Red-Boy, though less drained — to attend to matters more mundane, but nevertheless necessary. The labor dispute at his factory was finally settled without his workers going out on strike.

A slight breeze fluttered in from the Connecticut River, catching and ruffling the tall evergreens at Titan's Pier. Chris had just come in from chopping firewood, ready to plunk himself behind his dark desk and plan how to assist in Butler's campaign without alienating his Democratic friends. As he listened to the comforting ticks of the old grandfather clock at the far end of the room, he settled on the excuse he'd give his friends, that his efforts for Butler's campaign were contributions toward a higher purpose. They'd understand.

The rasping of the knocker on the heavy chestnut front door of the log house startled him. Marie rose from her embroidering on the living room couch and went to the door. The heavy door blocked her muffled conversation.

"Oh, honey! Oh my gosh!" exclaimed Marie, rushing over to his desk. As she reached to hand him the paper and envelope, her outstretched hand was trembling. "Honey! The man said that he had trouble finding us here because they went to our winter residence first."

He unfolded the paper that his wife had already opened —

*WESTERN UNION*
*TELEGRAPH*
*Received at 349 Dwight St., Holyoke, Mass.*
*168 Y 44 NL Leavenworth, Kansas August 13, 1926*

*Morning Eagle*
*Holyoke, Mass.*

*CONDITIONAL PARDON SIGNED ON SIXTH INSTANT ACCEPT SINCERE THANKS FOR YOUR HELP STOP PARDON WAS RETURNED TO WASHINGTON BUT NO WORD HAS BEEN RECEIVED TO RELEASE ME FOLKS ARE ALL SO ANXIOUS WILL YOU TRY AND URGE THEM AT WASHINGTON TO EXPEDITE MY RELEASE STOP I SHAKE YOUR HAND FROM MY HEART STOP.*

*Peter Stabs-By-Mistake*

"My God!" exclaimed the man, in one explosive burst. "This is unbelievable! My God!" He leapt to his feet.

Then, just as suddenly, the astonishment disappeared, his face turned ashen.

"Honey, what is it?" Marie asked, startled at her husband's unexpected pallor.

Glancing down at his desk drawer, Chris opened it, extracted a letter, and handed it to his wife without a word. His eyes were diverted. It was a letter from James Vielle, which had evidently been written for him by Oliver

Sanders. After quickly scanning the letter, her lips moving in soft whispers, Marie went back to her couch, sat down and stared at her husband.

Sinking back into his leather chair, Morning Eagle looked at his sits-be-side-him-woman. "Marie, I need to be on a train and in Cut Bank as soon as possible."

*United States Department of Justice*
*District of Columbia*

# AFFIDAVIT

I hereby certify that I am a custodian of the records of the Office of the Pardon Attorney, which is the repository for records concerning grants of presidential clemency. I further certify that I have caused a search to be made of the records of the Office of the Pardon Attorney. This search has revealed that on July 27, 1926, Peter Stabs-by-Mistake was granted a pardon on conditions similar to parole. A true copy of this pardon warrant is maintained in the records of the Office of the Pardon Attorney. I certify that the attached is a true copy of that copy.

*Given under my hand and seal of the Department of Justice this 24th day of July, 2002.*

*Roger C. Adams*

Roger C. Adams
Pardon Attorney

Red-Boys Conditional Pardon Granted by President Coolidge.

*Now, therefore, be it known, that I,* CALVIN COOLIDGE *, President of the United States of America, in consideration of the premises, divers other good and sufficient reasons me thereunto moving, do hereby* grant unto the said Peter Stabs-by-Mistake a pardon upon the following conditions, to-wit:

That hereafter the said Peter Stabs-by-Mistake shall commit no crime punishable under the laws of the United States; shall abstain from the possession and use of intoxicating liquor; shall not associate with persons of evil character; shall lead an orderly, industrious life; shall work and reside at all times where the Attorney General of the United States, through the Superintendent of Prisons of the Department of Justice, shall direct; and shall report his residence and occupation to the said Superintendent of Prisons between the first and fifth days of each month until excused therefrom by the President;

That the pardon shall be in force only after the said Peter Stabs-by-Mistake shall have agreed in writing to keep and perform the conditions upon which it is granted, and only so long as he shall keep and perform them;

That upon the failure of the said Peter Stabs-by-Mistake to keep and perform the forgoing conditions, as to which fact the judgment of the President of the United States for the time being shall be conclusive, the pardon shall become void, and the said Peter Stabs-by-Mistake shall be apprehended upon a warrant issued for that purpose by the President to any United States Marshal or Deputy United States Marshal, and forthwith committed to the United States Penitentiary at Leavenworth, Kansas, there to serve the remainder of his term of imprisonment.

*In testimony whereof I have hereunto signed my name and caused the seal of the Department of Justice to be affixed.*

*Done in the District of Columbia this* twenty-seventh *day of* July, *in the year of our Lord One Thousand Nine Hundred and* Twenty-six, *and of the Independence of the United States the One Hundred and* Fifty-first.

(seal)

Calvin Coolidge,

*By the President:*

Jno. G. Sargent,

*Attorney General.*

August 6th, 1926.

I, Peter Stabs-by-Mistake, the person to whom the foregoing pardon is granted, do hereby accept the same, subject to the conditions therein named, and I agree to keep, perform and abide by all said conditions.

Witness: John J. McConlouge
N. P. Timmons

Peter Stabs by Mistake.

# CALVIN COOLIDGE,

*President of the United States of America,*

**To all to whom these presents shall come, Greeting:**

**Whereas**

Peter Stabs-by-Mistake was convicted in the United States District Court for the Districtof Montana of the rape of an Indian woman on an Indian reservation, and on September twenty-sixth, 1921, was sentenced to imprisonment for twenty years in the United States Penitentiary at Leavenworth, Kansas; and,

Whereas it has been made to appear to me that the said Peter Stabs-by-Mistake is a fit object of Executive clemency:

President Coolidge's Conditional Pardon.

*List of pardons, commutations, and respites, etc., granted by the President during the fiscal year ending June 30, 1927*—Continued

| Name of applicant | District and offense | Sentence and date | Recommendation of Attorney General | Action of President, and date |
|---|---|---|---|---|
| Seymour Berman (44–435). | North Carolina, western. Transporting a stolen automobile interstate. | Oct. 6, 1925. 18 months at the National Training School for Boys, Washington, D. C. | The applicant, a boy sixteen and a half years of age, together with another boy, appropriated an automobile which they found on a vacant lot in New York City and proceeded to North Carolina. He was thoroughly repentant of his act, which was more in the nature of a boyish prank than one denoting criminality. The Attorney General concurred in the recommendations of the United States attorney and Judge Webb and advised that the sentence be commuted to expire at once. | July 21, 1926. Sentence commuted to expire at once. |
| Thomas Ryan (43–722). | Tennessee, eastern. Impersonating a Government officer. | Nov. 27, 1920. 1 year and 1 day in the United States penitentiary at Atlanta, Ga. | Petitioner was released on parole Sept. 1, 1921, and finally discharged from custody Oct. 17, 1921. His conduct since release was investigated by a special agent of the department, who reported that the applicant had steady employment, enjoyed a happy home life, had proven trustworthy to his employer, and was otherwise conducting himself in a law-abiding manner. The Attorney General advised that the applicant be granted a full and unconditional pardon for the purpose of restoring his civil rights. | July 22, 1926. Pardon granted to restore civil rights. |
| Manuel Vincent, jr. (44–419). | Hawaii. Adultery, and violation of the white slave traffic act. | Oct. 8, 1918. 3 years in the Oahu prison, at Honolulu, Hawaii. | Petitioner served his term, less the allowances for good conduct, and was released Jan. 28, 1921. It appeared that since release the applicant had done everything in his power to live a straightforward life and had been conducting himself in a moral and law-abiding manner. The Attorney General advised that he be granted a full and unconditional pardon for the purpose of restoring his civil rights. | Do. |
| Henry Bernst (44–245). | New York, western. Buying goods stolen from an interstate shipment. | June 2, 1919. 2 years in the United States penitentiary at Atlanta, Ga. | The applicant was released on parole June 11, 1920, and finally discharged from custody Jan. 19, 1921. As evidenced by very strong character affidavits and the report of a special agent of the department, the applicant appeared to have been conducting himself in a very satisfactory manner since his release. The Attorney General advised that he be granted a full and unconditional pardon for the purpose of restoring his civil rights. | Do. |
| Henry Margulies (44–326) | New York, northern. Conspiracy, and receiving and concealing dutiable goods which had been smuggled into the United States. | Dec. 14, 1925. 1 year and 3 months in the United States penitentiary at Atlanta, Ga. | The applicant made a full confession before being brought to trial and assisted the Government in bringing to justice the principal offender. He had undergone more than half of his sentence, and the United States attorney and the sentencing judge were of the opinion that clemency should be extended. The Attorney General advised that the sentence be commuted to expire at once. | July 24, 1926. Sentence commuted to expire at once. |
| Ercole Maglione (44–83). | California, southern. Conspiring to violate the Harrison Antinarcotic Act and the opium act. | Feb. 3, 1925. Two years in the United States penitentiary at Leavenworth, Kans., and a fine of $3. | It appeared that the culpability of the applicant was not as great as that of his codefendant, who received a similar sentence. Under the circumstances presented the Attorney General was of the opinion that a commutation of the sentence to 18 months was justifiable and so recommended. | July 26, 1926. Sentence commuted to 18 months, with the allowances for good conduct. |
| Peter Stabs-by-Mistake (43–686). | Montana. Rape of an Indian woman, on an Indian reservation. | Sept. 26, 1921. 20 years in the United States penitentiary at Leavenworth, Kans. | The offense committed does not appear to have been an aggravated one. The applicant had served an actual imprisonment of 4 years and approximately 8 months. The prosecuting attorney was of the opinion that the sentence was excessive and strongly recommended clemency. The Commissioner of Indian Affairs was also of the opinion that the sentence should be reduced, as were also the complaining witness and her parents. The Attorney General advised that the applicant be granted a pardon, upon conditions similar to a parole. | July 27, 1926. Pardon granted on conditions similar to parole. |
| Allen Merrill Young (42–451). | District of Columbia. Receiving stolen property. | Jan. 10, 1920. 5 years in the District of Columbia Reformatory, Lorton, Va. (Case appealed; judgment affirmed.) | The applicant had served an actual imprisonment of 14 months. His operations covered a period of less than 3 months, and he was not regarded as a confirmed criminal. His confinement was working an extreme hardship upon his family, and the Attorney General advised a commutation of the sentence to expire at once upon conditions similar to parole. | July 29, 1926. Sentence commuted to expire at once, on conditions similar to parole. |
| Abe Levin (44–320) | Illinois, northern. Conspiracy to violate the prohibition act. | May 5, 1925. 2 years in the United States penitentiary at Leavenworth, Kans., and a fine of $10,000. (Transferred to Atlanta Penitentiary Feb. 18, 1926.) | The applicant had since his confinement voluntarily and without any promise of reward, rendered service to the Government, and the Attorney General was of the opinion that a shortening of the sentence was justified. The applicant's offense, however, was a serious one, and the Attorney General recommended a conditional commutation to expire at once, the commutation to be upon conditions similar to parole. | Aug. 3, 1926. Sentence commuted to expire at once, on conditions similar to parole. |
| George J. Pastore (44–264). | New York, southern. Selling heroin in violation of the act of Dec. 17, 1914. | Oct. 3, 1922. 1 year and 1 day in the United States penitentiary at Atlanta, Ga. | Petitioner served his term, less the allowances for good conduct, and was released July 25, 1923. His conduct since release was investigated by a special agent of the department, who reported favorably. The Attorney General advised that the applicant be granted a full and unconditional pardon for the purpose of restoring his civil rights. | Aug. 11, 1926. Pardon granted to restore civil rights. |
| Donald Creekmore (44–153). | Tennessee, eastern. Conspiracy to steal, receive, have in possession, and conceal interstate freight and express. | July 1, 1925. 2 years in the United States penitentiary at Atlanta, Ga., a fine of $1,000, and costs. (Transferred to the industrial reformatory at Chillicothe, Ohio.) | Petitioner, together with 2 others, was found in possession of a quantity of cigarettes which had been stolen from an interstate shipment. One of his codefendants, after an imprisonment of 3 months and 2 days, was released on parole. The applicant was regarded as no more culpable than the other man and there was nothing to indicate that he was in any respect a seasoned criminal. The Attorney General concurred in the views of the United States attorney and trial judge that the prisoner had been sufficiently punished and advised that sentence be commuted to expire at once. | Aug. 11, 1926. Sentence commuted to expire at once. |
| T. G. Walker (44–422). | Kentucky, eastern. Having in possession counterfeit coins. | Apr. 8, 1902. 14 months in the United States penitentiary at Atlanta, Ga., and a fine of $200. (Suspended as to the fine.) | Petitioner served his term, less the allowances for good conduct, and was released Mar. 27, 1903. It appeared from the character affidavits submitted by a number of representative citizens that the applicant was regarded as a good business man and citizen. The Attorney General advised that he be granted a full and unconditional pardon for the purpose of restoring his civil rights. | Aug. 16, 1926. Pardon granted to restore civil rights. |
| Max A. Levy (44–302). | New York, southern. Selling, and aiding and abetting in the sale of narcotic drugs in violation of the act of Dec. 17, 1914. | July 27, 1921. A fine of $1,000. | The applicant duly paid his fine. His conduct since the commission of the offense was the subject of investigation by an agent of the department, who was of the opinion that he fully merited the restoration of civil rights. The Attorney General concurred in the favorable recommendations made and advised that the applicant be granted a full and unconditional pardon for the purpose of restoring his civil rights. | Do. |

artial list of pardons granted by the President in 1927, including conditional pardon granted for Peter Stabs-By-Mistake.

Drawing of golden eagle, courtesy of Joseph Wagner.

# XXIV

# The Hand Is Weak

He felt light-headed and took a deep breath. His heart was still beating too fast. Free...finally on The Outside...after five years behind that Wall. The Outside looked restless—color, lots of color and women and little ones moving, scurrying about in all directions. He boarded the train to Helena.

He held a brown paper bag containing some rolls and a sausage. After the food and the train fare, he had seventy-five cents left of his five dollars in prison "severance pay." In his other pocket were the instructions to meet Grorud. And his pardon.

His prison-made War Shield was carefully hidden between two pieces of taped cardboard. He clutched the Sun Painting close to him.

He couldn't sleep on the train. Most of the time he sat immobile, transfixed by the passing countryside, the other passengers, the new noises and freedom. He walked from one end of the train to the other just because he could.

The young Indian glanced around furtively at the others about to disembark and followed them onto the worn wooden station platform in Helena. He stood awkwardly, re-reading his instructions on where to meet the man he had never met, wondering how he was expected to greet him.

Grorud had broken his promise to come to Leavenworth. Is he gonna be here now? he worried.

The instructions said Grorud would meet him at a place called Power Block in Helena. He smiled a little. In one day he had come from cell Block

B to Power Block, as if being here miraculously re-established his power and status.

He squinted, scanning for something familiar, a knowing gesture. People everywhere, parents shouting, children yelling, pushing, running; it all thrilled him and made him nervous. He felt the glances, the glares—a lone Indian with long braids, in ill-fitting prison-issue street clothes, a white shirt and oversized brown pants and a worn pair of tight-fitting shoes. He felt foreign, vulnerable, not knowing what might be expected of him, starting completely over as if he were an apparition returned from the Ghost-Trail, back to visit the living.

He shut his eyes momentarily, trying to picture the rich familiar colors worn by his Elders, the feel of a pair of moccasins. His thoughts then turned to his more recent friends.

Was tough leavin' Big Ed, Gunny and the others...especially Coombs and Shake Spear, he thought. Tougher even than leavin' my buddies after the war.

Red-Boy found strange comfort thinking back to his friends as he opened his eyes.

They'll keep the Stick Game going for sure. The Vets'll protect Coombs' racket. Aaee, they'll make sure he stays cell boss. Wonder what those cowards are doin' now?

He had assured his poet-friend, Shake Spear, that he and Annie would write. He wished he were off to his Annie now rather than to meet Grorud.

He reached into his baggy pants pocket and pulled out the pardon from President Coolidge. He read it to reassure himself. He squeezed his eyes shut once more, then opened them wide as if to convince himself that the chattering strangers were not part of a dream.

A cloud of apprehension hung over him; something he might do, others would take offense, he'd be sent back. He felt the gloved hand of prison guards; someone grabbed his left shoulder. He spun around, clutching his War Shield, almost losing a grip on his paper bag. His eyes met those of a taller, wiry, gray-haired man.

"So good to see you, Peter. I'm Albert Grorud." The gentleman was smiling broadly, his hand extended.

"Yes...thank you," was all the startled Indian could say. He widened his eyes at the sudden appearance of the person who had been woven through Morning Eagle's letters, the man who had spoken with prison officials and people in Washington, D.C. Could this man—Morning Eagle's friend—have succeeded where his attorney at the trial, Ed Elliott, had failed? He noticed Grorud was dressed in an ill-fitting pair of gray pants and a short-sleeved shirt, the same drab clothing that all Anglos, at least all Anglo attorneys, seemed to wear, he decided.

"My car is right over here," the attorney offered. "I'm going to take you home right after I drop by my office."

Going home. The thought was all that had saved him. Now, the thought made his heart pound again.

Grorud's brand-new two-door, white-sidewalled Ford transported them to Grorud's Power Block office. The lawyer related how he had gotten a good trade-in for his colossal, too-expensive-to-run Cadillac. Red-Boy just listened.

The only questions Grorud asked the self-conscious young man during the drive to his office were about the prison food and the cardboard-covered object Red-Boy was carrying.

"Food was worse than in the war," Red-Boy replied. The cardboard contained a drawing, he told the counselor.

Red-Boy blinked hard as he took in Grorud's large book-lined office. The lawyer occupied a corner office with tall windows framed with dignified blue drapes. The counselor's antique, high-backed desk sat in the corner. The opposite wall was lined with books and more books with numbers on them. They looked so strange. Red-Boy wondered what was inside. Were whiteman's laws held there, hidden away? Was the whiteman's law about numbers? Did they count things differently than the Pikuni?

On the adjacent wall hung framed diplomas and other certificates from places far away. Grorud's War Shields, thought Red-Boy. A large, overstuffed green couch was shoved up next to the wall underneath the certificates and diplomas.

Grorud explained with an awkward grin that this was where he spent most of his time with clients when not busy with court appearances, trials and filing briefs. "One of the reasons I couldn't get down to Leavenworth as I promised," he said apologetically. "Lots of legal deadlines and such…all unexpected emergencies." The apology seemed weak. Red-Boy nodded. It didn't matter anymore.

Quickly returning a few phone calls and giving instructions to a plump, middle-aged woman who appeared as if she had, at one time, taught at boarding school somewhere, Grorud finally nodded and smiled at Peter. The young man sat in the middle of the green couch with his sack on one side and his cardboard-covered drawing on the other.

"Well, it's time to leave, Peter," Grorud finally announced with a broad smile. Red-Boy stood abruptly, not yet rid of the lock-step discipline inside Leavenworth. He worried how he would make conversation during the long trip to the reservation.

Finally, they were about to be on the road, the sun nearly overhead, first to East Glacier to pick up Bear Head and Red-Boy's old friend, James Vielle. Then, they would head on over through Browning and down home to Heart Butte. There, Red-Boy would reunite with Morning Eagle and his parents. From inside The Wall, he had learned that Thomas and Steals-In-The-Day-time-Woman had been working their land northeast of Heart Butte, when not visiting friends and relations in Cut Bank.

At last, Red-Boy asked what was most on his mind. "Mr. Grorud, how has Annie Running Crane been?"

The lanky attorney frowned slightly. "You know, I've been out of touch with the folks up there on the reservation lately."

Red-Boy followed the taller man down the hall, but in his mind's eye he pictured Annie nestled in his arms late at night inside his small log house at Heart Butte. She looked the same, the same soft, flowing black hair, the same slender graceful form, the same gentle finger-tip touch. Her eyes spoke of things that had gone wrong with the Bureau, plans to help their families, their Pikuni people. Their life together.

The blood pulsed and pounded at his temples like the push through the Argonne. He knew, then, that if he must die in the dark ambush of war, he would not do so with his back facing the enemy. The intensity of the throbbing in his head and the thumping of the blood through his heart made the dizziness return.

Worry crowded out the vision. Annie's letters had stopped coming. Would she still be his sits-beside-him-woman?

Quickly, Red-Boy knew what he must do. He would give his sits-beside-him-woman his War Shield when they met. It seemed to him the only fitting way for them to be united once again.

>>>→ • ←<<<

Grorud's car bounced and swayed as it made its way toward their stop at East Glacier Lodge. His client stared out, renewed by the snow-peaked humps of the Shining Mountain Rockies looming and framing a picturesque background. A strange encampment of lodges had been raised in front of the tourist lodge. A long iron horse rested on tracks near the lodge, the locomotive clanking and slowly hissing whispers of steamed impatience.

"Looks like a Great Northern has just pulled in with Eastern dudes," remarked Grorud.

Getting out of the car, they walked toward the encampment. All here for the Sun Dance, thought Red-Boy. Then he saw the tourists, streams of them, disembarking from the train, walking around the lodges. He recognized some locals—Piegans, some Bloods, Crees. They were hovering around the iron horse. The tourists were taking pictures with their black boxes while youngsters were laughing and scurrying about everywhere, even through the lodges.

Grorud explained that the white tourists were curious beings, traveling on the iron horse from the East, carrying with them their picture machines to "capture authentic Indians," Blackfeet hired by the Great Northern Railroad to camp outside the lodges built by the railroad.

Red-Boy's jaw tensed, sensing that these whitemen strangers were robbing his people of a certain privacy. Then he spotted some locals hawking "Authentic Indian" beads, tomahawks, jewelry, blankets, even pipes. The young Indian slowly shook his head.

So, economic survival on the reservation had come to this, he thought. First, surrendering to the Indian Office's farming and livestock-raising agenda, and land fraud schemes that had bankrupted his Nation and stolen tribal lands. Now pandering to the tourists promoted by monied railroad interests, which, for Red-Boy and many of the Elders, had somehow laid tracks through their reservation lands without thought of the word Treaty.

"This is a new thing, now, since you've been gone," offered the lawyer. The dark cloud surrounding Red-Boy's face told Grorud that he had better find Bear Head and James Vielle. Quick.

Walking a short distance to a grass-covered slope in front of the tourist
lodge, Grorud and Red-Boy stopped and noticed an old man sitting on the
grass, surrounded by small leather tipis. "Authentic Indian Tipis," the stenciled sign read.

James Vielle was seated just outside the little miniature tipi circle, having
concluded a sale with an "Eastern dude" who had made a purchase for his
daughter. His wife stood nearby, snapping her Kodak.

"Aaee! Bear Head. Sani tápe? (How are things?) What are you and Drags-
Behind doin'?" Red-Boy called.

Red Boy's casual, offhand manner surprised Grorud, as if the Indian had
only been gone a short time.

Old Bear Head looked over and cast a broad, sweeping grin, but said
nothing.

"Ó ki, Red-Boy. We're just havin' some fun at the whiteman's expense,"
James Vielle joked. "Iik so ka' pii." He took hold of Red-Boy's shoulders with
both hands and looked warmly at his friend. Nothing was said for a long few
minutes.

Finally speaking, Red-Boy greeted his friend of many winters.

"Aaeee, Drags-Behind, this is like a lariat-who-ropes-the-thunder. My
heart rises." They were both smiling now. Bear Head nodded approvingly.

Red-Boy glanced around the bustle of tourists, herding their gaggle of
children, then turned again to his old friend. "Looks like the whiteman Easterners have come in here and are makin' you beg." He paused, then shook his
head slowly. "Makes me angry."

"They think we're beggin'," Bear Head replied in his native Pikuni. "Actually, we're playin' an Old Ná pi trick on 'em," he winked. "At their expense, I
think," the old man grinned.

"What's Bear Head saying?" Grorud asked. Red-Boy slowly translated for
the lawyer. "How's this a trick?" the lawyer asked again.

"Them little tipis you see? They're from a whiteman store down in Helena," explained James Vielle. "Railroad brings 'em up here for us to sell." Red-
Boy shook his head as he translated.

"Pretty clever racket," Grorud laughed.

"We keep sellin' 'em and they keep payin' us," said Vielle.

Red-Boy remained skeptical. "How much does the whiteman businessman take?" he asked. No one answered. "So it's come to this, huh? The white-man's farmin' and sheep raisin', then sellin' little tipis to kids."

"Maybe you have a better plan, Red-Boy?" teased Bear Head, casting an amused look. Red-Boy nodded and smiled at his Elder.

Turning, he now asked his old friend, "Aaeee, Drags-Behind, where's yer bottle?"

The lanky Indian shrugged. "Ain't got one no more," he answered.

"We cured him of that." Red-Boy's mouth dropped open with an attempted question. "Couple 'a good sweats and he got Red Man's religion," joked Bear Head. Jim Vielle laughed.

"Just like what happened to you, Red-Boy," Vielle replied, nodding his approval to Bear Head.

Yet looking at his friend's worn and ruddy face, Red-Boy knew that perhaps James Vielle's battle for sobriety had been tougher than just a few sweats.

Grorud led the group away from Glacier Lodge to his car. On the way, Red-Boy caught sight of an obviously drunken mixed-blood badgering an elder. The two men were far enough away from the tourist lodge so as not to attract attention. The young drunk was yelling and cursing, a half-empty bot-tle raised high. He was wrestling and grabbing at the old man's money purse with his free hand, scattering coins everywhere.

Red-Boy suddenly started forward. Vielle and Grorud followed. Red-Boy confronted the young drunk. "You wouldn't pick on my grandfather that way," he muttered between his teeth.

Grorud firmly grabbed the Indian's shoulder. "No Red-Boy. Don't!"

The young ex-con instinctively whirled and glared at the tall lawyer.

"Listen, Peter," advised the lawyer. "You risk violating your conditional pardon if you get into trouble."

"He's right," Vielle said. "I'll take care of this.

Red-Boy lowered his eyes, glowering at the drunken man with dark contempt. "Coward," he muttered between clenched teeth.

Red-Boy scooped up the elder's prize. Vielle gave the drunk a firm shove. Red-Boy strode over to the old man and handed him his money.

»»→ • ←««

The fancy black Ford banged along the pot-holed dusty road, whipping up a thick, brown tail whose clouds hung in the air, marking their trail in the vastness of the bone-dry prairie. The car rolled and banged to the front of the small Heart Butte exchange store and livery post and came to a sudden stop. The occupants lurched forward as if being thrust upon this isolated outpost by an unexpected down draft.

The men walked the two miles from the outpost to the lodge of Thomas Stabs-By-Mistake.

Peter saw occasional Model-T Fords bouncing along lone, distant paths—for him, an odd sight.

"Them cars, they belong to the agents," offered James. "Indian Bureau claims it helps them git around the reservation quicker." He laughed.

"Yeah. And how many of the sick ones do they help in such a hurry?" scoffed Red-Boy.

"Unh," Bear Head intoned.

There were few circular lodges. Here and there, tiny cottonwood cabins and dilapidated, square-box clapboard houses dotted the dry landscape.

They passed an abandoned, rusted car lying on its side in front of one small clapboard. Shoeless children were climbing over and inside their steel horse, playing on it instead of with the ever-present dogs.

The notion struck Red-Boy, as he cast a sullen look at the whole scene, that perhaps some Indian agent or white rancher had liquored up a gullible Piegan to exchange his allotment land for the now-rusted hulk of an automobile.

Grazing lands seemed beaten down and chewed up. Even the clothes worn by the children and their parents seemed chewed up and worn ragged; colorless, torn shirts, shapeless baggy pants, or no pants at all.

Grorud explained that more public schools instead of mission schools had been added to the reservation. Red-Boy wondered how the children got to school, and if they were allowed to speak in their Pikuni dialect.

As always, Thomas's lodge stood steadfast, northeast of town inside a gently folding draw. The approaching foursome was first seen by Thomas's sits-beside-him-woman. She had been carefully, meticulously weeding and hoeing the now dry, dusty vegetable garden. For all intents and purposes, the little plot looked barren save for a few cornstalks, wilting green beans and patches of dry, cracked ground, pock-marked with holes where potatoes and turnips had been harvested.

Red-Boy's mother ran to the lodge flap and opened it, shouting something, then came running to greet them. Uncustomarily and unceremoniously his mother, sturdy as ever in her long gray trade cloth dress, ran as best she could with her lame leg.

Steals-In-The-Daytime-Woman smothered her son with a hug all the way to the lodge. His mother was crying now. Grorud felt awkward, embarrassed. He stood off to the side and waited patiently for instructions. The woman beckoned him and James Vielle to come inside.

Seated, as always, on his soft willow rest, Red-Boy's father stared at his son, eyes glistening, hands motionless at his sides. To his right sat Big Brave-Mountain Chief. Seated to Thomas's left was Ted Running Crane, holding the Medicine Pipe, mouth open as if about to utter a greeting to the lost warrior but unable to find the words. Morning Eagle sat opposite Red-Boy's father.

Morning Eagle turned and smiled broadly but said nothing. The others sat mute, their faces as ashen as the smoldering embers of the lodge fire in the center.

Time stood still. The men looked at Red-Boy and at each other. The air was silent. The Pikuni way.

Bear Head and Grorud sat by the lodge-flap, next to the grub box.

Red-Boy, still standing, touched the New Englander's outstretched hand and uttered, "My hand to you, Aapinakoi Píítaa. My heart sings to me."

The others seemed to be uttering an upward inflection of surprise and wonder, a strange song-like "A-a-a-a-e-e-e."

Then Red-Boy saw his mother's outstretched hand, holding his beaded necklace with buckskin bag. It had found its way from the courtroom in Great Falls to Steals-In-The-Daytime for safekeeping all these years. Tears fell freely as he took the necklace and embraced his mother.

Now, Chief Running Crane stood and approached Red-Boy, placing his right hand on the young Indian's shoulder. "My Heart is good towards you, Red-Boy," he said, looking the young man full in the face. Red-Boy knew instinctively that the truth had finally been spoken.

Completing the circle and meeting the eyes of all those present, Red-Boy's eyes once again connected with those of his father. The young warrior approached, arms outstretched as if sleepwalking, carefully seating himself beside his father. Tears came freely as their hands touched.

The others watched, now, as the father spoke with his son and the son spoke with his father, both speaking with naked hearts.

Several hours passed and the group finally took an evening meal of sarvis berries, turnips, some broiled beef chips and coffee. They passed the Medicine Pipe once again, clockwise, four times.

Mountain Chief then told of the little ones and of the Elders who had been taken by sickness, hunger, the freezing hand of Cold-Maker. He finally paused and nodded for Morning Eagle to speak.

Red-Boy leaned close and listened as Morning Eagle recounted how Cold-Maker had taken Chief Curly Bear the way of the ghost-trail to the Sand Hills. A long stillness followed, broken only by an occasional crackle from the lodge fire.

The conversation finally turned to Victor Black Looks.

Thomas spoke first and explained that the young man's Uncle Richard continued serving on the Tribal Council. Yet Richard Sanders was now clearly seen by the Elders and many of the younger half-bloods as a voice for the Indian Bureau, even though he and his nephew, Victor, had pretended to advocate for Red-Boy's release. Everyone knew it had not been straight talk.

Victor Black Looks' life had taken an abrupt downturn. Thanks to the efforts of James Vielle, Thomas, Running Crane and the other Elders, the government interpreter had been narrowly defeated for a coveted seat on the Tribal Council next to his Uncle Richard. Maxine's recent death and the guzzling effects of alcoholism were also wasting away her son, casting him evermore distant from his father and even from his Uncle Richard. Chief Running Crane explained all of these things to Red-Boy.

Then, Running Crane said something that startled, even shocked Red-Boy. His son-in-law, James Veille, had been elected to the Tribal Council in the last election. Red-Boy said nothing at first, only motioning assent with a nod of his head to his old friend, James Veille, wondering if he should ask about Annie.

His consternation was cut short when Morning Eagle jumped in and told him that James had married Running Crane's oldest daughter, Louise. They had two children, a girl they named Mollie and a little boy they named Peter.

Then, Morning Eagle ventured to tell him that James, with the help of Morning Eagle and others, was just beginning to organize a Boy Scout troop.

Red-Boy asked if Annie was helping to organize the troop.

He explained to the others that Annie had always been a good organizer, telling him which lodges to visit on which evenings and what to look for and report to the Indian Bureau.

He noticed that Running Crane was now rocking slowly back and forth, his face reflecting no emotion. Red-Boy wondered what was hidden underneath.

"How is your daughter, Annie, Chief Running Crane?" asked the young Indian politely. Annie's father continued rocking slowly backwards and forwards, expressionless.

"I have been five winters away and my heart misses your daughter. I wish to see her." Running Crane glanced over at the young man but said nothing, continuing to rock.

"Red-Boy, why don't you and I go for a ride," James Veille offered.

When outside, his friend added, "I must speak with a naked heart to you, now, Red-Boy." Let us ride out and speak together."

Indicating which horse to his friend, James Veille mounted his pony. Red-Boy felt a weakness in his legs but followed, nodding to the others that they would not be gone too long.

>>>→ • ←<<<

The two young Piegan warriors rode out on the grasslands, two old friends speaking of what had traveled by during the past five winters.

They rode past hoodoo outcroppings—green-gray and black sandstone-weathered pillars, transformed to a dark brown by Cold-Maker's harsh touch.

They slowed near a clump of fringed sagewort and rabbitbrush atop a gradually inclining dusty knoll. The hilltop overlooked an expanse of bluebunch wheatgrass.

They watched a golden eagle hold itself gracefully aloft, hunting, drifting and gliding through the prairie's warm updrafts and currents.

The eagle's eyes darted westward and bore witness to the Sun's fingertips touching the snow caps of the "Crown of the Rockies," casting a blazing sunset cape of silk. The wind whispered; the eagle followed its currents.

The eagle, its seven-foot wings outstretched, banked toward the two riderless horses, now—the men sitting cross-legged nearby.

One was telling his friend he had married the older sister of his friend's loved one. He and his wife had taken care of her younger sister when their mother had become too ill. The young woman had lived with them in the cabin that the two old friends had built at Heart Butte.

With bowed head, the other listened as he was told that the younger sister had become tubercular. When the disease had reached down from her lungs and took hold of her intestines, she imagined herself with child.

At first, the whiteman doctor had told them not to worry and left some medicine.

To distract her from her suffering and delirium, they complied with her wish to go in the evenings to where she could look up at the Star-That-Never-Moves.

She grew sicker and weaker. No doctor came. They listened to her hopes for the imagined new life she carried. She whispered over and over the father's name, telling them that he was away.

As she slipped into her final delirium, she called the name of her unborn baby, "star child."

Diving, the eagle saw the young warrior sink to the very floor of the prairie, his body curled, knowing now that life had left the young woman, his beloved.

Annie and her imaginary "star child" now walked the same Ghost-Trail as his first newborn.

Circling and soaring, the eagle sees the companions together now, holding on to each other. The ponies stand with heads bowed.

The Sun lowers behind the Crown of the Rockies, the golden eagle crosses the great Sky Fire's pink glaze, spreading and bleeding into a scarlet-purple shawl framing the shining whitecaps of the Rocky Mountains.

Close to sunset, the eagle soars on winds that do nothing to warm a heart frozen by grief.

The eagle screams as the young man draws a hunting knife away from his neck. The knife sweeps down, shearing off the long black braids. Released from his desperate grip, the knife falls as the young Indian covers his head with dirt in mourning.

Shadows lengthen, enveloping aspen parklands, creeping slowly across the vast landscape of foothills, enveloping the grays of fescue and bluegrass prairie.

In the dark, the Eagle slowly circles the Star-That-Never-Moves and the young man looks, unblinking, at the glowing bits embedded in a blackened ceiling of the world, imagining the young woman watching him now, seeing him within his cruel new prison, life lost without her soft presence.

Just before dawn, when the golden eagle returns he finds the young man resting there until the Sun breaks its light on a new day.

As the Sun's gentle hand touched and awoke the prairie, the two warriors opened their eyes.

And the morning eagle cried out and flew off, showing the two companions the pathway home.

Black and white photo of Red-Boy's silk painting encased in its silver-antiqued, hand carved wooden frame designed by the late Blackfeet Elder Tomas A. Blackweasel (Sikapiohkitopi-Gray Horse Rider).

# XXV

# The Giving-the-Shield Ceremony

D epression hung around Red-Boy like a leaden Buffalo robe that covered and completely smothered him. "Red-Boy, do not think of harming yourself, for the sorrow that is in your heart is always on your face." It was Aapinakoi Piítaa who reminded Red-Boy that he must grieve; but he must also live a good and true life of giving deeds because of the coups he had counted. Yet, to Red-Boy, counting coups seemed meaningless. His mind was indifferent to everything but loss.

It was Aapinakoi Piítaa who talked to Red-Boy of the time when they both saw Wolf Plume grieve as his younger brother Black Bull lay dying. And Aapinakoi Piítaa spoke of the depth of his own sorrow over Curly Bear's passing, yet how the old warrior's death had steeled his resolve to obtain Red-Boy's freedom.

Many sleeps were spent at the lodge of Thomas Stabs-By-Mistake with Red-Boy. James Vielle was constantly present to remind his friend of his new purpose—to be there, back at home, back on the reservation, working as he always wanted to work, doing the things his mind had foretold him that he and Annie would do someday when he was free.

Aapinakoi Piítaa told Red-Boy of the gifts Red-Boy possessed and brought back with him from the far-away places that would make him a leader of his people.

Still, Red-Boy's despair spoke louder—his aversion to food and being with anyone, his sleeplessness that blurred the world into a relentless gray overcast.

Early one morning, Red-Boy was quietly coaxed by Morning Eagle to ride out with him. For several hours they rode together into the hilly land, finally stopping and walking their mounts. Neither spoke for a long time.

"Red-Boy, I must tell you something now." Making sure the young man's eyes were with him, he continued. "It is the whiteman's custom to give one who receives a conditional pardon a free and full pardon after three years of probation. You must lead a good life, free from any trouble with the law. You must not mix with the Indian police. You must keep your distance from Victor Sanders."

Morning Eagle paused. Red-Boy looked at his whiteman friend, then lowered his head. The veteran's tired eyes had grown sunken and dark with a deep, burrowing hollowness that seeped and ached through him, slowing his gait and silencing his tongue.

The New Englander knew that sorrow would stay with the young man despite a full pardon. Still, he continued to talk straight with Red-Boy.

"You must be friends with all your neighbors and the priests here on the reservation. They can help you and recommend that you be given a full pardon." He paused again, looking Red-Boy full in the face.

"Now, I have one more thing to tell you. You must have a guardian to look out for you during these three years that you are leading an upright life on the reservation. I have asked Oliver Sanders to be your guardian for this time. He will help you in many ways."

Red-Boy suddenly turned a sharp eye on the older man. "Why the father of Black Looks, the coward who cheated me and fooled the others?"

"Red-Boy, I tell you that Oliver Sanders was very helpful to me and the others in getting your freedom. You know he does not approve of the ways of his son. You must make a new life for yourself here, Red-Boy."

The two men walked together in silence for a long time.

Finally, stopping full in his tracks, Morning Eagle faced Red-Boy, Peter Stabs-By-Mistake and said, "You must soar above Black Looks, above all the cowards. Red-Boy, you are a leader because you have an honest, truthful heart."

Then Morning Eagle paused and looked off into the distance toward the interior of the reservation and the eastern slope of the Shining Mountains where the warm breath of the Chinook wind would gather in late fall and winter, perhaps melting Snow-Maker's hand and freeing up the grazing land for a spell.

"Red-Boy, you are a powerful Piegan warrior who has served your country well. Your father is a chief. Your grandfather, Big Brave-Mountain Chief, and his father the great Mountain Chief, are your blood. Your heart grieves now, but with time your grief will be pushed down inside and a new strength will emerge from within. I know it."

Red-Boy looked long at his whiteman friend and knew he spoke from his heart; the same words he had heard from his father inside the Sweat Lodge long ago.

Listening to the man who, more than any other, had brought about his impossible freedom, Red-Boy knew what he must do.

That night he slept inside his father's lodge.

With sleep came the dream-talk of his blood relations.

》》→ • ←《《

"Now, I have something more to say," said the old warrior. Big Brave's arrow had made blood gush from the nostrils of many Buffalo. Red-Boy, now inside the Otter Medicine Tipi, heard his grandfather speak to him.

"It is about the War Shield that I will tell. To own a War Shield was the aim of all young Pikuni warriors. It was a great honor and the Shield was his most sacred possession. Only those who had brave hearts and who had joined war parties could earn one. When in camp, the Shield hung from a pole to the east of his lodge. It faced the place of rising Sun until Sun went away. Then it was taken into the tipi and hung from a lodge-pole. Its feathers were fluttered by the wind that came in at the smoke-flaps. When a warrior went the way of the Wolf-Trail, then his head rested upon his Shield in the grave.

"A young man who had been successful on the war path and who was respected by the people would carry his pipe to a Medicine Man or some old warrior and ask for a favor. After the pipe was smoked, the young man would say: 'I ask you to make a War Shield. That is why I bring my pipe. For what I ask, I will give you many blankets and robes.' If the favor was granted, the young man would sing in his heart.

"At the time of Giving-the-Shield ceremony, all the relations and friends of the young man were invited. Many songs of bravery, and Medicine-Songs-of-the-Shield were sung. Then came the giving. The giver slowly drew the Shield up over the painted body of his young friend so that all might see the presentation. The Shield was fastened to the young warrior's arm with buckskin thongs. The old warrior then gave him his blanket. The young brave was proud in his heart to own a War Shield, and a blanket that had belonged to an old man who had been successful on many war parties. He would carry the Shield in all battles. No arrow could go through it.

"Dream-Spirit told us to observe all the ceremonies of the War Shield, and how to paint our bodies when we carried it. Dream Spirit said that we must protect our Shields with outside covers of soft elk or deer skin. Dream-Spirit told us that the cover must never be removed or the Shield exposed to view until going into battle.

"Shield-Spirit was most powerful. He came close when the Piegans were fighting the enemy. Shield-Spirit killed harm that might come to our bodies. That is why we counted many coups in the war days."

Big Brave-Mountain Chief remained silent a long while. Then he announced, "That is all I have to say." He closed his eyes and was gone from Red-Boy's dream.

Red-Boy felt himself enveloped in the shining blue light of Dream-Spirit. From out of the light came her bright dark eyes, sparkling. He felt the velvety silk of her gentle touch. She called his name and as he looked into her eyes he knew why she had come to him.

$$\text{»»}\rightarrow \bullet \leftarrow\text{«««}$$

The next evening was the first day of the month when-the-leaves-turn-yellow, September, 1926. Cold-Maker's breath sent shivers through the little group, which sat huddled around the lodge fire after the evening meal. The Medicine Pipe was passed. Smoke from the lodge fire rose steadily through the top ear-flaps as the men spoke of deeds done, coups counted, of family and friends who had passed along the Ghost-Trail during the past five winters, of marriages and babies, of sickness and of plans for the future.

Everyone in the group—Mountain Chief, Thomas, Red-Boy, James Vielle, Bear Head and the other Elders—everyone, except perhaps Morning Eagle, knew that an important ceremony would soon take place before the New Englander journeyed once again to the land where the sun-first-rises.

At last, it was time.

"Now, Aapinakoi Píítaa, I have something I must say to you." The war veteran nodded solemnly to his father and his friend James. "As my father and mother have told me, you have lived among us and have become one of us, a Pikuni. Your deeds of honesty and courage have helped me use my powerful Medicine wisely. I did not die in the whiteman's prison."

He went to the back of the lodge and retrieved from behind his bedding a rectangular cardboard container. Carefully, he stripped the tape off the cardboard and held up his Sun Painting.

In silence, all eyes stared at the silk stretched within the wooden frame.

"Inside, I painted my War Shield. It protected me. I had the dream of my powerful Medicine. I dreamt of my ancestors, Big Brave and his father, Mountain Chief. I dreamt of a wild, kicking Black Horse. The Black Horse Medicine is my power. It saved my life. Later, inside the walls, Dream-Spirit told me how I must paint my War Shield to honor my ancestors."

Morning Eagle remembered when the Blood warrior, Black Looks, had told him the names of the warriors who had transferred the Bear-Medicine-Knife. It gave the recipient protection from death in battle. Morning Eagle knew that the Sun Painting held by Red-Boy meant the same.

"Now, Aapinakoi Píítaa," announced Thomas Stabs-By-Mistake, "we will start the ceremony. You will be given my son's War Shield for your bravery." He leaned back onto his willow rest, looking fully at Morning Eagle.

With glistening eyes, the businessman from Holyoke leaned forward and listened intently. It was Big Brave-Mountain Chief's turn to speak.

"Our brother, Aapinakoi Píítaa, you have gone into battle for us and you have been victorious. Your Otter Medicine Tipi, it brings you powerful Medicine." The elder chief then nodded to Red-Boy.

"Now, you must listen to my talk," said Red-Boy. "You must remember my words of the deeds of my grandfather and great-grandfather. They are the ones I have drawn on my War Shield, Morning Eagle. I have removed the cover of my War Shield. I remember the words of my grandfather, Big Brave... 'Never remove the War Shield cover until going into battle.' Now, together we go into battle for my people."

Morning Eagle slowly, solemnly nodded.

"I will listen and write your talk down, Red-Boy." Reaching over to his parfleche, Morning Eagle extracted a pad and pen and waited for the owner of the War Shield to recount for him the memories of his grandfather, Big Brave, and of his great-grandfather, Mountain Chief.

Red-Boy and Thomas Stabs-By-Mistake carefully recounted for Morning Eagle the days on the prairie in the times-that-are-far-back, when Mountain Chief was an infant, then a youngster, then an adolescent, then a young man — recounting the movement of his people. The horse-raiding parties, the pitched battles with the Cree and the Crow and the Kootenay and the Gros Ventre. And finally the slow, crushing onslaught of the big knives — the white-man — and the disappearance of the Buffalo.

With a steadiness of mind and purpose, Morning Eagle listened, writing everything down until the Sun's globe rose from the misty East.

(left to right) Chief Red-Boy, Thomas Stabs-By-Mistake and Morning Eagle (Aapinakoi Píítaa).

# Epilogue
## Heart Butte, Montana
## October 17, 1929

Three winters had passed. Peter Red-Boy had remained in Heart Butte, caring for his aging mother and father, working their farm—putting in wheat, grain and a garden, putting up hay for his horses. His full, absolute pardon had finally come through. In the meantime, he had become a Piegan Chief. Additional responsibilities occupied his time.

Red-Boy had befriended a young Montana lawyer by the name of Yessup, who had been hired by the Senate subcommittee investigating long-simmering accusations of mismanagement by Superintendent Campbell. By the end of 1928, Campbell was gone. Miggs had moved on. Yessup was rewarded by the incoming Hoover Administration with an appointment as Assistant U.S. Attorney.

Yet right now, Red-Boy's attention was drawn to the racket coming from within the Heart Butte Day School, where children ran about, scrambling and scurrying to see who could reach the door first for afternoon recess.

The children piled outside under the bright sun to play on the wooden ponies and lodge poles, using lengths of rawhide for jump rope. The older boys organized a Stick Game and the younger girls went off for a pretend lodge meal preparation. Some of the teenage girls worked on beading or sewing parfleches.

Watching over the bedlam of the younger children, the Indian Chief, now sporting long double braids, extracted a letter from the front pocket of his shirt. He read it a second time:

*My honored Piegan warrior*

*My heart is singing all the time while I write this word message to you. Your War Shield protects me wherever I go.*

*I am glad that you are able to write your letters to me. Four letters came by the iron horse. I read those letters to our troop here in Holyoke, Massachusetts. I told all of our Boy Scouts that your troop at Heart Butte is called Troop Number 7, Boy Scouts of America, Blackfeet Council. That is the name that the great council of New York gave to you. That is what the letter said because your dues are paid. Remember my brother, you are making the bows, arrows and quivers that we will sell for you so that all of your Little Buffaloes may pay their dues. Most important of all, you can make dance drums, moccasins, belts, War Bonnets, Sun Dance whistles, Medicine rattles and obtain Peace Pipes.*

*Now I will say something to you before I go. The door flaps on my Otter Medicine Tipi are always raised for you, my brother. For you, each day, I think good. After Snow-Maker leaves, I will see you at the Sun Dance during the Berry-Ripe-Moon (July). We will sing a song and pass the Medicine Pipe.*

*I know that Snow-Maker will make the winter moons long and hard. Our troop is sending boxes of warm clothing and school supplies for the Little Buffaloes. The crops may be short and many Pikuni people may cry out from hunger if the Chinook winds do not come. I will pray that the warm winds come.*

*Now I know that the great and merciful Spirit, Natose, is with you and I pray that you may see the young grass. I shake your hand from my heart.*

*Aapinakoi Píítaa*

Carefully folding the letter, the young Pikuni Chief tucked it back into his shirt pocket, remembering that a few summers earlier his friend had helped organize another Boy Scout troop at Havre, Montana—Troop 1, Boy Scouts of America, Rocky Boy Council. The Chippeway and Cree Boys, together with the Pikuni young Buffaloes, were now the newest members. He looked at his Little Buffaloes scampering and jumping about like wild ponies in the small school yard: Joe White Bear, Albert Big Dog, John Swift Hog, Little Wolf, Buffalo Child, Wolf Walker and a dozen others.

His old friend made a splendid Scout Master. The boys all liked and respected the lanky Jim Vielle, who always sported a rawhide band with a white feather and squinted his eyes at any of the Little Buffaloes who became too enthusiastic. Several young fathers of the Little Buffaloes were skilled patrol leaders and storytellers.

Soon the BIA teacher over at Browning would arrive and he, the Heart Butte Day School Principal, would introduce her to his charges.

The young principal reached over and dutifully bangle-dangled the day school recess bell back and forth. Two of his little charges began fighting over how many willow sticks each side had won in the "fancy gamblin" stick game. Lining them up in parade formation, his friend, the Scout Master who also taught at the Day School, marched them slowly inside, admonishing the feistiest of the little charges to "bury your tomahawks and keep your heads down on your desks for nap time or Old Napi will steal your recess."

Red-Boy had almost forgotten the other long lines and harsh words of the guards inside The Hot House back in Kansas. His friend Yessup had finally confided to him how his former boss, Miggs, and Campbell had used every opportunity to block the Indian's pardon.

Feeling demoralized and unappreciated after "being second-guessed by those damned politicians in D.C.," Miggs had finally decided to quit his post. Just last week, a relieved Yessup had informed Red-Boy that Miggs had signed a lucrative contract with a private Wall Street firm, bragging that by the end of the year he would be raking in a fortune on Wall Street instead of "prosecuting little nobodies out in Montana."

>>>→ • ←<<<

The young man caught sight of the Model-T bumping along. It stopped abruptly at the edge of the dirt road. He walked over to the woman's car. She greeted him with a smile.

Taking the young woman's hands in his, he fixed his eyes on her hair, her eyes.

"I am so happy you came," he whispered to her, embracing her warmly. He felt the soft touch of her back, the comforting press of her breasts.

She reached up and tenderly stroked the back of the young Chief's neck, whispering, "What are we standin' out here for?" They smiled at each other.

For a few minutes, the couple stood there outside the Heart Butte Day School saying nothing, listening to the little excited utterances inside growing louder.

Then, the young Piegan Chief looked over at his Black Appaloosa tethered to a lodge pole at the corner of the school. "Well, we're not the only ones standin' out here, I guess," he grinned.

Then, taking her hand, he led the young woman towards the open door.

"I'd like you to meet my Little Buffaloes, Áwákaasii-Pokaa," he said, as he gently led Marilyn Deer Child inside and closed the door.

*United States Department of Justice*
*District of Columbia*

## AFFIDAVIT

I hereby certify that I am a custodian of the records of the Office of the Pardon Attorney, which is the repository for records concerning grants of presidential clemency. I further certify that I have caused a search to be made of the records of the Office of the Pardon Attorney. This search has revealed that on October 17, 1929, Peter Stabs-by-Mistake was granted a pardon. A true copy of this pardon warrant is maintained in the records of the Office of the Pardon Attorney. I certify that the attached is a true copy of that copy.

*Given under my hand and seal of the Department of Justice this 2nd day of May, 2005.*

Roger C. Adams
Pardon Attorney

*Red-Boys full pardon granted by President Hoover.*

# Herbert Hoover,

## President of the United States of America,

## To all to whom these presents shall come, Greeting:

## Whereas —

Peter State By Mistake was convicted in the United States' District Court for the District of Montana of rape of an Indian woman upon the Blackfoot Indian Reservation, and on September twenty-sixth, 1921, was sentenced to imprisonment for twenty years at hard labor in the United States Penitentiary at Leavenworth, Kansas; and,

Whereas the said Peter State by Mistake began his sentence December fourth, 1921, and on July twenty-seventh, 1926, he was granted a conditional pardon by President Coolidge; and,

Whereas it has been made to appear to me that since his release the said Peter State by Mistake has conducted himself in a law-abiding manner;

**Now, therefore, be it known,** that I,

**Herbert Hoover,** *President of the United States of America,* *in consideration of the premises, divers other good and sufficient reasons me thereunto moving, do* hereby grant unto the said Peter Stabs By Mistake a full and unconditional pardon for the purpose of releasing him from the requirements of his conditional pardon and of restoring his civil rights.

**In testimony whereof** *I have hereunto signed my name and caused the seal of the Department of Justice to be affixed.*

**Done** *in the District of Columbia this* seventeenth *day of* October, *in the year of our Lord One Thousand Nine Hundred and* twenty-nine, *and of the Independence of the United States the One Hundred and* fifty-fourth.

*By the President:*

Herbert Hoover

Attorney General.

# Glossary of Selected Blackfeet Terms

*(Instead of translated as complete words, the Blackfeet rendition is broken into syllables or is hyphenated for ease of pronunciation. Some proper Blackfeet names are broken into hyphenated syllables)*

| *TERMS (ANGLO)* | *ANGLO TO BLACKFEET* |
|---|---|
| 1. Bear | Ki áá yo |
| 2. Blackfeet (US)<br>Blackfoot (Canadian) | Siksika |
| 3. Bloods—Blackfeet band living in Canada | Ki naa wa (short for many Chiefs or the Tribe of many Chiefs) or Aá pai ai ta pi wa (Weasel People); Kái naa wa (Blood relatives) |
| 4. Buffalo jump | Piss kan (Anglicized as Piskun) |
| 5. Buffalo stone—sacred, petrified Buffalo stone | Iniskim (Anglicized); Ii-niss-kimm |
| 6. "Come here" | Anglicized as Poxapot; Pooh sa poot |
| 7. Count Coup | I naa maah ka (He got himself a gun) wa (He counted coup) |
| 8. The Crazy Dog Society | Ka nát tsoomi tai ksi (the traditional Blackfeet Police) |
| 9. The Creator | Ápi sto too ki (Our Maker; God) or Sspo mi tá pi (Above Person; Heavenly Spirits) or Iih tsi pái ta pii yo pa (The cause or giver of life) or Ná pi (Old Man or Creator), depending upon context |
| Creator | Naa to yi ta pi |
| 10. The Doves | Kak koi ksi (Blackfeet society and traditional rival of the Crazy Dog Society) |

11. Fish      Ma míí (wa — the Fish)

12. Glacier Park      Crown-of-the-Rockies; Aawah kais skááh kowa (playland; implied as vacation land)

13. Good      Sokape; So kap ak kaa (he is my good friend); iik sokape — very good friend (pronounced "eeksokapee"; [alt., iik so ka' pii] Ma tso wáp ákkaa (he is my very good friend)

14. "Goodbye" or "Enough"      Ki ta ko ta mattsin (I'll see you again); Ki á nni a yi (enough; that's it)

15. Greetings, hello      Okee or Oki (preferred); Ó ki

16. Lodge      Oyie; Mo-yis (dwelling/ lodge); nii-tó' yis (tipi/lodge; native dwelling)

17. Moon      Kokomíkisomm

18. Morning Star      Ii pi só waahs or Aa pi só wooh ta

19. Mysterious (Medicine) Man      Naa to wá pi naa (Holy Man; Spiritual); or Naa tó yi naims skaa kii (Holy Medicine Pipe Woman)

20. Napi      Ná pi (Old Man; Creator or Blackfeet trickster, depending upon the context); Na pí (denotes friend)

21. Otter      Áím mó níí si

22. Parfleche      soo-tsí-maan

23. Peigan (Canada; Pii ká ni)      Piegan Pi-ka-ni (Montana Blackfeet; Pikáni)

24. Pemmican      móó-kaa-kin

25. Piercing — insertion of skewers into the chest-part of Sun Dance ceremony to give thanks to Natose for surviving sickness or battles      Aa wah ka nioh si (sewing one's self; pierce with needle)

26. Pikuni (Anglo)      Pi-ká-ni or Pii ká ni; plural is Pii ka ii ksi or Pi ka ni ksi

27. Red Man — native or Indian      Mi ko tsi naa (Red Man — Native or American Indian); Nii tsí ta pi wa (literal: real person, i.e. the physical person as opposed to the person's spirit)

| | |
|---|---|
| 28. Rocky Mountains | Shiny Mountains; Saa kó ko toi ii sta ki stsi (the Blackfeet expression denotes a shiny reflective quality like glass) |
| 29. The Rocky Mountains | Backbone-of-the world; Mii stá ki stsi |
| 30. "Squaw" | Algonquain word; a colloquial term used by early Anglo trappers and settlers when referring to Indian women; in modern usage, a term of disrespect and sexual derision when referring to an Indian woman or girl; an epithet never used in polite company or among family members. |
| 31. Sun Dance | Oa kaan |
| 32. Sweat Lodge | (I)sstsii yss kaan; (I) denotes older sound or syllable which has been dropped from modern usage |
| 33. The Sun—giver of life to all living things | Natose; Naa-tósi (The Holy One) |
| 34. Tomorrow | aa pi ná kosi (tomorrow); aa pi ná koi (morning) |
| 35. Turtle | Sspo píi (wa—the Turtle) |
| 36. "Unh" | an expression of protest, anger or acknowledgment, depending upon the inflection given |
| 37. Vision quest | Ii tsi yi si |
| 38. Whiteman (one word) | Náá pii koan |
| 39. Wife | Sits-beside-him-woman; Ip pi taam (elderly wife/spouse) |
| 40. Wind Warm Winds from the South | Chinook; Siks so po or (Canadian term) I koo pii so po |
| 41. Cold arctic winds from the North | Cold-Maker; Ais-sto-yiims-staa-wa |

| MONTHS of YEAR | BLACKFEET MOONS | BLACKFEET TRANSLATION |
|---|---|---|
| November 1st | Moon, Wind Moon (Pikuni: last of October - first of November when geese fly south) | So po ki sómm (wind moon); Ii tao' t stoyi wa (when it turns cold; winter) |
| December | Moon of the first warm wind (Chinook) | Ist tsi tsai si'ks so po (the first warm Chinook wind) |
| January | When the jack rabbit whistles at night | Omah ká attsi stai ksi itai ka tsi maa yaa wa |
| February | Heavy snow moon (Pikuni: Hunger or when Buffalo calves are black) | Sá om mi tsi ki' somm (deceiving moon, re variable weather; extremely inclement) |
| March | When the geese fly north (Pikuni: when ice breaks up on rivers) | Sa' áí ksi i to' too yi (when the geese arrive) |
| April | Grass begins to grow | Ma tsi yik ka pi sai ki' somm (moon of the frogs) or Ma tó yih koi i táí sáis ski wa (when the grass grows) |
| May | When leaves come out | Sa yii pa' si (leaf out) or So yoo po ka' si (blossom) |
| June | Much water (Pikuni: moon of high water) | O' ka ko yii ki' somm (moon of floods) |
| July | Berry ripe moon | Mii nii stsi o tsi tai' tsih ip or i' tso yi (ripe/cooked, Canadian) |
| August | Home moon | Aah kia pi ksi stsi koi stsi (going home days) |
| September | When leaves turn colors | So yoo po kiistsi ii ta wa pa pittsko yi; Ii táó ma ta pa pitts sko (leaves change color) |
| October | Leaf falling moon | Ii tsin ni si' yi soo yóó po kii stsi |

# INDEX

# Acknowledgments

With the advent of the Lewis and Clark Bicentennial from 2004-2006 comes this story—an allegory of the heartbreaking suffering and struggle, yet ultimate survival, of a Native people—of the Blackfeet who, upon discovering Lewis and Clark, were chronicled as the only people who had a violent encounter with President Jefferson's Corps of Discovery. Sadly, over time, it was the Blackfeet people who became the recipients of a long trail of violence prompted by the incursion of the whiteman.

It happened at the end of the nineteenth century and the beginning of the twentieth century, after the destruction of the Buffalo, which had formed such an integral part of the Blackfeet way of life. Blackfeet culture—its oral tradition and legends and even its language—began to disappear to "christianization" and "assimilation" of the reservation Indians with the "civilized" whiteman's culture.

Sensing this, a few prominent white men travelled out West and lived among the Indian tribes of the plains, individuals such as James Willard Schultz, whose Blackfeet name was Apikani, and Walter McClintock. They transcribed into written language the disappearing Indian cultures—their oral traditions—including the Blackfeet language, legends and religion.

Most notably, McClintock's work, *The Old North Trail*, describes for us the religious Sun Dance ceremony of the Blackfeet as well as their customs and way of life. McClintock had come West with Gifford Pinchot to explore the western territories preparatory to President Theodore Roosevelt's dedication of vast tracks of land as national monuments.

Following in this tradition, my great-uncle Christian F. Schuster—a wealthy Massachusetts businessman who knew President Calvin Coolidge—journeyed west on the iron horse during the 1920s and 30s to live among his

Piegan-Pikuni friends in Montana. He soon befriended James Willard Schultz. Christian Schuster was adopted by Chief Curly Bear of the Blackfeet tribe on his birthday, September 4, 1923, at Glacier National Park, a ceremony witnessed by important Blackfeet Elders and James Willard Schultz. Chris was given the Blackfeet name Morning Eagle (Aapinakoi Píítaa). Later, he was also adopted by the Apinakwi Pits tribe.

A prominent leader of the Boy Scouts of America in New England, Morning Eagle actively pursued establishing Scout troops among the Plains Indians.

Morning Eagle witnessed the bone-crushing poverty and soul-wasting disease among the Blackfeet Indians during the early part of the twentieth century, all occurring while the Indian Bureau and other government agencies cynically refused to pull aside the curtain-veil of ignorance and indifference toward Native people.

Out of the rubbing together of Anglos with the Blackfeet and other Native cultures and races during the "Roaring Twenties," a deeper story has been forged about the rich diversity and struggles of American people as a whole — the soul-fabric of our Nation.

Thanks to the wisdom of such Blackfeet Elders as Curly Bear, the language, customs and legends of the Blackfeet people — some of the great oral traditions handed down from generation to generation — have been transcribed. Indian Chiefs and Elders familiar with the traditional way knew that their culture would die unless these Anglos, who had the gift of the written language, were adopted. They knew these Anglos would carry forth, in written form, their Indian culture.

The title of this historical fiction work is adopted from the Indian writings, stories, legends and ethnicity studies of my great-uncle Morning Eagle. Many of the Blackfeet and other Indian cultural and ceremonial artifacts that were given to my great-uncle are now on display at Indian and Anglo museums, most notably on the East Coast at the Smithsonian National Museum of the American Indian in New York City and Washington D.C., at the Smithsonian.

This novel of historical fiction is based on the life story of Red-Boy, Peter Stabs-By-Mistake, a young Blackfeet man who was convicted of rape, and who was granted a conditional pardon by President Coolidge and later a full pardon by President Hoover through the efforts of Morning Eagle.

The fictionalized service of Red-Boy in World War I is a tribute to the thirty-five Blackfeet Natives who enlisted and fought in the Great War. Like all First Nation People, many thousands of American Indians enlisted in the U.S. Armed Forces and fought in the Great War but were not granted U.S. citizenship until 1924.

The front cover of the book is a photograph of the actual painting attributed to Peter Stabs-By-Mistake and given to my great-uncle out of gratitude for the pardon obtained through my great-uncle's efforts.

The names of historic figures – chiefs and important tribal members and band names – have not been changed. However, many of the accounts of events in their lives are fictional. Some event sequences (including prison events) have been altered or fictionalized, a few names have been changed, and fictional characters have been created. This was done not with the intention of distorting the truth but to form the plot, to give honor to the survival and adaptation of the Blackfeet and, in all instances, to protect the honor of Blackfeet family names as well as Blackfeet culture and tradition.

Portions of many of Morning Eagle's stories, legend accounts and interviews with tribal Elders have been incorporated into the story. Where they have been incorporated, they have been edited or slightly altered to fit the pattern and tempo of the story, where appropriate.

As an Anglo writer, I do not pretend to know the mind of Indian people, least of all the mind of a young Blackfeet man who lived during the 1920s and was incarcerated at Leavenworth Penitentiary. However, I have written this story in the spirit of my great-uncle. Any mistakes, cultural or otherwise, are entirely my own and I accept full responsibility for them. Any insight this work of historical fiction may shed upon the culture and faith of Native people—most specifically the Blackfeet and other Native people living in Montana—I owe to those Blackfeet in Montana who have assisted me with cultural issues and have lent their unqualified cooperation in providing invaluable background material, which was essential in compiling this story.

One American Indian whom I have never met, but whose writings provided inspiration and tremendous insight in shaping my story, is Leonard Peltier, an American Indian Movement leader. As Curly Bear Wagner has so aptly stated, "*Sun-Painted Man* is a unique story because we find ourselves sitting there in prison with Peter—the same way we sit beside Indian people like Leonard Peltier, set up at Leavenworth Prison." I wish to thank Mr. Peltier for the opportunity to read and to meditate on his book *Prison Writings: My life is My Sun Dance* (Harvey Arden, Ed. St. Martin's Griffin, NY, 1999), written while an inmate at Leavenworth Prison. I recommend his book to all those who are kind enough to read *Sun-Painted Man.*

Paralleling Leonard Peltier's plight, the 1921 trial of Peter Stabs-By-Mistake was one of the first significant off-reservation prosecutions of a Blackfeet Indian under the Major Crimes Act. This statute was enacted by Congress following the US Supreme Court's reversal of the murder conviction in *Ex-Parte Crow Dog.*

I wish to thank the following individuals and organizations whose help and assistance was most instrumental in writing this story:

Heather Munday, Dechen Bartso and the late Pat Rouse, all of whom typed and assembled the manuscript; Linda Bowden, for her excellent finish editing; The Blackfeet Heritage Program in Browning, Montana; Chairman Earl Old Person, Blackfeet Business Tribal Council; The George Gustav Heye Center, National Museum of the American Indian; Delores Magee, Enrollment, Blackfeet Nation; Professor William Farr, University of Montana; Ms. Jo Wojnarowski and Ms. Irene Kronin, South Hadley Historical Society; Mr. and Mrs. Edward Alford, South Hadley, Massachusetts; The Connecticut Historical Society; Ms. Elise Feeley, Forbes Library, Northampton, Massachusetts; Ms. Lynne Augare, Administrative Assistant, Browning Public Schools, Blackfeet Heritage Program; Ms. Donna E. McCrea, Archives and Special Collections of the University of Montana – Missoula; National Archives and Records Administration – Pacific Alaska Region, Seattle, WA and Central Plains Region, Kansas City, MO; Mr. Roger C. Adams, Pardon Attorney, U.S. Department of Justice.

I am especially indebted to the late Thomas A. Blackweasel (Gray Horse Rider: August 4, 1935-August 26, 2005), a full-blood Blackfeet Elder, and his wife Doreen, both members of the Board of Directors of the Glenbow Museum in Calgary, Alberta, and Ms. Vicki Privett of Arcadia, Indiana. Both Mr. Blackweasel, a Native historian, orthographer and linguist of the Blackfeet language, and his wife gave generously of their time and invaluable knowledge and wisdom. I am also indebted to Gerald T. Conaty, Ph.D., Senior Curator of Ethnology at Glenbow Museum.

I especially wish to thank Mrs. Jean Billedeaux, Ms. Roxanne DeMarce, Ms. Phonda Pepion, Joseph Wagner and Ms. Joanna Basha of the Going-to-the-Sun Institute, and Darrell Kipp, founder/director, Cuts Wood Immersion School, for generously giving of their time and honest, forthright guidance with the many language, cultural and historical issues.

I owe a special debt of gratitude to Barbara Lear, my editor, for assisting me in making this historical fiction novel move in directions that, I hope, will meaningfully touch the reader.

I also wish to thank Portland, Oregon writer Tim Brown for painstakingly reviewing the manuscript and for his skillful, thoughtful "constructive criticism," which as any writer knows, is an invaluable gift. I also thank Jennifer R. Dalglish for her review of the manuscript and thoughtful comments.

I wish to thank my friend, mentor and senior law partner, Roger F. Dierking, for his kind encouragement and help throughout this project. Special thanks also to my Vietnam veteran buddy, Ed Olsen, who listened to me "talk out" the story while we walked many hundreds of miles on Portland's Esplanade.

A special debt of deepest gratitude I owe to my very good friend and brother Curly Bear Wagner, founder and director of the Going-To-The-Sun Institute. (Please See Special Memorial Dedication)

I also give heartfelt thanks to the Clear Light Publishing family for their kind generosity of interest, patience and time — most especially Harmon Houghton, Publisher, Marcia Keegan, Editor, Lee More, Editor, and Gregory Lucero, designer and typographer.

Most importantly, I owe an immeasurable debt of gratitude to my family, for their support- to my wife Barbara and two sons, Chris and Matt, whose love and encouragement have always sustained me. My special gratitude also goes to my mother, Ruth E. Schuster, my brother Bob and sister Peggy, and to my extended family for their love and encouragement.

Finally, I owe a special debt of gratitude to my great-uncle, Christian F. Schuster — Morning Eagle — in whose memory and spirit I wrote this story.

»»—→ • ←—««

In every sense, this novel of historical fiction is a collaborative effort — my great-uncle Morning Eagle's spirit-tribute, through me, to the tenacity of Native people he loved — people who have survived the unrelenting depredations of hunger and starvation, disease and alcoholism and a Curtain of Indifference which, for far too long, has hidden the Light of Renaissance.